CHILDREN
of the
STARS

OTHER BOOKS BY MARIO ESCOBAR

Auschwitz Lullaby
Remember Me (coming September 2020)

CHILDREN

of the

STARS

A NOVEL

MARIO ESCOBAR

THOMAS NELSON
Since 1798

Translator: Gretchen Abernathy
Spanish Editor-in-Chief: Graciela Lelli
Spanish Editor: Juan Carlos Martín Cobano
English Editor: Jocelyn Bailey

Thomas Nelson titles may be purchased in bulk for educational, business, fund-raising, or sales promotional use. For information, please email SpecialMarkets@ThomasNelson.com.

ISBN 978-0-7852-3479-1 (hardcover)
ISBN 978-0-7852-3517-0 (international edition)
ISBN 978-0-7852-3300-8 (e-book)
ISBN 978-0-7852-3299-5 (downloadable audio)
ISBN 978-0-7852-3303-9 (trade paper)

Library of Congress Cataloging-in-Publication Data

CIP data is available upon request.

20 21 22 23 24 LSC   10 9 8 7 6 5 4 3 2 1

*To my wonderful family, Elisabeth, Andrea, and Alejandro,
who joined me in the transformative experience of Le
Chambon-sur-Lignon that became this book.
To the women and men of France who saved tens of
thousands of Jews, political refugees, and stateless
souls from the clutches of the Third Reich.*

Anyone who saves a life is as if he saved an entire world.

—TALMUD, MISHNAH SANHEDRIN 4:5

A Note from the Author

The book *Children of the Stars* has given me the chance to return to the mysterious territory of childhood. As we grow up, we lose the perspective of that magnificent discovery of being born and contemplating everything around us with the eyes of a child. Every inch that distances us from the ground pushes us irrevocably and farther away from the world we dreamed of changing but that we are now mostly content to endure. This book is about just that: the capacity we have as human beings to transform the world in each generation, when the balances are zeroed out and, for better or worse, everything begins again.

Children of the Stars is a tribute to the power of everyday men and women to change reality. Centuries have hammered into us that people are simply a passive element in the unfolding of history, but civil resistance has often been the only thing capable of holding out against tyranny and oppression. From the plebian rebellions in ancient Rome to the American Revolution, from the pacifist movements for independence in India to the end of racial segregation in the United States, the power of the common man and woman is what has changed the world.

The first time I entered the lush valleys surrounding Le Chambon-sur-Lignon, I thought I had stumbled upon paradise: small villages built of granite with a rainbow of painted wooden shutters, ancient hotels with their façades blackened by a hundred cruel winters, bucolic farms spread out between dense forests of beech and fir trees that absorbed and mellowed the intense light of summer. Something had happened here that changed history and that I knew, somehow, would also transform me.

The story of the children saved by the residents of Le Chambon-sur-Lignon and many surrounding towns was unknown for quite a long time. After World War II, the French preferred to forget the Vichy regime and the persecution of those the collaborators called "pariahs" and "undesirables." But in 1989, the documentary *Weapons of the Spirit* brought to light this beautiful story based on real events.

Children of the Stars is the story of Jacob and Moses Stein—the unforgettable protagonists of this novel who, armed only with innocence, become young heroes against evil.

MADRID, JULY 1, 2016

Prologue

Paris
May 23, 1941

"Every generation nurses the hope that the world will begin anew."
Those were the last words his father had said in the train station. The man had crouched down on his haunches in his ironed gray suit to be on Moses's level. The child looked out with his big black eyes and sighed, not understanding what his father meant. The station filled with strangely sugary-smelling white smoke. His mother watched with tear-swollen eyes, and her cheeks were so red she looked as if she had just scaled a mountain. Moses could still remember her delicate white gloves, the damp, cold feel of that spring, and the sensation that his little world was ripping apart. His father attempted a smile beneath his thin brown mustache, but it ended up a tortured grimace. Moses clung to his mother's legs. Jana

smoothed the boy's blond hair and bent down. She took her son's chubby, rosy cheeks in her hands and kissed him with her dark lips, her tears mixing with the child's.

Jacob pulled at his brother. A light steam emanated from the engine's wheels, and the train gave a final whistle as if the huge frame of metal and wood were sighing in grief over the souls it had to separate. Aunt Judith hugged Jacob's chest, both protective and worried. All around, German soldiers moved like moths attracted by the light. They had neglected to pin the yellow stars to their chest that morning. Judith feared the Nazis could detect them with a single stony blue glance.

Eleazar and Jana turned away. Their coats swirled among the crowd of people with hands waving goodbye to other loved ones. In the midst of that boundless ocean of raised arms, Jacob and Moses saw their parents melt away until they disappeared completely. Moses clung to his aunt's hand with a ferocity intent on keeping her beside him. Judith turned her head and looked at her nephew's short bowl cut, the blond hair gleaming in the sun that filtered through the station's skylights. Then she looked at the other child, Jacob, with his dark brown curly hair. His big black eyes were set in a serious, angry expression, nearly rageful. The night before he had begged their parents to take them away from Paris, vowing that they would be good and behave, but Eleazar and Jana could not bring the children with them until they had a safe place to hide. Nothing bad would happen to the children in Paris, and Aunt Judith was too old to flee. She had taken them in six years before when the family could no longer endure the pressure in Berlin. Aunt Judith was more French than German; nobody would bother her.

They left the station as the sky began to turn leaden blue and the first cold drops spilled over the stone pavement. Judith opened her green umbrella and the three huddled together silently in the futile effort to avoid the downpour. They arrived soaked at Judith's tiny apartment on the other side of Paris, just where the city's beauty faded into a scabby, gray scene that made the glamour of cafés and fine restaurants seem like a distant mirage. They had taken the metro and then the noisy, rusty tram. The two boys had sat in the wooden seat at the front while their aunt sat just behind and allowed her eyes to relax their efforts against tears.

Moses studied his brother, whose brow was still furrowed. Jacob's freckles blurred together with raindrops and his frowning red lips were tensed to bursting. Moses did not understand the world. Jacob always called him "clueless," but the younger boy did understand that whatever had happened was bad enough to make their parents leave them. They had never been alone before. Moses still believed his mother was an extension of himself. At night, despite his father's grumbling, he slept pressed up against her, as the mere proximity of her skin calmed him. Her smell was the only perfume Moses could stand, and he knew he would always be safe as long as her lovely green eyes watched him.

As the boy had looked out through the dirty windows of the tram, the ghostly figures of the pedestrians jumbled together with the delivery trucks and old wagons that left the streets littered and rank with the droppings of their workhorses. This was his world. He had been born in Germany, but he recalled nothing of his home country. His mother still spoke to him in their native tongue, though he always answered in French, thus somehow making a statement against the place they had been forced to flee. Where would they go now? He felt like the world was closing at his feet, like when school-mates avoided him at recess, apparently struck with fear or nausea at the sight of the yellow star on his chest. "Children of the yellow star" is what people called them. To Moses, stars were the lights God had created so that night would not swallow everything up. Yet the world now seemed orphaned of stars, dark and cold like the wardrobe where he would hide to trick his parents and from which he always jumped out as soon as possible so the immense blackness did not devour him completely.

PART 1

Chapter 1

J acob helped his brother get ready. He had been doing it for so long he went through the motions mechanically. They hardly talked as Jacob pulled off Moses's pajamas and helped him into his pants, shirt, and shoes. Moses was quiet with a lost, indifferent expression that sometimes broke Jacob's heart. Jacob knew Moses was old enough to get dressed on his own, but this was one way he could show his younger brother he was not alone, that they would stay together until the end and would be back with their parents as soon as possible.

Spring had gone by quickly enough, but the hot summer promised to drag on. Today was the first day of summer vacation. Aunt Judith left very early in the morning for work, and they were to fix breakfast, straighten up the apartment, buy food at the market, and go to the synagogue for bar mitzvah preparation. Their aunt insisted on it since Jacob was almost old enough to assume the bar mitzvah responsibilities of Jewish laws. He, however, thought it was all nonsense. Their parents had never taken them to the synagogue, and Eleazar and Jana themselves had known practically nothing about Judaism until they got to Paris. But Aunt Judith had always been devout and became even more so after her husband died in the Great War.

Jacob got his brother dressed and helped him wash his face. Then they both went to the kitchen, whose blue tiles were now dull from decades of scrubbing. The table, painted sky blue, had seen better days, but it held a basket with a few slices of black bread and cheese. Jacob poured some milk, heated it over the sputtering gas stove, and served it in two steaming bowls.

Moses ate as if safeguarding his breakfast from bread robbers all around. At eight years old, hardly a moment went by when he did not feel rapaciously hungry. Jacob was just as capable of eating everything in sight, which forced Judith to keep the pantry locked. Each day she set out their humble rations for breakfast and lunch and at night prepared a frugal supper of soup light on noodles or vegetables in a cream sauce. It was scant fare for two boys in their prime growing years, but the German occupation was exhausting the country's reserves.

In the summer of 1940, the French, especially Parisians, had fled en masse to the southern parts of the country, but most had returned home months later as they saw that the German occupation was not as barbaric as they had imagined. Jacob's family had not left the city then, despite being German exiles, but his father had taken the precaution of seeking refuge in his sister's house, hoping they would not easily raise Nazi suspicion.

Jacob knew that his family was doubly cursed: his father had been active in the Socialist Party and had written satirical tracts against the Nazis for years, not to mention that both Eleazar and Jana were Jewish—a damnable race according to the National Socialists.

Paris was under the direct control of the Germans, represented by Field Marshal Wilhelm Keitel, and the Nazis had exploited and exhausted the populace. By the spring of 1942, it was nearly impossible to find coffee, sugar, soap, bread, oil, or butter. Fortunately, Aunt Judith worked for an aristocratic family that, compliments of the black market, was always well stocked and gave her some of the basic supplies that would have been impossible to acquire with her ration card.

After their meager breakfast, the brothers headed out. The previous night had been muggy, and the morning foretold an infernal heat. The boys ran down the stairs. The intense yellow of the Star of David shone brightly against their worn-out shirts, endlessly mended by their aunt.

The four sections of the apartment building, lined with windows, walled in the interior courtyard. From there they would pass through an archway and an outer gate leading to the street. Each side of the square building had its own staircase. As soon as Moses and Jacob stepped into the courtyard, they sensed something was wrong. They ran to the street. More than twenty dark buses with white roofs stood parked up and down the sidewalks. People swirled around as French police officers with white gloves and nightsticks herded them into the buses.

A chill ran all the way up Jacob's spine, and he grabbed hold of Moses's hand so tightly the younger child made a noise and tried to pull away.

"Don't let go of my hand!" Jacob growled, yanking his brother back toward the building. He knit his eyebrows together.

They were reentering the building when the doorwoman, leaning on her broom, sneered down at them and hollered to the gendarmes, "Aren't you going to take these Jewish rats?"

The boys looked at each other and took off running toward their stairway. Three of the policemen heard the doorwoman's raucous calling and saw the boys dashing toward the other side of the courtyard. The corporal gestured with his hand, and the other two ran after the boys, blowing their whistles and waving their nightsticks all the while.

The boys raced along the unvarnished wooden floor and the worn-down steps with broken boards, unable to keep their feet from pounding with terrible volume. The police looked up when they got to the stairwell. The corporal took the elevator and the other two agents started up the stairs.

Jacob and Moses panted as they approached the apartment door. Moses reached for the doorknob, but Jacob pulled him, and they ran toward the roof. They had spent countless hours there among the clotheslines, hiding among the hanging sheets, shooting doves with their slingshot, and staring at the city on the other side of the Seine.

When they reached the wooden door that led to the roof, they paused past the threshold, hands on their knees as they gasped for air. Then Jacob led them to the edge of the building. The roofs stretched out in an interminable succession of flat black spaces, terra-cotta tiles, and spacious terraces some Parisians utilized for growing vegetables. The brothers climbed up a rusted ladder attached to an adjacent wall and walked tentatively among the roof tiles of a neighboring building.

The police watched them from the roof of Judith's apartment building. The corporal, winded despite having taken the elevator, blew his whistle again.

Jacob turned for a moment to judge the distance between the men dressed in black and themselves—instinctively, like a deer wondering how close the hounds are.

The younger two gendarmes awkwardly climbed up the ladder and resumed the chase, breaking half a dozen roof tiles as they closed the gap second by second.

Jacob stepped between two tiles and felt something crack. His leg fell through a hole, and searing pain shot up his shin. When he managed to pull his leg out, blood poured down into his dingy white socks. Moses helped him get to his feet again, and they kept running to the last building on the block. A chasm of more than seven feet separated the last rooftop from the next building.

Moses glanced at their pursuers and then at the abyss shining with the intense light of summer. Despite the light of day, a cavernous darkness below seemed eager to swallow anything that dared fall into it. Moses turned his bewildered look to Jacob, at a loss for what to do.

His brother reacted quickly. Just below them there was a small terrace. From there, a ledge circled the building toward the main road. Perhaps they could reach a house, then the street, then try to get lost in the crowd. Without a second thought, Joseph jumped and turned to help Moses, arms outstretched. Just as the younger child began to leap, a pair of hands grabbed his legs. He twisted and hit the rooftop hard.

"Jacob!" Moses screamed, trapped.

For a moment, Jacob did not know what to do. He could not abandon his brother, but if he went back up on the rooftop, they would both fall into the police's hands. He did not understand why, but his parents had warned him about the Nazis sending Jews to concentration camps in Germany and Poland.

The corporal leaned out over the rooftop and saw Moses from the ledge.

"Stop it, you brat!" he bellowed as he grabbed the younger boy from the other policeman, held him by an ankle, and dangled him over the roof.

"No!" Jacob yelled.

His brother's face was purple with terror, and he flailed like a fish yanked out of water.

"Come back up here. You don't want your brother to fall, do you?" the corporal called with mocking as he held Moses a little farther over the edge.

Jacob's heart beat harder and faster than ever in his life. He could feel it in his temples and in the tips of his fingers through his clenched fists. His breath abandoned him. He raised his hands and tried to scream, but nothing came out.

"Get up here now! You and your people have wasted enough of our time today!"

In the sunken eyes of the corporal the boy could see a hatred he could not understand, but he had seen it often over the past few months. He climbed back up the wall toward the roof and stood before the corporal.

The corporal was a tall, heavy-set man whose stomach threatened to burst from his uniform jacket with every breath. His hat sagged to the side, and the knot of his tie was half undone. In his red face, his brown mustache quivered as his lips frowned and spat out words.

Once Jacob came up from the terrace, the corporal let Moses fall with a thud onto the rooftop. The other two gendarmes grabbed both boys by the arms and carried them between them back to the first building. They descended in the elevator and returned to the courtyard.

The doorwoman smiled as they passed, as if the capture of the two brothers had brightened her day. The old woman spat at them and shrieked, "Foreign communist scum! I won't have another Jew in my building!"

Jacob gave her a hard, defiant stare. He knew her well. She was a lying busybody. A few months prior, Aunt Judith had helped the doorwoman acquire ration cards. The woman could neither read nor write and had a disabled son who rarely left their apartment. Occasionally on a nice afternoon, she would labor to get him out to the courtyard and sit him down while the boy, crippled and blind, shook all the while.

Moses had not yet recovered from the terror of dangling over the roof, and he turned his eyes toward the woman. Though she always yelled at them when they ran in and out of the building or bothered the neighbors with their shouts or the noise of pounding up and down the stairs, they had never done anything to her.

The street still teemed with people, and the buses were already half full. The gendarmes shoved the women, hit the children, and brusquely hurried the older people along. There were very few young men. Most had been in hiding for months. The helpless throng, compelled by fear and uncertainty, moved like a flock of silent sheep about to be sacrificed, unable to imagine that the police of the freest country on earth were sending them off to the slaughterhouse before the impassive gaze of friends and neighbors.

The buses roared to life as Moses stared mesmerized out the window. He felt the odd sensation of going on a field trip. Beside him, Jacob studied the terrified faces of the other passengers, all of whom avoided one another's eyes, as if they felt invisible under the scorn of a world to which they no longer belonged.

Chapter 2

Paris
July 16, 1942

The buses came to a stop in front of a large building. The gendarmes jumped out of their cars and stood in a line to prevent the Jews from slipping off to nearby streets. The sun was beating down on the buses, draining the passengers' energy. Yet Jacob and Moses kept their eyes on the Eiffel Tower, situated behind them. Looking at it made their present reality seem less real.

The French police beat the metal doors of the buses for the drivers to open up. The passengers looked around. No one wanted to be the first to get off the bus. They had held collective silence on the way there, and now uncertainty had taken such a hold of their souls that resignation seemed the only viable response to their unexpected arrest. Most were foreigners, though some French Jews had fallen into the spiderweb woven around them. An elderly gentleman dressed in a work uniform stood and addressed the frightened passengers.

"We need to stay calm. Surely the French are bringing us here to protect us. This country would never let them deport us to Germany. We may be occupied and the German hordes may rule our lives, but the values of the Republic still stand."

One of the few young men on the bus pushed the older man aside and stared defiantly at the rest of the passengers. "Are you stupid sheep or human beings? Haven't you noticed that since the occupation began the French government has registered us in their files, forbidden us from working in most trades, and forced us to wear these stars like they do in Germany? What's waiting for us in there is prison. Then they will send us north by train."

A woman dressed in a nice gray suit and blue hat made to leave the bus. The younger man stood in her way, but she pushed him aside. "Let me by. Don't intimidate these poor people. We have no idea what's waiting for us, but haven't we always been persecuted? Yet somehow we survive?"

The rest of the passengers filled the aisle and pushed and shoved their way toward the door. Outside the buses, a long line of women, men, and children marched slowly toward a set of enormous doors. Above them hung a sign with stylized letters: VÉL D'HIV.

Jacob and Moses knew the place. Their father had taken them there once to watch a bicycle race. The velodrome allowed Parisians to enjoy cycling competitions throughout the winter, and all sorts of events were held there.

A boy sitting behind them leaned forward and asked, "You're the Stein brothers, aren't you?"

Jacob and Moses turned to look at him. It was a relief to know someone in the crowd of strangers. "Yes," Jacob said, getting to his feet. They were the last ones in the line that had formed in the bus aisle.

"I'm Joseph, the plumber's son," the boy said. "We used to study together in the synagogue, but lately my father has let me go with him to his jobs. You haven't seen him here, have you?"

"No, you're the only person we've recognized today," Jacob said.

"This morning they beat on the door of our house. My father went out with a wrench in his hands, but he left it in the foyer when he saw it was the gendarmes. They told us to bring one blanket and one shirt per person, nothing else. But we got separated when we got to the buses."

Jacob answered in kind. "They didn't come looking for us, but the doorwoman of our building started hollering, and a few policemen ran after us. We tried to get away on the rooftops, but they chased us down."

A gendarme stuck his head through the door and shouted, "Get out here, you little rats!"

Terrified, the boys ran to the door. Moses caught the eyes of the bus driver for a moment before the man lowered his head. It had been the worst job the man had ever had to do. He did not know what the gendarmes planned to do with these people, but he was ashamed that the French collaborated with the Nazis. Since occupation, he had tried to slip under the radar. Union members and anyone who spoke out for other political parties were accused of high treason against France.

Jacob exited the bus first and faced the gendarme. The policeman scowled and indicated with his nightstick where they should walk. In the brief moments the boys had remained on the bus, most people had already entered the stadium. Moses clung to his brother's hand, and Joseph followed the rest of the crowd down a wide hall-way. As they reached the end, they heard a murmur that grew to a deafening roar. They entered the enormous dome and looked at the stands. Then their eyes wandered to the slanted racetrack and the long rectangle in the center where a few Red Cross tents stood.

"Oh no," Moses whimpered. His jaw dropped, and his eyes struggled to take in the enormous space. He only vaguely remembered the time they had come to the velodrome with their father.

"There are thousands of people here," Joseph said, incredulous. It would be nigh impossible to find his family.

A government worker seated at a wooden desk motioned to them. The three boys walked toward him in single file.

"First and last name," the man demanded without looking up. Round spectacles attached to his jacket by a chain balanced precariously on his narrow nose. "Are you deaf?" he barked when they did not answer immediately.

"Why have you brought us here?" Jacob asked. The man set down his pen and crossed his arms at the boy's insolence. He finally looked at them.

"Where are your parents? Didn't they teach you any respect?" he growled.

Jacob's temper shot up. "Respect? You drag us out of our homes at the crack of dawn, force us to come here, and lock us up like animals. You really expect us to be respectful?" His voice had risen to a shout.

When a nearby gendarme heard the boy's tone, he pulled out his nightstick and approached with a menacing scowl. Moses grabbed Jacob's shirt from behind and jerked him back just in time. The nightstick crashed down onto the table, and as the policeman raised it to strike again, the three boys fled into the crowd. The officer chased them, but when the boys hid among the throng, several men closed in around him. "Is there a problem, officer?"

The gendarme saw the futility in inciting further rebellion. The brats would not be escaping any time soon; there would be time enough to find them.

Jacob looked back and saw the gendarme returning to the door. Then he regretted losing his temper. Perhaps he could have learned if Aunt Judith was there or he could have even contacted her somehow.

"What are we going to do?" Moses whined, catching his breath.

"I don't know," Jacob said. Moses threw himself into his brother's arms and began to cry. His quiet sobs were a whisper amid the murmur of the crowd all around. Jacob looked up. Light poured through the enormous glass panes of the ceiling. As they stood at the foot of the racetrack, he recalled that Sunday morning in the velodrome with his father a few years back, just before the Nazis invaded France. He remembered how sweat poured off the racers while the crowd cheered them on. Back then, the stadium was a magical place for Jacob. Now it was a cage, a tomb that brooked no escape.

"I have to find my parents," Joseph said, turning to walk away.

"Wait," Jacob called. "We'll help you. Our aunt might be here too." The boys began walking along the edge of the racetrack. People had lain down, trying to get comfortable on it. The heat was oppressive. As the day progressed, the place would surely become like an oven.

Moses saw a woman standing alone with twin boys. She wept as her face turned from one child to the other and back again. A little farther on, an elderly man dressed only in his underwear laughed hysterically as his wife attempted to dress him again. Children ran every which way, exploring the area. The world seemed to have been turned upside down, as if the war had twisted both young and old into grotesque reflections of themselves.

Jacob kept his hand on Moses's shoulder. He did not want to get separated, and nothing guaranteed they would find each other again if they did.

The crowd slowly began to quiet, like a wheat field returning little by little to a calm after the violent buffeting of a storm. The constant murmur dwindled. People had lost interest in talking, complaining, or entreating the gendarmes. They just wanted a place to rest, but the most comfortable areas had already been claimed by the strongest adults. A handful of nurses appeared at the lower doors and headed for the tents in the middle of the track. They closed themselves in to evaluate the situation.

Just then they heard a loud thud. The three boys turned to look, unsure of what it could be. A cry of horror arose, which turned to shouts of panic. People scrambled to get away from something or someone. Jacob stood on the handrail and stretched to get a look. The bloodied body of a woman twitched on the wooden racetrack and began to slide down it, leaving behind a trail of blood.

"What's happening?" Moses asked.

Before the younger child could get a look, Jacob pushed him back, away from the track. Moses protested and made for the rail again, but Jacob clapped one hand over Moses's eyes and tugged him back with the other.

They heard more of the loud thuds. The cries of terror welled up like a hurricane wind. Jacob, his eyes still tinged with the sight of blood, knew he had to get his brother out of there as quickly as possible. It was the closest he had ever come to hell on earth. Together they ran for the hallways that led to the different seating tiers. They were on a mission: find Joseph's family and try to learn what had become of Aunt Judith so they could escape the velodrome before it was too late.

Chapter 3

Paris
July 16, 1942

The day would not end. The velodrome's detainees were hungry, thirsty, and tired. Babies and children wailed about the heat. The nurses tried to hand out the little bit of milk they had to mothers who screamed and fought over it. The suffocating air compelled most men to strip to their undershirts, and women fanned their children with hats, paper, or anything they could find. Many people wandered in search of lost loved ones, shouting out names with aggrieved monotony. Elsewhere, families huddled together nibbling their last remnants of food.

Jacob, Moses, and Joseph walked without stopping. Four hours later, they had covered the hospital tent, every stairway, and the highest tiers of the building. The French police remained stationed at the doors but did not venture into the stands or racetrack. Men bearing stretchers had removed the bodies of the suicide victims, though the bloodstains continued to dry on the wooden circuit.

"We've looked everywhere . . . I don't think your family's here, Joseph," Jacob said. His friend's face grew cloudy. A few silent tears fell before Joseph wiped them with his dirty hand and dropped his head.

Jacob knew exactly how he felt. His parents' departure over a year ago had left a void within him. Loneliness and insecurity came out in night sweats when his own shouting for his mother awakened him.

"Cheer up. That might be good news." Jacob rested his hands on Joseph's shoulders.

"But if they aren't here"—Joseph sniffed—"where can they be?"

An older man dressed impeccably in a double-breasted gray suit stood up and approached the boys. He had overheard their interaction. He took off his glasses and knelt down. "They've taken some people to the Drancy camp, just a few miles northeast of Paris. Your family might be there. You should tell one of the Red Cross volunteers or one of the workers."

Joseph fought to hold back his tears. The lump in his throat made it hard to breathe. "Thank you, sir," he managed.

The three boys walked away from the man, and Jacob turned to his friend. "Don't even think about it. Your family might be at that other place, but you won't be able to help anybody if they take you to where your family is."

"What do you mean? What can we do to help?"

"Escape." Jacob let the word out in a whisper.

The idea had not even occurred to Joseph. In the last few hours, they had covered nearly every inch of the velodrome. The exits were guarded, and aside from the high glass roof, they'd found no way to get out. Trying to escape would be lunacy.

"But how can we get out of here?" Moses asked.

"There's got to be a way to do it without raising suspicion," Jacob said firmly, convincing himself as he spoke.

Joseph shrugged. "Well, even if so, then where would we go?"

"We'll look for Aunt Judith. She'll know what to do," Jacob said. He knew it was a simple answer, but he was the kind of person who faced problems one at a time.

The boy raised his eyes and beheld the stadium in a new light. He had to find its weak point—and fast.

"Jacob, I'm thirsty," Moses complained for the hundredth time. His face was pale and his lips dry and pasty. They looked toward the Red Cross tents.

"We should get some food and water," Jacob said, heading down the ramp.

"There are sinks in the bathroom," Joseph said, following.

"Haven't you noticed the bathrooms in this place? They stink like nothing else! I wouldn't go in there for all the gold in the world!" Moses declared.

Jacob pointed to the tents. "They'll give us water."

When the boys reached the lowest level of the velodrome, French policemen stood at the center of the track. They surrounded the Red Cross volunteers, ensuring that no one could steal the meager amount of food that remained in the stadium.

"Where do you think you are going?" one of the officers asked when he saw the three children approach.

"We haven't had anything to eat or drink all day," Jacob said, adopting his most pitiful face.

The gendarme was very young. His uniform was so new and bright it must have come from the cleaner's that day. At first he frowned—but when he saw that none of his fellow gendarmes were looking, he took some bread out of his pocket and gave it to the boys. "In the basement you'll find some fire hoses where you can get fresh water. That's the door," he said, pointing to a small opening concealed in the concrete wall at the base of a stairwell.

The three boys descended the stairs and opened the door cautiously, hoping not to rouse suspicion. They closed it behind them and stood groping in the dark until Jacob's hand moved over the cold, damp wall and found a switch. A dim light flicked on. The bulb was caked with dirt and cast only sparse, dusty light.

It was the first time since they had been forced into the velodrome that they did not feel the suffocating July heat. The bowels of the stadium maintained a low temperature, and it almost felt cool. They walked down a long hall, turning on lights as they went, and came to two hydrants.

Jacob struggled to turn a giant bolt, and water leaked from the hose. Moses grabbed it and started drinking greedily. His thirst slaked, Joseph took a turn, and then Jacob.

The three boys sat on pieces of rubble left over from some past mishap in the building and divided up the bread from the gendarme. It was not much, but it abated their hunger for a moment.

"I think we discovered the best spot in the velodrome!" Joseph said, almost triumphantly.

Jacob looked around. It was a horrible basement, dark and rank, but compared to the inferno above them, it felt like paradise. "This doesn't change our plans," he said. "We need to get out of here as soon as possible. You need to find your family, and we've got to find

Aunt Judith. If it turns out your family is in that other camp, you'd be better off staying with us. When the war is over, I'm sure the Germans will send everybody back home. I've heard Hitler wants us all as cheap labor while his soldiers are fighting on the front, but after that, they won't need us anymore."

Joseph recovered his serious tone. "I'd rather be with my family, even in an internment camp."

Jacob could understand. He would travel the world over to be with his parents again, even if it meant being stuck right back in the same horrible situation. He missed them—missed them bitterly— their laughter, their games, just walking along enjoying a pretty afternoon together. A familiar knot started to form in Jacob's throat. Before Eleazar and Jana had gone into hiding, he had spent eleven years with his parents. And now he had to face something like this alone. What could they do? How would he keep his brother alive? Questions ran through his brain while the two younger boys bantered, as if their situation were not yet truly dire.

"Okay, I get it. If it's the best solution after all, we'll take you to the camp at Drancy, wherever that is, but you could also just stay with our aunt."

"What makes you think she isn't locked up somewhere too?" Joseph asked.

"My aunt wasn't registered as a Jew. I already told you, they captured us because the doorwoman started hollering."

"But you're wearing the yellow star," Joseph objected.

"Yes, to be able to go to school and in case they stop us on the street, but we're registered at a different address. That's why I think our aunt is probably still free," Jacob explained.

The three boys sat quietly. Then they heard Moses's stomach growl, and all burst out laughing.

"What we really need is more food," Jacob joked, trying to change the subject.

They crept up from the basement as carefully as they had entered and closed the door silently. Night had fallen in the velodrome. They picked their way around the tents. At this hour they saw just a couple police agents smoking off to one side of the stadium, and the boys took advantage of the moment to creep into one of the tents. There they found stacks and stacks of half-opened boxes of food: canned goods, loaves of bread, crates of fruit.

Moses was incensed. "If there's so much food here, why are they making everybody go hungry?"

"I bet they don't know how long we'll be here, so first they want people to eat up whatever they brought with them," Joseph said.

"Well, we didn't bring anything. So we'd better stock up," Jacob said. The boys filled their pockets with food, then crept out of the tent and back to their hideout.

Jacob pulled out the knife he used for whittling and making figurines. He opened a can of green beans, and they ate with their fingers. The momentary fun kept them giggling.

They slept after their makeshift supper, but Jacob woke after a few hours and decided to explore the basement tunnels. The dim lighting spooked him, but he needed to know if the bowels of the velodrome held a way out. The light bulbs reached only so far down the long hallways of various pipes and tubing. Eventually the darkness made further exploration impossible. He retraced his steps back to the entryway and carefully opened a door that led to a small room. He turned on the light. Hanging on the wall and inside a carpenter's desk he found several tools and an oil lamp. He searched the little drawers of the desk until they revealed a half-full box of matches. Nervously, he struck the match and watched the flame slowly rise from the center of the lamp. The intensity of light from the short wick surprised him. It reminded him of hope: almost insignificant, but enough to guide a person's way.

Jacob left the closet silently, but before he reached the tunnels, he heard his brother's voice. "Where are you going?" Moses asked, starting to panic. Separation from the one person he had left was the worst fate the boy could imagine.

Jacob motioned for Moses to join him. He could still remember when Moses was born, all pink skin and chubby cheeks. But he had cried all the time. When he learned to walk, Moses followed Jacob everywhere and copied his every move. There in the basement, Moses was Jacob's shadow.

Jacob found it difficult and even awkward to be "an example," as his mother had always called him, but he also felt proud. He knew he was no one worth imitating or admiring, but for Moses he was a veritable hero.

The two brothers walked timidly down the gallery. Any little noise startled them. Two or three times they surprised rats that dashed off or cockroaches that fled down the pipes. Typically, the boys were not afraid of such creatures. In their aunt's apartment building, they had made a game of stomping on bugs in dark corners of the courtyard at night and hunting rats with their slingshot. But being surrounded by them in the dark was another matter altogether.

Minutes later, Moses jerked with a panicked question. "Do you know how to get back? We've taken so many turns I don't know where we are."

"Don't worry, I've been keeping track of the turns. We're closer than you think," Jacob reassured him, though he had his own doubts.

They kept walking, not knowing exactly what they were looking for. Half an hour later, they were back at the entrance to the basement. Joseph was sitting up, hands covering his sobbing face.

"What's wrong, Joseph?" Jacob asked.

The boy lifted his head just above his hands. The redness of his eyes and the expression of utter sadness threatened to swallow them all in grief. "I thought you'd left me. I was afraid . . . alone again."

Jacob knelt down and reached for Joseph. Through the hug, he could feel his friend's body, both cold and sweaty, and hear the sobs right next to his ear. Something like tenderness flooded him. He had always received care from others. His parents were supposed to take care of him, encourage him, embrace him; but now he was starting to see what it meant to care for others, to be the one who offered comfort.

In the months since their parents had left, Jacob had taken care of his brother but had not known how to express what he felt. Perhaps he was too busy trying to hide his feelings, not wanting to break down in front of Moses. He had to be the strong one. He had presumed his brother needed security more than affection.

"We're never going to leave you. I promise. We're alone too. But now we have each other. Nothing's going to stop us. I'm not afraid of those Boche or of the gendarmes. We'll see our families again. I swear we will."

Moses joined the hug and the boys fell asleep again, dreaming of their previous life, the days of drifting off curled up next to their parents as life passed by in its merry little stream.

Chapter 4

Paris
July 17, 1942

The sound of footfalls overhead woke them. Jacob's neck was stiff with the strain of having been sleeping at an odd angle for hours. Moses had to go to the bathroom badly, and Joseph was ravenous.

"Go back there to pee. It's cleaner than going in those rancid bathrooms upstairs," his older brother told him.

Moses moved to where the light turned into the darkness and sighed with relief as his bladder emptied.

The three boys crept back upstairs to the stadium and were surprised to find that the crowd from the day before had grown. The velodrome was a beehive being shaken by the beekeeper. The stands crawled with people, and the echo of voices was a resounding buzz.

A young man in a white uniform approached the boys and stuck out his arm to stop them. "Where are you going? Are you alone?"

The three boys looked up. A young, dark-skinned man with shiny, gelled hair and a carefully trimmed mustache frowned down at them. "Yes, sir," they answered.

"Call me Dr. Michelle. Aren't your parents with you?" he asked again.

"No, Dr. Michelle."

"Unbelievable. These people are animals. What a disgrace. Where have human rights, basic human decency gone? That senile, fanatical marshal is the worst thing that could have happened to France."

The boys were dumbfounded. No one talked like that about Marshal Pétain, the country's savior and chief of state in unoccupied France.

"Don't worry, we'll be fine," Joseph said, drawing away from the man.

"There's a section for lost children. I'll take you there." The doctor took Moses's hand.

"It's okay. We can find it on our own," Jacob answered, his mind calculating how to escape as soon as they were out of the man's sight. No one had documented their arrival yet, and they might still have a chance of slipping away unnoticed.

Just then, the French police officer who had taken them to the government official's table the day before passed by.

"Gendarme," called Dr. Michelle, "take these boys to the section for lost children."

The officer recognized the boys, and Jacob saw the fury in his eyes. The man smiled, his enormous double chin stretching up to reveal the golden buttons of his combat jacket underneath. "Of course, Doctor. I'll leave them in good hands."

The gendarme grabbed the two older boys by the collars of their shirts, and Moses followed, terrified.

"There's no call to escort them like that. They aren't criminals," the doctor said, frowning again.

"Well, we don't want them getting lost in the crowd now, do we?" the gendarme retorted.

Jacob thought about calling out to the doctor but feared it would be even worse if the man knew the boys had not even been registered.

The officer dragged them up the main stairway to the first level of stands but, before heading for the section for lost children, shoved them into the locker rooms where only police were allowed. "Now you can all pay me back at the same time," he snarled.

The boys were petrified. Jacob knew they had to do something to get away from the man. No one would care what happened to three abandoned children. The people in the stadium were concerned with their own problems already.

"We're really sorry for what happened yesterday. We were really scared. Really, we're sorry," Moses stammered.

The gendarme locked the door and loosened his grip on the boys, who fled to the opposite corner of the room. They instinctively bunched up together through some distant hope of safety in numbers. The officer drew out his nightstick and a switchblade. "We happen to have an overabundance of Jewish refuse at the moment. No one will notice if a couple brats go missing." He smiled as he spoke.

"Sir, do whatever you want to me, but the others are innocent," Jacob pleaded, taking a step forward.

"You think I'm in the mood to bargain? When you three leave here it'll be for the hospital or for the cemetery for Jewish pigs."

Jacob remembered his own knife and checked his pants pocket.

He took it out and waved it at the policeman, who guffawed. "What do you think you're going to do with that little toothpick? You don't think I've taken down tougher guys than you?"

"Yeah, you're real brave, attacking a few helpless children," Jacob said. On the ground he spotted a police jacket, which he snatched up and wrapped around his left hand for protection.

"Pests must be eliminated," the gendarme replied, taking a step forward.

The nightstick came down hard but only brushed Jacob's hand. Then the boy managed to wedge his knife into the policeman's sleeve. The gendarme roared and lunged, but Jacob ducked and scampered to the door. He tried to force it open, but it would not yield.

The officer reached for Moses and grabbed him with his knife-wielding hand. Moses whimpered in terror as more tears fell.

"You'd better give up, buddy, if you don't want your little prig brother to have a bad time," the policeman called to Jacob, breathing hard.

"Let my brother go, you pig!" Jacob screamed in fury.

Moses seized the moment to bite the policeman's hand as hard as he could, and the gendarme pulled his hand back with a howl. Joseph jumped on the man's back, but the gendarme whirled around like a madman with the child clinging to his neck. Moses kicked him hard in the groin, bringing him to his knees with another howl. Jacob sent his knee firmly into the man's face, and the other boys pummeled him with all their strength.

Before long the policeman had collapsed on the floor. Jacob searched him for the key to the door, opened it, and the boys flew out of the room. They did not stop running until they were as far as possible from the gendarme. They climbed to the top tier of stands and mixed in with a group of children playing games led by a few women trying to make their confinement a little less unbearable.

"What are we going to do?" Joseph whispered to his friends.

"We've got to be more careful, stay out of sight, figure something out at night. We've just . . . We've got to get out of here," Jacob said.

Moses was still white as a sheet. "I'm scared," he said.

"Don't worry," Jacob consoled him. "I won't let them do anything to you." Then he quirked an eyebrow. "Hey, did you see his face when you kicked him in the crotch? You're a real hero!"

The three boys grinned. At least they had escaped uninjured. When they had fully calmed down, they snuck back to their hideout in the basement of the velodrome.

Once night had fallen and the buzz of voices had quieted, they reemerged from their hiding place. They hoped the gendarme would not be out at those hours of the night, much less after the beating the man had endured. But they needed to stock up on food for their escape before the police searched the entire stadium to find the boys who had beaten an officer.

Jacob crept to the food tent, taking care that he was not being watched, and slipped in as the other two boys stood guard. On the left, Joseph watched the main entrance and the stands. Any sign of alarm would complicate things. Moses kept his eyes on the lower entryway and the guards who made their rounds.

All around they heard the background noise of the whining, crying, and coughing of thousands of prisoners crammed together inside the stadium. The main stadium lights were off, but the emergency lights and some from the main track remained lit.

It left Joseph in a stupor to see the masses of people spent by hunger, heat, and fear. He wondered if they could at least find refuge for a few hours in dreams, clinging like shipwreck victims to the vanishing remains of life. He imagined his parents and siblings in a place like the velodrome, then tried to get the picture out of his mind.

Moses heard a wail and saw a dirty, naked little girl crying and moving all around her mother. Her eyes were swollen and tears made a mess of her face, the part not covered by matted blond hair. The mother looked to be asleep, but when the child knelt and shook her, Moses understood the woman was dead. All around them slept an indifferent crowd. The dehumanizing objectives of the cruel French police and the Germans for the terrified, humiliated masses were being met.

A chill ran up Moses's entire body. Then he felt a hand dig into his shoulder. He did not want to look around, but the dark uniform left no room for doubt. "I knew the rats would come out sooner or later," a voice growled. Fat, sweaty fingers grasped Moses's clothes, and the boy felt something slice through his thin shirt. He screamed, and two more policemen approached. Joseph turned at the noise and saw his friend's face, his eyes bulging in terror. There was nothing Joseph could do. He fled to the stands to hide in the shadows.

Jacob's heart skipped several beats when he heard his brother's scream. He hesitated. If he ran to help him, he would surely be caught—but he could not leave Moses alone. He peered through a hole in the tent's fabric and watched policemen running toward the scene. To his horror, the gendarme they had encountered was dragging his brother away. He crouched behind the boxes of food a few moments before slipping out of the tent. Everything was still, no gendarmes in sight. Jacob's chest closed in on him. He recalled his promise to his parents to never leave Moses and to keep him safe. Jacob crumpled to the floor and started to weep.

Footsteps approached, and a figure knelt beside him, waiting for Jacob to lift his head. "What's going on?"

It was the voice of the doctor from earlier in the day. His brow was furrowed, and his glasses seemed attached to his long, curved nose.

Jacob spluttered between sobs. "They . . . took . . . him . . ."

"Who?"

"My brother." He buried his head again.

"The policemen gather up all the abandoned children. We can't have you wandering around out of control. This is a dangerous place." Michelle's tone was so calming that Jacob's breathing began to normalize.

"That man, the gendarme, he brought us to the velodrome. We escaped, and he's been looking for us. This morning he tried to kill us, but we managed to get away. Now I don't know what he'll do to my brother."

"The gendarmes are just pawns. The government sent them to do the dirty work, but a lot of them detest what they've been forced to do." The doctor touched the boy's chin to raise it.

"You're only saying that because you're not a Jew. They hate us. The French hate us."

The doctor pulled back the flap of his white jacket and revealed a yellow Star of David. The child dissolved into tears again and threw himself onto the man. Michelle fought off the knot in his own throat. He was a French Jew but had volunteered his services in the velodrome to aid the unfortunate prisoners.

"My family has been in this country since the sixteenth century," he explained, supporting Jacob in his arms. "I'm more French than most of the people who spit at me as I walk down the street. They kicked us out of Spain centuries ago, as though we were the plague, but France welcomed us. It wasn't easy at first, but my family settled in Paris and ran drugstores and pharmacies, up until my grandfather, who became a doctor. We've fought and died for the Republic. We believe in her eternal values, and we know this dark hour will pass. Hard times show what people are really made of. This trial won't destroy us. It'll make us a better, stronger country. I may never get to see it, nor any of these people"—he gestured to the stands—"but France will shake off this barbaric, evil yoke and begin again."

Tears streamed down the doctor's face, deepening his thin wrinkles and making him look older in Jacob's eyes. Two strangers had achieved a rare moment of connection, and it demanded silence.

Michelle took a deep breath and made to stand, recovering the energy that drove him to serve in that wasteland. "I'll help you find your brother," he said.

Joseph appeared beside them all of a sudden, a worried, hesitant look on his face. At first he thought the doctor had captured Jacob and was preparing to hand him over to the police, but the tears on the man's face gave him the confidence to approach.

The doctor continued, "I know a gendarme sergeant who can give us a hand. Follow me, but stay a bit behind."

They headed for the stairs and slowly walked up to the second tier, then to one of the rooms at the back of the velodrome.

"Wait here," the doctor said, sticking his hands in his pockets and walking off.

"Can we trust him?" Joseph asked as soon as Michelle was out of sight.

Jacob shrugged. "We've got no choice. We're not supposed to trust strangers, but there's nobody here in this huge stadium *but* strangers."

The two boys stood facing the dark hallway with their ears attuned for any sound of approach. They grew impatient the longer the doctor delayed. Joseph drummed his fingers on the wall, and Jacob fiddled with his knife. Finally, they heard voices, then steps, and saw two figures emerging from the darkness.

Jacob and Joseph straightened up. One of the men was a gendarme. "I knew we shouldn't have trusted him," Joseph hissed.

Michelle raised his hands to calm them. The braids on the officer's jacket shimmered, and the children understood he was a sergeant. The boys stiffened in fear when the two men stopped before them.

"Your brother," the doctor said, "is not in the section of lost children."

"What?"

"The sergeant believes he may have been transported to the commissary, but I imagine he's still in the building. We must find him before anything happens to him," Michelle said, glancing at the sergeant.

"I can't put my men on this job, but I can ask some friends to help us. The velodrome is large, but it only has a few private rooms," the sergeant explained.

Jacob felt his heart breaking into shards of glass, slicing at him from within, making breath impossible.

"We're going to find him," the doctor said. His frail encouragement fell flat, and Jacob burst into tears. He knew that hatred was an unbeatable force in the heart of a wicked man. Every second that went by, his brother was in more danger. He took off running down the halls of the stadium, his heart pounding in his ears with a furious thrum.

Chapter 5

Darkness allied itself to fear that night. Jacob ran from one place to the next, stopped short when he saw a boy that looked like his brother in the crowd, then recommenced his frantic search. It was almost impossible for the doctor to keep up with him. Finally they reached the uppermost tier. The rows of seats swarmed with people even though this was the hottest area in the velodrome. Not even the hint of a breeze stirred, and the nearness of the Seine only increased the humidity.

Jacob stared into faces darkened both by the lack of light and exhaustion. He scoured the bathrooms and searched the few empty seats he could find, then sat down on a bench jutting out into the main hall.

"He's not here," he said flatly as the doctor approached, panting.

"He's got to be somewhere," Michelle insisted. Though the stadium was enormous, there were only a limited number of hiding places.

"The only place we haven't gone is . . . Of course!" Jacob shouted, jumping to his feet again.

"Where now?"

"The basement. The gendarme took him to the basement!"

Jacob tore down the stairs and came upon Joseph and the sergeant on their way up. The banging of feet on the stairway reverberated louder as the rest of the group followed Jacob down. Minutes later, on the ground floor, Jacob tried to pull open the basement door—yet it would not budge. The sergeant and a few of the gendarmes that had joined them tried as well, but it was locked from the inside.

"Surely there's another way in?" Jacob asked the air, frantic. They looked all around but saw no other possible way into the basement.

"Maybe from the bathrooms?" suggested one of the policemen. They all ran back up to the main floor and searched the bathroom hand over hand for any out-of-the-way door. Despite the nauseating stench, Jacob threw himself on the ground to leave no square inch unexplored.

"And we're sure they didn't take the child from the building?" Michelle asked the sergeant.

"No, they would have presented a transfer slip. Besides, it's too soon."

One of the gendarmes raised his arms and hollered for everyone to come. "Look here!" The group ran toward him and saw two handles sticking out of a metal plate in the floor. Two of the men managed to lift it, revealing a sort of tunnel. One of the gendarmes shone his flashlight into the darkness inside. "There's no way to know where it—"

Jacob wasted no time. He grabbed the flashlight from the man's hand and jumped down into the tunnel, with Joseph right behind him. They fell onto a damp, cold floor, then stood and shone the light all around them. "It looks just like the tunnel I was in the other night," Jacob said.

The boys walked as fast as they could, nearly losing track of the many turns they took, but Jacob kept his eyes on the pipes that looked like the ones he had seen in his first foray into the basement's inner workings. They walked for a while before the tunnel changed and became more like a hallway. Seeing a light at the end, they proceeded with care.

Jacob feared the worst when he heard voices and cries of pain. He pulled out his pocketknife and, pressed against the wall, made his way carefully toward the room at the entryway ahead. Joseph followed close behind. Jacob turned to Joseph ever so briefly and motioned for absolute silence. The door before them was ajar.

The boys crouched down and peered through the crack. They saw the large back of the gendarme, but no sign of Moses. The officer took a few steps backward, just in front of the door. Jacob shoved it with all his might. The wooden door knocked into the gendarme, throwing him off balance, and the two boys shot into the room. Moses was there—wearing almost nothing but the belt marks on his back. When the gendarme made to stand, Joseph pummeled and kicked him to give Jacob and Moses a moment to escape. But as they ran, the gendarme grabbed Joseph's leg. The boy fought with all his strength and planted his foot in the man's eyes. The officer collapsed, and the three boys took off running into the darkness of the basement.

Minutes later, hoping they were a safe distance away from the gendarme, they paused to catch their breath and turned on the flashlight.

"We've got to get out of here," Jacob said, his voice unsteady. "The gendarmes will register us and then send us somewhere else."

Moses stood looking at him, speechless. His pants were bunched up and twisted, his shirt was on inside out, and his face was blotched with screaming red. Jacob reached for and held his sobbing brother.

"The worst is over," Jacob soothed him, stroking his hair. "We're together again. That's all that matters."

"I . . . I was so scared. He was . . . He was crazy. I thought he was going to . . . to kill . . ." Moses stammered and gasped for breath.

"Shh, shh. It's okay now," Jacob said in his calmest voice. Moses's breathing evened, the rising of his chest echoing the fall of his brother's in a soothing rhythm. They had been still for several minutes, and all three boys felt a little cold. The past few hours had left them drenched in sweat, and in the stillness it turned into a chill.

"Do you think these tunnels have an exit to the outside?" Joseph wondered aloud.

Jacob turned the flashlight onto their friend. He seemed even paler than when they first met him, and his shirt was damp with sweat. Jacob had only seen Joseph a few times before, and only ever in the synagogue—but since they had found each other here in the velodrome, he had started to become another kind of brother.

Jacob grabbed the Star of David his aunt had tacked onto his shirt and yanked it off. He threw it onto the basement floor and stomped on it. The other two boys followed his example. They entered near hysterics trampling the symbol of their shame and oppression.

"That is the last time I'll ever wear it." The absoluteness in Jacob's voice cut through the energy of the younger boys. Then he turned the flashlight into the darkness, which could not be chased away but could be split open by the light. As hope could destroy doubt, the ray of the flashlight would be enough to guide them to freedom.

They walked down several tunnels and started to hear the noises of toilets being flushed. "People are waking up," Joseph observed. Then they heard the rush of water through the pipes.

"Water will lead to the sewers," Jacob said. "If we follow it, we might find an exit." The boys quickened their pace. When they were unsure where to go next, they stood still, listening to discern the direction of the flowing water. They heard voices in the distance but tried to ignore them, focusing on the water that might lead them out.

Jacob spotted some pricks of light in the ceiling of the tunnel and some metal rungs in the wall. "It looks like a sewer drain," he said. The boys looked around them before deciding to climb the ladder.

"What happens if we're coming up too close to the velodrome and a gendarme sees us?" Joseph asked.

"We'll just have to run. They'll be able to see us since it's daytime, but we can try to get lost in a crowd," Jacob answered.

"But our clothes are disgusting. We'll stand out. Plus, you can see where the star used to be," Joseph countered, touching his chest.

"Well, we'll head for empty streets. First, let's try to find my aunt at her apartment. Then we'll go to your family's house so you can get cleaned up. After that, we'll go with you to find them like we promised."

Joseph studied his friend's face, as much as the darkness would allow. The confidence in Jacob's words breathed an inner strength into Joseph like he had never felt before.

"Isn't it strange to you that your aunt hasn't come looking for you?" he asked.

Jacob shrugged. "Don't forget, nobody registered us. There's no record of us being here, and we weren't on any list."

"Yeah, but people saw you get on the buses. Someone must have told her what happened," Joseph insisted.

"They took tons of people and shipped them off to who knows

where. I'm not surprised she hasn't been able to find us. But we'll find her. She'll tell us what to do." Jacob nodded firmly.

Moses, calmer now, piped up. "Aunt Judith is really brave. She'll take care of us." He pressed a small hand to his sore body, but at least he could breathe again. As the policeman beat him, his mind had instead focused upon Jacob coming to save him and taking him to their parents.

Jacob went up first. When he reached the round lid, he pushed gently. It was much heavier than he expected, and he would need help to budge it. "Come on up," he said to Joseph.

The two boys worked together, barely balanced on the metal rungs of the ladder as their only support, and pushed on the lid of the manhole. They managed to pry up one side and slowly budge the lid to the side.

They inched the lid a little farther out of the way, and Jacob stole a glance around. Fortunately, the manhole was located neither in the middle of the street nor in a highly visible area. The velodrome was directly in front of them. He and Joseph slid the lid open enough to allow them room to climb out. Blinded by the light, Moses watched from below, and the fresh air reminded him that a world beyond the tunnels did exist.

"Come up quick," Jacob called.

After climbing up onto the street, the three boys walked down the sidewalk in front of the building. Gendarmes stood all around, but no one paid them much attention. As soon as they rounded the corner, they broke into a run. They had no idea where they were going, but when they saw the Eiffel Tower ahead, it beckoned like a lighthouse leading them home.

Chapter 6

The city seemed to have transformed during the two days the boys had been sequestered in the velodrome. The degree of indifference among Parisians was even more visible after the raid. The sad fate of misfortune retreated, leaving the rest unscathed and somehow immunized against pain and suffering. The passersby hardly glanced at the three little vagabonds. Since the occupation, unkempt children roaming the streets was not an uncommon sight. Little by little, poverty and hunger had spread throughout both the occupied and free zones of the country, but most French focused upon how things would get better soon. The Great War had been much harder than this, and they had come out stronger.

The boys made their way down the clean and empty streets. They went by foot, not daring to take a train or bus. The police could detain them easily on public transportation, and the boys had no identification with them.

After an exhausting three-hour walk, they finally saw the street where Jacob and Moses had spent the greater part of their existence—their own little world where the frontiers of their imagination had seemed safe and stable. They walked beyond their school building toward the synagogue. The wooden doors—scorched black and still smelling of smoke—were open, showing the disarray within. Jacob thought of Rabbi Ezekiel, the young man with the curly beard and kind face. He knew the rabbi was German like the Steins, and there would be little hope of finding him there. If the man had not been taken, he would be somewhere safer, in hiding.

They walked by the bakery, which was closed, and the butcher's and several other stores before reaching their apartment building. The large gate leading to the inner courtyard was wide open. They snuck through the narrow pass by the doorwoman's lookout as quickly as they could. They could not risk her betraying them to the police again.

They crept up the stairs, unsure of which tenants they could trust. All the Jewish residents had fled or been taken. *And we surely can't trust the non-Jews,* Jacob thought as he climbed the worn wooden steps. A tempting thought flickered through his brain: What if it had all been a bad dream? Maybe his parents and Aunt Judith would be waiting for them at the apartment, as if nothing out of the ordinary had happened.

When they got to the door, Jacob felt in his pockets. He still had the key. He opened the door and slipped into the front hallway. It was dark inside. In the summer, only afternoon sunlight made its way into the apartment, and even then only in the living room and his aunt's bedroom. The long wooden floorboards creaked as they walked, alerting any and every neighbor that someone was home. They decided to take off their shoes. No trace of their aunt remained in the living room, the kitchen, or the bathroom. They went into her bedroom, the one place off-limits to them in the house. The bed was made, and her clothing was still neatly arranged. Judith's old brown suitcase lay atop the wardrobe.

"She hasn't left," Moses said, pointing to the suitcase.

"No, she might be at work. Maybe it would be better for us to stay here and rest until nighttime," Jacob suggested.

"But I thought we were going to my house and then you'd help me find the other camp where they took prisoners." Joseph's chin trembled.

The two brothers looked at their friend. They had finally gotten somewhere they knew, where they felt moderately safe, but he was still not home and had no real certainty about the whereabouts of his family. Being that alone in the world was the worst thing that had ever happened to him. No one cared about him. If he disappeared right then and there, his life would have vanished like noonday fog.

"We will. I promised you. But first we've got to know what's happened with my aunt," Jacob assured him.

While the two younger boys went to look for food in the kitchen, Jacob searched the drawers of his aunt's bureau and then brought the suitcase down. He opened it carefully and looked inside. To his surprise, it was full of old photographs—yellowed letters in white envelopes with red-and-blue trim, all bundled together with red yarn; some newer envelopes; several maps of France; some money; and the personal documents and identification for each of the three of them. Jacob slipped a picture of his mother into his pocket, then flipped through the yellowed letters. The handwriting on the envelopes was a lovely, slanted script in dark ink. It looked like a woman's writing, in German. Perhaps they were letters from his grandmother. The newer, loose envelopes had no names on them, but they did bear a return address: Place de la Liberté, Valence, France. The address was completely foreign to Jacob. He unfolded one of the maps he had left on the bed and studied it a good while before he found a little city with that name south of Lyon. It was clear on the other side of the country from Paris, far to the southeast. He opened one of the letters and began to read:

Valence, May 5, 1942

Dear Judith,

Spring has come quickly, but not even its eternal vitality can coax a smile out of us. A mother should never be separated from her children, her very soul. But I thank heaven at least they've got you.

I imagine Jacob is taking good care of Moses. He's always been so responsible, though he's on the cusp of when his body and mind will begin their unceasing war to control the awkward adolescent self. Sometimes it's hard for me to watch him grow. He's no longer the little boy who would crawl into bed with us on Saturday mornings and jump up and down on Eleazar, laughing his little head off.

Since we left Paris, your brother has not been the same. His shoulders are stooped, his face a constant picture of defeat. The war has amputated his heart. He cannot keep suffering so much for all of us.

We've found work, at least for the first part of spring. It'll be enough for the train tickets. Things are calmer here than in Paris, but the air itself seems to be on edge, like when a storm is coming and you can almost feel the electricity in the atmosphere.

We get news about new raids in occupied France. It seems we wretched foreigners will never find peace anywhere. It is proving to be extremely difficult for us to get visas for any country at all. Eleazar has twice been to Marseille. The consulates are overwhelmed, and the number of visas for exiled Jews are severely reduced. Even so, we hope to obtain papers for all four of us.

We desperately hope you change your mind and decide to join us. I know how deeply you love France. Your mind and heart belong in Paris, but no one in the city is safe with the Germans ready to pounce. And your employers won't stay much longer if things continue in the direction they're headed.

I trust Moses is as sweet and handsome as ever. His lips have the grace of his grandmother, always smiling, his heart spilling over with goodness.

Kiss the boys for me. Tell them how much we love them, that we think of them constantly every day, and that we will be together again soon.

Your loving sister-in-law,
Jana

Jacob's eyes and face turned dark with the grime from his shirtsleeve as he wiped away his tears. He sighed. Loneliness was starker when the heart wandered down memory's paths. He looked at the half-dozen letters and thought twice before reading another. Finally, he settled on taking the last letter, as if the words in between were of no import.

He read the beginning quickly, torn between wanting to make the letter last and hoping to know how his parents were. His chest contracted as he reached the last few paragraphs.

A cry escaped before he clapped his hands over his mouth. He did not want to upset Moses, but it would be almost impossible to hide his grief. Did his eyes deceive him, or had he just read that his parents were planning to go to South America without them? Surely not . . . This could not be. He also knew that in the past year so many things had happened that the only truly impossible thing was for more unexpected things *not* to happen. The brothers had to find them as soon as possible, but they would have to cross France to do it.

He remembered when the world consisted of their house, his days at school, walks with his father, and nights snuggled up to his mother—when everything was a game, and holding his father's strong hand gave him a calmness he had found nowhere else. Jacob felt like an eagle perched at the edge of its nest just before diving into the infinite abyss below. Would his wings let them take flight? Would they be able to float through the unknown before them?

He put the letter in his pocket, dried his face, and went to the kitchen. Moses and Joseph were playing a game on the wooden table. Jacob glanced at the pantry and saw that Moses had managed to remove Aunt Judith's lock. The younger boys had eaten nearly all that was left of Judith's meager stores. Hunger and sadness were at war within Jacob, but upon seeing the bits of cheese and the half loaf of bread on the table, his stomach won. Then he drank as much water as his belly could hold. Approaching something like fullness, he said, "I actually think it would be better for us to go to your house, Joseph. It's not that far away. Then we can come back here to see if my aunt is home."

Joseph nodded, feeling the panic of the raid wash over him again.

"Moses, you've got to shower first. I'll find you some clothes," Jacob said.

"Shower? No way. I can do that when we get back."

"The Germans will smell you a mile away. The idea is for no one to notice us, so we're all three going to shower before we leave here."

Moses grumbled but moved toward the bathroom. Jacob went to their room and found clean outfits, walking shoes, warm clothes, hats, and the packs they used when they would go for walks in the countryside.

"What's all that for?" Joseph asked.

"We might have a long journey ahead of us. I found some letters in Aunt Judith's things, and it looks like our parents finally got visas and were hoping to leave at the end of the—"

"Without you?" Joseph interrupted.

"They couldn't get visas for us. They wanted to go to South America and then send for us, but they have no idea what's happened the last few days here in Paris."

Joseph nodded. "So you want to go find them?"

"If my aunt comes back, we could go with her. But if she's not here anymore, we'll have to try it anyway."

Joseph buried his hands in his hair, closed his eyes, and shook his head. It was too much to take in. "And you thought I was crazy for trying to find my parents at the other camp? There's no way you can travel around the country on your own."

Jacob knew his friend was right. Traveling through France right now would be suicidal. But he could not give up. He would walk until his strength ran out, searching for his parents.

"It's worth a shot," he answered, with all the conviction that innocent confidence could muster—at the age when dreams and reality were still jumbled together and recklessness was still a kind of bravery.

Chapter 7

Paris
July 18, 1942

The shower and food refreshed them, though the boys were bleary
from not having slept since their fitful rest in the velodrome
basement two nights before. They cautiously left the apartment,
walking with short, light steps over the floorboards of the landings.
When they reached the courtyard, they took care that no one saw
them leave. Once in the street, they stuck their hands in their pockets and tried to appear like boys just whiling away the time before
supper. No one paid them any attention. One of the advantages of
being children was being completely invisible to most adults.

The building where Joseph lived was much older and more run-
down than Aunt Judith's. The brick façade was blackened from proximity to the nearby factories. Several of the windows had broken

glass, and the dirty shutters, many only partially attached, made them look like eyes wide open in desperation. But for Joseph, it was home.

They walked up the stone stairway. Some steps had crumbled, and the rickety bannister offered flimsy support as they climbed. They reached the third floor and saw an apartment door open. Joseph began to cry at the doorway.

The floor was wet and littered with newspaper, with things thrown everywhere. The mattresses had been removed from the bedrooms, and the clothing strewn about tightened the noose of desolation around Joseph's heart.

Jacob and Moses followed Joseph into what had been his room. Broken toys and dirty clothes had been scattered around at will.

So this was not his home anymore after all. The walls still enclosed his memories, but the soul had been removed. All the birthdays with a simple cake made by his mother, the steamy aromas of soup made by his grandmother, the squabbling and laughter punctuating family meals, the absurd assumption that they would always be happy . . . Everything was gone. They had never had money, but they'd always had one another. There is no greater wealth than love; but when the wrenching force of fate crushes affection, the misery of love's lack turns people into shadows of themselves.

Joseph fell to the floor, gripping his stomach and weeping. He felt as though knives were stabbing him. Jacob and Moses were afraid his wailing would alert the neighbors, but they did not silence him. They offered what comfort they could.

"The important thing is that your family is okay. Tomorrow we'll go to that camp at Drancy. I'm sure you'll see them again. At least they're not too far away," Moses said. Yet sadness descended upon him as he heard his own words. Jacob wanted to go look for their parents, but Moses was terrified. Since leaving Germany, he had rarely been outside the place where his aunt lived. Running all over France seemed like madness. The only thing that made it bearable was that he would be with Jacob.

No one spoke for a while. Then Moses sat down and started fiddling with some little lead soldiers that were damaged. Jacob finally broke the stillness. "Do you need to get any clothes? We shouldn't stay here long."

"Do you think your aunt will be back?" Joseph asked, stuffing a few belongings into a backpack.

"I don't know. The house was quiet, like she hadn't been there for a while. The furniture had dust on it, and Aunt Judith doesn't tolerate dust. The kitchen looked abandoned too . . . I don't know. Maybe she's been out looking for us this whole time, or maybe they took her. I think we should stay there tonight. And if she doesn't come back, we'll get you to that other camp and then head south."

Jacob's voice was so quiet it startled Joseph. Jacob always tried to encourage the others, but he seemed to be running out of steam. Joseph had seen Jacob stand up for his brother on more than one occasion when nasty schoolboys were roughing Moses up because of his yellow star. Yet, as he zipped his backpack closed, Joseph wondered if the atmosphere of his apartment and the fear surrounding them had taken a toll on Jacob.

"Okay, let's go," Joseph said, throwing his backpack over his shoulders. They walked down the hallway, and Joseph saw his father's hat hanging on a nail behind the door. "I should keep this," he said, settling it on his head. Contact with something that belonged to his father filled him anew with dread, but he swallowed hard and walked out to the landing.

Joseph kept his eyes glued to the narrowing vision of his apartment as the door closed behind them. He knew his old life was over and that things would never be the same.

They went down the empty staircase to the entryway. Just as they started down the street, Joseph glanced back. Fearing he would be turned into a pillar of salt like Lot's wife, the boy could not resist one last look at what remained of his world.

Innocence can only be lost once. The eyes of the boy now beheld something unknown. The bright colors of his childhood had turned to gray, the magic morphing into the dark reality that now held everything in its merciless grip. Becoming conscious of himself, a boy turns away from the lost paradise of childhood and becomes one more soul to whom the gates of Eden are forever closed.

Before the three boys reached Aunt Judith's apartment building again, they noted the heightened activity in the streets. Many of their former neighbors were Jews, but the non-Jews who remained carried on, indifferent toward the lot that had befallen their former friends, neighbors, students, employees, and clients.

Jacob found the normalcy shocking. Within a matter of hours, no one recalled his existence, no one was concerned. It was as if he had never even been born.

Jacob told Moses to go ahead and spy out the approach to their apartment building. Moses went to the corner, took a few cautious steps beyond the threshold, and saw the doorwoman. Her back was to him. His pulse shot up, and he ran back to the other boys.

"She's in her lookout," Moses said, eyes wide.

"Okay, okay, think. What are we going to do? When she's at the entryway, she can stay there for hours . . ." Jacob's mind ran through all the possible scenarios.

"I don't think she'd recognize me," Joseph said. "I could distract her, and once you two are in, I'll sneak in after you."

Jacob shook his head. "It's too dangerous. That woman is the devil incarnate. You know what she did to us."

Joseph's chest rose with determination. "I'll take my chances. Leave it to me." He was eager to help. Danger sometimes was the best sign that life carried on. It was better to stare fear in the face than hide in a hole.

Joseph took his hat off and went up to the doorwoman. His friends could not see him, but they could hear him faintly.

"Could you help me, ma'am? I think I've gotten turned around. My Aunt Clara is waiting for me on Rue Nollet. Is it nearby?"

The woman turned her dark brown eyes on him, not hiding the annoyance she felt when anyone asked for help. She stood, opened the green door, and stepped down to the cobblestones of the entryway. "It's not far. You have to go down to the end of the street," she said, pointing vaguely.

"To the right or to the left?" Joseph asked, stepping toward the road. He needed to draw the doorwoman away from the entrance without her seeing his friends.

The woman frowned. She was heavy and preferred not to move from the door. Supposedly she swept the courtyard and mopped the stairs, but no one had ever seen her do it. She heaved herself forward, over the threshold, and Jacob and Moses seized the moment of her back being turned to them and dashed behind her into the courtyard. Once behind the wall, they paused to quiet their breathing and let their heartbeats slow.

"Watch out, sir!" Joseph cried out as a noisy truck bearing casks of wine chugged down the street too close to them. The doorwoman turned and flinched, and Joseph skittered through the gate. By the time the doorwoman turned back to the lost boy, recovering from the fright, there was no one there.

"Little brat!" she yelled, arms raised. Her sweaty, white flesh jiggled beneath her coarse black dress. She hefted herself slowly back toward the lookout.

The three boys giggled as they made their way up the stairs. With the key in the door to their aunt's apartment, they heard a noise behind them. They turned, terrified, but it was not the greasy face of the doorwoman. Instead, it was the sweet face of Margot, the woman who lived right below them. She was a loner who preferred cats to other adult company, but she did like to give sweets to children and sing along to old songs on her gramophone. Jacob and Moses had spent many a night listening to her through the floorboards.

"Ms. Margot!" Moses greeted her with a smile.

"My dear children," she said, holding out her soft, pale hands. "Are you looking for your aunt? Come into my apartment. Let's not talk here in the hallway."

With difficulty, the woman made her way down the set of half-turn stairs. She opened her lock with a large key and stood aside for the boys to pass, and they went to the living room and settled on a couch. Margot came in a few minutes later, holding a tray.

"I've brought you some pastries and milk. An old woman doesn't eat much, and you are growing boys."

The boys eyed the food greedily but did not move. Margot placed the silver tray on the table and motioned for them to help themselves. That was all the invitation needed. The three boys gobbled up the food and downed all the milk in their glasses. Margot watched them quietly, pleased. She waited until they were finished before speaking again.

"So you have come looking for your aunt Judith?" she asked the brothers.

"Yes, ma'am," Jacob answered. Margot's smile faded, and she

looked down at the floor. She swallowed hard, took a deep breath, and chose her words carefully.

"The day of the raid was terrible. I never imagined anything like that could happen here. You boys know I've been a teacher for forty years. In fact, I taught literature at the same school you attended before the Nazis came to Paris."

Jacob and Moses nodded, crumbs around their mouths. The little feast had perked them up.

"From my window I watched them take all those poor people away. When I saw Moses's little blond head, I just broke down and wept. I so admired your parents, and you boys have always been so sweet and respectful to me. I've known your aunt for ages—a wonderful woman." It always took Margot a while to get to the point. The boys kept quiet but were getting impatient. "After that beast of a woman denounced you," she continued, "I heard the race up the stairs—how you went out to the roof, how the gendarmes chased you—and I prayed you would escape to safety. Speaking of which," she said, interrupting herself, "where have you been the past few days?"

"Locked up with thousands of other people in the velodrome," Jacob answered.

"The velodrome? Where they have the bicycle races?" Margot asked, incredulous.

"Yes, there in the stadium."

"Unbelievable," she muttered, looking for confirmation from the cat she cradled in her lap. "The world has gone absolutely mad."

"So have you seen Aunt Judith?" Moses broke in.

"Yes, that's what I wanted to talk to you about. Your aunt came back a few hours later. I heard her go in the apartment—"

They all four jumped at the sound of loud rapping at the door. Silence fell. Margot got slowly to her feet and went to the hallway, gesturing for the children to stay quiet. She peered through the peephole and saw two gendarmes shuffling uneasily before her door.

Chapter 8

Paris
July 18, 1942

Margot took a deep breath and opened the door just a crack. "Madame, pardon the interruption, but the doorwoman called us. Some of the tenants have heard voices coming from the apartment upstairs," said the gendarme, still breathing heavily from his trip up the stairs.

Margot waited a moment. She never lied, yet she could not let the children be taken.

"I'm so sorry. It's my fault. Two of my cats got out. Sometimes they get into my neighbor's apartment. I actually have keys, so I went up to get them. That must be what people heard."

"Could you let us in upstairs so we can have a look? It will only take a moment," the older gendarme said. The younger one gave him a look of annoyance.

"Why, yes, of course," Margot responded, rustling through a drawer in the table beside the door, looking for the key to Judith's apartment. She opened the door just wide enough to pass through and hand the key to the gendarmes.

The gendarme continued, "A lot of the Jews have tried to hide in their neighbors' and friends' houses, and we've got to round up the last of them. They'll be shipped out of France soon."

"Is that so? Away from France?"

"Yes, the Germans need them to work, it seems. They've got too many men on the Russian front, and they need manpower to make weapons in the factories," the gendarme confirmed.

Margot nodded and crossed her arms. The agent's answer had convinced her. As the gendarme walked upstairs, she shut the door again and sighed with relief. She went to the living room and held a finger to her lips. "Not a word! The gendarmes are upstairs."

"My backpack!" Jacob whispered, horrified. "I left it up there. They'll see it, and there were some really important things in it . . ."

"Let's just hope they don't take anything," Margot said.

They heard footsteps above them, the sound of doors opening and closing. Moments later, the two men knocked again at Margot's door.

"Thank you for the key, ma'am. Do you know if anyone's been up there in the past couple of days?" the older officer asked, his face clouded with concern.

"It's difficult to say. Like I said, there was a woman living up there, but I haven't heard anything for a few days and, I'll tell you one thing, though my hearing's not what it once was, down here you can hear a pin fall from upstairs. You should have heard those children who used to live up there. The way they would tear from one end of the apartment to the other—never a moment's peace!"

The gendarme nodded. "We saw a backpack on one of the beds. It had some food and a few maps. It seems suspicious."

"Well, all I know is that the day of the raid, everyone had to get out fast. I imagine one of those boys left it, didn't have time to grab it."

The officer frowned. Perhaps the old woman was telling the truth, but the number of coincidences was mounting. "Would you mind if we came in? I'm rather thirsty," he said as an excuse.

"Of course you can come in," Margot answered loudly.

Jacob, Moses, and Joseph hid in the bathroom before the men entered the living room.

"Do you live alone?" the gendarme asked, seeing the three glasses of milk and crumbs on the table.

"Oh, no, I have my cats. Don't you see the mess they've made?" she chuckled, tidying up the table.

"And you serve them milk in glasses?" It was more a statement than a question.

"They're my babies. An old woman like me needs something to dote on." She buried her nose into the neck of a tabby to hide her nerves. The gendarme grunted, and Margot looked up. "What can I bring you to drink?"

"No need, we should be getting along," the younger gendarme insisted.

Margot followed them to the door with her short, arthritic steps.

"If you hear anything about the tenants upstairs, please call for us immediately," the older officer said at the threshold.

"Anything for France, officer." Margot nodded.

When the door finally clicked closed, Margot let out a long breath. Her body was sticky with sweat, and her head spun. She was sure her blood pressure was through the roof, but she was proud to have helped the poor young boys. She would not be one of the French who licked the boots of their occupiers, such as Jacques Doriot or Marcel Déat—one-time leftists who supported Marshal Wilhelm Keitel and General Charles Huntziger, the actual rulers of France, though Huntziger had not lasted long.

She called the boys to come out of the bathroom. Their faces were white as a sheet. "Did they suspect anything?" Jacob asked.

"They suspect something, but they won't come back unless someone calls them. They're tired, and they'll be busy hunting down thousands of people who've gone into hiding." Margot's voice was weaker and more serious now. She went to the window. Through the lace curtain she could see the gendarmes stopping at the doorwoman's lookout to talk for a moment. They looked back up at Margot's apartment, but she was out of their range of vision. "They've said something to the doorwoman," she continued. "You boys can't stay here much longer, but you shouldn't start out at night either. Sleep here, then head out first thing in the morning."

The three boys went back to the couch. Each boy's stomach was a ball of nerves, but they managed to eat the crackers she brought them.

"Where is my aunt?" Moses asked. His sad face belied his desperate need to see an adult he could trust.

Margot dropped into her chair. She was worn out. The circles around her eyes were darker than before the police officers' visit, and her wavy gray hair was tousled. She had run her hands through it a number of times in an effort to calm down.

"She came back around noon. Apparently the family she worked for had been taken away. Since she herself wasn't registered on any list, she had managed to escape, but . . ."

"Please, just tell us what happened," Moses pleaded, his voice tremulous.

"Good old Judith, such a generous soul. This is destroying the best of us," Margot said, her head bowed.

"What happened?" Jacob demanded.

Margot looked up with her bright eyes. She took a deep breath and sipped her cold tea. "She came back at noon. She looked for you all over the house, called for you, wept out loud. I went up to see her, but she wouldn't let me in. I begged her to calm down, told her things would work out, that they weren't going to hurt innocent children. She told me I had no idea what the Nazis were capable of. I reminded her we are in France, the gendarmes would take care of them . . . but she was desperate and was shouting . . ."

Moses started to cry. Jacob thought his brother should not hear any more. This terrible war would destroy all the good that was left in the world.

"That witch of a doorwoman called the gendarmes. Half a dozen of them came barreling up the stairs. I hid because I was a coward . . ." Margot trailed off into tears.

"There was nothing you could've done," Jacob said, soothingly.

"She started screaming from the other side of the door, and I just hid down here in my apartment. I heard them banging at the door, heard Judith's steps, heard the gendarmes ordering her to open up. Finally the gendarmes broke her door open, and I heard Judith running fast. More steps, and then in the courtyard . . ." Margot could barely continue. "There was a loud noise, like a sack of flour had dropped from the ceiling. I looked out the window, the same window I was just looking out. Your aunt was there, facedown, her foot still twitching when I saw her. The gendarmes ran down and called for a doctor, but she was already dead. The next day, the doorwoman cleaned up the blood, but you can still see the stain . . . as if some part of her isn't ready to leave this place."

Tears streamed down Moses's face. He did not really understand what death was, but he knew it meant a separation that lasted forever. Judith had been a second mother to them. She may not have been overly tender or affectionate, but she looked after them, stayed up all night with them when they were sick, and gave them everything she had.

Jacob swiped at the tears that dripped down his nose. This loss made him more determined than ever to set off in search of their parents. Joseph stayed silent, wondering how his family was, hoping they were alive and well.

"Do you understand?" Margot asked. "A woman like her, dead, murdered by this despicable Vichy regime, murdered by all those who have surrendered their souls and looked the other way. The worst friend of the truth is silence. The worst lie in the world is that ordinary people are powerless against tyranny."

Jacob stood and looked out the window. From that height, the dark stain could still be seen, proof of the power a person's actions have over life. The stain was all they had left of their aunt.

"We're heading south. There's a city we've got to get to. I don't want to tell you where, but it's south of Lyon," Jacob said calmly.

"But Lyon is so far. You'll never make it. The Nazis are controlling all movement . . . the train stations, the roads, everything. And there's a border between occupied and unoccupied France."

"It doesn't matter. We have to find our parents."

The old woman was quiet, thoughtful. Then she reached out for Jacob and said, "In Versailles, I have an old friend who restores art. He has a safe-conduct permit that lets him travel around France freely. I'll ask him to at least get you out of Paris. He might be able to get you as far as the border with unoccupied France, near Bourges. There's a famous cathedral there, the perfect excuse to justify a visit to the city during the holiday."

"But first, tomorrow, we have to take Joseph to the camp at Drancy. We think his family is there," Jacob said.

"If you go there, the Nazis will take you prisoner," the old woman said, turning to him.

"I don't care, ma'am. I just want to be with my family."

"Judith told me what the Germans did in Dachau. Her father was taken there in 1937. I think that's why she threw herself out the window. She knew what they would do to her." Margot winced as she spoke but prayed her words would get through to the child.

But Joseph's look was determined. He knew that life would be pointless without his family. What would he do all alone in the world? "I'd rather go through whatever they're going through with them. I know you can't understand, but it's what I've decided. Most people value freedom and life, but for me, it's all worthless without my family. Existing without them would be a kind of slavery. Suffering with them, I'll be with them forever."

The boy's words touched them all deeply. Margot was surprised at how grown-up he sounded. Yet she knew that war changed people. It made the things that actually mattered shine like gold nuggets amid the dust of daily life.

Margot nodded to Jacob. "I'll get your backpack. I doubt the police will be back up here. You boys will sleep, and I'll keep watch tonight. First thing in the morning, I'll telephone my friend, and he'll be waiting for you."

"Can we trust him?" Jacob asked. He was not convinced about the plan. Getting out of the occupied zone would increase their chances for survival, but anyone and everyone might be a collaborator.

"There are so few people in the world one can trust fully. But one of them is this friend. I'll write a note for you to give him." Margot walked slowly from the living room to the landing outside the door and up the stairs to get the backpack. For a few moments, the three boys were alone.

"Can we trust her?" Joseph asked.

Jacob shrugged. "She's always been nice to us. Plus, she just put her neck on the line for us."

"Margot is a good woman," Moses said. "She always gives me candy."

The two older boys snickered. Moses held limited criteria for evaluating people, but in this case they were all in agreement. Margot seemed trustworthy.

The old woman returned a few minutes later, carrying the backpack in one hand as if it were weighed down with bricks. She hoisted it onto the dining room table and, smiling for the first time, said, "Tomorrow will be a long day. We'd best have a light supper and get to bed."

The meal was brief. They spoke little as they shared a loaf of rye bread and a can of sardines. Margot prepared the bedroom for them, and the boys laid down fully dressed. A clean bed, no matter how narrow it was for three boys crammed together, was a delicious luxury. Their eyes were closing before the light went out. But then Moses whispered to Jacob, "Do you think we'll see Mother and Father again?"

Jacob looked at him through the darkness. Moses's eyes were shining bright like a cat's. He did not want to lie to his brother or give him false hope, but Jacob really believed their family would be reunited. Stroking the boy's hair, he answered, "Nothing's going to stop us from seeing them. I swear to you, we'll cross heaven and earth to get to them. Father always told me that nothing was impossible—that if we had faith and worked hard, we could achieve anything we put our minds to."

"It didn't work out that way for Aunt Judith. She preferred to end her life . . ." Moses felt the tears pricking at his eyes again.

"But we're going to make it. Margot is helping us, her friend is going to get us to the unoccupied zone . . . It's like an angel is watching over us," Jacob said, still stroking his brother's head.

"I trust you, Jacob. I'm never going to leave your side. Thank you for not leaving me in the velodrome."

The two boys hugged until sleep overcame them. Nightmarish monsters tried to trap them that restless night, but their innocent minds escaped and flew off to the world of dreams, where everything is possible and nothing lasts forever.

Chapter 9

Paris
July 19, 1942

To get to the street, they had to pass by the doorwoman's lookout again. Usually there was no one around that early in the morning. Jacob was the first one to scout things out. Stealing a glance through the window of her lookout, he could see no sign of her. He was just about to wave Moses and Joseph through when a hand grabbed his shirt.

"You piece of trash! I knew you'd come back. The police didn't find you, but I did. It's too bad you didn't all jump out the window like your two-faced aunt." The woman's mouth was twisted into a gleeful snarl.

Jacob tried to twist free, but the doorwoman tightened her grip. "Why do you hate us?" he cried. "We haven't done anything to you!"

"You're filthy little foreign rats. Your family showed up acting all hoity-toity, looking down on the rest of us. Jews always think they're better than everybody else. Well, now you're getting what was coming to you," she said. Jacob was distracted by the saliva bubbles at the corners of her mouth.

"But my aunt helped you with your son. She—"

"I don't need your pity," the woman cut in. "The gendarmes will take care of you." With her free hand she opened the window of her lookout and reached for the telephone. Joseph ran up at full speed and pushed the woman with all his might. The door she leaned against gave way and she lost her balance, stumbling down the stairs that led to her basement apartment. Jacob peered in and saw the doorwoman's face covered with blood, but she was moving.

"We've got to get out of here," Joseph said, shaking Jacob to snap him out of his stupor.

"But we've got to call a doctor," Jacob said, confused.

"There's no time. They'll come help her. We've got to go before anyone sees us."

The three boys ran toward the gate and walked down the street as nonchalantly as they could manage, not looking back. Without fully realizing it, they had started on their journey and had no idea where it would take them.

They headed for the train. At that hour, the cars were packed, and three boys could slip in and out without being noticed. They stuffed themselves into the car near the door. The trip would only last about twenty minutes, even with all the stops for people to get on and off.

Joseph studied the manual laborers and office workers. Their faces were set and cold. Life went on despite Nazi occupation and mass arrests. All those "good citizens" looked the other way when a neighbor or a childhood friend disappeared without a trace. They were powerless to stop it, and the powerlessness led to an entrenched in-difference. They were better off not getting involved and just praying to heaven that they were not next. Joseph barely contained his im-pulse to scream at the top of his lungs, to wake them all up from their self-absorption, but he knew it would do no good. Just trying to get by, that amorphous mass of people followed the song of the sirens that lured them to the rocks.

They got off the train near the Drancy camp. Margot had told them the Jews were in an officially protected housing complex. If he could not find his parents there, Joseph would have to search the Hotel Cahen d'Anvers, the Austerlitz train station, the Levitan furniture warehouse, the wharf in Bercy, and the Rue de Faubourg. The French authorities had turned all of those locations into improvised intern-ment camps to house the imprisoned Jews.

They walked for several minutes before coming to an area with few buildings except for an enormous U-shaped structure. From a dis-tance, it looked like a big apartment building, but the barbed-wire fence and wooden lookout towers indicated otherwise.

Joseph was ready to walk right up, but Jacob stuck his hand out and caught him. "Are you sure you want to do this? Once you go up to that fence, it's over. You'll never come out."

"My family's in there. What would you do if you were in my place?" Joseph asked, squinting with sadness.

"I don't know. I get it that you want to be with them, but they might not even be in there. They may have been sent to Germany already."

"It's a risk I have to take. Thank you for helping me the past few days. Thank you so much. You've made me feel that at least I mat-tered to someone."

The three boys embraced. Jacob and Moses watched as their friend walked slowly up to the watchtower. Joseph felt like his feet were made of lead. He knew he was somehow turning his back on life, but he had chosen to be with his people. Humans are nothing more than the sum of their affections and the connections they make in life. When those ties break, loneliness destroys what little is left in an uninhabited heart.

Joseph went up to the gendarme. After they exchanged words, the policeman opened the gate and the boy walked forward. Jacob and Moses heard a commotion of voices, and a man and a woman ran toward Joseph. The three embraced like shipwreck victims clinging to fate's driftwood. Jacob and Moses glimpsed Joseph's eyes from above his father's shoulder, full of gratitude. He was where he needed to be, nestled into the hearts of those who loved him.

Jacob and Moses turned and walked back to the train station. They would head back downtown and transfer at the Gare de Lyon station to a train that would take them to Versailles. Their heads still hung low by the time they got to the stop near Drancy. In a way, they envied Joseph. They did not really need freedom; all they wanted was to find their family. Boarding the train, Jacob was lost in thought. At the age when concepts like the origin of the world, religion, and fatherland were nothing more than empty words, when the only country that matters to you is your mother's welcoming lap, your father's face lighting up when he sees you, or your arm slung over your brother's shoulder, home is wherever your family is.

They arrived at Gare de Lyon and headed for the next train platform, but there were German soldiers everywhere. At the head of each platform the soldiers stopped people at random and demanded to see their papers. Though not every traveler was being stopped, Jacob and Moses could not run the risk of being discovered.

"What do we do?" Moses cried, his voice lilting up in worry.

Jacob looked at the doors. Gendarmes and soldiers were stationed at every entry and exit for the trains. Then he looked at the platform again and shrugged. "We'll just have to risk it," he said, and headed for their train.

Moses followed, nervous. They walked slowly, their gaze glued in front. People all around were passing briskly or pushing to try to make the train on time. When they got to the checkpoint, the brothers took a deep breath, as if preparing to dive into the ocean. They held their breath and walked forward.

"Boys!" a soldier shouted in a thick German accent. They heard the voice but were unsure whether to turn around or keep walking. "You, boys, come here!" the voice repeated, this time with more authority.

Jacob stopped, and Moses followed his lead. They turned until the freckled face of the German was in sight. The young soldier smiled. His perfect features reminded them of angels they had seen in pictures at school or in paintings in the Louvre when their parents had taken them.

"You dropped this," the German said, holding out a map. "Your backpack's open." The soldier stuffed the map in and zipped up Jacob's pack.

"Thank you, sir," Jacob managed to splutter.

"Where are you two headed all alone?"

The boys looked at each other. They did not know how to answer, but Jacob thought it was probably best to tell the truth. "We're going to Versailles. Our uncle is waiting for us, to take us to our parents."

The soldier smiled again, pulled a cigarette out of his combat jacket, and lit up. He looked around for a moment, then gestured for them to continue. The boys walked on without looking back. Once at the train, they got on the first car they came to. It seemed that the only people heading to Versailles right then were tourists, German soldiers, and government employees.

The boys sat in the most out-of-the-way compartment they could find and, for the first time in what felt like forever, they did nothing more than sit and stare out the window. Little by little, the dense city streets gave way to forests and fields yellowed by the July heat. They could hear the snorting of the steam engine, the pistons that themselves seemed to whistle as the train chugged toward one of the most beautiful places on earth. Jacob and Moses had never been inside the great palace, but their parents had told them how Louis XIV had constructed—in order to avoid his own subjects—his own personal Eden, a magical combination of exquisite buildings and luxuriant gardens.

"France is so big," Moses said, agape at all that his eyes were seeing. Until very recently, his world had been comprised of the five streets around his aunt's apartment and a few vague memories of downtown Paris.

"Bigger than you can even imagine," Jacob answered. He relaxed, his head propped against the wooden back of the seat, and his eyes glued to the bright colors of the Parisian outskirts.

"The city where we're going . . . Is it very far?" Moses asked.

"Yes. It might take us days to get there."

"So what will we eat, and where will we sleep?" Moses's stomach growled to accentuate his question. His hunger, never far from the surface, was growing uncomfortable.

"Margot gave me some francs, and I took some money from Aunt Judith. When it runs out, we'll just have to trust people to help us."

"Trust strangers?" Moses's raised tone registered his perplexed surprise. All his life he had been taught not to talk with people he did not know, especially when away from home.

"We've got to. Margot, her friend in Versailles . . . Many people don't support what's going on."

"Why do they want to take us away? What did we do?"

Jacob did not know how to answer those questions. He had heard his parents and aunt talk about how the Nazis hated the Jews, but he had never been able to figure out why. "I don't know. Some people say we killed Christ." It was all he could think of to offer.

"Who?" Moses asked, surprised.

"The God of the Christians. He was crucified, and they blame us. Other people hate us because we always overcome or because we have a lot of money . . ." Jacob was stretching hard to come up with reasons.

"But," Moses interrupted, "we never did anything to that Christ guy, right? And we don't have a lot of money or live in a fancy palace."

"No, but once people begin to hate, they stop asking questions. Stop using their brains. They just look down on other people," Jacob answered.

"What is hate? Like when you don't like someone?" Moses's face scrunched up in confusion.

Jacob did not really understand what hate was either. But maybe it was what he had felt when he saw that gendarme beating his brother. "It's like the opposite of love. When you love somebody, you put up with things that bother you about them. You get over things. When you hate them, you can't stand anything they do, even if they're try-ing to help you. The doorwoman hates us. She can't stand the sight of us, and she doesn't want us to be happy. When there are more people who hate than people who love, then there are wars, which make hate grow until it destroys everything."

They began to see the first roadways of Versailles. The wide-open boulevards were nothing like the streets in the neighborhood where the boys had lived with their aunt. They got off the train and walked toward the palace. Three huge avenues converged in an enormous plaza that seemed like it must be the center of the world. As they walked, neat brick walls and slate rooftops shot up in impressive beauty. Two buildings that looked like Roman temples flanked a set of golden gates, and behind them stood a monstrosity of a building with windows and roof trimmed in gold.

Jacob and Moses stood looking with mouths agape. They were drawn toward the imposing central gate, where both Germans and French gendarmes were stationed. Jacob approached a policeman and, his voice trembling, said, "Excuse me, sir, we are looking for our uncle, Raoul Leduc, the art restorer?"

The gendarme frowned at the boys, smoothed his blond mustache, then entered the sentry box and made a phone call. He returned a few minutes later.

"Mr. Leduc is waiting for you in the workshops at the back. Go around the building to the left until you get to a black door. Ask for him there."

"Thank you, sir," Jacob said, already on his way toward the workshop with Moses in tow.

"This place is for one person to live in?" Moses asked, still awed by the building.

"Back in the day, the kings of France used to live here, but nobody does anymore. The revolutionaries killed them all."

"Really? Why?"

Jacob summarized what he could recall from his history classes: "All the common people were really poor, and the kings were really rich. One day the people got fed up, cut off the king's head, and created the Republic."

Moses nodded as if it made all the sense in the world, though the details of economics and politics eluded him. When they reached the black door, they rapped with the gold knocker and then waited.

A few minutes later, the large wooden door cracked open. From the dark entryway emerged a thin face with sunken cheeks and two days' worth of stubble. The man wore squared glasses at the tip of his nose, and his thin blond hair was combed over to one side of his head.

"The brothers. You'd better come in."

It was dark inside, and the boys' eyes took time to adjust. They walked blinking and squinting toward a room lit with artificial lighting. The air was cool but heavy for being closed in. They could practically chew the odors of varnish, paint, and plaster.

"Margot called me this morning," he began. "All the arrangements will be ready soon, though I always say that these sorts of things take time. I've had to make an urgent call to the secretary to the bishop of the cathedral in Bourges for them to make a formal request for me to restore one of their works. He sent a telegram to the post office, and I had to go there. I've lost almost an entire day's work. Come, I want to show you something." He gestured for them to follow. His stained, white smock was too large for him, as if the man had shrunk since first using it. The boys could make out a brown shirt, bow tie, and vest under the smock. His shoes were dirty, and his pants sagged such that he was nearly walking on the cuffs.

He led them to a small courtyard. The enormous windows of the walls around them reflected the dazzling July sun, and the boys' eyes once again struggled to adapt. Leduc, on the other hand, seemed unfazed. He pointed. "That's my van, the Citroën. It has a false floor in the back. It's not very large and not at all comfortable, but you'll have to stay in there when we go through bigger towns and any checkpoints. I know where the checkpoints are. The soldiers and gendarmes have seen me come and go many times. This is how we've gotten several Allied pilots, dissidents, Jews, and Spaniard republicans to the unoccupied zone. I've never taken children. I won't lie: I don't like the idea. Childhood is a disease cured only by age, but while it lasts, everyone suffers."

The boys looked at each other, unsure how to respond but sure the man would not care to hear their response anyhow. "Thank you for helping us," Jacob said.

"Don't thank me. Somebody's got to do something. Just look around at Versailles. The place is falling to pieces. These Teutonic barbarians want to destroy our beautiful country. They hate us. Never mind that they may be right about a few things. We can't let them plunder or humiliate us anymore. It's madness."

Jacob looked toward Moses. Margot's friend seemed a tad strange, but he was their only hope for getting across occupied France without being discovered.

"Are you hungry? What an absurd question," Leduc muttered to himself. "Children are always hungry. I was a child once, though not for long. Thank God my mother made me toe the line very young."

The boys nodded in silence.

"There's some bread and cheese on the table. Margot didn't give me much time to gather food. I won't be taking you into inns or restaurants. Everyone will ask what in the world an old fud like me is doing running around France with two boys at a time like this. You do know what's going on in the world, yes?"

Jacob presumed this was another rhetorical question, but Leduc scrunched up his brow and bent down to look right in Jacob's face. "Do you?" he insisted. Then, gesturing to two old, round wooden chairs, he said, "Sit down and eat."

"No, Mr. Leduc, we don't know," Jacob answered, cutting a slice of bread and some cheese with his pocketknife. He passed them to Moses and looked back up at the art restorer.

"The British have held the Germans at El-Alamein. If the Allies recover North Africa, it won't be long 'til they skip up to France. The Americans have bombed several German cities, and the Nazis are stalled in Russia. Do you know what this means?" he asked, eyebrows raised.

"That France will be free again soon?" Jacob ventured.

"Not so soon, boy. What it means is that things are going to get even uglier. They'll have to get worse before they can get better. The French must unite. At first, when your enemy's boot is on your neck, before there's much pressure, you don't notice you're getting destroyed. But when the pressure increases, the only option is to pull your neck back or bite the foot that's crushing you. Our beloved country is currently governed by a bunch of lapdogs, accomplices the whole lot of them. Do you understand, boy?"

"Yes, sir."

"Well, eat your bread. We'll leave in an hour. I've got to finish something first. They'll be by any minute to pick up this figurine, and it needs another touch," Leduc said, pointing to a beautiful golden statue.

"It's beautiful," Moses said with his mouth full.

"The Sun King liked everything to be gold. He believed he was the brightest star that gave light to all. He was a foolish, selfish Bourbon, but at least he had good taste," Leduc quipped, examining the piece.

An hour later, the vehicle was ready. Leduc slid back a wooden panel and told them to get into the small compartment. "Don't move, don't talk, don't make any noise. I'll let you know when you can speak. Do you understand?"

"Yes, Mr. Leduc," the brothers said in unison.

They heard the motor rev to life, and the Citroën lurched forward.

The cobblestone pavement forced the narrow wheels left and right in their stuttering attempt to go straight. Moses felt like he was suffocating in the enclosed heat. Jacob tried to fan him with the map from his backpack, but they had little room to move.

They spent an hour that felt like many more closed up in the narrow, stifling compartment. When Leduc pulled back the panel and let them out on a country road somewhere between Orsay and Les Ulis, the boys' faces had reached a new level of pallor.

There was room enough for all three to sit up front, with little Moses in the middle. Jacob focused on the endless road ahead, lined with trees that had witnessed hundreds of years of passengers. Moses's eyes followed the course of green trees. The bright, clear sunlight attempted to break through the dense forest, sparkling gold wherever it slipped between clumps of leaves.

"We'll stop at Artenay in about three hours and sleep at the church there. The priest has helped me out several times before," Leduc said.

Jacob and Moses just nodded in silence. The journey was wearisome, and their nerves were shot from the constant state of vigilance. Moses nodded off en route. When they arrived at the small town, Jacob was fascinated by the stark lines of a huge windmill juxtaposed against a church dome: rounded, then shooting up into a steeple, with an embedded clock. They parked a few blocks behind the church and walked through the dark streets to the rectory. Leduc rapped lightly at the door, and they were greeted first by the barking of a little dog and then by a red-haired, red-cheeked man in a black cassock with a napkin tied around his neck.

"My dear Leduc, just in time for supper. You know we country folk turn in early for the night. And who have you brought me this time? Come in, come in, let's speak indoors."

The priest glanced around before closing the door, then led them to the kitchen table. There was a plate with a half-eaten supper, a glass of red wine, and a fruit bowl filled with apples.

"The priesthood is a lonesome trade. I can offer you some marinated beef and potatoes from a nearby farm, as well as some white bread, which is hard to come by these days. The village's baker is a faithful Catholic. The Germans carry off most of the flour and bread, but our baker always manages to keep some back."

The boys sat down, but Leduc stopped them with, "Go wash up," though he himself made no move to stand. The boys wandered off where the priest pointed, and the two men began to speak. "They're brothers, and it's best I don't say any more about them. I don't even know much myself. The less we know, the less they can get out of us if we're apprehended."

"I understand," the priest nodded. "They look so young. To my knowledge, you've not transported children before."

"Things are getting nasty in Paris. I've concluded that the Nazis are like rats. They nest and reproduce easily, they steal, they spread their diseases of intolerance and racism—and when the ship starts to sink, they get even more dangerous, more daring. They know they'll have hell to pay, so they're taking as many innocent lives down with them as they can," Leduc said.

"They're the very spawn of the devil. They commit their outrages here too. As if robbing all the food weren't enough, they rape the farmers' daughters and then detain anyone who complains. You think the police do anything about it? They don't lift a finger, Leduc. Just a bunch of lackeys."

The boys returned and sat down at the table. The priest blessed the food, and they ate in silence.

"My children," the priest said after a while, "God in his goodness has blessed me with a bit of leftover cake. It's not much, but I wonder if you boys like chocolate?"

Moses reached eagerly for the cake the priest held out, but Jacob gave him a severe look. "No, it's all right, let him eat," the priest said. "None of us knows when our time will come, especially these days. Who knows if we'll even see tomorrow, and if we do, what there may be to eat. Let's enjoy the moment while we can: *Carpe diem, quam minimum credula postero,*" he said as naturally as if Latin were his native tongue.

Leduc translated for them: "Seize the day; put little trust in tomorrow."

The boys accepted a piece each. Their lips were smudged dark with the sweet, creamy stuff, and a kind of happiness stole through them. It was a marvelous elixir of life that restored their hope, even if only for a moment.

The priest was pleased. "Sometimes we chase big dreams, but the most important things happen right where we are, today. The sound of the wind in the trees outside, the fragrance of meat being cooked, the perfume of the flowers swaying in the morning breeze, the bright sun, the clouds giving us their shade in the blue sky . . . Never forget that happiness takes the shape of the puzzle pieces of our lives. A piece might be missing, but we keep making the world we dream of. I once was a great lover of soccer. How I longed to be out playing in the field. I was one of the top players in seminary! I can't play anymore, but I still relish the chance of seeing a game when I travel to Paris, and I help the village boys when they need a coach or a referee. The secret is in the small things . . ." His voice trailed off and he sighed deeply, folding his hands in his lap.

"Ah, you religious types are all hedonists," said Laduc. "Eat, sleep, enjoy. Real pleasure is contemplating the big absolute truths: beauty, love, friendship—"

"I couldn't agree more," interrupted the priest, "but these boys need to sleep. The back room is empty. It's nice and quiet and cool."

Laduc nodded to the boys. "We'll head out at dawn."

The priest rose slowly. His youth had faded so gradually that he was still taken aback at times by the pains and afflictions of age.

The boys went into the sparse, white-walled room. It held a simple chair and a bed with a metal frame and a white crocheted cover.

"You'll sleep in your clothes?" the priest asked.

"It's all we have," Jacob answered.

"Well, sleep the best you can. I'm sure that in the long life ahead you'll find better lodgings elsewhere. God tempers the wind to the shorn lamb." He set a lit candle on the chair and left the room.

Jacob and Moses pulled off their shoes, folded up their pants, and dropped onto the mattress like deadweights. Jacob shifted to blow out the candle.

"What odd people," said Moses. "We're complete strangers, but they're helping us, risking their lives for us. And even though they hate us."

"What makes you think they hate us?"

"Didn't you tell me the Christians, like the priest, think we killed their God?" Moses asked, still trying to get the facts straight.

"That's just something people say. People who are smart and educated don't think that. Leduc and the priest are helping us because they love France."

"But don't the gendarmes love France too?"

"Well, I guess in a way, yes. You know what? We always have to choose between love and fear. If we choose fear, our lives and our choices are going to turn out bad. We won't be doing our best, we won't even do what we wish we did, because we'll just be trying to survive.

But if we choose love, it'll be a risky, bumpy ride. Death may find us before it's time, but it will have been worth it," Jacob reasoned.

"Like when I tried swimming in the river. I didn't know how, but I really, really wanted to learn. I almost drowned, but then I got the hang of it."

"Exactly, Moses. You can't learn to swim unless you're willing to risk drowning. Keeping your distance from water might keep you safe for a while, but it also keeps you far away from the things that are really worth it."

Moses pondered everything in the dark. He thought his brother was the smartest person on earth. Often he had overheard teachers tell their parents how bright Jacob was. Jacob liked to read their father's books and stay up listening to the adults talking about politics, literature, or the theater. "You're really smart," was all he could think to say.

Jacob chuckled. Intelligence seemed rather irrelevant in the world they were now living in. He somehow understood that what really made the world go round was power and violence. "Let's go to sleep. Tomorrow will be a really long day, and we'll have to get back in that hole."

"Again?" Moses complained.

"'Fraid so."

"We're a lot closer to Mother and Father now, aren't we?"

"Nothing's going to stop us from seeing them again, I already promised you, and—"

"A Stein never breaks a promise," Moses finished. It had been their father's refrain.

Silence settled between them, and Jacob was left alone with his thoughts. A family was much more than a group of people united by blood. More than anything, it was the thin thread that kept the present linked to the past. Memories and memory itself kept both worlds together, which is why he and Moses had to keep remembering. As long as they did, Aunt Judith would still be alive and their parents would always be with them. Jacob let his quiet tears fall to dry on the pillow. He tried to imagine what had gone through his aunt's mind as she plummeted from the window to the courtyard below. Had she been scared? Of course she had, but he was sure that, at least for a fraction of a second, she had thought about them, about how she had left them alone and had not kept her promise. *A Stein never breaks a promise,* he thought, as sleep loosened the grip on his consciousness. He repeated the phrase until words could no longer penetrate the thin veil of darkness, and he slept.

Chapter 10

The night passed too quickly. Before light began to turn the sky, the boys found themselves once again hidden in the false floor of the Citroën, heading toward Nouan-le-Fuzelier. Leduc hummed through his repertoire of songs while Jacob and Moses felt every dip and pothole in the back road that Leduc had taken to avoid most of the checkpoints and curious looks. A few hours in, in the middle of a forest, he slowed down, pulled off onto a lane that led into a field, and let the boys out to have breakfast.

Moses unfolded himself from the back of the van first and promptly vomited on the grass. Jacob rubbed his brother's back until the nausea passed and Moses could stand up again.

"Do we really have to ride in the compartment the whole time?

Yesterday it was only 'til we got farther outside of Paris," Jacob asked, frustrated.

"The priest told me last night that they're even stricter at the checkpoints now. In the past few weeks, several Allied pilots have been shot down in the area, and the Germans are looking for them. There's a whole Resistance network helping them escape. We're not part of the partisans, but the gendarmes and Nazi soldiers are combing the countryside trying to flush them out," Leduc explained, folding some of the leftover meat from the night before into some bread.

"But we aren't pilots. You could tell the soldiers at the checkpoints that we're your nephews, and . . ."

Leduc frowned. The children were a nuisance, and the boy was being ungrateful. Leduc was risking his life to help them, but he swallowed back his comments and focused on his sandwich. There was less and less food with each passing day. His excursions into the countryside at least provided him with a bit more variety than he usually got in the city.

"I'd rather not run that risk. Perhaps it would be better if I dropped you off in the next town and returned to Versailles," he said, chewing slowly.

Jacob nodded solemnly. "I don't mean to sound like a brat. We understand what you're risking by taking us to the unoccupied zone, but my brother is just a kid. He can't stay locked up in there."

Fearful, Moses looked at the man. Leduc shrugged and said, "Fine, take the risk, but I assure you that getting deported to Germany is no pleasure cruise. During the Great War, I fought at Verdun, and the Germans captured me. I was locked up in a hole for almost two years in northern Germany. The Boche might seem like serious, conscientious folk, but they treated us like the scum of the earth. The winters were unbearable—no warm clothes and what I had on my feet one could hardly call shoes. And they forced us to work fixing the roads or in heavy factory jobs. It was torture, truly. I'd rather die than fall into their hands again." His face was dark and he looked at something very, very far away.

"I'm so sorry," Jacob said. His family was German. In another lifetime, they would have been Leduc's enemies. Evil had a way of transcending nationality and clan, becoming a darkness that overshadowed everything.

"They're just memories. I always knew we'd face each other again, but I have the feeling that it's different this time. The issue is not the victory of some empires over others, or the survival of the French Republic's values. This time we're fighting a kind of evil the world has never known before. Totalitarianism on the left and the right is after the same thing: destroy everything good in human beings and turn them into cogs in an infernal machine that makes the world a very terrible place."

The boys stared at him with wide, confused eyes. They could not follow him completely but understood the gist of what he said. In the interminable discussions around the dinner table at Aunt Judith's apartment, their parents, aunt, and other adult friends had talked about the Nazis and their leader, Adolf Hitler, and the power of evil to corrupt everything it touched. The power the führer held over the masses was not natural. The adults had said that he seemed like a magician doing devious tricks.

They all three got into the front seat again. Leduc started the engine and guided the van down the rough lane flanked by beech trees that led them back to the road. The tall lines of trees on both sides of the road enclosed and protected them from the intense sun. They were quiet for a long time. Leduc no longer hummed, but Jacob and Moses felt much happier than they had been when hidden.

"When we see our parents, we'll tell them all you've done for us," Moses said. "And when the war's over, we'll come visit you. It'll be nice to spend time with you in Versailles. You can show us the palace and the gardens."

Leduc's mouth twitched in an attempt to smile, but he doubted he would see the end of the war. If the gendarmes and the Gestapo did not find him, then hunger, disease, or old age would. "Old men don't make plans for the future. Everything happens here and now, you see? Who knows what will become of me within a few hours. I've been alone my whole life. Art is my family. The paintings, the statues—they're with me every day, and I can only be who I really am with them. This world . . . It scares me," he said, puzzled at his revelations to two Jewish kids.

Leduc's mother had raised him Catholic, and he had never known his father, who died of heart complications when Leduc was not yet four years old. From as early an age as memory could register, he recalled his mother's black dress, the closed curtains that let in only the vaguest hint of light, and the dark smells of bitter coffee and garlic in his home. They lived comfortably enough on his father's state employee pension. They spent little money and never traveled, but at least his mother allowed him to study at the École nationale supérieure des Beaux-Arts, the French National School of Fine Arts. She appreciated his sketches and his ability to shape things. As a young man, Leduc was not socially skilled, but he had a special connection with works of art, which is why he believed in the absolute values. He did not believe in his mother's God, that jealous, vindictive punisher. He had never felt much love, affection, or tenderness. For him, life was a simple chain in which each person's link had its own work to be done, and when one was finished, one's link simply stopped existing.

Leduc continued, "Childhood, as I already told you, is a disease that passes soon enough. I don't believe that children are happier than adults; they just don't yet understand how the world works. First we glorify our parents, then the future and our youth, then our work and glory itself. But the only thing that really lasts is the grave and oblivion. I'm sorry, boys, but in these matters I cannot be an optimist, much less in the times we're living in."

Jacob chewed on what the man said. Leduc was not so different from their father. Eleazar also thought life was a series of misfortunes that led inexorably to death. But Eleazar had not always thought that way. Jana had told Jacob how, when he was younger, Eleazar had been a successful playwright. He was invited to all the literary circles of Berlin's salons and open houses among the educated. His works were hailed by both critics and the public, until Nazism left him in the streets. Eleazar loved his children dearly, but he could not forget who he had been or how suddenly his crash had come.

As they headed south, the landscape became an interminable succession of thick forests. Broken up by a series of small lakes, everything was green and humid, and the villages they passed looked to be very small and poor. It was a kind of impoverished France few knew existed. Life was hard here, and making it from one day to the next was a great challenge. For the inhabitants of the region, war and peace were hardly distinguishable. In many ways, survival itself was already in open, constant conflict with life.

Leduc slowed as they approached a gas station he knew well. He always stopped there to fill up. There were few vehicles in the area, and it was too easy to run out of gas and be stranded in the middle of nowhere. He stopped before a rusted pump. A tilted sign hanging on a timid nail read CFP: Compagnie Française des Pétroles.

A young man with a dirty shirt and blue oil-stained overalls stepped out of the wooden shack behind the pump, spat a wad of tobacco onto the ground, and walked up to the van.

"André, how are you? Could you fill it up?" Leduc said, stepping a few feet away to light a cigarette. Jacob and Moses had not seen him smoke before. Their parents did not smoke, and they hated the smell.

"You want one?" Leduc offered the employee.

"Thank you, sir." André took it, steadied it behind his ear, and kept filling up the tank.

"How are things around here, staying calm?"

"Oh, as calm as ever. Summer is hot, but that's nothing new. The wetlands send up sultry clouds, and the mosquitos near drive us mad. But in winter it's as cold as hell is hot."

"Many checkpoints?"

"The Boche seem agitated, like a beehive after you poke it. Better keep your distance from them. They come around here and leave without paying. The boss is full up with it, but there's nothing to be done."

"Of course. Well, thank you, and I hope summer's not too hard on you."

"You'd best stay off the highway. Go around by Jargeau. They're stopping everybody in Orleans. Lots of Jews trying to get to Switzerland and Spain, but they're hunting them down like rabbits."

Leduc just nodded, flushed. He got in the car and paused longer than usual before starting the engine. They rolled out of the service station and changed routes for the detour. He could not understand why the Nazis would be watching that route, which traversed the heart of France. The natural path to Spain from Paris was through Bordeaux, then cutting through French Basque Country. Leduc presumed the Jews were scrambling to get into unoccupied France, though the Vichy regime detained them and sent them back to the German-controlled side if they were not French nationals.

Jacob and Moses listened intently to the entire exchange and grew scared.

"I'm sorry, but you've got to get in the back again," Leduc said. The children complied without hesitation and were silent for some time. As they approached Jargeau, Leduc spotted a checkpoint crossing the river. He slowed down and approached carefully.

A German soldier with a machine gun raised a hand for the van to stop at the base of the bridge. Leduc braked but did not turn off the motor. Two Germans came up wearing the distinctive collar of the Feldgendarmerie. The one with the corporal's braid saluted Leduc. The van's nameplate bearing "Palace of Versailles" was helpful when it came to checkpoints.

"Your papers, sir, and authorization for free movement throughout occupied France."

Leduc tried to remain calm. He opened the glove compartment, took out the papers, handed them over, and looked gravely at the German. The soldier flipped through them, went to a white-and-red sentry box, and came back a few minutes later. "We'll need to inspect the van," he announced.

Leduc pursed his lips. They hardly ever searched him. "Is something out of order with my papers?" he asked.

"No, sir, but we're on high alert. Orders are orders." The German's face was stony.

Leduc got out and walked around to the back. He opened the doors as wide as they would go and stepped back. The soldiers looked inside. There was a wooden sculpture wrapped in paper, some strips of wood, and a toolbox. One of the soldiers made to step inside, and the art restorer said in perfect German, "But what do you think you're doing? That sculpture is French patrimony!"

The soldier halted, surprised at such impertinence from a skinny little Frenchman—and in impeccable German. The corporal's look bore a hole in Leduc. "How do you come to speak our language?"

"I spent some time near Hamburg."

"Well. We will search the vehicle. Those are the orders."

"It's a work of art, and you can see there's nothing else there," Leduc complained.

At the end of the bridge they heard a car screech to a halt and saw it backing up furiously. The Feldgendarmerie lost interest in Leduc and turned to the fleeing car.

"Can I go?" Leduc asked in German, but there was no response. He shut the trunk and shifted into drive quickly. The vehicle was slow to respond, like a cranky old man. But little by little it picked up speed. Sweat beaded where hair had once covered Leduc's forehead, and his back and neckline were damp. His heart raced, and his mouth tasted bitter, like a premonition of vomit. He took the first lane he could find off the main road. The surface was very rough, but he hardly noticed the jostling. He had forgotten about the children in the back. He was entirely ready to die but absolutely not ready to be captured again. He swore to himself this would be the last journey he took. He could help in other ways, but not on these high-stakes missions. Good times had come and gone in France. The Germans were no longer there on vacation, and the repression only get much worse.

After more driving, when the dense woods had calmed his nerves some, Leduc stopped the car and rested his head on the steering wheel. He panted as if he had been running. Then he remembered something, lifted his spinning head, and walked to the back of the van. He ran his hand over the gun he had put in his belt after leaving the checkpoint, then opened the panel for the boys to get out.

"You'll have to make the rest of the journey on your own. You're less than sixty-five miles from Bourges, and you can stop at the house of the pharmacist Magné. His house is in Nouan-le-Fuzelier, near the town hall. It's a stone house with red shutters, and the apothecary is on the ground floor."

"You're just leaving us here?" Jacob asked. "But . . . it will take us days to get to Bourges. We'll have to sleep outside, we have no food or water . . ."

Leduc went to the front of the van, retrieved a sausage, some bread, a piece of chocolate, and a few other supplies. "Here, it's all I have."

Moses shook his head. "We can't eat pork. We're Jewish."

"Curse it all, then. I don't care what you Jews do or don't eat!"

"We should get to the town within two hours if we keep driving, right?" Jacob tried reasoning. "Could you at least take us that far? Then we'd be halfway there. You can rest for the night and then return to Versailles. Maybe this pharmacist, Magné, will have a good idea for what we should do. Surely it's not the first time something like this has happened."

Leduc tried to think, but he was having trouble concentrating. He studied the boys: their dirty faces, cuts all over their legs, skinny bodies, and an eternal sadness haunting their eyes. "I'm a complete fool. Get in the car before I change my mind. I'm an art restorer, not a hero."

The boys hopped into their hideout in the back before he could reconsider. Leduc stepped on the gas and, for the first time in their journey, the vehicle responded immediately.

It seemed the Citröen would break down at any moment. Worried, Moses kept looking at Jacob, even though he could barely see his brother in the darkness of their compartment. They covered the distance to the town as quickly as he could. Going around turns, the shocks groaned, and the vehicle tilted dangerously from one side to the other. Leduc sighed with relief as the town came into view. It was a small village built near a canal, and an enormous Norman tower loomed above the church. There was still plenty of daylight. The few houses were painted white, the windows framed in bright red brick that glinted in the light of the hot summer day. It was hot, and the air coming through the Citröen's windows was powerless to cool off the sweating boys, closed in as they were.

Leduc got out of the car and walked into the pharmacy without waiting for the boys. He wanted to be rid of them as soon as possible. The refugees passed from hand to hand like hot potatoes, or more like live, hot coals wrested from flames. Helping a Jew—the slightest touch of the coal—could lead to incarceration or deportation. Fear is an irrational anguish. Once firmly rooted in the human heart, it stays until destruction is complete.

Jacob and his brother crawled out from the back of the van and stood at the pharmacy door, watching Leduc arguing with a man inside the building. Then Leduc brushed by them with hardly a glance, got into the van, and drove away.

The pharmacist motioned for the boys to enter. He flipped the sign on the door to show Closed and kindly asked them to follow the spiral staircase to the upstairs apartment. They soon found themselves in a small living room, where they took a seat on a comfortable leather couch and studied their surroundings and their new host.

The house was small but pleasant, nicely decorated. The pharmacist Magné was about sixty years old, with gray hair, sideburns that went down almost to his chin, and deep blue eyes. He seemed calm and quiet despite the recent argument. Smiling, he said, "I'm sorry, nothing like this has happened to us before. Before the occupation, we all just minded our own business. Many of us fought in the Great War and came back alive, but we're simple civilians. Fear moves about unchecked. Sometimes we fall into its grip, and it can send us over the edge. But don't worry. I'll carry out the promise from your contact in Paris. I don't even know you, but I can't let you stay this far away from your goal. I just hope Leduc can calm down and get back to Versailles safely, or else we'll all end up detained."

"Thank you, Mr. Magné," Jacob said, starting to breathe evenly again. He tried his best to remain calm, but he was nothing more than a frightened, abandoned child.

"My wife will return from church in half an hour. She'll fix you something hot to eat and give you pajamas and a clean set of clothes. Our appearance is important. Our occupiers see Jews and those they call 'asocial' to be mere animals. So as much as we can look like respectable humans, the better for us." He sighed, the weight of it all sagging his brow, and said, "I'm so sorry, children."

Jacob tried to cheer up their current savior. "Mr. Leduc brought us this far. We'll make it; we'll reach our destination. We're so grateful for your hospitality."

Magné nodded and stood. His spotless suit was of very fine cloth. Despite the heat, he had been wearing the jacket, which he removed and placed over a chair. He went to a room off the living room and returned with a large box that he placed on the floor.

The children looked up, curious about what it might contain. The pharmacist carefully opened the cardboard lid. Jacob and Moses were delighted at what they saw inside: toys. Beautiful, new toys.

"My sons left to study at the university in Orleans a long time ago," the pharmacist explained. "One joined the army right as the war began and is a prisoner in Germany. The other is trying to finish his studies. They were very careful with their things, and we've kept them."

Moses let out a whoop. They could be children again. He and Jacob threw themselves onto the floor and started pulling the figurines out one by one. Their eyes shone with a happiness that momentarily flushed the sadness out. The pharmacist smiled and got down on his knees as well. The three of them played at the Napoleonic wars until they heard the door open.

Mrs. Magné looked younger than her husband. Her heart jumped at the scene before her. Time had rewound and there were her husband and boys giggling and playing on the floor. She did not interrupt. She watched a moment, then went to the kitchen and started heating up the food. She returned wearing a white apron and intending to send the boys to take a bath, but she just watched them for a while instead. Finally, she interrupted. "Boys, you'll need to wash up before supper."

Jacob and Moses looked up, smiling and relaxed. A pretty woman in an apron was telling them to get cleaned up, and they felt as if they were with their mother again. But Mrs. Magné was thinner, her hair dark brown, and her face a darker complexion. She was not their mother. "You may call me Marie," she said, her smile lighting up her face.

"I'm Jacob, and this is Moses."

"How about I help Moses with his bath, and then it'll be your turn," she said, still smiling. Moses looked to Jacob for confirmation. At his brother's nod of approval, he took the woman's hand. It was soft and warm, like a mother. He gratefully let himself be led to the bathroom and saw the large white tub. Marie put in something that made bubbles form under the faucet and let the warm water fill high. Moses made little clicks of excitement, his eyes dancing as he watched.

Marie helped him undress, then picked him up and gently let him down into the tub. The brief moment of being lifted in the air recalled the muscle memory of his parents, the enjoyment of being held by someone who loved him. The water seemed too hot at first, but the bubbles and steam worked their way into his bruises, cuts, and all the pent-up tension, relaxing him.

Marie washed his white skin like fine china. Moses could sense her tenderness. A gentle touch spoke more than a thousand words of cheer, the language coming through fingertips and the thrill of nerves that respond, alive again. Moses closed his eyes and let his breath out. Time had stopped for him in that forgotten spot in France, halfway to his destiny, yet still so far from his parents. He opened his eyes to see the woman's face right in front of his, tears coursing down her cheeks in transparent rivulets.

"Are you all right?" the boy asked. "I'm sorry if I'm bothering you."

"Dear, you couldn't bother me even if you tried. It just makes me remember taking care of my boys when they were young. It's hard work to be a mother, but very gratifying. We give everything we've got for the new life, and then we have to learn to let it fly away. Real love means letting your children go."

Moses could not follow her train of thought, but her words sounded pretty, like a summer sunset when the sky seems to burn up until the darkness cools the flames.

Moses stood, and Marie helped him get out of the tub. She dried him thoroughly, her eyes drinking in every detail of his face. "Mothers are alike, my boy. It doesn't matter that you aren't my son. I can't *not* take care of a child who shows up and needs help."

She helped him get into a white nightshirt and asked him to call his brother.

Jacob entered, hesitant. He was twelve and knew how to give himself a bath. Marie smiled knowingly and, as she got up from the wooden stool, said, "Never fear, I just wanted to tell you to take advantage while the water's hot. Here's a clean towel. Dinner will be ready in ten minutes."

Jacob looked at the tub and had to rub his eyes to make sure what he was seeing was real. After Marie left, he got in slowly, leaning back and closing his eyes. Time passed, and he thought of nothing. He was exhausted from thinking all the time.

When he finished, he found his brother and the Magnés sitting at the table. Waiting for them on the blue tablecloth were bowls of boiled potatoes, peas, corn, and stewed beef. The boys ate cautiously under the smiling gaze of their hosts.

"Aren't you going to eat?" Moses asked them.

"We'll eat later," Magné answered. He put his arm over his wife's shoulder and pulled her a little closer to him.

After supper, they sat on the couch again, and Magné read a few chapters from Jules Verne's *Dick Sand, A Captain at Fifteen*. Marie then led the children to a bedroom. "I hope you rest well. The angels are watching over you."

"They watch over Jews too?" Moses asked. Jacob elbowed him under the sheets.

"Of course they watch over little Jewish boys," she said with a chuckle.

Alone, and despite their exhaustion, the brothers whispered together. The extreme ups and downs of the day made it difficult to fall asleep.

"Mrs. Magné is really nice. She reminds me of Mother," Moses said.

"Me too. It feels like we're in a real home again." Jacob could sense Moses nodding. "But we should sleep. There's still a long way to go." He snuggled up to Moses, knowing that his brother needed human contact in order to sleep well. Smelling the clean sheets, ancient memories of their house in Germany flitted before him, vague re-collections of things being good, having enough of everything. It made no difference to him that his parents were impoverished for-eigners. Jacob just wanted to be with them and feel safe again.

Chapter 11

Nouan-le-Fuzelier
July 21, 1942

A rooster crowed, waking Jacob. He looked at the darkness still lying thick over the room, turned over, and went back to sleep. It was a gentle sleep, without the startled anxiety of the past few nights. His weary body recognized that it was safe again. The shutters were mostly closed, but eventually sunlight broke into the room, and Jacob sat up, stretching in bed. Moses's angel face was still in the world of dreams. Their mother always said that true peace was a sleeping child's face. Jacob envied Moses in a way. His younger brother could still dwell in the mysterious land of his imagination, where reality was relative and details mattered little. Moses could still pretend he was in other places or simply reinterpret his surroundings into a fantasy that insulated him from the cruel facts. Jacob fiercely wanted to protect his brother's innocence and stretch out the time of sweetness that never returned once it passed.

Moses, too, stretched in bed, and the sheet fell away. Jacob covered him back up, but it did not last. Moses sat up and reached his arms high, smiling the wide smile he had not shown in quite some time. "I'm hungry," he pronounced.

Jacob laughed, his chin propped between his hands, elbows resting on the bed. "You're always hungry."

"Look who's talking!" Moses shot back.

They picked up the clean clothes folded over the chair—practically new shirts and two pairs of shorts with suspenders. They were most pleased to see the dark brown shoes, which were nicer than any they had ever worn.

They left the spare bedroom and headed for the kitchen, drawn by the delicious aroma of crepes Marie was making. The boys smacked their lips as they sat down at the table already set with two glasses of milk, bread spread with jam, and a bit of coffee.

"Do you drink coffee, Jacob?" Marie asked.

The boy was unsure how to answer. The truth was he had never tried it, but he nodded and watched as Marie poured just a touch into his milk, hardly even enough to change the color. She then flipped the last of the crepes out of the skillet and set the steaming plate on the table. "And do you boys like chocolate?" she asked.

Their heads bobbed, as if controlled by an automatic spring. She drizzled a robust portion onto the crepes and sat down with them.

Jacob and Moses set about the task with concentrated dedication, hardly pausing to breathe until they were stuffed. Then they leaned back against their chairs, hands on their contented bellies, and sighed with a somewhat dazed look.

"So I take it you enjoyed your breakfast?" Marie chuckled. "It's been quite a while since I've cooked crepes. Pierre, that is, Mr. Magné, doesn't care for them, and our boys live far away." As she explained, her eyes grew troubled with the anxiety that accompanied the memories.

"They were amazing!" Moses said, his face stained with chocolate.

Jacob wiped his brother's face, then took a sip of the milky coffee. It tasted bitter at first, after the crepes, but Marie offered him a pinch of sugar, and he loved the combination. Perhaps growing up meant having new experiences and making decisions. Jacob longed to grow up, to become an adult, yet he was still drawn to so much from childhood, and he did not want to give up his playing.

"Mrs. Magné, I thought we'd be leaving soon, but no one came to wake us up this morning."

"Pierre is totally tied up. We had not been planning on taking a trip, you see. With the way Mr. Leduc . . . Well, it's been an unfortunate occurrence. We've never had anything like this happen before."

"Have you been helping . . . people . . . for a long time?" Jacob asked.

"Since the Germans arrived in France. Once the Nazis entered Paris, countless people fled to the south. They were afraid of retaliation. Nearly every rural area swelled up with refugees, but after the first few months, most Parisians returned home. Since then, there's been a constant trickle of people who needed to escape or just preferred to be in the unoccupied zone, or Allied pilots the Nazis have shot down. Someone comes through our home pretty much every week. We don't usually keep people here. We have a small farm just outside of town. If we house someone here, people start asking questions and meddling, but what happened yesterday was an exception. On the other hand, children don't stand out as much. They're practically invisible to most adults."

"Children are a nuisance," Moses said with all seriousness.

"But why would you say that?" Marie asked, with a curious smile.

"We're just a burden. Adults think we're loud, wild, and inconvenient." Moses spoke with utter sincerity.

"Dear me, well, that must be because the adults don't remember when they were children," she answered.

"When do you think we'll leave?" Jacob asked.

"Perhaps tomorrow, or the day after next, at the latest. Are you in a hurry?"

Jacob shook his head. "No, but our parents are waiting for us."

Marie nodded with a long face, then got up, served herself some black coffee, and looked out the window. It was cloudy. Dark storm clouds moved in from the north, making the hot air feel stifling. "It's going to rain," she said at last. "Probably tomorrow as well. Pierre will tell us when it's best to leave. He also wanted to make sure Mr. Leduc had not been captured or given anyone away."

She took another sip of steaming coffee, then fished in her white apron, pulling out a small key that she contemplated for a moment.

"Would you children like to see the playroom our boys used to use?" she asked, her voice chipper once again.

Despite their eagerness, Jacob and Moses were slow to get to their feet, the bounteous breakfast having required most of their energy. They followed Marie to a stairwell, listening to their collective footfalls on the wooden steps that took them to a spacious attic. Inside they saw a fully assembled electric train set up to run through a model town. There were swords, armor, and all sorts of toys.

"Why don't you play up here until lunch?" she suggested. "No one will hear you. The house next door is vacant." She left them to their imaginations.

Jacob and Moses raced to the train and spent the morning lost in play.

"Wow," Moses finally said, unable to shake the feeling of disbelief. "I've never seen a room like this."

Jacob nodded, his hands busy with everything they could touch. "But we should leave tomorrow. I don't want to get there too late."

"Why do you say that?"

"Well, we don't know how long Mother and Father will be in Valence. Maybe they'll have to flee from there and, if they learn that Aunt Judith is dead, maybe they would try to go look for us," Jacob said.

"Oh, I hadn't thought of that." The seriousness had returned to Moses's voice.

"If we leave two days from now, I hope we get there before the end of the month. It's just that news travels faster than we can."

"What will we do when we get to Bourges? It's not even halfway there." Despite the toys, Moses was discouraged again.

"We'll figure something out. We've got some money. Maybe we could take a bus or the train."

"Wouldn't that be dangerous?"

"I'm guessing that things are a little better in the unoccupied zone."

The boys sat on the attic floor and were suddenly hungry again. The gray light coming through the window depressed them.

Then Moses asked, "Do you think Joseph is okay?"

"Yeah, sure, he wanted to be with his family."

"But what will happen to all those people?"

"I have no idea. Maybe they'll go to Germany." Jacob wished the subject would change.

"If they capture us, will they send us back to the velodrome?"

"They're not going to capture us, Moses. I promise you." He put his arm around his brother, as much for his own sake as for the younger boy's. Sometimes Jacob needed to feel his brother close.

At the sound of Marie calling them for lunch, they pounded down the stairs, washed their hands, and sat hopefully at the table.

The Magnés seemed to be in very good moods, smiling, friendly, offering to help. The food was again delicious and plenteous. They all moved to the couches again before Magné returned to the pharmacy.

Jacob once more voiced his constant thought: "When will we leave?" No sooner had he spoken than the first flashes of lightning sparkled and the sky opened up with thunderous rain. The rushing sound and the heavy humidity held them in silence for a while. It was pleasant to hear the splatting against the exterior of the house as the sky watered the dry land all around.

"In a few days. Storms are very troublesome for driving," Magné answered.

His vagueness did not satisfy Jacob. The boy wanted detailed plans and was not content with general ideas, but he also did not want to press further. He decided to wait until dinner.

The afternoon was pleasant. Marie turned on the lights, and the boys played contentedly, noting how the heat abated some with the rain. Magné returned just before six in the evening.

Marie emerged from the kitchen, where she had spent the past few hours, and called to the boys. "Take your baths before supper."

Moses smiled, recalling the delicious experience of his bath. Marie got a clean towel, filled the tub, and called Moses, and they repeated the proceedings from the day before. Moses closed his eyes and nearly fell asleep in the comforting water.

"Would you like to stay with us a bit longer?" Marie asked.

Moses opened his eyes, looked at Marie's sweet face, and asked, "But would my brother stay as well?"

"Of course, I was meaning both of you. You could stay with us for the summer. In the winter we could take you to the city where your parents are. After the raids in Paris, the roads are being heavily watched. If we wait for things to calm down a bit, it'll be safer for everyone. You two can play every day, and we'll tell the neighbors you're the children of one of Pierre's cousins. We can go to the farm on the weekends. We've got horses, and sheep . . ."

The idea sounded marvelous to Moses. He was tired of traveling, of meeting new people, of being terrified by the sight of German uniforms. Spending summer vacation with the Magnés seemed like the perfect idea.

Marie helped Moses get out of the tub, dried his hair carefully, and helped him get dressed. Jacob followed but did not take long to get cleaned up and ready for supper. When they got to the dining room, the meal was already served: carrot soup, codfish, and apple pie for dessert.

"How has the afternoon been?" Magné asked.

"Great! We played upstairs the whole time," Moses said. His face was relaxed, the tension and sadness having been replaced with contentment.

"Mr. Magné," Jacob began, "after lunch you said we would set out in a couple of days. I don't want to sound ungrateful, but we'd like to leave tomorrow. We want to find our parents as soon as we can." His wide eyes turned fully upon the pharmacist.

Marie threw a worried look at her husband and gently squeezed his elbow. The man cleared his throat and said, "We were thinking you might stay with us for a time. I've learned that the roads are being watched to hunt down and capture every possible Jew. The Germans are out in full force. Traveling through occupied France is extremely dangerous."

His words did not deter Jacob, who took a few sips of soup and then spoke again. "I'm really sorry to cause trouble, but I'm afraid our parents will try to look for us in Paris when they hear what's happened in the city. I don't want to lose their trail. If we get there and they've left, I won't know where to look for them next."

"I understand." Magné nodded. "We could contact them. We have ways, and that way they could know where you are."

"Mr. Magné, the timing isn't the only thing. It's that we haven't seen them for over a year. We miss them and need to be with them," Jacob said, unable to keep the emotion from his voice. It was the first time he had spoken aloud what he had felt for so long in his heart.

The couple was quiet, unsure how to respond.

Moses, who had been silent up to then, said, "But we could stay for the summer. We're safe here."

Jacob cut him with a glance. How could his brother say such things? "We are not staying. A few toys may be all you need, but our parents are worried about us."

Moses was quiet, then his eyes welled with tears. "I'm sorry," he whispered, wiping his face with his sleeve.

"It's not Moses's fault," Marie intervened. "I mentioned to him it would be better for you to stay for the summer. It's so dangerous to travel right now."

Jacob jumped up so forcefully his chair fell backward. "We're not toys to keep you entertained, Mrs. Magné. We have a family. If you can't take us, we'll leave tomorrow on foot," he declared.

In agony, Moses looked at their benefactors, stood up, and followed his brother to the bedroom. Jacob lay stiffly on the bed, face-up, his arms crossed and his lips pressed tightly together. Moses sat beside him and, swallowing back his tears, said, "I'm sorry, Jacob."

"You're just a kid. No way can you understand."

Crying again, Moses repeated, "I'm sorry."

"Here you've gotten kindness and safety, so of course you don't want to leave."

Moses nodded and said, "But Mother and Father are probably scared, and they'll think something's happened to us. You're right, we should go tomorrow." He slid down next to Jacob, who put his arm around him. They stayed that way on top of the bed until sleep overcame them.

The next morning, before sunrise, Magné knocked on their door. They had a simple breakfast, packed their bookbags with some provisions, and headed down the spiral staircase in silence. Before opening the door to the street, Jacob put his hand on the pharmacist's shoulder.

"I want to say I'm sorry. I didn't mean to offend you. We're just so worried. And we're so grateful for your hospitality and that you'd put yourself at risk for us."

"Don't worry about it. We're happy we can help," Magné said, though without feeling.

"Please tell Mrs. Magné thank you. She's been so kind to us."

Magné nodded, and they went out to the street. The ground was still wet and the morning slightly cool. Magné opened a door, took a gray covering off his car, and pulled it out into the street. He got out again, closed the garage door, and motioned for the boys to get in. It was a Renault Juvaquatre, shiny and seemingly new. They were unaware of Marie watching them from behind the curtains upstairs. Her heart was heavy for them—so alone, so helpless. She hoped they would find their parents but knew that the war had already taken so many loved ones. Europe was wandering aimlessly, led by a few fanatics crazed for power and wealth while millions raised a collective lament to heaven. She thought of her own sons, tried to imagine seeing them safe and well again; attempted to believe that happy, peaceful times would come once more, that life would flow effortlessly toward the immense ocean of all the good feelings and goodwill that make the world a livable place.

Chapter 12

They drove most of the way in silence. Jacob and Moses intuited that the Magnés simply missed their sons and had wanted to shelter these new boys as long as they could. In a way, it would have been a good choice. They had no way of knowing if their parents were still in Valence, if they had perhaps gone to look for the boys in Paris, or if they had ended up sailing to South America. If Jana and Eleazar were still in Valence, there was no guarantee they could take care of their children again.

From the back seat, Moses stared at the forests and lakes that little by little gave way to wide, cultivated fields and empty prairies. As they approached Bourges, the impressive towers of the cathedral began to grow in the distance. The building was the pride of the entire region and one of the most breathtaking churches in France.

"We're almost there," Magné said.

The children were openmouthed at the sight of the medieval city with its half-timbered houses with plaster walls. They turned off the main road and came to a small plaza near the church of Saint-Pierre. They parked the car, one of the few visible in the area, and walked toward an ancient-looking house. Magné took great strides, as if anxious to rid himself of a troublesome burden. With two fingers he knocked with the rusty knocker on the door.

They heard footsteps on a wooden floor, then the door creaked open loudly. An elderly woman with a face crisscrossed in wrinkles received them with little to-do. Magné, Jacob, and Moses followed her down a narrow hallway. The dusty, musty walls had seen better days. The woman led them to a small room, muttering something they could not hear.

"The collier Bonnay is a good man," Magné said at last. "He's a widower. His wife died two years ago, and his sons are around your ages. I don't think you'll be able to stay long, but he will help you figure out how to get into the unoccupied zone and then to Valence."

"Thank you, Mr. Magné. Again, please tell your wife how grateful we are," Jacob reiterated.

The small room was stiflingly warm, and the thought of staying there long put Jacob on edge. He would rather spend the night, then leave immediately the next day.

The collier was busy with deliveries at the moment, but a dark-haired boy poked his round, cross face through the door.

"Father won't be back 'til lunch," the boy said, pronouncing the words rather awkwardly, as if a toddler were speaking through the body of an older child. He was a bit shorter than Moses but looked hardy enough.

"What's your name?" Moses asked, eager to see someone near his age.

"Paul," the boy answered.

"I'm Moses."

The old woman, who up to now had remained silent, said, "You boys go play out back 'til your father gets here."

Moses ran, following Paul out to the small yard, but Jacob preferred to stay and wait.

"You can go out too," the woman said.

"Thank you, but I'd rather wait here," Jacob answered.

She turned to Magné. "Sir, you can go now. My son will take charge of the boys."

Magné hesitated a moment, then put his hat on and knelt to say goodbye to Jacob.

"I want you to know we're not angry with you. We understand what you're feeling. You have a noble desire. But if you ever need any help at all, write or call us. Here's our address and phone number. If you find yourselves in trouble, though, destroy this paper. Do you understand?"

Jacob sighed and tried to hold back his tears. The Magnés were some of the kindest people he had ever met. Their home and family had been a refuge in the midst of danger.

"I will, Mr. Magné. Thank you." He stood and hugged the pharmacist, who, tense at first, eased into it and returned the embrace.

"You and your brother are good boys, and things will turn out for you. It may be that this world just gets messier, but you'll always be able to find good people in it. There are more generous hearts than we might think."

Magné stepped out of the room and covered the distance through the hallway to the door with his great strides. He was tempted to try to take the boys to Valence himself, but he knew it would be impossible. If the Germans did not stop him at the checkpoints, then the gendarmes would. It was better to let fate play out as it would.

For hundreds of years, the confident stone church of Saint-Pierre had seen generations come and go, all the while safeguarding its grandeur and mysteries. It now seemed to laugh at the smallness of Pierre Magné and his goodwill. But in Jacob's eyes, looking through the dirty windows of the Bonnay home, the man was a veritable giant.

At noon, the grandmother served them a light lunch of soup with noodles and beef sausage that was past its prime. It was nothing like the delicacies at the Magnés' home. The collier's children slept in a damp room with a large straw-mattress bed and a broken mirror. There were no toys besides a slingshot and a sort of scooter their father had put together with wheels and a wooden steering wheel.

When they heard the front door, Paul tore down the stairs and threw himself into his father's arms. Bonnay was a middle-aged man with a beard and a blue sailor's cap. His shirt was blackened with soot from the bags of coal he transported all day.

"You're going to stain your clothes, son."

The boy, heedless, nestled his face further into his father's neck. Jacob and Moses felt hollow as they watched. How long had it been since they had hugged their father?

"And you two are the boys?" Bonnay asked with his deep voice.

"Yes, sir, good afternoon. I'm Jacob, and this is my brother, Moses."

"You're here a bit later than I expected. Unfortunately, just yesterday a small group of refugees crossed over into the unoccupied zone. They were hidden in a transport truck and made it near to Vichy, but the truck has come and gone, and there's no way they can take you now." He sounded annoyed.

"It wasn't in our control," Jacob apologized.

"Of course not. You can stay here as long as you need to. We'll find a solution. You'll go with my son Marcel to help me at work, and the younger two will stay here at home. From now on your names are Jean and"—he pointed to Moses—"Martin."

Marcel stepped forward from his father's shadow. He was taller than Jacob and had much wider shoulders though he was slightly younger. His blue eyes and long, curly blond hair were dazzling despite the soot stains on his face.

"You boys go play a bit before supper. Tomorrow we'll have to be up very early, but it would be better for you not to go out in those nice clothes. People will wonder. Grandmother will get you some of Marcel and Paul's clothes," Bonnay told his guests.

Jacob and Moses changed quickly. They were eager to get out and run through the streets of a new town, a new place to explore. The sons of the collier would be the perfect hosts. Paul opened the front door, and they all four ran down a narrow road toward the Auron River. Huge trees separated the old road that followed the river's edge toward an old mill with a waterwheel. The boys sat on the bank and started throwing rocks into the water.

"Where are you from?" asked Marcel, who—with a clean face and clean clothes—now looked like an eleven-year-old boy.

"We lived in Paris, and now we're going to the unoccupied zone," Jacob said.

"Everybody wants to leave, and I don't get it. Beyond the fields of Bourges, the grass is just as green and the sky is just as blue as here."

Jacob knew Marcel was right. He had never understood what borders did, much less one that split a single country into two parts.

"Well, we don't really care what they call that side of France. We're just looking for our parents."

"Why did they leave you?" Marcel asked, grabbing a handful of dry grass and choosing a piece to chew.

Moses frowned. "They didn't just abandon us. They left us with Aunt Judith."

"Where's your aunt?" Paul asked. Paul had already decided Moses was the best thing to happen to him.

"Um . . ." Moses looked down, preferring to avoid the truth. "We're not sure."

"You want to go into the mill? You can see the river really close from the window, and it's a good spot to aim at the birds in the trees," Paul said, trying to cheer his new friend.

The boys ran to the old stone bridge. The arch looked weary, but it had withstood the current of water for hundreds of years and would endure many more.

The walls of the building itself were barely standing, and the roof had fallen in ages ago. The old millstone was the last remaining vestige of the place's one-time function. They went up to the window and watched the current. In the summer, the river flowed more slowly, and the boys could see the rocks at the bottom, even under the thick shade of the trees.

Marcel aimed at a bird perched on a branch overhead, but Jacob jostled his arm to wreck his aim.

"Hey, what'd you do that for?" Marcel complained.

"That bird didn't do anything to you, and you're not going to eat it. So why do you want to kill it?" Jacob's tone took Marcel aback.

"Well, why not? It's just a bird. There are thousands of them."

"That's not a good enough reason." Jacob huffed.

"Oh yeah? Says who?" Marcel stuck his face right into Jacob's and bumped the older boy with his chest.

"Quit fighting," Paul intervened. "I'll tell Father."

"You little snitch!" Marcel turned and pushed Paul hard. The boy lost his balance and fell through a gap in the wall to the lower part of the millhouse, to where the old waterwheel still turned with its paddles. Only a few teeth remained in the wheel, but Paul's shirt got caught in one, and the force of the water started to lift him. "Help me!" he cried.

Not stopping to think, Jacob threw himself into the water and caught Paul by his clothes. But the wheel kept turning and pulling him upward, where he would eventually be trapped within the gearworks.

Marcel watched, helpless, from above. He did not know how to swim, but he rummaged among the remains of the millhouse until he found an old rope. He tied it to one of the standing wooden supports of the building and threw it into the water.

Jacob grabbed the rope and yanked hard on Paul, but his shirt was stuck in the wheel. Paul tried to rip the shirt, but the fabric wouldn't budge.

Moses tossed them a stick to jam up the wheel. It would not withstand the force of the water for long, but maybe it would give them a few seconds. Jacob jammed the stick in, and the wheel groaned to a halt. It gave Jacob both the time and the leverage to yank Paul free. The younger boy clung to him as Jacob hoisted them both back into the millhouse with the rope.

Despite the heat of the day, Paul trembled with cold and fright. Marcel folded him into his arms. "Thank you," he said, looking at Jacob. "I owe you."

Just then they were startled by the sound of footsteps. The four boys withdrew to the darkest recesses of the millhouse. They heard voices, then two blond boys appeared and went up to the window.

"It's the Germans," Marcel whispered in Jacob's ear.

"Germans?" Jacob's blood froze.

"The sons of the commander and the captain of the garrison. They've come for the summer," Marcel explained.

"Do you know them?"

"Nobody goes near them. We call them the dirty Germans. Normally their nanny or a soldier is with them. I've never seen them alone before."

The German boys said something in their language and then laughed, but they were startled into silence by the sound of a board creaking in the shadowed part of the millhouse. One of them pulled out his slingshot and fired into the dark.

"Ouch!" Moses yelled, when the pebble whacked his neck.

"Who's there?" one of the German boys asked in a thick accent.

Marcel stepped out into the light with his slingshot raised. He was much bigger than the two German boys. "What are you doing in our hideout, you little Deutsch maggots?"

The boys froze, but before Marcel could fire at them, Jacob grabbed his arm.

"Leave them alone."

Marcel frowned. He could not understand this rich city boy. The whole world knew the Germans were the enemy.

"They're kids just like us. The war is between adults," Jacob said.

The German boys threw down their slingshots in surrender. They looked truly frightened. Their parents had warned them about lurking dangers, but they had run off at a moment when no one was looking in order to explore the old mill.

"We're not going to hurt you," Jacob said in German.

Their eyes widened in disbelief.

Marcel's did too. "You speak German?" He was incredulous.

"Yeah," was all the explanation Jacob gave.

"We didn't mean to hurt you," the older boy said to Jacob.

"You can go, and don't forget your slingshots."

"Thanks," the boys said in unison. But before leaving they turned back and asked, "Do you want to play?"

The four boys looked at one another. It was one thing to not attack the Germans, but it was another thing altogether to play with them. Moses finally stepped forward and said, "Sure, we can play, but we should go outside. It's kind of dangerous in this millhouse. Paul just fell."

The Germans nodded. They knew French, so games with their new playmates would come easy.

Sometime later, the church bells rang out loudly, and Paul reminded them to go home for supper.

"Will you be back here tomorrow?" one of the German boys asked.

"I'm not sure. We've got some things to do," Jacob answered.

"How do you know German?" the smaller boy asked.

"I learned it in school." Jacob found a lie more prudent than the truth.

"You sound German. You don't have an accent. So we'll try to come back tomorrow at the same time, and I'll bring a ball," said the older boy, before turning and running off toward the commander's residence.

Jacob, Moses, Paul, and Marcel ran back toward the Bonnay house. As they neared the plaza, Jacob could not stop berating himself for his critical error. Surely the boys would tell their parents they had met a boy who spoke German. He did not know what had made him do it, but it was too late now. He would have to warn Bonnay of the risk they were now running.

Once home, they washed up and waited impatiently for supper. Jacob could hardly eat, however. When Bonnay went out to the patio to smoke his pipe, Jacob followed him.

"Mr. Bonnay, may I speak with you?"

The man grunted and then patted the stair with his hand for the boy to sit. "What is it, my boy? I hope you haven't gotten into trouble on your first day."

"I'm afraid I have. We ran into two German boys near the river. Marcel threatened them with his slingshot . . ."

"Well done. My Marcel doesn't put up with these blasted Deutsch." Bonnay smiled proudly.

"Yes, but I stopped him, and I spoke to them in German to calm everything down."

"You did what?" he said, taking his pipe out and turning toward the boy.

"I spoke to them in German."

"To the children of the commander and the captain of the garrison? Have you lost your mind?"

Bonnay scratched at his scalp. His hair badly needed to be cut. The gray was steadily encroaching upon his bushy brown head.

"I'm sorry," Jacob said.

"Well, there's no way around it. We'll all have to leave tonight. My mother can stay. She's in no danger. We'll take my coal truck and take a shortcut over the lines. It's by cattle trail . . ."

"I'm really sorry," Jacob repeated, on the verge of tears. He hated himself for putting this family at risk.

"Calm down, lad. Many times I've thought about crossing over.

The Nazis are stealing coal from me every day, and I've thought one too many times about shooting the whole lot of them. The boys are the only reason I haven't done it yet. I've got family in Roanne. From there you can go to Lyon. Then it's not far to Valence, just over sixty miles."

Bonnay stood up. He seemed even taller and stronger than the first time Jacob saw him.

"Marcel, Paul, come!" he called as he entered the house. He put out his pipe and emptied it in the kitchen.

"What is it, Father?" Marcel asked.

"We're going to Roanne tonight to see our cousins. It's been a long time since we visited Uncle Fabien."

Marcel and Paul stared at him, puzzled. Since their mother's death two years ago, they had never left home.

"We're leaving in the middle of the night?" Marcel asked, connecting the dots. "Is it because of those German boys?" Then he grabbed Jacob's collar. "You little Jews, you—"

Bonnay's great hand pushed Marcel, and he fell flat on his back. "You will never speak like that again, do you hear me? In our family, there are no Jews or Christians. We're socialists, and all people are our brothers and sisters." He pointed at the boy with his pipe to mark the seriousness of his words.

Bonnay went upstairs and spoke briefly with his mother. After filling two small suitcases, he lifted a wooden plank and retrieved his savings. It was not much, but it would be enough to start a new life somewhere else. For years, he and his wife had scrimped to save enough to send their boys to good schools—but none of that mattered now. What chances did a collier's sons have in a world ruled by Nazi swine? Such thoughts ran through his mind as he put on his coat and secured the money in a secret pocket in his pants.

The boys were waiting downstairs. They were dressed, including shoes, and holding their jackets. Jacob had gotten his bookbag from the room.

"I won't miss these old walls too much. We've been very happy in this house, for sure, but also rather unlucky. Your poor mother worked herself to the bone trying to turn this pigsty into a home, but she's not here anymore." Bonnay's eyes focused on something far away, but only for a moment. Then he picked up the suitcases again.

The truck was parked at the back, and not a soul walked the streets. The mandatory curfew forbade the townspeople from venturing out at night. They had to get out of the city as soon as they could. And no one knew the country roads like a coal man.

All five of them piled into the cab. The two younger boys sat by Bonnay, and the older boys beside them. It took them a while to get settled, then Bonnay turned the ignition. The vehicle roared in the surrounding silence, and Bonnay looked around through the dirty windows nervously. None of the neighbors were looking out their windows. He eased the car into gear and started out slow, leaving the plaza and heading for the road that ran along the river. If they could just get a few miles down, the Germans would have no way of finding them. The night was so clear he could drive without the headlights.

He managed to sneak through the narrow streets of Bourges, then take a smaller road that ran along some cornfields. There he sped up to get away from occupied France and to the made-up border that turned half of the French into Hitler's slaves and the other half into his bootlicking subjects.

The truck sped through the prairies and cornfields. As soon as they got to the unoccupied zone, it would be less dangerous. He had their papers in order and could say he was taking his nephews back home after a visit.

As the truck drove away, a group of Germans advanced lightly toward the church of Saint-Pierre. A sergeant knocked at the Bonnay home. It took the elderly Mrs. Bonnay some time to put on her robe and make her way down the steep stairs and through the hallway. When she opened the door, the Germans pushed her aside and began searching the house. Smarting, the woman went to the small living room and sat down to wait.

The sergeant entered and in basic French asked, "Where are the children?"

"What children?" she asked quietly. She was calm. At her age, death was more a gift than a threat.

"The one who speaks German."

"My grandchildren don't speak German. A week ago they went to see their cousins in Orleans." This kind of lying, anything to throw them off a scent, came easy to her.

"You're lying. They were playing today down by the river." The sergeant grabbed the front of her gown.

"I'm not afraid of you. I'm just an old woman," she said.

The sergeant dropped her. They were wasting their time. He considered sending a search party, but it was late, they had not eaten, and this whole row was over some children. He would look for them tomorrow. *The little fish always slip through the net*, he thought, then pushed the grandmother down hard for good measure.

The soldiers left the house in disarray, and the grandmother listened to their boots on the stone pavement of the plaza until they faded away on the main road. She got to her feet slowly, closed the front door, and went to her room. She prayed for her son and grandchildren. She knew the cost of war—her uncle in the war with Prussia, one son in the Great War—and she desperately hoped God would spare her one remaining son. She had little left to give the world. It had been a difficult life: poverty, hunger, death, and sadness were etched into her face and looked out through her downcast, cataract-clouded eyes. Yet for some reason just then she had the fleeting sensation of the first dance she shared with the man who became her husband. The vibrancy and hope of youth still nested in her worn-out heart. She understood immortality to be becoming young again, shaking off the smothering mantle of age, as one shakes off dirty, threadbare clothes, and running toward all those who had gone before her. She closed her eyes and saw her husband's smile, her mother's freckled face, the grin of her dead son, the blundering frame of her uncle. She longed for the paradise of the gone generations, where time made no difference and tears did not exist.

Under the star-studded night sky in France, at some point in the middle of the mountains, the world still felt like a happy place, where joy and peace orchestrated the lives of the inhabitants. It was a secret place, surrounded by dense forests and green meadows, where the monster of war seemingly had not yet arrived.

PART 2

Chapter 13

The *clickety-clack* of the truck lulled the boys to sleep, and Bonnay fought hard to stay awake at the wheel. Since the beginning of the war, and especially since his wife's death, the care of the family fell almost entirely on his shoulders. His mother helped as she could, but her age limited her. The children were well behaved, and he knew he was lucky in that regard. Paul was a tenderheart with an eternal smile that brightened up their dull lives and breathed hope back into them. He was so much like his mother, Marguerite. Both of them could fill a room with their joyful presence. For years, Bonnay and his wife had fostered big dreams in their hearts, but death was a rude awakening. The hopes of commoners are abruptly cut off when the current of history changes direction and drags them where they could never have dreamed of going.

Love had found them when they were still young enough to have one foot in the fairytale land of innocence. The children of manual laborers were never allowed to draw out the season of childhood, but when the young Bonnay would leave his father's coal yard, he would dash to Marguerite's school. They would run through the city to the cathedral and play in the yard around the huge building, chasing each other up and down the stairs before sharing an ice-cream cone in the park. When it rained, they would walk around inside the cathedral, stealing glances at each other as they studied the enchanting stained-glass windows that turned all the light into magic rainbows. Before they were eighteen, they got married in the chapel at Saint-Pierre. It was the only time in his life that Bonnay had put on a suit, and it was the last time he attended a service. He was an atheist and Marguerite, Catholic, but Bonnay respected that she wanted them to be married by the Church.

After Marcel arrived, they started saving. They wanted their son to become a doctor, or maybe an architect, but none of that mattered anymore.

Sometimes life shrinks and plans fall apart. Making it from one day to the next is hard enough, and feeding four mouths is a miracle.

The sun started to light up the yellowed fields around them. Spring had brought copious rains after a bitterly cold winter, and now the raging heat seemed intent on burning up the life that had worked so hard to be reborn.

Paul turned to his father and gifted him with Marguerite's smile. Bonnay's heart was pierced with the knowledge that he was carrying in his beat-up truck everything he loved. He felt like the richest man on earth. Everything he needed fit into two suitcases, because those two boys were his whole world. Being a father meant renouncing his own hopes and putting everything he had into the dreams of his children.

"Good morning, Paul."

"Good morning, Father," Paul said, rubbing his eyes.

"Are you hungry?" Bonnay dug with one hand into a bag behind his seat.

"I'm starving! I could eat a horse," the boy answered with another smile.

Bonnay held out a chunk of bread and a piece of beef sausage, and Paul made short work of it. The smell of food woke the other boys, and they all had their breakfast. The collier enjoyed watching them eat, though he did not partake himself, not wanting their supplies to run out before they reached his brother-in-law's home. Since Marguerite's death, the families had not seen each other. Bonnay was not beloved by Marguerite's family. They had always thought their daughter and sister deserved someone better. Bonnay himself felt the same; his wife had been much better than he. Still, Marguerite's brother had always offered to help if they ever needed it. Bonnay did not like asking for favors, but the safety of his sons was more important than his pride.

"How much farther?" Moses asked. Though he had been on the road for many days now, he was still not used to long car trips.

"Not too far. We had to take a long detour, but we should be there by tonight. My brother-in-law has a lovely farm outside of Roanne. I don't know how things have gone for him since the German invasion, but he's always been a survivor."

Just then the truck gave a great lurch. A piece of bread jumped out of Moses's hand as if it were alive, and the boys howled with laughter. A big hole in the road threatened to stall them, but Bonnay regained control of the truck and they continued on.

Cropland surrounded them as far as they could see. This region was much more fertile than the fields they knew. The cities were brighter, and the people happier and more friendly the closer they traveled to the Mediterranean. Bonnay preferred the bogs and rustling branches of the thick forests in his department of Cher. He loved the wine from his region and the brilliant, flashing colors of their autumn.

The truck spluttered its way toward the outskirts of Céron. From there, Bonnay intended to head down and enter Roanne from the north. He was not sure if gendarmes would be stationed all around, but he doubted they would come across Germans.

For the next few hours, he avoided all towns and cities. He feared they would run out of gas, and he feared for the truck. It was sturdy enough to deliver coal all around Bourges, but Bonnay had not taken it onto a highway for years, much less the back roads they traveled, which were paved with old, uneven cobblestones or nothing at all—roads no one had tended for decades. Finally, they approached Roanne—an industrial city that produced paper and textiles and had a huge factory for tanks and Citröen cars.

Bonnay turned down a road that ran along the Loire River and led to the farm of his brother-in-law, Fabien. As the truck chugged up the drive, Bonnay noted that things must be going very well for Fabien. Large buildings lined the drive, which ended at a beautiful, newly built villa. He parked right in front of the door, and a woman dressed in a maid's uniform came out to greet them. She wore a white bonnet and an impeccable apron.

"The collier," she said matter-of-factly.

"We'd like to see Mr. Fabien Aline," Bonnay answered, ignoring the scorn on the woman's face.

"We've not ordered any coal. We have plenty left from the winter, and we do business with Mr. Darras," she said, not letting Bonnay explain. His worn-out clothes, black nails, and rough hands were calling card enough for her.

"No, you don't understand," Bonnay started, trying not to lose his patience.

A well-dressed gentleman in a spotless white suit walked out of the house. He smoked a long, thin cigarette, and a dapper felt hat covered part of his gray hair.

"What's going on, Suzanne?" he asked.

"This man is trying to sell us coal." She waved her hand toward the truck.

The gentleman frowned as he studied the visitors, his thin brows forming a nearly perfect golden arch. "Good heavens, it's my brother-in-law!"

Fabien walked forward and hugged Bonnay lightly so as not to stain his wool suit. Bonnay was overwhelmed and confused. He had never seen Fabien dressed like this. He wondered how people could change in such a short time.

"Have you brought the boys? Alice and little Fabien will be delighted to see their cousins. It's been over two years. I see you're still in the family business."

"Yes," Bonnay answered, "though it seems you've done much better for yourself than I have."

"Oh, the world is a farce, the human comedy and all that. Things are always changing."

The children got out of the truck. Marcel remembered his uncle, though the last time he had seen him, the man had been dressed in the black of mourning. He could also remember his aunt, who was younger than her husband, with blond hair and lavender blue eyes.

"These are the boys? How they have grown!" Fabien exclaimed. But when he saw the two other boys, he turned a puzzled look to Bonnay.

"They're some friends of Marcel and Paul's. We invited them to come enjoy a few days off with us," he lied. He would explain the reason for their trip later.

"Well, come in, come in. Clotilde is in town doing some shopping. She's not too big a fan of the country anymore. In fact, we live in Roanne during the winter. The children are in their piano lessons, but they'll come out to see you before long," Fabien said, his ringed hand guiding Bonnay through the door.

They went inside and walked to the back of the house to a large porch that faced the river. They could hear a piano in the background. The garden was full of flowers and lush trees, a veritable orchard.

The two men sat at a light wooden table, and the children headed for the swings that hung from an enormous walnut tree.

"I admit I'm surprised," Bonnay began. "I see you've done very well for yourself."

"Raising cattle and crops is hard work, and it's hard to find good help. We've got a lot of French, but most of our workers are Spaniards."

"Spaniards?" Bonnay asked, perplexed.

Fabien nodded. "A lot of them came this way after the civil war. They were running from hunger and Franco's regime. They're hard workers, though not very disciplined. At first I wasn't sure about them, some being communists and unionists, but all they care about is sending money to their families in Spain. It seems the situation is rather dire there."

"I'm not so sure things are much better here, at least not in the occupied zone," Bonnay said.

"You know the rain doesn't fall to everyone's liking. In Vichy, things don't seem to be so bad. At least someone finally took control of the country. The Masons and the Jews were destroying France, but Marshal Pétain will get our glory back."

The maid arrived with a silver tray and placed several glasses and a crystal jar of lemonade on the table. Fabien served his brother-in-law and then took a glass for himself.

Bonnay cleared his throat. "We may not see things eye to eye, but I haven't come to discuss politics. I need to spend some time here. I can work anywhere you put me on the farm. You know I'm not afraid to work." He picked up his glass and took a sip. The cool, sweet liquid revived him. He had not eaten since the night before, and it was nearly suppertime.

"Of course you can work here, and your oldest boy too. He looks strong as an ox, just like his father. Paul looks to be more delicate, like our beloved Marguerite. How I miss her. She left us too soon. The world was robbed of an angel. By the time my doctor friend arrived, it was too late." Fabien's tone of reproach was not lost on Bonnay.

"Your sister was too selfless. She thought only of us and nothing of herself. When the Germans came, everything was in chaos. We hardly had enough to eat, and we were helping the refugees that fled Paris. By the time I knew she was sick, the tuberculosis was already too far along."

"It's true, my sister had a Christian heart of gold. I imagine that means nothing to a socialist like yourself, but to those of us who believe . . ."

"But you were a socialist yourself!" Bonnay's ire began to rise.

"The key word there is *were*. We all change. Things are different now. With determination, a man can make a fortune and change his destiny," Fabien said, watching the children play.

"Are you part of the Rassemblement National Populaire now?"

"Yes. Marcel Déat was once a socialist, too, but a long time ago he figured out that the future of the world held something else. Don't you realize that everything has changed? Communism was leading us toward disaster. It all sounds so pretty, sharing everything equally, but human beings aren't motivated by altruism. What really drives us is ambition." As Fabien spoke, he gesticulated as if delivering a speech to a crowd.

"There's no doubt things have changed. You can tell that by just looking around."

Fabien's children came out to the porch and stared at the strange, dirty man sitting with their father, then looked toward the children.

"They are your cousins. Go say hello."

The girl smiled, but the boy stayed quiet and inexpressive. He hardly remembered the existence of cousins. The girl ran off to the big tree, then her brother reluctantly followed.

When the four boys saw two children dressed in white running toward them, they halted their games, though Moses and Paul were still moving on the swings with the momentum of their brothers' pushes.

"Marcel? Paul? Don't you remember me?" the girl asked. Alice was twelve years old. Her white skin was so thin that blue veins showed through. Her hands were delicate and her fingers long. Little Fabien was also pale, but his face was covered in freckles. His hair was a dark red, almost brown.

"Hello, cousin," Marcel said, though without much enthusiasm.

Paul studied them as his swing kept moving, then he jumped off and went up to the boy. They were almost the same height, but that was the only similarity between them. Their clothing, facial expressions, and skin tone were in contrast. Paul smiled and asked, "So you're Fabien?"

The boy did not respond. Rather, he turned and walked toward the river.

"What's got into him?" Marcel asked.

"He's just shy, and he doesn't remember you. You came to see us the summer before the war, when we lived in our old house. We had so much fun together. I sure do miss your mother," Alice said, greeting her cousins with the three official kisses. When she took note of the other two boys, she stood expectantly before them.

Marcel introduced them, using the fake names his father had given them. "These are our friends, Jean and Martin."

"Are you friends from school?" Alice asked, intrigued.

"Nah, I don't go anymore. I've got to help my father with the business. Times are hard," the boy said, though he did not really understand his father's oft-used expression.

"Hard?" Alice was curious. "You mean because of the war? I'm sad about what's happening because of the Russian communists, but it won't last long. That's what Father says."

"So what do you like to play here?" Jacob asked while Moses and Paul went to see what Fabien was doing by the river.

"We ride horses, read, play the piano, swim in the river . . ."

"You can swim in the river?" Marcel asked, as if it were the best news he had heard in weeks.

"Of course! A little farther up there's a small beach. The water is really cold, but with it being so hot outside, you'll get warmed up soon enough."

"Could we go swimming now?" Jacob asked.

"Sure. But we should leave the younger boys here. I don't want to have to watch them."

The three of them started walking. Alice's father owned about twenty-five acres along the wide river. There was an island just up from where the house sat and a lovely little beach surrounded by trees.

"Nobody else comes here. It's part of our farm," Alice explained.

The boys kicked off their shoes and dipped their toes in the water. Alice took off her white dress, revealing a black swimsuit that covered almost all of her back and shoulders and went down almost to her knees. Jacob pulled off his shirt and pants. He was about to take off his underwear when Alice cried out, "What are you doing?"

"I'm going to swim," he answered, perplexed.

"Without your underwear?" she asked.

"Don't be an idiot," Marcel said, slapping Jacob's neck.

The boys jumped in with their long underwear and the girl with her swimsuit. Jacob went under time and time again, loving the sensation of quiet under the water. He wondered if this was what it had felt like to be in his mother's womb, and he felt as if he were going back there somehow, becoming an indivisible part of her again. When he resurfaced, he saw Alice's wet hair falling down her back, which stood out even paler against the black swimsuit.

Jacob could not understand why some of his friends were so interested in girls. He found most of them to be boring, conceited, and too delicate to be any good at games. He tended to avoid them. Besides, since he only had a brother, girls were so foreign to him that he ended up treating them with indifference. He recalled how in the last school year, after he had been kicked out of public school and sent to the school for Jews, he'd met a black girl named Sophie. She had big dark eyes, and everyone teased him that Sophie was his girlfriend, even though they had never even spoken to each other. Some of the older girls even joked about having a wedding for them on the playground.

"What's up? You're staring at my cousin," Marcel said, jabbing his elbow into Jacob's ribs. Without realizing it, Jacob had indeed been staring.

"Don't be stupid. I don't even like girls." Then Jacob dunked his friend.

Marcel seemed to have gotten over his anger at Jacob's stupidity for speaking in German to the German boys at the mill. The surprise journey had been fun and exciting for him. This was certainly better than hauling bags of coal and enduring the old ladies who pinched his cheeks with their bony fingers and gave him paltry tips.

Alice stretched out on a rock while the boys continued to splash each other. On the porch, the men talked politics until Fabien's wife arrived and it was time to prepare for supper.

The maid had set the table in the formal dining room. Bonnay interpreted this as a display of his brother-in-law's wealth and power rather than a gesture of hospitality.

The men sat together at one end of the table with Clotilde, the mistress of the house. The children sat at the other end, closest to the yard. After saying grace, Fabien poured the adults a very expensive Bordeaux wine.

Clotilde smiled and said, "I hope you enjoy the supper. We weren't expecting you."

She was truly beautiful. She was still young enough that her youthful features won out over the lines and contours of the adult in her. Her well-proportioned body swayed beneath her elegant evening gown. Fabien had changed to a dark jacket, and Bonnay had put on his newer shirt, less-worn brown pants, and a vest.

"Your hospitality is more than adequate," Bonnay said, trying to be as kind as possible. He knew this would be the last time they sat at that table, being nothing more than lowly working-class people.

They sipped the delicate consommé. "Fabien tells me you've

come to Roanne looking for work. Are things that bad in the occupied zone?" Clotilde asked, taking a bite of the exquisite charbroiled duck.

"The world is always hard for people who don't go along with it. I don't like the Germans or those who collaborate with them, though we all have to answer to our own consciences for our actions," Bonnay answered curtly.

"I understand. It's a constant battle between adapting or dying," the woman proffered.

"I thought conscience was something only we believers had," Fabien joked.

"According to Hitler, conscience is something the Jews made up. I may be an atheist, but I've got a conscience, perhaps even more than the whole Vichy government that makes a show of religious bigotry while handing the Jews over to the Nazis. It's Christian charity, you see," Bonnay said. He regretted his words before they were even out of his mouth.

"I'm sure the führer is right, as always," Fabien slipped in, provocatively.

Clotilde shifted. "Who are the other children?"

"Just some kids that have lost their parents. I'm helping them out until they're back with their family." Suddenly Bonnay stood up and let his napkin drop to the table. "I . . . well, I believe I made a mistake by coming here. I apologize for the inconvenience. We'll leave right away."

"Don't be an idiot," Fabien said. "You may be a miserable failure, a stuck-up, arrogant, socialist collier, but those are my nephews. I won't let them go hungry or anything worse. Sit down. We don't have to agree on politics in order to eat dinner in peace."

Bonnay looked at the children, who had all turned and looked at the adults at the sound of raised voices. They looked exhausted, especially the younger boys. It would be better for him to swallow his pride, keep his mouth shut, and work for a season in his brother-in-law's estate until things calmed down. He sat back down.

"I don't want you to misinterpret me. I'm very happy for you that things are going so well. But one day this war will be over, and it will not be pretty for the collaborators."

"Thank you for your concern, but money always wins. The Nazis may lose this war, especially now that the North Americans have joined the fray, but France is their ally. I'm not doing anything wrong. I just export beef, lamb, and chicken for the German army. I'm not making weapons like others in Roanne do. I'm just a merchant who sells his goods to the highest bidder," Fabien said, regaining his composure.

Clotilde took his hand and turned her earnest eyes toward Bonnay. "My husband is an honorable man and a wonderful father."

"Your sister loved you so much. You were her little brother. For her sake, it's best we behave like civilized men," Bonnay said to settle the matter.

Fabien nodded. "The only thing I ask is that you be honest. Who are those children? With the times we're living in, I don't want undesirables under my roof. It could put my business at risk."

"I'll take them away tomorrow, then I'll come back and work on your farm for room and board for my boys. We'll sleep with the rest of your workers, but don't do anything to them. They've suffered enough already." The resignation in his tone surprised Fabien and Clotilde.

"We would never do anything to them, but we need to know who is staying in our house. You must understand. There are plenty of rooms in our home. You won't stay with the other workers. We have the same blood as your children," Clotilde answered.

Bonnay was silent for a long moment, hesitating. Finally, he spoke.

"They're Jewish boys, looking for their parents. They fled from Paris. Now you know what's happening all over occupied France."

"There have been raids here too," Fabien said.

"Here? The Vichy government is handing the Jews over to the Germans?" Bonnay asked, taken aback.

"The government had no choice. The Germans have pressed them into it. But only the foreign Jews. And they turn a blind eye to those who take refuge at Marseille and the coast. Up to now, the authorities have let anyone who wanted to leave France go. But the war is entering a new phase, and they fear an invasion from the Mediterranean," Fabien said.

"What does that have to do with the Jews?" Bonnay asked.

"The Nazis think they are potential enemies, dangerous communists. They won't stop until they're all locked up. There's nothing we can do for the poor things," Clotilde said.

"Yes, we can do something for them. They're people just like we are," Bonnay protested.

"Well, nothing's going to happen just because a couple of kids spend a few nights here, but they can't stay," Fabien said. The discussion was over.

They passed the rest of the meal in silence. After dessert, the children were shown to rooms, and the men found themselves alone again.

"Cigar?" Fabien offered.

Bonnay hesitated but finally took the fine Havana cigar. There had been precious few occasions when he had been able to enjoy any cigar at all.

"All of this"—Fabien waved to indicate the house, the wealth, the land beyond the spacious yard—"I've gotten in two years' time. My hands are clean, but I've known how to take advantage of opportunities."

"Congratulations."

"But there's money to be made for you too. The Germans need loads of coal to transport their materials, not to speak of all the deportations. You've got the contacts and know how the business works. We could be partners in a new company that supplies raw materials. You wouldn't have to cough up a single franc for start-up costs. Besides, you could keep thirty percent of all the earnings. It would be a good deal," Fabien said, settling back into his chair on the wide porch.

The idea took Bonnay by complete surprise. He remained standing. The cool breeze coming from the river cleared away the wine and the argument from dinner. His brother-in-law had always looked down on him, treated him like a nobody. The generous offer came as quite a shock.

"I'm not sure what to say."

"Just think about it tonight. Tomorrow you can give me an answer. Sometimes it's best to consult with the pillow on these matters."

The two men stared at the clear, dark sky for some time. The stars seemed brighter than ever, the universe indifferent to human miseries, as if all the wars and petty personal ambitions were tiny specks of dust.

Bonnay got up, said goodnight, and headed to his room. His sons were in the room right beside him, joined by a bathroom. He let out a deep sigh, looking at the canopy bed with its gold curtains and silk sheets. All of this could be his. The boys could study, have a promising future, and his wife's hopes would not have been for naught.

Fully dressed, he fell onto the bed. The soft mattress, the silk cradling his skin . . . He could get used to this. Then his eyes closed, and Bonnay fell fast asleep.

Chapter 14

Roanne
July 24, 1942

Jacob woke with a start. He felt like his chest was about to explode. He panted, and flashes of scenes from his nightmare left him shaking. He slowly calmed down and told himself it was just a bad dream. He looked over, where Moses slept peacefully. It was still night, but it would be light soon. His throat was dry. He turned toward the nightstand, searching for a glass of water. Then he went to the bathroom, turned on the faucet, and lapped up a few sips. Hearing voices, he went out to the hall.

The voices came from one of the rooms at the back of the house. It sounded like an argument, which was odd at that time of the predawn morning.

"You don't understand. It could be dangerous," a woman said.

"It's only for one more night. He promised he would take them away. We might be able to set up a good business. Later, we'll see how to actually split the profits."

"You have to protect your interests. If anyone in the government or any of the Germans find out you're hiding Jews, everything you've worked for will disappear in a snap," the woman said.

"No one's going to find out," the man said, clearly losing patience.

A chill ran up Jacob's spine. He slipped back to the room he shared with Moses and woke his brother.

"We've got to go. I don't want Mr. Bonnay to get into trouble because of us. We've already caused him enough problems."

Moses stared at him, still half asleep. He had no idea what Jacob was talking about, but he got dressed quickly. They crept down the stairs and were halfway out the door when they heard a voice behind them.

"Where are you going so early?"

They turned and saw the mistress of the house. She wore a lovely pink suit, and her hair was pulled back in a bun. Despite the early hour, she was fully dressed, as if she had been standing at the ready all night.

"We just wanted to go out and play a bit. We're used to getting up before dawn."

"But you must be hungry," she said. "You'd better eat something."

The brothers hesitated, but Clotilde put her soft hands on their backs and led them toward the kitchen. She opened the door and said sweetly, "Go on and eat whatever you'd like. There are croissants, cake, and fruit."

Moses moved forward, but Jacob grabbed his arm. Yet Clotilde took advantage of their movement to give them a push forward. Then she shut and locked the door.

They were in total darkness. From the mixture of smells, it seemed like they were in a pantry. Jacob beat on the door awhile, then kicked it, then threw himself on the ground and started weeping.

"What's going on?" Moses had no idea what was happening.

"That woman's going to call the gendarmes. I overheard a conversation she had with Marcel and Paul's uncle."

"Why would she do that?"

"She's afraid they'll be found out for helping us."

At that, Moses began to cry. The impenetrable darkness was oppressive, and his brother's words terrified him. What would become of them? Surely they would never see their parents again.

Meanwhile, Bonnay awoke refreshed. He had not slept so well in years. He usually woke two or three times a night. The early morning was the time he most missed his wife, though they had their best talks at night. It was too hard to find any time the rest of the day with the kids being little and both of them working nonstop.

The shower water relaxed him even more. Bonnay dressed slowly, without the typical early morning rush, and went out to the huge upstairs hallway covered in rugs. He met his sons as he was going downstairs and they were running up to meet him.

"Good morning, boys. I hope you slept as well as I did."

"Father, we can't find Jacob or Moses anywhere," Marcel said.

Bonnay's eyebrows knit together, and he looked all around to make sure no one was watching them.

"I told you not to use their names," he whispered severely.

"But they're gone!" Paul cried.

"This is a huge house, not to speak of the yard outside. They're bound to turn up any moment. Surely they'll come to the dining room when they get hungry."

"No, we've looked everywhere, and our cousins haven't seen them either."

Bonnay went downstairs to search the living room, the dining room, the music room, the porch. Back inside, he searched the spacious entryway. He found no sign of the boys.

Clotilde emerged then from the kitchen. Impatiently, Paul asked, "Have you seen our friends?"

She smiled as if his question were cute. "Oh, they left early this morning. I gave them some food for their journey. It seemed they did not want to stay here any longer. They were anxious to find their parents. They wanted to take the first train to Lyon. At least, that's what they said."

Bonnay stopped in his tracks. It seemed very odd that the boys would have gone off just like that, without even saying goodbye to Marcel and Paul.

Just then Fabien descended the stairs, grinning widely. He came up to them and put his hands on his brother-in-law's shoulders.

"We've got so much to do. This morning we'll go to the notary. I've already called my lawyers to formalize the terms of the limited partnership. I'm sure that, within a year, once you've got a house like this, you'll thank me for making you a rich man."

The collier looked at his children. Caressing Paul's face, which bore a concerned look, he said, "I'm sure they're fine. They were with us for a while, but they've decided to continue their journey."

Fabien put his hand on Bonnay's back and the two men went toward the door. The chauffeur was already waiting for them outside in a Mercedes.

The boys watched their father walk away. They could not believe he was unconcerned for their friends.

"All right, young men, you must have your breakfast. I'm sure you woke up hungry. Your cousins have already eaten," their aunt said with a forced smile. She made every effort to hide her disgust that such vermin were mixing with her refined children.

Like many children, the boys had a sixth sense that detected intentions and what lived in people's hearts. They saw something in their aunt's expression that made them uncomfortable.

"Come now, your food is ready in the dining room," she insisted, gesturing for them to hurry up and get to eating.

Marcel and Paul followed her to the dining room, but as soon as she turned to leave, Marcel discreetly followed her. Paul hesitated but then joined his brother.

"Where are we going?" he whispered. Marcel motioned for him to keep quiet. They watched their aunt go into the kitchen and then followed.

"What are you doing?" Paul asked again.

"I think Aunt Clotilde knows where Jacob and Moses are."

Paul scrunched up his face. He could not understand why his aunt would do anything bad to his friends.

Clotilde came back out of the kitchen, a set of keys tinkling at her side. Marcel stared at them a moment, then said to Paul, "Call to her. While you talk to her, I'll try to steal the keys."

Paul stepped forward and stopped his aunt in the middle of the hallway. Marcel slipped out behind the door and stood just behind her.

"What's going on, Paul? Have you already finished eating?" she asked with annoyance.

"Yes, but I can't find Alice or Fabien. The house is so big . . ."

Marcel managed to slip the keys from Clotilde without jingling them, then tiptoed away.

"But don't worry, I'll find them!" Paul said, turning and running away.

Clotilde was puzzled but went on about her tasks. The gendarmes would arrive any minute, and she did not want the inconvenience of those children to make her lose her whole morning.

Paul caught back up with his brother, who was examining the keys one by one. "If they're locked up somewhere," Marcel said, "it'll be where only the maids go, since she knows we wouldn't look for them there."

Marcel tried each door one by one until he found one that was locked. Then he tried several keys until the lock finally gave way.

Jacob tumbled out of the room so fast he knocked Marcel over. Moses followed, armed with a stick he had found.

"What happened to you?" Paul asked the boys.

"Your aunt locked us up," Jacob said.

"You have to get out of here right away. I bet she called the gendarmes."

The boys headed for the door, but then Jacob remembered his backpack.

"I'll go get it, and you just get out of here," Marcel said. He ran back to the pantry as fast as he could. On his way out again, he found himself standing face-to-face with his aunt.

"What do you think you're doing?"

He pushed her hard and ran to the door. The others were waiting for him, jittering with impatience. They could see a cloud of dust at the end of the drive. "A car is coming," Jacob said.

They ran through the cornfields, then along the river. If they followed the current, it would lead them to Roanne. "You've already done so much for us," Jacob said through ragged breaths. "You'd better get back to the house."

"No, we'll go with you to the city. I know where the train station is. We were here a couple of years ago. When the train leaves the station, it goes really slow, and you can jump on it and get to Lyon. You'll have to avoid the ticket collector and make sure you jump off before you get to the last station," Marcel said, panting.

Jacob hugged his friend, and Moses hugged Paul. "Thank you," he said.

"We're your friends." Marcel shrugged.

They ran farther along the river's edge. The vegetation protected them from being seen from the road, but they knew they did not have much time. The gendarmes would not be slow to pick up their trail. Besides, their pursuers had a car, and the boys would soon lose their advantage.

They slowed and walked for some time until they reached the city center. They turned up Avenue Gambetta and walked until they saw the great mustard-yellow station. "We have to get to the tracks," Marcel said, pointing toward the end of the road.

"How will we know which is the right train?" Jacob asked.

"Each train has a sign, and we'll be able to see it from the tracks."

They ran again until the station was behind them, crossed the street, jumped a fence, and went down to the tracks. Minutes later they heard a train slowly approaching. They let the engine go by and saw the sign: Lyon. They waited a little longer, so they would not hop on the very first cars where travelers would see them and alert the inspector.

"It's going fast," Moses said, watching the train picking up speed with each passing second.

"You'd better go for it now," Marcel said, breathless.

The two brothers began running alongside the train. When they reached a good speed, Jacob jumped and grabbed a handle between two cars. Moses kept running, but the train sped up, and no matter how fast he went, Moses could not reach Jacob's out-stretched hand.

"Come on! You've got to jump now or else you won't be able to!" Jacob yelled, on the verge of panic.

Moses started to lose ground, and the train moved away from him little by little. Then he felt someone grab him from behind and run with him. It was Marcel. He had seen what was happening and knew Moses would never make it on his own. He picked the younger boy up, ran as fast as he could, and threw Moses with a great heave toward his brother. Moses flew suspended in the air for the briefest of seconds before Jacob clutched him and pulled him onto the little platform. Recovering their breath, they waved goodbye to Marcel and Paul.

As they watched the train fade away into the distance, Marcel turned toward his brother. "Let's go to the station," he said.

"Why? We're already going to be in trouble for what we've done."

"We have to help them gain some time."

Paul did not understand what his brother meant, but he dutifully followed to the train platforms. They hopped up on the nearest one and walked to the main entryway. The gendarmes rushed over as soon as they saw them.

"Did you think you would get far? Come with us to the gendarmerie," a policeman said, his strong fists clenching the boys' arms.

Marcel kicked his leg hard, and the man instinctively let go. The boys ran to the exit and slipped away into the streets as half a dozen gendarmes ran after them.

Running through the peaceful roads of Roanne, Marcel could not help but smile. He was imagining his friends on the train to Lyon, just a bit closer to their parents, which made him feel victorious. He would probably never see them again, but he would always carry them in his heart. Neither time nor distance could make him forget them. Jacob and Moses were two brave souls who had decided to face their destiny with everything they had, and he was sure nothing would hold them back.

Chapter 15

The wind blew in their faces as if announcing their impending arrival. Jacob and Moses knew Lyon was just a little over sixty miles from Valence and that the river that escorted them from afar, the Rhône, was the same river that refreshed the city where their parents were.

Jacob pointed out the current of the water to his brother through the little window of the car they had slipped into. He got lost in thought about how the water he had seen seconds before was moving faster than the old wooden train run by a steam engine that laboriously chugged them toward what they hoped would be the final layover of their journey.

At times, Jacob wondered how they had been able to come so far. Without the help of so many people risking their lives day after day to protect the persecuted—pariahs of the land so universally despised—they would never have made it that far. It had been a harrowing journey. Paris now felt like a distant memory, as if they had never even lived there. All Jacob and Moses had was the present—the past was a dense fog they could never return to, hardly even in their memory—and the future seemed so uncertain they dared not imagine their lives beyond this moment.

In one sense, childhood is an eternal present. The road traveled is just a few feet beyond the starting point, and the end goal seems so far away that it gives the false sense of eternity that the young always feel.

Moses looked out again at the ripe fields, the patches of forests, and the spread-out towns with white, peaceful-looking houses. He thought about how huge the world was. He tried to imagine what the ocean was like, how it would feel to climb the high Swiss mountains, or how the coasts of Africa appeared. In the past few days, his vision of the world had expanded so greatly that, on the one hand, he felt insignificant, and on the other, he felt the fascinating power of soaring in his imagination, regardless of what was happening all around them. His brother, however, seemed overwhelmed by worry and the certainty of constant danger, the anguish of what might happen to Moses, or the fear that their parents would no longer be at the only address they had for them.

"What will happen if we're all alone in the world?" Moses asked, not looking at Jacob. He seemed lucidly aware that what they were going through was an agonizing flight from death, not an exciting adventure.

The question felt like an uppercut to Jacob's jaw. He wanted his brother to remain unaware of the realities that were more and more unbearable for him. "We're not alone in the world," he said. "We'll find Mother and Father." His voice was firm as he tried to convince himself of his own words.

"Don't lie to me," Moses whispered. "We're in a war. I know what that means. I also know our parents will have found out what happened to Aunt Judith, and maybe they went back home. So what will we do if we don't find them?" His question throbbed with pain. His eyes watered, but Moses willed them not to spill over.

"We'll keep looking. We'll move heaven and earth to find them," Jacob said, though he could see his answers no longer convinced his brother.

"For how long? What if we look for them forever and never see them again?" Moses finally began to cry.

"Well, I'll always be here. You can't get rid of me that easily," Jacob joked.

"You're an idiot," Moses said, punching his shoulder.

"We'll work, we'll get out of France, far away from the Nazis, go somewhere safe . . ."

Moses looked up. "Is there somewhere safe for us?"

Again, the child's question reverberated in his ears. Jacob wondered the same thing. Just over a year ago, anywhere their parents took them seemed like a safe place. But in that moment, everywhere on earth felt dangerous.

Their stomachs growled. They had not, after all, had any breakfast, and even though they had eaten a huge dinner the night before, they were very hungry. Jacob checked his backpack. They still had a few tins of food and some hard bread. They ate in silence but had hardly begun to digest the food when at the end of the aisle they saw a man dressed in black.

"The ticket inspector," Moses whispered, pointing down the aisle. The boys gathered their things quickly and walked in the opposite direction. They went from car to car until they reached the last one.

"What do we do now?"

"I'm not sure how much time is left until Lyon," Jacob said. Right then the train seemed to be going faster than it had the rest of the journey. They looked out at the ground whizzing by as they left the world they had known and catapulted toward an uncertain future.

"You aren't thinking about jumping, Jacob."

Jacob shrugged. "I can't think of any other option."

Moses saw a ladder that led to the roof, tapped Joseph on the shoulder, and pointed up. "I bet he won't find us if we stay up there the rest of the journey."

"But that's even more dangerous than jumping off while in motion," Jacob said. He was not a fan of heights.

"Come on, we don't have much time."

Jacob started up slowly, suddenly sweaty and feeling the racing beat of his heart. He looked to one side, saw the landscape rushing by, and felt like he was in a free fall. He took a deep breath and kept climbing.

Moses followed, pushing Jacob with his head to move him along. The inspector could look out at any moment. When they were on the roof of the car, they felt the full blast of the wind and the *clickety-clack* of the train. They threw themselves down, clinging to the top of the ladder, and waited.

The inspector came out onto the final platform, glanced around, then returned to the car, the door banging shut behind him.

"Let's go back down," Jacob pleaded. The terror on his face startled Moses.

"Let's wait just a little longer," Moses said. It was not smart to go down too quickly. The inspector could be anywhere.

"I've got to get down," Jacob said, his face pale and his stomach turning over.

Jacob descended much faster than he had gone up the ladder and collapsed onto the floor of the platform. Eventually he noticed his brother descending with a smile. "So I found something I'm better at than you!" Moses joked.

They stayed there on the platform for another hour, waiting for the train to close in on Lyon. Despite the heat, the breeze was cool. As they approached the forested region, the heat was less unbearable than in the plains and marshy areas they had traversed in recent days.

A sign on a nearby roadway let them know they were not far from Lyon. The train slowed as they entered the city limits, and when the boys spotted the station ahead, they jumped.

The train was already moving at a slow pace, so the impact of the jump was minimal. Even so, Moses banged his legs on the track and sat for a while, rubbing the spot that hurt.

"Come on," Jacob said. "We need to get away from the tracks."

"Will we do this again to get to Valence?" Moses asked.

"Let's sneak up to the station and check out the trains and schedules. We've got nothing to lose by trying it," Jacob said, smiling. He felt very proud of having gotten so far along by themselves. No one had helped them on the last leg of their journey. Then he wondered what had happened to Marcel and Paul, though he shook the thought away. Surely, after a reprimand, they would be returned to their father. Jacob hoped that the uncle would protect his own flesh and blood, even if only to keep his name clear of scandal. He knew that a lot of people did the right thing out of fear of what would happen if they did not, instead of out of true love for others or due to some higher sense of justice. Jacob mused on all of this as the boys picked their way to the station.

They entered the great hall and went up to the board that displayed the train schedules. After a few minutes of studying, they deciphered the abbreviations and saw that a train to Valence would be leaving early the next morning.

"So what do we do until tomorrow morning?" Moses asked.

Jacob shrugged. "Look for somewhere to rest."

They had never slept on the streets before. Even on the worst days during their search for their parents they had found some sort of food and some sort of roof over their heads. But in Lyon, they were completely on their own.

They knew that if they went to a park, someone might see them and report them. The police would waste no time in arresting them and asking what they were doing so far from home. Finally, they decided to try out what looked like an abandoned house near the train tracks.

Through the open door they saw no furniture inside, but most of the windows still had their glass. It seemed like a decent place to take shelter for the night. They fashioned a sleeping mat of sorts from the many old newspapers they found lying around the house.

"This place creeps me out," Moses said.

"Don't worry, I'll stay up and keep watch. I can sleep on the train tomorrow," Jacob said. He did not like the place either. He would rather stay up and make sure they did not miss the train instead of sleep in such a place.

The hours passed slowly. Jacob began to nod off, sleep finally overcoming him. He was resting peacefully when a noise startled him. He lifted his head and saw movement in the shadows. He shook

Moses. Before they had laid down for the night, Jacob had checked to see if there was a back door, and he thought they should make a run for it now out the back. But before they could move, noises surrounded them.

Moses woke in fright and screamed. Still dazed, he thought the shadows all around him were ghosts, but one of them flicked open a cigarette lighter and lit up part of the room.

The dirty, angry face of a boy was inches from his face, and Moses screamed again. The boy clamped his hand over Moses's mouth. "Shut up, you little rat! Do you want all the guards from the station to come running?" The boy had a strange accent, but his words were enough to quiet Moses.

"What do you want?" Jacob asked, trying to disguise his terror.

"First, every penny you've got. Then your shoes and that backpack. If you behave, I might let you go after that, but if you make me angry, I'll slit your throats. Nobody's going to care about two little vagabonds sleeping in an abandoned house." His voice was hoarse, punctuated by dry, staccato laughter.

The three others with him also laughed. Moses was trembling beyond control and feared he would wet himself.

Jacob made every effort to master his fear. "We'll give you the money, but we need our shoes and clothes, and a couple of papers that won't do you any good."

The youth grabbed Jacob by the collar and pulled him to his feet. "You trying to make a deal with me? You think you've got gumption? You're a piece of trash to talk like that, but I'll teach you a lesson."

Seeing that all the attention was on Jacob, Moses kicked the thief hard in the groin. The boy went to his knees with a cry. In the second it took his cronies to react, Jacob and Moses dashed to the back door and disappeared into the darkness. They hid behind a cargo train and caught their breath, still not believing they had managed to get away alive.

"The backpack! I left the backpack!" Jacob moaned in a whisper.

"So what? They were going to kill us," Moses said. He was still unable to control his trembling, but he was proud of his daring act.

"The letters are in there, Mother and Father's letters. I've got the money with me, but the letters are the only thing we had left of them. I have to go back," he said, trying to stand.

"But they're going to kill you," Moses warned. "Soon we'll see Mother and Father face-to-face, so what do we need their letters for?" His brother was being irrational.

"Their address is in the letters," Jacob said, his head hung low.

"Didn't you memorize it?"

"I can't remember it."

"You read them a zillion times. When you've calmed down, I'm sure it'll come back to you," Moses said.

Jacob tried to be still and quiet and willed his mind recall the address. He could call up every word of the letters, seeing them on the page in his mind like a photograph. But the return address on the envelope was fuzzy.

They had come so close, yet hope had vanished again. He began to cry. Those white envelopes were the only thing that proved their parents were real, were alive, could be found in a real place—that they were not ghosts or figments of his childish imagination. His mother's stylized script was what kept her alive in Jacob's mind, the ink that ran a touch lazily at the end of her signature. His memory was so weak, so fragile, so capricious, always subject to the inexorable march of time.

"And her picture," he mumbled between tears. But then he searched his pockets and found the picture was there.

At his brother's words, Moses tried to call up his parents' faces, and his breath caught when he could not. He could still recall his mother's smell and his father's voice, but their faces were just out of reach. They were like two voids, slowly being consumed by nothingness while forgetfulness gnawed away at the thin thread that tethered them to the world of the living.

Chapter 16

Lyon
July 25, 1942

Neither of the boys was able to sleep for what remained of that night. They were terrified that the thugs who had stolen their backpack would return at any moment. Jacob leaned against the metal wheel of the train car and looked back and forth, back and forth. Moses closed his eyes and tried to sleep, but he woke with a start each time.

They felt better as soon as the sun started to rise. It would not be too long before the train left the station. They might even be with their parents in a few hours, and all of this would seem like a bad dream. Jacob tried again to remember the name of the street and the house number. He knew the letters by heart and could see them when he closed his eyes, but he cursed himself for not having paid as much attention to the envelopes.

"I'm hungry," Moses said, getting to his feet. He spied the abandoned house from their spot among the train cars.

"Don't even think about it," Jacob warned, knowing what his brother was thinking.

"But maybe they threw out some food."

"I seriously doubt that anyone in their situation would throw out canned meat and bread."

Moses knew his brother was right, but sometimes it was better to make completely sure.

"The train will leave in about twenty minutes. We'd better hide nearby so we can jump on as it's moving, like last time," Jacob said, changing the subject.

The brothers walked along the tracks. Very few people milled around the station that early in the morning. The train heading to Valence carried goods, not passengers, but that was all the better for them, as they would not have to hide from an inspector.

Soon they saw the train creeping toward them. It was a much older steam engine than the one on the passenger train from Lyon, and it would be easy to hop on and hide in one of the cars. The journey to Valence would be longer, but they would arrive before nightfall.

They ran alongside and jumped into the fourth car, and no one seemed to take notice. They had inadvertently chosen an empty cattle car that had already delivered its goods of cows or sheep to Lyon.

"I can't breathe!" Moses said, pinching his nose. The stench was unbearable.

"You'll get used to it in a while."

Moses winced and felt like he was going to vomit, but he knew Jacob was usually right. They were so exhausted that the steady rocking of the train soon lulled them to sleep, bunched up together.

Straw covering the floor offered some cushion, and a full two hours passed before they woke.

Jacob's eyes opened, and he stretched and yawned. "I really needed that sleep." Then he set about studying the train car. It was rather dark, the only light filtering in through the wooden slats of the walls.

"What are you looking for? Do you think there might be food?" Moses asked, joining his brother.

"Who knows, maybe we'll find some leftover grain they gave the animals. I think I'd eat just about anything right now."

After a fruitless search, Jacob found some newspapers in a corner. He pushed them aside slowly and saw something. It was a book, a little journal, with a pencil stuck between the pages.

He took it and they moved closer to the door where they had entered the car, to a spot with more light. They sat, and Moses leaned back on Jacob and drifted off to sleep again. Jacob opened the book to the first blank page and started to write something when he noticed the long, delicate writing of perhaps a woman. He flipped back a few pages and then started reading at the beginning. He was surprised to see the date was very recent, just a few weeks prior. There was a location he did not recognize: Rivesaltes Camp. The owner of the diary was a woman named Gemma Durieu. As Jacob read and was drawn in by the young woman's words, he realized how similar their stories were:

> We got here from Perpignan just a few days ago, and it already feels like months. Life in the camp is hard. Spring is hot and rainy this year. If there's wind, it blows clouds of dust that make it impossible to breathe. We spend all day shut up inside the suffocating houses with dirt floors and glassless windows. Then it rains really hard,

and everything becomes a huge mud pit. It's horrible. We can't go out to get food, use the disgusting bathrooms at the end of the street, or stand for roll call without sinking into the mud. I've had to pull my boots out by hand several times. Some people say summer is even worse, though we'll be gone by the time the heat really cranks up. They're sending us Jews up north to work in factories for the Germans. At least time will go quickly if we're working and it won't feel like time is standing still and we're slaves to nothingness . . .

The last few weeks, so many trains have come and gone. We'll be next. A lot of them have taken our friends and neighbors, the people I would see on the streets back home, but I hardly recognize them now. Their clothes are torn apart, and the people are so skinny. Thank God the Quakers and the Red Cross bring us some food. At least this unending hunger sometimes lets us sleep and dream. Only in the arms of Morpheus are we really free . . .

They've made us get into long lines, separated by age and sex, then they put us on trucks to take us to the train station. For me, leaving is better than staying, though a lot of people are afraid of what will happen. At least *something* is happening, and the monotony becomes curiosity. I'm still alone. I lost sight of my family back when they arrested us. People have told me there are lots of camps, and maybe we'll find our families up north. I cry myself to sleep most nights. I feel like an orphan. I never knew what loneliness and fear were 'til now. Everything terrifies me, even going outside in broad daylight or the heavy rains of early summer. It's starting to get really hot now. Sometimes it feels like being underwater, but it's heat instead of water, and I try to get my head above the surface to breathe before the burning smothers me . . .

I had no idea they would ship us in a cattle car. Camp life was already horrible. There were absolutely no comforts of daily living, and hardly any food, but at least we were considered human beings. This cattle car reeks of feces, sweat, and urine. Sometimes I think I can't take it anymore. I'm so alone, so afraid . . .

We've been traveling for three endless days now. We're hungry, we've barely slept, and many of the people crammed in here are sick. I've wondered if they aren't actually taking us anywhere, but we'll just travel back and forth until we all die, as if our final station is death itself . . .

Now the train has stopped on an unused track. I see nothing around us. I can hear the doors of the other cars banging open, many voices, dogs, shouting, and heat, it's so unbearably hot . . .

The diary cut off there, midsentence, as if someone had ripped the journal out of the girl's hand and thrown it into the corner. Jacob tried to make sense of what he had read. He could not understand all of it, and the chilling, abrupt ending confused him especially. He wondered if something like this had happened to Joseph. Then Jacob thought about his parents. Had they been arrested and sent up north? It turned out that Jews in the unoccupied zone were also being held in camps and sent to Germany.

"What are you thinking about?" Moses asked, waking to find Jacob holding the diary.

"Nothing," Jacob lied. He did not want Moses to worry, especially now that they were so close to Valence and their parents.

"What's in the journal?" he asked, curious.

"Just ideas, the things the girl who lost the diary was thinking about. It wouldn't interest you."

"Well, you've been reading it for hours." Moses frowned.

"I've got nothing else to do." Joseph stood up and opened the train car door a bit to look out at the scenery. The trees stretched for miles around. There were more hills and mountains than in Lyon, though he could also see grain fields and animals grazing in pastures.

"I'm so hungry," Moses complained, coming up to Jacob.

"Me too. Maybe Mother will cook supper for us tonight." Jacob smiled at the thought. He desperately wanted to believe they had reached the end of their long journey, though he was afraid their parents would have left already, or afraid he would not be able to find the right street. Regardless, he figured Valence would be small enough. They would find them eventually.

They spent the next few hours watching the scenery. The cool wind from the surrounding forests cleared their heads, and they grew more and more nervous as time passed.

Moses could not hold it in any longer. "Have you remembered the name of the street?"

"I don't think it was a street, but more like a plaza . . ."

"A plaza? Well, at least there can't be that many plazas in one city," Moses said, somewhat encouraged.

"Yeah, and it was something like republic, or equality, or fraternity . . ."

"Liberty," Moses offered, filling in the third value of the French motto.

"Yeah, it was the Place de la Liberté, Liberty Plaza!" Jacob answered, thrilled to have finally remembered the name. Now they just had to get there. They would find their parents in no time.

The train was following a river and, little by little, the houses that had been few and far between became denser until it seemed they were traveling on the outskirts of a city. The river split the city in two, though most of the city fell east of the river, the side the train was on. They passed through a few neighborhoods before the train entered a railway section with enormous storage vessels. On the other side of a fence, the boys glimpsed pale, uninspiring buildings. They looked like poor imitations of the more decorative buildings in Lyon. The whole place had a gray, provincial air about it.

The train began to slow as it drew near the station, which was sloughing off its yellow and white paint. Despite the deterioration, it was the most beautiful city in the world to Jacob and Moses. Euphoric, they jumped out before the train came to a halt.

Making their way through the tracks toward the station, they came out on a narrow road covered by thick trees. They did not know where to go next. Finally, Jacob went up to a street vendor who pushed a heavy cart laden with vegetables.

"Sir, could you tell us how to get to the Place de la Liberté?"

The street vendor studied them with his little eyes barely visible below the bill of his cap. He had a salt-and-pepper mustache and wore a dark apron over an old suit.

"You go north up that street, Avenue Victor Hugo, until you reach the main boulevard, then it becomes Rue Emile Augier. Keep going north. You can't miss it. The plaza is at the end, on the left."

"Thank you so much, sir!" Jacob hollered as the boys ran toward the avenue the man had pointed to. Within minutes they were standing on Place de la Liberté. It was an elegant rectangle with lively buildings, including a theater on one side painted with bright, shining colors.

Jacob just stood and looked at the place his parents had lived all that time. His eyes were seeing the same buildings, trees, and cobblestones they had seen, his feet were standing on the same ground they had walked. The knot in his throat threatened to burst. He wanted to hug them, have their embrace wash away the memories of the last ten days.

"What number is it?" Moses asked, impatient.

Jacob pointed to a three-story, green building. If he remembered correctly, they lived in the top floor, in the attic apartment. The boys stared at the outside of the building for a while, then began to walk. Rather, it felt like they floated, every nerve tingling with terrified hope. At the door, they looked up. Taking a deep breath, they pushed it open and walked into the cool entryway.

Chapter 17

Jacob's and Moses's legs were filled with sand as they made their slow way up to the attic. The stairway was clean. The black handrail was not dusty, and the stairs shone as if recently stained. It was a much nicer building than the apartment they had shared with Aunt Judith the last few years. The cities in the farther reaches of the country seemed less worn-out by the pressure of the war, as if the ugly cloud that stretched thickly over Paris and northern France had not yet arrived in full force farther south. Jacob briefly thought that Valence was more like the country his parents had fallen in love with and where they had hoped to make a fresh start and which, since the arrival of the Nazis with their threats and lies, had become gray and prosaic, like an endless, monotonous silent film.

They were out of breath when they reached the final landing. They stared at the dark wooden door, the huge golden peephole, and the round, black doorbell. They looked at each other, unsure of what to do. A soul can long so deeply for its happiness that it fears the truth will rear up and ruin the moment it has envisioned thousands of times. Finally, Joseph touched the doorbell lightly, almost caressing it. After the ringing noise, he drew his hand back quickly, waited with his arms behind his back, and then felt his brother's sweaty hand grabbing his own.

The door opened slowly, and a soft light flowed out onto the dark landing. A tall, stocky figure appeared. The man wore an old red silk dressing gown, matching slippers, and white linen pants underneath.

The person leaned down a bit to study the visitors more closely, then took off his glasses and folded them over the pocket of his robe. "Who exactly are you?" he asked after a long silence, as if he had tried but failed to recognize them.

The children were speechless. Their eyes stung, and their skin grew redder by the second. Had they tried to speak, the words would have died before leaving their throats.

"Do you know what time it is? I'm having supper. I don't know what you're after. If you're just going to stand there staring, I'm sorry, but I cannot waste any more time." The man started to close the door, but Jacob's arm shot out to keep it from latching. The man's eyebrows lifted, more from curiosity than anger.

"We're the children of Eleazar and Jana Stein. They sent us letters from this address. We've come from very far away to find them. Can you tell us where they are?"

The door swung back open, the man's curiosity fully awakened now by the child's words. He stared at the boys in shock as if they were ghosts. "Come in, good gracious, come in!" he urged. His shock had turned to worry.

The boys stepped into the small entryway, then followed the man down a hallway to a large living room with a sloped ceiling. The furniture seemed relatively new and gave off an intense smell of varnished wood.

"Oh my, oh my, oh my!" the man groaned. The weight of this news bubbled out of him but had no clear words of its own. He motioned for them to sit and brought them glasses of water and some cookies. They accepted eagerly, and the man watched the boys pick up and eat even the crumbs that fell to their dirty pants.

"So you are Jana and Eleazar's boys. How did you get here? Did someone bring you?"

The fact that this man knew their parents was an enormous relief to Jacob and Moses. Lately they had begun to wonder if their parents really existed after all or if they were just two orphans who had made them up to keep them on a journey toward an impossible goal.

Moses asked the most natural question in the world: "Where are our parents?" The frustration he had felt when the man first opened the door started to abate, and at least Moses's stomach was no longer rebelling loudly and he had received a soft and comfortable seat.

The old man studied the boys again. Their faces were blackened with filth, their hair a mess, their clothes stained, and their shoes ruined. But they were most certainly the same boys Jana had shown him in the little picture she always kept with her.

"Sweetheart, your mother is the sweetest, most beautiful, wonderful woman in the world. That's why she has such adorable children. She has told me so much about you both. She missed you terribly every day. I've seen her weep countless tears sitting in the same spot where you're sitting now. For her, living apart from you two was like having her heart cut out of her. It was different for your father. He surely suffered as much as she, but he was focused on a goal that did not allow him to show any feeling."

The old man was quiet then. He bit his lips, swallowing back the emotion starting to block his throat. He stood abruptly and drew close to the boys. "Your parents adore you. You are the most important thing in the world to them. Never forget that."

His words were so definite that they scared Jacob. He sensed the old man was trying to tell them something he dared not speak aloud, hoping for them to intuit it instead.

"They aren't here?" Jacob asked, though it was more of a statement than a question.

"No, they aren't here. For shame, it's a misfortune—like a Greek tragedy. Tragedy, no, it's an epic saga. They left two weeks ago. I was to send you a letter, but I've been unable to leave the house until just yesterday. As soon as they left, I fell gravely ill and nearly died. I moved here to be more comfortable and isolated. I manage this house. I was staying on the bottom floor, but the noise, the renters, everything got to me. I think it was your parents' leaving that made me sick. I loved them as if they were my own children, you see. The children I never had." The man's eyes were wet.

"What did they say in the letter?" Jacob asked, impatient.

"I don't have it anymore. I gave it to the theater director, who promised to send it, but I don't know if he already has. I can call him," he said, reaching for the phone. He dialed a number and waited.

The boys looked at each other. Moses grabbed Jacob's hand.

"Mr. Perrot, please. I need to speak with him urgently." The man cupped his hand over the receiver and looked back at the boys. He heard a sound and motioned for them to be calm, that it would be all right.

"What's happening?" Moses asked Jacob, scared. Jacob put his finger to his lips for Moses to keep quiet, though he, too, was anxious to know what was happening.

"Yes, I understand, I understand. Some boys will be dropping by in a bit for a letter. Thank you very much."

The man hung up the phone and said, "I don't think he's taken the letter to the post office yet. It seems the director hasn't left the theater all day. You'll have to go get it there. It's the building right in front. The director, Mr. Perrot, will give you the letter. Take it and come back here right away. Don't speak to anyone, you understand?"

The boys nodded and stood up. The man walked them to the door and watched them dash down the stairs.

Out on the street, the afternoon light had begun to fade, and the street lamps were lighting up one by one. They saw the theater directly in front. It was not very big, but it was painted a pleasing light yellow and had a balcony and a gable roof supported by two columns that gave the building the feel of a classic temple. The red door looked to be closed, but Jacob and Moses went up the stairs and pushed it open without knocking.

A middle-aged man dressed in a blue usher's uniform with gold buttons stopped them in the vestibule. "Where are you going, boys?" he asked, eyeing their disheveled appearance.

"Mr. Perrot has an envelope for us," Moses answered.

"Mr. Perrot just left," the usher responded.

"Where did he go?" Jacob could not keep the nerves out of his voice.

"I imagine he went home, though he had some errands to run first."

"But they just called him," Jacob protested.

"I know nothing more than what I've just said. The theater is closed, so you shouldn't be in here," he said, shooing them toward the door.

"Where does Mr. Perrot live? We have to find him right away!" Jacob insisted.

The usher sighed. He wanted to lock up the place, but reluctantly he walked them out and pointed down a street. "He usually heads to the right, but he was carrying some mail. The post office is at the end of the street. I imagine he's there by now."

At those words, the boys were off in a flash. A little light remained in the sky, and only a few people walked the streets. They veered right without running into anyone and saw the symbol for the post office at the end of the way. Seconds later they were panting at the door. They burst inside and saw one older woman and one elderly man with a nice hat and a light brown suit.

"Mr. Perrot!" Jacob called, trying to catch his breath.

The man turned. He held a cane in one hand, and in the other, half a dozen letters. The post office employee eyed the children suspiciously and was about to send them out when the gentleman smiled and let the woman go ahead of him in line.

"Do tell me what I can do for you," Perrot said, imagining that the children would not have run so fast to shout at him in the middle of the post office for no good reason.

"Eleazar and Jana Stein are our parents," Jacob whispered.

"Oh dear me." He took a step back. "Come, come, let's be on our way."

They all three walked out to the street and sat on a bench.

"I was just about to mail a letter to you and your aunt. Why aren't you in Paris?" he asked, puzzled.

The boys were still trying to regain their breath, and they did not take their eyes off the letters held in the man's gloved hand.

"There was a big raid, and we were picked up by accident. After we escaped, we couldn't find our aunt, and we've traveled many days to get here."

Perrot gestured in dismay. "But your parents left two weeks ago. They wrote you a letter, but poor Mr. Vipond has been too ill, and he finally asked me to send it. If you had come even five minutes later, I wouldn't have been able to help you." He sighed with relief and started thumbing through the letters. He handed them a long envelope trimmed in red and blue.

"You don't know where they were going?" Jacob asked, opening the envelope.

"No, they didn't want anyone to know, in case the police came looking for them. Until recently, things have been pretty calm here, but in the past few weeks the gendarmes have begun asking for identification from foreigners and have even detained some."

Jacob opened the letter nervously and recognized his mother's handwriting. He did not know if he should read it then or wait until he and Moses were alone.

"Your parents worked for the theater. Mr. Vipond introduced them to me several months ago. As soon as I heard your father's name, I knew who he was. I was familiar with his work as a playwright. He helped me adapt a few plays, and your mother designed costumes, though I know she also wrote. I was so sad to see them go. Do you boys need help? How did you get here?"

"Lots of people have helped us along the way, though we had to make the last part of the journey on our own. We thought this would be the end of it, but we'll have to keep searching." Jacob let out a long sigh.

"I can give you some money. I imagine you can stay in Mr. Vipond's building tonight. He's a very interesting person. In his younger days he was a great actor, but he'll tell you all about that. Allow me to walk you back to his home. It's already nighttime, and it's not good for two boys to be out alone. This is a small town, and people will talk."

"Don't worry about it," Jacob said. "We remember the way and don't want to lose any more time." But the director insisted. They were an odd trio on the way back to the plaza—one finely dressed gentleman with a mahogany cane and two dirty children with torn clothes. At the front door, Perrot took off his hat, revealing a bald head on top with just a ruffle of thin, white hair around the back.

"If you need anything," he said, "you can usually find me at the theater. My house is very near the post office. Mr. Vipond can give you the address. I'm so pleased you've made it here safe and sound. These are very dangerous times." He put his hat back on and bid them goodnight.

Jacob and Moses walked up the stairs slowly. They were eager to read the letter but wanted to wait until they were inside and could savor their parents' words like a delicate treat. Then they would figure out how to continue their search.

Vipond opened the door with a swoosh and pulled them inside urgently. "For heaven's sake, I told you this was a Greek tragedy. Didn't you see the men coming up the stairs?"

"No, who?" Moses answered. Vipond led them to the living room again, where it was dark. He turned on a light so dim it barely allowed them to see one another's faces.

"Two inspectors came by. Someone reported you in Roanne. They traced you to Lyon and found some letters from your parents near the station, which led them to this address. They riddled me with questions, but I told them the truth, that your parents had left two weeks ago. They asked about you two, but I swore I'd never seen you. I'm sure they'll be back. They did not seem convinced."

Terror overtook them again. They thought they had thrown the gendarmes off their trail, but Marcel and Paul's powerful relatives wanted to see them locked up.

"You can sleep here tonight," Vipond said, "but tomorrow we'll have to find somewhere safer. Thank God you didn't run into them on your way back here."

Moses's legs were twitching. He had to go to the bathroom. Dipond noticed and said, "You'd better wash up. I'll give you t-shirts to sleep in. I don't have any other clothes that will fit you, but I can wash what you're wearing. In this heat it'll be dry by tomorrow." He led them to the small bathroom and handed them towels, then picked up the clothes they tossed out to the hallway.

"Where are Mother and Father?" Moses asked, desperate, once they were finally alone.

"I have the letter, but let's read it tonight in bed," Jacob said.

"I can't take it anymore. I'm so nervous."

"Me, too, but I don't want to read it in a bathroom while supper is waiting for us. Let's be patient. Just another hour and we'll know where they've gone," Jacob said. The room filled with steam as he fixed a bath for his brother. Moses sank into the water and tried to relax. After the last few days of fleeing and being hunted, sleeping in the abandoned house or in a disgusting train car, Vipond's apartment reminded him of the Magnés' house in Nouan-le-Fuzelier.

"You've got to finish up, Moses. I need to go," Jacob said. Moses took his time but finally dragged himself out and stood shivering until Jacob wrapped him in a towel. Moses sat on a white stool and waited for Jacob, thinking about their parents all the while. His parents had been in this apartment just two weeks ago. The boy did not understand why he could not simply transport himself to wherever he wanted, whenever he wanted. The limitations of time and space were

absurd in the world of his mind. If he closed his eyes, he could imagine himself in the Far East, in a jungle, or climbing a snowy Tibetan
mountain. He tried to remember his father's face. They had no photograph of him, and his features were blurry in Moses's mind. It grew
harder and harder by the day to make out anything recognizable.

Jacob sank into the bathtub and stared at the white ceiling, then
played with the suds awhile. He did not want to alarm his brother, but
he did not think they could travel all over the rest of the country by
themselves. The last stretches of their journey had been so difficult,
and they had been in serious danger. Plus, now the police were
looking for them. Jacob tried to relax his mind but failed. He was
gripped by fear that something would happen to Moses. He groped
for the prayers he had learned at the synagogue, but they were mere
babbling on his tongue. He got out of the bath and dried off. When
the boys threw on Vipond's nightshirts, they cracked into laughter.

"Take a look at yourself!" Jacob told Moses.

They stood side by side facing the mirror. The nightshirts posi-
tively engulfed them. Still smiling, they went out to the hallway and
were greeted by the aroma of soup and beef. In the living room, they
saw the table was already set, the soup steaming. The old man sat,
forcing a smile.

"Have a seat or it'll get cold. I thought something warm might
calm your nerves. I imagine you've had quite a day," Vipond said.

The boys sat and waited for Vipond to begin. As soon as the spoon
reached his mouth, Jacob and Moses tore into their bowls. They
spoke little during the meal, and when they had finished, Vipond
retrieved some cheeses from the kitchen by way of dessert.

"So did you find Mr. Perrot? He's a good man."

"Yes, but he'd already left by the time we got there. Fortunately,
he hadn't put the letter in the post yet."

"And if you'd found him at the theater, you likely would've run into the inspectors. It seems Providence is on your side," Vipond said with a twinkle in his eye as he bit into one of the cheeses.

"Mr. Perrot told us you were an actor," Moses said. Jacob kicked him under the table to shush him.

"Oh, yes. Sometimes one feels one has lived several different lives. When I was young, I went to Paris, full of dreams. I grew up in Lyon and ever since I was little I'd wanted to act on stage, but my father was a respected notary and demanded that I study law. I convinced him to send me to the Sorbonne in Paris, and I managed to fool him, because I never went to a single class. I joined a theater troupe at the university and then tried out for a play at the Théâtre de la Porte Saint-Martin. It was a bit part, but I got the job. From that moment on, I knew I'd been born to be on stage. The applause, the spotlights, the jitters just before the curtain was raised . . . It was magical. I could be whoever I wanted to be. One day I was the king of France. The next, a beggar falling in love with a princess."

Moses's smile widened as the man talked. "How wonderful! I wish I were an actor!" he said.

"Well," Vipond said, looking at the child, "it wasn't all wonderful. Actors face plenty of hardships. We have our ups and downs. When I left the stage, people hated me. The world is an unpredictable place. One morning they treat you like a god, and by nightfall you're the scum of the earth."

"The same thing happens to authors," Jacob intervened. "At least, that's what Father always said."

"Mm-hmm, but at least they don't ever get booed off stage." Vipond nodded. He took another bite of cheese and stared off into the distance, seeing the curtain calls of Paris.

"How were our mother and father?" Moses asked.

"Well, they missed you, but this place was nicer than their first lodgings. It's more comfortable here, and they could work at the theater. You should've seen your father's smile. His face lit up at every performance. He truly looked younger than when they first got here. Your mother was glad to see him happy again, but they missed you two so much . . . Every afternoon we would sit and talk for a while over tea. They would tell me all about your young adventures, the messes you got yourselves in, the silly or clever things you would say. You're embedded deep in their hearts, boys. You're very lucky. Most mothers love their children, but your mother couldn't *live* without you. The day your father told her they'd gotten their papers, she wept and wept. I said goodbye at the door of this building. She was wearing a lovely pink suit and black shoes and carrying a matching black bag. She looked like a movie star—but not in her eyes. They were sunken and sad, melancholic. Those eyes searched for you everywhere, hoping you'd magically show up somehow. It's as though she knew you were on your way."

The boys were sad again. The food had calmed their raging appetites, but their souls needed the nourishment only found in a mother's arms. Moses closed his eyes and tried to envision her in that pretty pink suit. The sun was shining on her, as if she were strutting down a fashion catwalk in Paris.

Their sadness was not lost on Vipond. Gathering up the dishes, he said, "You'd better get some rest. This old man's stories only bring sadness."

Jacob and Moses excused themselves from the table, and Vipond led them to their room. There was a nice double bed and a window in the roof that sloped all the way down to the floor.

"I trust you'll sleep well tonight. I'm sure your parents, wherever they are, are watching over you." Their host gently closed the door.

As soon as they were alone, Jacob went to the lamp on the nightstand. Moses was glued to him, as if he needed physical contact before hearing their parents' words.

Jacob's eyes rested on the elongated letters and quick script of his mother's writing. In the combination of signs he recognized a harmony that went beyond the simple meanings of the words. The cramped, quick writing looked like their mother's heart spilling over onto the page, an inexhaustible torrent of love.

Moses tugged at Jacob's sleeve, impatient.

"All right, all right," Jacob said. He drew out the moment because the abyss opening before them was greater than the comfort any letter could give.

My dear boys,

One of the first things we learn in life is that we have almost no control over our actions. Time goes quickly, and it feels like existence slips away from us, out of control and sometimes cruel. Meanwhile we're just trying to be happy.

I've been thinking about writing you for so long, but I don't know how to explain what compels us to go farther away from you. Sometimes love and hope have to separate in order to live in the same heart.

Aunt Judith already knows that we're planning to leave, that we hope to see you soon, that we are trying to have you join us as soon as possible. The world is pointless without you two. When you were born, I ceased to belong to myself. I became a slave to the feelings I have for you. You are my air, the sun that lights my morning, and the only place I want to come home to.

Your father loves you deeply, more than he loves his work, even more than he loves me, though he's given up so much for me.

Every day I look for ways to shorten this trip and bring this dismal separation to a very quick end.

Judith will give you the details. In a few days we're heading for Argentina. Our boat is called the *Esmeralda*, and it will take a few weeks to reach Buenos Aires. We'll stop at a few ports before docking in Argentina. I'll try to write you from each stop. Your father is working on the papers for us to send for you as soon as we find work there. Meanwhile, don't worry about us. Aunt Judith loves you very much and will take good care of you.

I love you with all my strength, and every day I dream of seeing you. I promise to never, ever leave you again. We'll be together forever.

Your loving mother,

Jana

Tears made it hard for Jacob to read the last few words. As he read aloud, he could hear his mother's voice whispering the words in his ear.

"They went to South America?" Moses stuttered.

"Yes, but we'll join them," Jacob said, hugging Moses's trembling little body.

"But South America . . . It's so far away. It's taken us a long time to get around this part of France. Plus, there's a huge ocean between us. We'll never make it, Jacob. We've lost them forever."

"No, listen to me." Jacob took his brother's face in his hands. "We've made it this far. Nothing will stop us. We'll travel heaven and earth 'til we find them."

Moses wanted to believe him. But he could not stand the separation any longer. He was lost, lost in the anguish of loneliness, and the hope of seeing his parents again had gone up in smoke.

Jacob gently brushed his tears away, then started singing an old lullaby—one their mother had sung to them when they could not sleep. He listened to his brother's breathing for a while, his rapidly beating heart, his desperate sighing, but it all eventually slowed and quieted. Silence took over like a hot, burning wind. Jacob turned the light off and stared at the reflection that came in from the window. He tried to encourage himself, to convince himself they could make it. But he could not find the words to dispel his fear.

Chapter 18

Valence
July 26, 1942

Vipond woke Jacob and Moses very early. He had slept little, waking with a start at every little noise, afraid the police had come to take the children away. He felt it was his sacred duty to protect them. He owed it to Jana and Eleazar.

Jacob woke up right away, but they had to drag Moses out of bed. He was so tired, and the soft mattress had managed to relax him completely. Both boys' ears were still ringing with the sound of their mother's words in the letter. Right then, their parents were crossing the ocean on their way to Argentina, some place so far away the children could hardly believe it was real.

"Boys, you've got to get dressed and eat breakfast quickly. I'll be surprised if the police don't come back around," Vipond said to speed them up. He had already set out orange juice, milk, and some pastries—all luxuries in those days.

Jacob and Moses slipped into their clean, ironed clothes, and they looked like normal boys again, no longer like little fugitives. They sat down and devoured the very last crumbs of the bread, jam, and pastries that Vipond placed before them.

Their host enjoyed watching them eat. He was quite lonely. After Jana and Eleazar had gone, the few strands that kept him tied to life seemed broken forever. He had no idea how much longer he had left to live, and he did not care. He had already enjoyed all the beautiful things existence could offer and was just waiting to die.

"We've come up with a plan to keep you safe until things calm down. I don't think they'll go to too much trouble to hunt down two children, but as long as they're receiving orders from the prefect, they'll surely come back to bother us."

Jacob and Moses looked up attentively.

Vipond continued, "There's a room in the theater that doesn't get much use. It was designed as short-term quarters for actors or artists who would be staying in the city, though it's rarely been used for that purpose either. A mother and her daughter are living there now, but they'll be moving in a few days. Don't worry, there's more than enough space, and they are fine people." He took their plates into the kitchen and returned with a map.

Intrigued, Jacob and Moses pored over the names of towns and cities, mountains and rivers so neatly labeled.

"We're here in Valence." The old man pointed. "In a few days, you could be in Marseille, the port city where boats travel to Spain and other parts of the world. Mr. Perrot and I will see to all your expenses and your papers."

Jacob smiled. He never imagined that complete strangers would do so much for them. He grasped the risk they were taking. Even though they were in the unoccupied zone, either of them could end up in a detention camp of the Vichy government and lose their jobs and their property. "Thank you so much for helping us," Jacob said. He could tell Vipond had cared about his parents in a special way.

"Life is about giving your soul for the outcasts of the land, those the world rejects and denies even the right to live." The man's words heartened the boys. It was so easy to get dragged along by the tides of history, to justify indifference with prudence, cowardice with sanity. Finding someone who was truly brave filled Jacob and Moses with a peaceful sort of awe.

The doorbell rang, and they all three jumped. Vipond went to the door and was relieved to see Perrot through the peephole.

Jacob understood it was time for them to go. "Thank you again for everything," he said.

Vipond ruffled their hair and a momentary joy flashed through his eyes. "Your mother gave me the love I had lost. Other than Mr. Perrot, no one remembers or cares about this old man anymore. But Jana has a way of seeing deep inside people. I owe it to her to carry on, and now her boys give me the strength to put one foot in front of the other."

Perrot urged them to get moving. It was not wise to stand talking on the landing. They slowly descended the stairs and crossed the crowded street. No one paid them much attention. They seemed like a grandfather taking his grandkids out for a walk. They entered the theater through the side door and saw the usher. The uniformed man stood up straighter when he saw the director.

"Close the door, Alexandre."

Perrot led them up a somewhat concealed spiral staircase to the left, behind the stage. It put them out into a curious room that seemed suspended in the air. It was wide but had no bathroom. They would have to use the facilities in the dressing rooms.

There two people sat on a quilt draped over the wide, cushion-covered bed. One was a woman in her forties with dark hair, a thin, curved nose, and big brown eyes. Beside her was a girl of some twelve years. Her hair was so blond it almost seemed white, and the intensity of her emerald green eyes made it hard to look away.

"Mrs. Emdem, allow me to introduce Jacob and Moses Stein," Perrot said, taking off his hat.

"How do you do, gentlemen? This is my daughter Anna. Anna, introduce yourself," the woman said, lightly touching the girl's shoulder.

Anna looked up timidly. They had been on the run and in hiding for a very long time. Interactions with strangers were few and far between, and even less so with children of her own age. "Hello," she managed.

Jacob stood staring with a smile glued to his face. He finally reacted after Moses elbowed him in the back. "Hi, Anna."

"I'd better leave you. Mrs. Emdem, you'll be able to move along in a few days. You can lead a more normal life in the village. Here, danger lurks at every corner."

"We're so grateful for your help, Mr. Perrot."

"Oh, speak nothing of it. In a few hours, we'll send up some lunch. We've got rehearsal this afternoon, so I must ask you to be as quiet as possible. There are some books in French, German, and Spanish on that shelf, boys, and some toys in the chest. Plus, you can look out the skylight. Boys need time in the sunshine!"

Perrot made his leave, and Jacob and Moses spent a few very awkward moments unsure of what to do or say. Finally, Moses walked over to the toy chest and started pulling things out. Jacob joined him. On the one hand, he wanted to play; on the other, it seemed childish to him. He did not want Anna to think he was a little kid. His scruples vanished, however, when the girl approached and sat beside them on the floor in her resplendent white dress.

For over an hour they played without many words, as if the act of playing itself built trust between them. Finally, Anna looked at Jacob and, with a smile full of perfect pearls of teeth, asked, "Where are you from?"

"We've come from Paris, though our parents are German," Jacob answered.

"I know a bit of German. We're from a city in the Netherlands, in the north, very close to the German border," she said.

"I can speak German too. My brother understands it but doesn't speak it."

"Your brother is adorable. He's like a little doll." At this comment, Moses blushed, but happily.

"Have you been here long?" Jacob asked.

"The journey through France has been horrific. We left the Netherlands a few months ago. The Germans were starting to detain Jews, and we thought it would be safer to get out. My father was already in France, but he couldn't get permission for us to travel with him. He ended up buying false documents. We wanted to go to Canada because we have family there, but the Germans wouldn't let us leave the Netherlands. We made it to Paris almost two months ago, but we couldn't find my father. They had arrested him and sent him to Germany. We were all alone, in a foreign country and without much money. Thank God, some Jewish friends told us about an organization that was helping hide our people. They took us south to Lyon. They wanted to get us to Marseille, but I guess things are getting ugly there too." The girl rattled off the story as if from rote memory, with little emotion.

Jacob heard his own story reflected in Anna's. Their lives sounded foreign to themselves, as if belonging to people in a film. They could hardly recognize themselves even in a mirror. In their minds, they were still happy, carefree children who loved their parents, went to school, and played every chance they got.

"Is there any place left to hide? We're trying to get to South America. Our parents are in Argentina."

"I think that's the only safe place anymore. The only thing that can stop the Nazis is that huge ocean." She ducked her head, real emotion finally surfacing.

When she looked back up, her eyes locked with Jacob's, and he experienced an entirely new sensation: something like a tickling in his guts, followed by suffocating heat, and then terror.

"Are you okay?" Anna asked.

He nodded resolutely, though his flushed face contradicted the movement. "Let's just keep playing."

So they did, until lunchtime. Just before noon, Perrot came upstairs with a tray. Lunch was nothing spectacular, but the four of them sat down gratefully at the small table. Jacob and Moses sat on the edge of the bed while the mother and daughter took the two wooden chairs.

"Were you traveling by yourselves?" Mrs. Emdem asked.

Jacob nodded. "Yes. Our aunt died in the raid in Paris a few days ago."

"I saw it in the papers. It sounds terrible. Fortunately, we had left the city by then, even though I didn't want to. I was holding on to the hope that my husband would show up, though I knew they had taken him. But sometimes we humans run on false illusions and absurd hopes." Mrs. Emdem's melancholy cast an even more somber shadow over the meal.

"But we're alive, Mother. We're free, and we're going to a wonderful place," Anna said, attempting cheer. Her mother nodded and stroked her hair, then continued eating in silence.

Jacob was intrigued. "Where are you going?"

The girl and her mother looked at each other before answering. They did not know if they were allowed to speak of it. Finally, Anna said, "We're going to Le Chambon-sur-Lignon. It's a French commune in the Haute-Loire department, in the region of Auvergne."

"I've never heard of that place," Jacob said, shrugging.

"It's very secluded," Anna continued cautiously, "and surrounded by mountains. People used to spend summer holidays around there, but since the war started, it's become a kind of refuge, a sanctuary for refugees. Nobody asks where you're from or what your religion is. It's a place where people are once again just that—people."

It sounded like a fairytale to Jacob. He had worn a yellow star on his chest. He had been spit on, insulted, hit. Everybody everywhere cared about what country you were from, what your religion was, and how much money you had.

"It sounds like a wonderful place," said Moses, who up to then had been quiet.

"It is." Anna nodded. "And we'll be there 'til the war is over."

"But what if the Nazis win?" Jacob asked.

Anna gave him an exasperated look, annoyed at his insistence, though Jacob was only trying to help her be aware of the dangers all around them. They had to realize no place was really safe.

"I'm sorry, I'm not trying to bother you. I've never heard of that place. I was just curious," he said, apologetically.

Mrs. Emdem smiled, gave Anna a calming hug, then said, "So where are you boys headed?"

Moses piped up. "We're going to Argentina, where we'll meet back up with our parents."

"How wonderful. I'm sure you'll be with them quite soon."

Jacob was quiet for a while, then turned back to Anna. "Why do you think that town is so special? I've been in many towns all over France now, and I've run into good people, bad people, brave people, and cowards. So what makes that village different?"

Despite his tone, Jacob's question riled her, but she took a deep breath and tried to answer calmly enough. "Not everybody is the same. The people of that village and the surrounding villages have refused to obey Marshal Pétain. The children don't wear yellow stars, and they don't have to give the Nazi salute. I can go to school with the other children and just live a normal life. If the Nazis win the war, the world they rule won't be worth living in. So death will be better anyhow. Sometimes we think existence is better than dying, but that's not always the case."

"Anna," her mother said, "I don't like the way you're talking."

"I know, you're right, but sometimes it seems like death *is* the best option, even though we never give up hope. France is no longer the nation of freedom and fraternity. It's better that you're getting out of the country, Jacob and Moses," Anna said. An awkward silence followed. Jacob was sorry he had asked. Ms. Emdem changed the subject. She preferred that the few days her daughter would have in the company of other children would not be marked by such un-pleasantness.

The afternoon passed quietly. Moses and Anna played, but Jacob read a Dumas novel in French. For a few hours he could lose himself and all the fear, relax, and let his imagination unfold in the seventeenth century.

After a frugal supper, they prepared for bed. By nightfall the women were in the bed, while the boys slept on a straw mattress on the floor.

Around midnight, Jacob awoke and went to the skylight in the roof. The stars were shining so brightly they looked like they had been painted onto a black canvas.

"Are you okay?" he heard in a whispered voice at his back. He turned and saw Anna. Her hair fell around her shoulders, spilling over her pink nightgown. In the starlight, the perfect features of her face seemed carved in marble.

"I just couldn't sleep."

"Me neither."

"I'm sorry about my questions earlier tonight. I didn't mean to upset you. Really we're just looking for a place like that, too, but I've given up on believing it might exist."

The girl nodded. "Sometimes faith is the only way forward."

"I don't even know what faith is," Jacob said, confused.

"Having faith is trusting," she explained.

Jacob was at a loss. "Trusting who?"

"In God, of course. Aren't you a Jew?"

"Well, my parents were Jews, but we never talked about things like that. My aunt was more religious, but the only things I know about being Jewish are what they taught me this summer in the synagogue, and I didn't go for long. I know we're a chosen race, that God set us apart from other nations and that we should worship him, that he's the only true God . . . but I don't understand any of that stuff. What did he choose us for? For other people to hunt us down and hate us? My father's an atheist. He believes the world is just a beautiful coincidence and that we are just animals with powers of reason."

"It's fine if your father thinks that, but I believe God is watching over us and taking care of us, though sometimes I don't feel like he is. Come on, there's somewhere I want to show you."

Anna led him down the spiral staircase to the theater stage. Despite the darkness, Jacob felt safe beside her. They went into a small room, and she heaved something up. Taking his hand, she led him back to the stage. The auditorium was completely lit up. The golden box seats with red curtains shimmered with magic. Rows of burgundy seats were lined up like an army on the main floor, and the curtain was fully opened. They walked right to center stage and looked up.

"It's beautiful!" Jacob exclaimed.

"Beauty is one of the things that helps me keep believing. Humans are capable of creating something like this. Beauty is all around us, though we don't always recognize it."

Jacob looked at her. The intense shining of her eyes again threatened to trap him forever. He brushed his cheek against hers and felt the warmth of her face. "You're beautiful," he said, "but what I like best about you is your desire to keep living. I mean, I hardly know you, but I don't like the thought of leaving you."

"Come with us to Le Chambon-sur-Lignon. When the war is over, you can find your parents. They're not giving out visas anymore in Marseille. It's too dangerous." Her tone was pleading.

Jacob was quiet, just enjoying the moment, finally feeling like the protagonist of his own life.

Chapter 19

Valence
August 8, 1942

Anna and her mother left the day after Jacob and Moses had met them. A transport truck came by in the evening. They hardly had time to say goodbye, but Jacob grabbed the girl's hand and promised they would see each other again. It was an impulsive promise, driven by the desire to make destiny bend to their preference for once, but when the brothers were alone again, Jacob broke down and wept. Moses tried to console him. He knew that their ups and downs were like free-falling into desperation only to rebound up with hope and anticipation.

Over the next few days, Perrot's kindnesses and visits from Vipond made them feel at least a little less lost. But being shut indoors was wearisome. Though they ventured out at night to explore the building and dress up as cowboys, soldiers, or ancient Romans, each day felt longer and more exasperating.

One night, when August had already doled out a few days of its suffocating heat, their two benefactors met with them. They brought a nice dinner, as if celebrating a special occasion.

"Well, this will be your last night in the city," Perrot said, unable to hide the reason for the dinner any longer.

Jacob's face lit up. "Have you gotten the visas?" Moses, seated, started bouncing at the foot of the bed, until they understood from the look on Vipond's face that their celebration was premature.

"Marseille is besieged with gendarmes and immigration police. Even the Gestapo is combing the city. The politics of tolerance in the unoccupied zone has apparently come to an end. We hear news of raids everywhere, and even some of the ambassadors are scared. It is utterly impossible to get a visa in these circumstances," Perrot said, his face downcast.

"Don't worry about it. At least you tried. We'll go to Spain, then. We might have better luck there," Jacob offered.

"You wouldn't even make it to Avignon. The roads are pock-marked with checkpoints. We don't want you to end up in a concentration camp. We've heard reports of the horrendous conditions at the camps, and the authorities are sending the Jews to Germany. We'll keep trying to find a way to get you to Argentina, but in the meantime, we've got to get you somewhere safe, somewhere you can be outside and breathe fresh air, play with other children, and live peacefully. The Nazis might kill us all, but we're not going to just lie down and let them step on our necks. Each day you spend here, the Nazis are winning in a way. Early tomorrow morning you'll leave for the valley region in south-central France," Vipond explained.

Jacob frowned and crossed his arms. He would rather fall into the hands of the Nazis than give up searching for his parents.

Perrot read Jacob's face. "We promise we will keep trying. Perhaps before the year is over, you'll be sailing to South America. But to try it now would be suicide," he said.

Moses looked at Jacob and waited to see how he would respond. Moses would do whatever Jacob said. They would never be separated.

"So where is this wonderful place?" Jacob said.

"The village of Le Chambon-sur-Lignon, where Anna and Mrs. Emdem went. They've been there over a week and seem happy," Vipond said.

At that, a surprised little half smile crept over Jacob's face. They could be with Anna. He had been thinking about her every day, unable to forget her. "Le Chambon-sur-Lignon, you say?" he asked, to make sure.

"Yes. There's a Protestant pastor there, André Trocmé. We've spoken with him, and you boys can stay in the village for a few months. Jacob, you'll be staying in the Maison des Roches with other boys your age. Moses, you'll stay with a farmer's family," Perrot said.

"You want to separate us? But I promised my parents I'd take care of Moses." Jacob was distraught again.

"You'll see each other every week, especially on Saturdays and Sundays. He'll be just fine. It's better this way, and we haven't found any other solutions. This is just a provisional step, for a few weeks, a few months at the most," Perrot said, hoping to console him.

Moses grabbed Jacob's hand. "We should go there. We can't stay locked up here anymore. Plus, it's dangerous. Mr. Vipond and Mr. Perrot will get us out of France as soon as they can."

Jacob studied Moses's face. He knew his brother was right. "Okay, we'll go to Le Chambon-sur-Lignon. But if you don't think you can get us out of the country before the end of the year, we'll try to find our own way."

The men smiled at Jacob's determination, his brave commitment to keep his word.

"Then let's finish supper before it's all cold," Vipond said. It would be hard to say goodbye to the boys, but it was not safe for them in Valence.

They finished eating, chatting pleasantly enough, then the men bid the boys goodnight. It took Jacob and Moses a long time to fall asleep. Partly they ached to get outside the four walls of what had become a quaint, comfortable prison, but the thought of being in danger again was terrifying.

"I just really want to see Mother and Father," Moses groaned, knowing that the impending journey would further cement the separation.

"Look, it feels like the moment of joining them again is moving farther away, but really, each day we're a bit closer. Mr. Perrot told me the Germans are starting to lose in North Africa and that they haven't been able to advance in Russia for a long time. They're going to lose the war. It won't be long before we'll be able to travel again." Jacob was feeling more optimistic than usual, and he wanted to cheer Moses up. He knew his little brother's hold on their parents was growing more and more tenuous and that it would not be long before it would feel to him as if they had never existed at all.

"I hope so. I hope the Allies give the Boche a good thrashing," Moses said with all seriousness.

Jacob cracked up at the comment. After all, they themselves were German. "Go to sleep," Jacob said.

Moses turned over, but Jacob stayed faceup, thinking about Anna. He noticed how his heart thumped louder when she crossed his mind. So he would get to see her again after all, as he had promised. The journey would be worth it, even if he only spent the briefest second by her side. Somewhere between waking and sleeping he dreamed of coming back to France after the war and bringing Anna to Argentina with his family. They would be happy in Buenos Aires, a land of freedom and plenty. Nobody would care if they were Jewish, German, or Dutch. With the dying embers of lucidity, he understood that happiness was comprised of small decisions that move you closer to your dreams. Before you could be happy, you had to imagine life as an exciting novel with a happy ending.

Chapter 20

The next morning, a man dressed in a work uniform was waiting for them at the door of the theater beside an idling, old Renault van. Before they left, Perrot came up and put his hands on their shoulders. "Be patient, my boys. You'll be hearing from us soon. We'll do everything we can to get you to your parents in South America."

Vipond was there as well. He knelt down with difficulty to be level with Moses. "You're a brave dreamer, Moses. Don't ever forget that you'll always be able to accomplish what you put your mind to."

He slowly got back to his feet and met Jacob's eyes. "Take care of your brother. Don't make any rash decisions. Trust us and be patient. Sometimes, we have to wait a long time for the best things in life."

Jacob smiled, knowing he was right. Vipond kissed their cheeks several times and swallowed back his tears. "May God watch over you," he said, then put his hand over his mouth.

Vipond and Perrot walked the boys to the car. Jacob crawled into the front seat and Moses into the back. The old van was rusty but still had patches of its original gray paint. The driver remained silent as he shifted into gear and headed west. It would take them a few hours to reach Le Chambon-sur-Lignon from Valence. The roads were in poor shape, full of curves and drop-offs. In winter, the route they traveled would be nearly impassable. The people of the region were used to being isolated, and they spent summers storing the firewood and food they would need for their long winters.

The van driver was a hard, unexpressive local. He was fulfilling his duty but showed neither satisfaction nor displeasure regarding his task. After centuries of persecution and living isolated in a harsh, poor land, the Protestants of the region had developed a very thick protective layer. It was not easy to get through to them, to fit in and become one of them. But once they accepted an outsider, that small group of minimalists would put their lives on the line for what they considered just or for those who were persecuted outcasts.

The landscape slowly changed. The forests scattered around Valence grew into giant green waves that washed over everything. It looked like the van was charting its own course through the vegetation growing on either side of the road. The undergrowth was so thick and the trees so robust that little light got through. The sunny August day felt more like a late fall afternoon.

They went through very few towns, saw only a handful of farms, and counted on one hand the number of houses surrounded by clearings in the monotonous green blanket. Some time before reaching Le Chambon-sur-Lignon, the first meadows started opening up the countryside and allowed them a bit more perspective. Cows grazed indifferently as the noisy vehicle momentarily altered the encompassing peace that reigned in the valley region.

They went through Saint-Agrève, which seemed completely deserted even though it was near lunchtime. Dense forests reclaimed the landscape until, just beyond a tight curve, the first houses began to appear. They were spread out at first, granite structures with white shutters, then fell into rows that led to the main streets of the village where the buildings were somewhat taller, with stores on the ground floors. Unlike Saint-Agrève, the streets here were bustling. The well-dressed mixed with peasants selling their wares, and restaurants served food both inside and out on flower-filled terraces.

People seemed to walk unhurriedly and smiling while banners boasting the colors of France waved overhead as if it were a national holiday. For the first time in their entire journey, the driver addressed the boys. "Tomorrow, the Vichy's minister of youth, Georges Lamirand, and the prefect, Robert Bach, will be coming to visit. It seems the old marshal doesn't dare venture beyond Le Puy-en-Velay. He visited the Black Madonna and hightailed it back to Vichy like the devil himself was after him. We've no use for folk like him around here."

The man's harsh tone frightened Jacob and Moses a bit, but as he spoke, they realized he was just a simple, down-to-earth peasant worn-out by Pétain's empty promises.

"I'll leave you in Pastor Trocmé's house. He'll see to you. Take care with your manners. He's still got some of his mother's German blood, and he doesn't put up with insolence."

The boys' faces grew serious, startled by the warning, which made the driver chuckle. They drove through town, then down a hill and parked in front of a simple granite church. The driver got out and retrieved the two suitcases Vipond had packed for the boys. Vipond had also included a sizable sum of money, in case things went poorly and they had to escape quickly.

They all three walked toward the church. An inscription above the door read *"Aimez-vous les uns les autres"*: love one another. A round, unlit stained-glass window and gabled bell tower were the church's only adornments. Two rounded windows on each side of the dark wooden door completed the simple, inviting look of the place.

The driver went inside, removed his hat, and headed for the pastor's office. Fearfully, the children followed. The church's sober exterior was matched by the austere vestibule. They went up a couple stairs and entered a simple office. A small, dark table and bookshelves were the only furniture, while wall hangings of stylized Scripture verses hung on the walls. Piles of pamphlets and New Testaments rested on the table.

Seated at the table was a thin man in a simple, clean, well-pressed suit. They walked in as he read and saw his thinning, blond hair starting to turn gray. When he looked up, his clear, expressive eyes instantly set Jacob and Moses at ease. He smiled, revealing two dimples in his pale cheeks and making his round glasses bob up just a bit. The pastor set his pen down on the table.

"Pastor Trocmé, I've brought the boys from Valence, sent by Mr. Perrot and Mr. Vipond," the driver announced, his hat in his hands. The soft voice he used in the church was quite different from his loud, rough voice in the van.

"Thank you, Marc," the pastor responded quietly.

The driver left them and Jacob and Moses stood alone before the pastor.

"I can't say I'm happy to see you. If you're here, it's because you're running from something. Furthermore, I don't see your parents. I think Mr. Vipond and Mr. Perrot mentioned they were in Argentina. I hope your stay in our humble village will help you forget just a bit about the war and the difficult things you've likely had to face. Please, have a seat," he said.

"Thank you, sir . . . pastor," Jacob answered, unsure how to address the man.

Trocmé smiled and asked them for some information about themselves, then stood and walked to the windows. It was cloudy, and inside the church it was cold. Trocmé was wearing his jacket and a little red bow tie, which added a splash of color to his somber suit. With his light, smooth gait he walked back toward the boys.

"You know it will be necessary to live separately for a time. We don't have any families that can take you both. The Arnauds will take care of you, Moses. They have two boys around your age and live about two miles outside of town on a lovely little farm. I'm sure you'll enjoy living with them. Every day you'll come into town for school and can see your brother on Saturdays at Boy Scout meetings and on Sundays at church."

Jacob was very nervous at the thought of separating from his brother. He tried to speak calmly. "Is there no other option? You can tell the family I'll do anything. I'm strong, and I could help them out however they need."

"I'm sorry, but it just isn't possible. You'll stay in the Maison des Roches. Soon my cousin Daniel will be one of the caretakers there. He'll be helping us with our school L'École Nouvelle Cévenol. All the other houses are full. Last year, your brother would've been able to stay at the Maison d'enfance, but there's no more room in the boardinghouses. Many people have come our way in recent weeks, fleeing the violence in Paris."

A young man in an even simpler suit appeared just then. Other than a prominent forelock, his hair was very short. He stood next to Trocmé and smiled at the boys.

"Here we have Jacob and Moses Stein," Trocmé said.

"Hello, boys. A few days from now we're having a soccer game. Do you like to play ball?"

"Oh yes!" Moses answered.

"Wonderful. You'll make a lot of friends here and will learn so much," the young man said.

Trocmé gestured toward the man. "This is my friend and colleague, Edouard Theis."

"I'm so pleased to meet you," Theis said, shaking hands with the boys. Then, turning to Trocmé, he said, "Could we speak for a moment?"

The two men stepped aside and spoke in low voices.

"Regarding Lamirand and Bach's visit tomorrow, the town council has appointed Pastor Marcel Jeannet to speak. Nobody wants more problems."

"The politicians are the ones who always cause the problems. At least the marshal isn't coming. But I think Lamirand is a hard nut to crack," Trocmé answered.

"Will the youth stay in line?"

"Who can say? People are understandably upset about what's been happening in Paris."

"This isn't the time or place, André. Until now, the prefect has turned a blind eye, but we don't know for how much longer."

"You know all the pressures we've been dealing with, but we must always speak the truth and demand justice. It's what we teach the children, so we can't stop them if they believe it's necessary to do just that."

"May God save us all," Theis said with a short intake of breath, followed by a smile.

"No one is guaranteed a future. Every action has a consequence. But so does inaction."

The young man clamped a hand on Trocmé's shoulder, gave a nod to the boys, and left the office as quietly as he had entered. Trocmé turned back to the children and smiled again.

"My wife, Magda, has lunch waiting for us. I presume you are hungry? Let's go to my house. Mr. Arnaud will be by in a bit to pick up Moses, and one of the caretakers will come by this afternoon for you, Jacob."

They walked through the chapel, which was wider than the boys had imagined. Imposingly tall Ionic columns atop wide pedestals supported a barrel vault. Dark wooden pews lined each side of the central aisle, which led up to a raised platform. The back wall was paneled in dark wood, and jutting out from it was the main pulpit, covered with a curious overhanging roof. The great stones lining the floor absorbed the sound of their footsteps as they walked down the center aisle toward the back door. A narrow walk connected the chapel with the parsonage.

Magda was in the kitchen with an older woman. Several children were reading and playing in the living room, taking advantage of what light the cloudy day let through.

"These are my children—Nelly, Jean-Pierre, Jacques, and Daniel," the pastor explained. Except for the girl, all of them were younger than Moses.

The children greeted them with an unenthusiastic "Hello." They were used to the daily carousel of newcomers.

Just then a thin, darker-complexioned woman with a long braid of hair came out of the kitchen. "Hello there, you must be Jacob and Moses, right?" she said.

The boys were impressed that she knew their names. The woman looked tired. Dark circles made her otherwise large eyes look smaller than they really were.

"I'll be going now," said the other woman.

"Thank you so much for everything," Magda said to her, smiling.

The family sat down at the table and began eating in silence. After a while, and to Jacob's great surprise, Moses timidly raised his hand.

"Sir, there's something I don't understand," Moses said.

Trocmé smiled. "What's that?"

"Everyone calls you 'Pasture.' Do you raise cows or sheep?"

The whole table erupted in giggles, especially the Trocmé children. Moses scrunched his eyes up and hung his head.

"They call me 'Pastor' because I'm like a shepherd for people, and I lead them to safe *pasture* in God's good earth. It's a very good question, Moses."

Jean-Pierre looked at the new boy sitting beside him and showed him some marbles in his pocket. It did not go unnoticed by his mother.

"What's that? You know very well: No toys at the table!"

"Mother, it's just some marbles."

"But they're filthy from having been on the floor, I daresay."

"Yes, Mother." Then the child returned to his soup.

Just as they finished eating, they heard a car drive up, and Trocmé got to his feet. They all gathered at the door of the house. A van even older and more beat-up than the one that had brought Jacob and Moses was idling right in front of the door. A dark-complexioned man with dark eyes and a wrinkled face greeted Trocmé.

"This is Mr. Arnaud. Moses, we'll see you on Saturday," he said, trying to calm the boy. Moses had run to Jacob and was clinging to him in tears.

Jacob wrestled to master himself and, hoping to soothe his brother, said, "It's all right. You can go with him. You'll be fine."

"Don't leave me, please!" Moses begged.

"I'm never going to leave you. Even if the world caves in all around us, I'm not leaving you, brother." They hugged and kissed each other's cheeks. It was the first time they had ever been truly separated in their lives. Jacob had existed before his brother was born but could remember nothing of import that did not involve Moses. All they had was each other. When the small figure of his brother drew away and entered the vehicle, Jacob felt a ripping sensation in his heart. He forced the tears back and waved goodbye. Moments later, the van was gone.

Trocmé put his hand on Jacob's shoulder. Jacob allowed himself to be embraced, and all the pent-up tears came gushing forth.

"You'll see him in just a few days. He'll be all right. You've been living in hell for several weeks, but you're here now, and nothing bad will happen to you. I give you my word."

The sincerity of André Trocmé's words calmed Jacob. There was something in the man's eyes, a depth of goodness Jacob had never seen before. His soul was hovering just beyond the pupils.

Jacob thought about Anna and what she had said. For her, Le Chambon-sur-Lignon was much more than an out-of-the-way French village. It was a secret mountain, the last place in Europe where people could carry on as people—the last place human beings could live together in harmony.

Chapter 21

Le Chambon-sur-Lignon
August 10, 1942

The sun was out in full force to greet the prefect, Robert Bach, and the minister of youth, Georges Lamirand. Yet the sun was the only thing to receive with open arms the two men and their entourage of officials and collaborators.

Villagers did not turn out in droves in anticipation of the visit. The Vichy regime had enjoyed early success among many conservative peasants who were not aligned with the excesses of the Republic, but it had not taken Pétain's supporters long to realize that the old marshal was nothing but a puppet in Nazi hands. André Trocmé, Edouard Theis, Charles Guillon, Louis Comte, and most of the region's leaders had systematically opposed the measures imposed from Vichy. Prefect Bach had warned them several times, but neither civil nor religious leaders were willing to submit to Nazi authority, nor that of their French collaborators.

Some of the schools and children's homes had come out to attend the celebration so as not to cause offense to the authorities. Jacob was in the first row next to Edouard, who rested his right hand on the boy's shoulder. Jacob was nervous. It was his first time to attend a public event since fleeing Paris. The number of people made him feel jittery. Being surrounded by even a moderate crowd recalled the multitudes crammed into the velodrome a few weeks prior.

Lamirand showed up in Le Chambon-sur-Lignon wearing his blue uniform and black leather boots, and beside him the prefect Robert Bach wore a stern frown and crossed his arms. Before lunch at the YMCA's Camp Joubert, the Vichy's minister of youth stood before the few residents gathered to receive him. He began to speak:

"Dear citizens and residents of the commune of Le Chambon-sur-Lignon, it is my great pleasure to greet you on behalf of our president, his excellency Philippe Pétain, marshal of France and hero of the Great War. Our illustrious leader saved us from the disasters of the First World War through his military acumen, and now he has saved the nation from all those who treacherously ensnared her in war against Germany. The values of the Republic had been undermined. The immoral government run by Masons, Jews, and communists had driven our motto of liberty, equality, and fraternity into the ground. Thus, our esteemed leader has forged more solid principles based on deeper values, values that arise from our Christian beliefs and our tradition of freedom. Work, family, and homeland are now the backbone of our nation. Those who do not love France, who are not keeping anxious watch for her impending renewal, have no place in this new country."

There was a long silence, then Lamirand raised his right hand and saluted those gathered before him.

"Youth are the future of France. Le Chambon-sur-Lignon is doing admirable work with her youth. For years they have been taught Christian values, the love of nature, and the greatness of our beautiful nation. Today I want to recognize your efforts and encourage all organizations and associations to join with the government in a united effort to fight for a new France: all united through the youth work camps of France, Les Chantiers de la Jeunesse, for the good of our nation and the glory of the marshal."

Half-hearted, obligatory applause could be heard from one or two spots in the paltry gathering. The minister pursed his lips, and the prefect took the floor to quickly pass over the awkwardness.

"Beloved citizens of Le Chambon-sur-Lignon: the long tradition of aid, protection, and refuge of your beautiful lands brings honor to France. The love of your leaders for peace and nonviolence is an example for the entire country. Yet we are at a crossroads in history. Each and every one of us must decide which side we are on. We cannot remain neutral or be silent before those who seek the complete destruction of France or those who, from outside our country, strut alongside our enemies. Friends and citizens, the marshal is the only cure for the moral disease of our beloved land. I beg you, as Christians and Frenchmen, to join the great work to rebuild our dear country."

"La Marseillaise" started playing, but the swell of voices joined in unison could not quiet the awkwardness of the village's palpable rejection of the Vichy invitation.

"Now let's eat!" cried one of the women who had been tasked with preparing the food.

The authorities were led to the main table. Pastor Trocmé was seated next to the prefect, with Edouard Theis at his side. As a matter of protocol, Theis's wife, an American, was seated as far from the officials as possible. Lamirand was on the other side of Bach, and beside him was the Swiss pastor Marcel Jeannet, who would preach at the religious service following the meal.

Jacob took several plates and headed to the lead table. His legs shook as he approached the minister, who was dressed in a fascist uniform.

"Thank you for the food, lad," Lamirand said. He then turned to shout at both sides of the table: "Here are French youth at their finest, the purity of our race and the strength of our Christian beliefs."

Jacob's face burned red like a tomato. He withdrew, even more nervous than before, and tried to make himself scarce.

"Pastor Trocmé, what I said moments ago was in earnest," Bach said quietly to Trocmé. "The Germans are pressuring us. We can no longer look the other way. You must give me a list with all the foreign refugees of Jewish descent."

Trocmé opted for the path of evasion. "I'm not sure I follow you."

"Oh, I think you do. You've been sheltering hundreds of foreign Jews for a couple of years now. We've received several anonymous reports of how you and the other pastors are inciting the population to civil disobedience. This is unacceptable. If you supply us the list of foreign Jews, you can continue serving the others without further interference." The prefect's threatening tone had the effect of transforming Trocmé's peaceful semblance into one of indignant anger. The pastor took a deep breath and allowed Bach to continue.

"You have forty-eight hours to give me that list. These people aren't your church members; they aren't even Christians. I can appreciate your zeal, but to save a few, you're putting all at risk."

"I don't differentiate between foreigners and French nationals, nor do I concern myself with their beliefs. To me, they are refugees, people fleeing from war and death. My parish is the world, and each person is my neighbor. I am sorry, but I will not be giving you any list," Trocmé said, mastering his tone.

"Very well. You'll be hearing from us soon. We will alert your superiors of your position, which compromises the safety of all French Protestants. Do not forget that your first duty is to protect your own. They have suffered enough throughout history."

Lamirand turned toward Trocmé and Bach. He had overheard part of the exchange and was preparing his remarks when Magda, carrying a pot of soup, accidently sloshed some onto the minister's back. The broth burned the man and stained his recently pressed uniform jacket. Furious, he turned a raging look on Magda but checked the ire and forced a smile. It was nothing, not to worry.

"Oh, I'm terribly sorry, do forgive me," she apologized profusely.

The meal drew to a close, and Trocmé was first to get up from the table. He could not abide another second at the prefect's side. He ran into one of the teachers from the school, who grabbed his arm. "The students are going to do it," the teacher said in a low voice.

"May it be as God desires. We cannot deny our consciences," Trocmé answered, searching for Magda.

The group of officials stood up from the table and started making their way toward the church, but they had hardly taken ten steps when a group of students placed themselves before the minister and the prefect.

"Mr. Minister of Youth, we would like to give you this letter of protest."

The bodyguards stepped in the way, but Lamirand waved them aside.

"A letter of protest?" he asked.

"Yes. In light of recent events in Paris and in other cities of our great country, regarding the illegal detention of people due to their religion. Our laws and tradition prohibit persecuting people for their beliefs," the youth said. His voice grew in confidence as he spoke, losing its initial tremble.

Other young people dressed in blue shirts began to boo the group of students. Lamirand cut in. "Policy toward the Jews is not my area. I'm the minister of youth."

"Sir, you are a member of the government and, as such, are responsible for the government's decisions," the student answered.

"That was in the occupied zone," Bach cut in, attempting to end the conversation.

"But there are raids in the unoccupied zone as well. Plus, your government should have protested the inhuman treatment inflicted on hundreds of children that share our nationality. Not to speak of human rights."

Lamirand stretched out his gloved hand and snatched the letter. He gave a perfunctory smile and kept walking. The event had become such a public disaster that Bach was tempted to call off the final ceremony of the day, but he thought a bit of calm would perhaps improve the bitter taste sure to be left in the minister's mouth.

They traversed the tree-lined avenue and went straight for the church, passing the crowded aisles toward the platform at the front. The Swiss pastor, Marcel Jeannet, waited impatiently in the pulpit.

Jacob sat in the second row with the other students, directly behind the government officials. Despite the crowd, a deathly silence reigned. Then Jeannet invited the congregation to stand. They said a brief prayer and then sang a hymn.

"Please take your seats," Jeannet said. The young Swiss pastor looked around at all those gathered. *It seems no one wants to miss this sermon*, he thought, nervously arranging his notes.

"Dear brothers, sisters, and friends, what gathers us here today is much more than our ideologies, beliefs, or opinions. We are in the house of God with one purpose: for his truth to inspire us, as it has done up until now, in the task of serving the youth of France. We are pleased to hear of the government's interest in the youth. Each generation of young people fashions its own destiny, and this new generation has suffered the sting of war and violence.

"Therefore, I would like to congratulate the teachers, educators, and pedagogues who day in, day out seek to shape the youth that have joined us this afternoon."

The church remained quiet enough to hear a pin drop. Latecomers stood at the back of the chapel and spilled into the side aisles, standing.

"Christians and all men of goodwill always find themselves facing the same predicament: Should we obey men rather than God? The Bible certainly exhorts us to respect those in authority, because they have been established by God. Yet when the state passes laws that go against the laws of God and human rights, our duty is to say, 'No.'"

A murmur ran through the crowd. The prefect buried his head in his hands. The final ceremony had turned out far worse than he had imagined.

"The state is not nor can it be above the laws of God, nor above human rights. The state's duty is to protect its citizens, regardless of their faith, ideology, or origins. Here today, we are all French; we are all free; we are all brothers. Perhaps outside this valley, on the other side of these forests, men kill each other over these matters. But not in our towns. We Protestants were persecuted and nearly wiped out by the enemies of our faith. We fought against them, but today we know that our weapons are of the Spirit. Peace, harmony, and coexisting in community will always be the identifying marks of this valley. As long as we have life and breath, we will love our neighbors as ourselves. In this house, there are no Jews or Gentiles, no slaves or freemen. There are only children of God."

The gathered crowd stood and applauded while the government officials remained seated. Jacob watched Theis's face and then Trocmé's. The men were euphoric, as if they had just won a hard-fought struggle.

Bach and Lamirand made a hasty exit, and silence ensued. Theis leaned over to Trocmé and said, "They're out like the devil's after them."

"They'll be back, Edouard. We must prepare for the worst."

Jacob did not understand the pastor's words, but as soon as the officials were out of the church, the crowd breathed a collective sigh of relief and began talking again. Trocmé stood before them and motioned for silence.

"Moderation, restraint, and prudence! Let us not provoke. We have many people to protect."

The gathered crowd calmed down and, bidding farewell to their pastors, left the church little by little. Making his way against the current of those exiting, a man with long, unkempt hair, rings around his eyes, and a face as pale as death came up to Trocmé.

"Pastor Trocmé," he said, "My name is Albert Camus. I've been in the village a few days now. I came to heal from some medical problems with my lungs. I want to congratulate you."

Trocmé raised his brows. "I've done nothing extraordinary. It was Pastor Jeannet who spoke."

"But I know what you're doing here, in this place. I admire and respect you for it. I hope your example spreads to the rest of the country." The man's smile pleasantly counteracted his pallid expression.

"My dear Albert, look around at these people," Trocmé answered, gesturing to the crowd as they dispersed from the church. "They are the real heroes: the baker, the pharmacist, the hotel owner, the day laborer, the peasant. They lead tranquil lives. They could get through this war without upheaval, but they have chosen to love. Love is always risky."

"Absolutely, especially in the tides of today, the fascist plague that besieges us," Camus answered.

"That's not even the main problem. The real tide—the plague, as you call it—is hatred in the human heart. The only way to fight it is with love. We detected this wave of hatred several years ago, when Hitler rose to power in Germany, but no one wanted to listen. Now we can barely contain it. They've sown their hatred and violence everywhere and have shaped an entire generation with it. Let us withstand the wave and sow love, my friend."

Albert Camus smiled again, despite the heaviness in his diseased lungs. Trocmé's words rekindled his hope. In the past few weeks he had sensed death's proximity so acutely. He shook the pastor's hand, then left the building with the rest of the congregation.

One of the caregivers from Jacob's boardinghouse came up, patted Trocmé on the back, then smiled at Jacob. "The Arnauds are here, and they've brought Moses. Would you like to see him?"

Jacob's face lit up. The few hours of their separation had felt like an eternity. Outside the church building, the Arnauds came up to them. "This is Jacob, Moses's brother," the caregiver said.

"It's a pleasure to meet you, Jacob. I'm Martha, and this is my husband, Lorik. We'll take good care of your brother. You can come see him whenever you'd like," said the blond-haired woman, who wore an austere black dress.

"Thank you, ma'am," Jacob said. At a nod from his caregiver, Jacob ran off toward Moses.

"Jacob!" Moses cried for the whole world. "It's my brother!"

They hugged and stood talking together while the crowd continued to disperse. After a few minutes, the caregiver motioned for Jacob to return to the boys' home, and the brothers said goodbye.

Jacob and the caregiver walked toward the boardinghouse, enjoying the pleasant evening. The afternoon sky was lit up with a special brilliance. "Your brother will be all right," the caregiver said. "The Arnauds are Darbyites, from the Plymouth Brethren Church. They live very simply, but they are good people and hard workers."

Jacob smiled at him. Since their arrival in Le Chambon-sur-Lignon, he had not stopped thinking about Anna. He had looked for her in the crowd that day but had not spotted her. He asked, "Do you know a woman and her daughter who came just a few weeks ago? They're Dutch. Maria and Anna Emdem?"

The caregiver turned a surprised face to the boy. "Anna will be one of your classmates at school. You'll see her tomorrow morning. How do you know her?"

"We happened to meet in Valence and became friends."

The rest of the short walk passed in silence. Jacob could not wait to see Anna the next day. He felt the strange combination of his legs turning to jelly and his body floating through the air. She had been right: This village really did seem like a paradise, somewhere to forget the war and all the fear.

Chapter 22

A loud knock on the door woke Jacob with a start. He looked all around. It was still dark outside, and he hurried to get dressed by feel and go downstairs to see what was happening. A few care-givers and some of the older boys were in the living room, as well as Auguste Bohny, a caregiver from another boardinghouse.

"First, they came to the children's house and asked for Mr. Steckler," Bohny was saying. "I told them he wasn't there, that he was at the Wasp's Nest. Then they went there, found him, and ordered him to get dressed. I took that opportunity to get the children in our house ready and hide them. When the gendarmes returned, they were furi-ous. They wanted to see the children. I came to see you as soon as I could. You'd better take them all into the woods."

"But our school has protected status with the government," one of the caregivers objected. "I don't see how they could come and make demands here."

"It doesn't matter anymore. The prefect from Le Puy has sent the gendarmes. He wants to find the foreign Jews and turn them over to the Germans. If he doesn't meet a certain quota, it will look bad for him, and he knows we've got many sheltered here."

Jacob was coming down the stairs as he heard Bohny. He had his pants and shoes on but was still buttoning his shirt.

"Boys, lead the younger kids into the forest. Don't come back until someone gives you a signal."

Jacob was startled. "But what will happen to the children being housed with families?"

"I don't think anything will happen. The gendarmes are searching schools, children's homes, and boardinghouses."

"But my brother is really close to one boardinghouse, the Shelter." Jacob's voice trembled as all the old fear returned.

"We can't alert all the homes and farms because there are dozens of them. If the gendarmes go to the Arnauds' farm, Martha and Lorik will know what to do," Bohny said. They had no more time to waste talking.

Jacob finished buttoning his shirt and went outside. Heedless of the dark, he ran as fast as he could toward the Arnaud farm. Despite what Bohny had said, Jacob had to make sure nothing happened to Moses.

"Where are you going?" one of the older boys called after him.

"I'll meet back up with you when I make sure my brother's okay," Jacob called back. He ran down several streets. Windows in some of the hotels were lit up, and Jacob saw their inhabitants rushing half-dressed into the woods. There were a couple small buses parked in the town hall square. Then he heard voices and whistles being blown. His heart was beating nearly out of his chest, and he was running out of breath, but he pushed on until he reached a dirt road. The house at the end was not very big. It was a one-story, slate-roof house with a shed right beside it. Before he reached the front, he heard voices and saw the reflection of lantern lights. Jacob took cover. Two gendarmes were walking right up to the house.

At first Jacob was paralyzed with fear. The gendarmes would soon knock on the door. There were no lights on inside, and the family had not been warned of the raid taking place in the village.

After hesitating a moment, Jacob ran and tripped up the hill a bit away from the dirt road, among the trees. By the time he managed to reach the barn, the gendarmes were just a few yards from the door. Jacob made a dash for the back of the house and climbed in through an open window.

"Moses?" he whispered, but there was no answer. Jacob had climbed into the kitchen. He ran to a bedroom and opened it. The farmer's children were sleeping peacefully. The farmer and his wife were in the other bedroom. Jacob realized Moses must be sleeping in a room in the barn. Though they had seen each other several times since their separation, Moses had never mentioned where he slept, perhaps so Jacob would not worry. Jacob climbed back out the window just as the gendarmes began beating on the door. He slipped through the narrow area separating the two buildings and entered the barn, creeping blindly toward the middle. He started to call for his brother.

"Moses. Moses," he said as loudly as he dared. Outside, he could hear the noise of voices and furniture being moved.

"Jacob? What's going on?"

"Get dressed, we have to get out of here now!" Moses threw on his clothes as they heard the sound of voices approaching. Jacob climbed the ladder to where his brother was.

"Is there another way out?" he asked anxiously.

"Yes, through the window." Moses pointed to a small opening. He shimmied out first, and Jacob followed. They had just thumped down to the ground when they heard the gendarmes enter the barn. As the boys fled up the hill, the tall grass grabbed at their legs. They tripped over rocks and fallen branches, but they did not slow down. The sound of dogs barking reached them from below. The gendarmes must have found Moses's clothes in the barn and were coming after them.

Jacob had spent several afternoons wandering the hills and forests with his classmates, but it was still dark, and he was too scared to gather his bearings. His only thought was to get farther in.

The barking of the dogs grew louder now. Moses tripped and cut his leg badly. Tears came, and he whimpered, "I don't think I can walk."

Jacob spied a house not too far away, up the hill. He helped Moses stand and, hobbling, they reached the door. They knocked, and shortly thereafter an elderly woman opened up. "What is it, boys?" she asked.

"The gendarmes, they're after us."

The woman took in Moses's leg at a glance and ushered them in. She moved a cupboard, and they saw a door hidden in the wood paneling of the wall. She opened it and said, "Go up the stairs and don't make a peep."

The boys went up as fast as they could and entered a long, low room. They could not even stand upright, and they were not alone. An elderly couple waited at the back. Jacob could not see their faces, but he could hear them breathing.

Below, they heard the gendarmes beating on the door. The woman took her time in opening.

"What's all the fuss so early in the morning? Has there been a fire?" she asked, put out.

"We're looking for some fugitives. They came up the mountain, but the dogs have lost their trail," one of the gendarmes said.

"And what does this have to do with me? I'm an old widow who lives alone. You've scared me half to death."

"May we come in?" the same gendarme asked.

"I've told you, there's no one else here, but the police don't believe the word of decent folk anymore. Come in and have a look around. I'm going to make some coffee." She left the door open and went to the kitchen. Keeping her cool, she made the coffee as strong and fast as she could to throw off the dogs' noses.

The boys and the couple crouching upstairs could hear the boots of the gendarmes clomping over the wooden floor. The police searched for a good while. The smell of coffee filled the house as the coffeepot hissed.

"Would you like some coffee?" the woman asked.

"Thank you, ma'am. We left Le Puy at three o'clock this morning. A cup would do us good."

She poured them steaming mugs. The gendarmes sent the dogs outside and stood in the doorway. One of them addressed the woman.

"Don't think it's easy for us to go after innocent people. Most of them are children, or mothers and elderly folk. It breaks our hearts to arrest them, but it's our duty."

The woman replied, "We must always act according to our conscience, no matter our occupation."

Jacob heard a drop of liquid nearby and then a rush. With horror, he realized the poor woman near him had lost control of her bladder due to the fright. The urine spread out over the wooden floor and entered the cracks between the wood. Jacob peered through a tiny hole down into the living room. The gendarmes stood talking with the woman, their backs to the living room. Jacob looked in the other direction and saw the first drops fall from the ceiling onto the table.

"Oh no," he whispered, then clamped his hand over his mouth, terrified of being heard.

"Thank you for the coffee, and I'm sorry we disturbed you," the first gendarme said, nodding and replacing his cap. The woman was closing the door when the other officer turned and ran back to the table with the mug in his hand. He set it down and said, "Forgive me, I nearly walked away with your cup."

Drops of yellow liquid fell just inches from the cup, but the gendarme seemed not to have noticed. But the old woman did. Her eyes flicked from the table to the ceiling, and she turned pale, gripping the door for stability. The gendarme ran out and she closed the door behind him, leaning on it and letting out a long sigh.

A few minutes later, after watching the gendarmes walk sufficiently far away, she whispered for them to come down. The children came first, followed by the elderly couple. The man had to help the woman. She was still dressed in her nightgown and looked both angry and ashamed. Her husband turned gentle eyes toward her.

"It's all right. We were frightened, and your body just reacted that way. It couldn't be helped."

Tears of exasperation coated her cheeks. "But I wet myself like a little girl!"

"Don't worry about it. Come, I'll help you get cleaned up."

The couple went toward the bedroom while Jacob, Moses, and their hostess watched.

"What's the point of staying alive?" the old woman bemoaned.

"I'm just a clumsy old fool, good for nothing. We should've stayed in Lyon. Just let me die once and for all." Her husband embraced her and started to cry as well.

"Sweetie, sweetie, no, don't say those things. We're together. We'll always be together."

"Just let me go. Let me die!"

Jacob and Moses were stunned, and their eyes pricked with tears. The desperation was like that in the velodrome: terrified people crammed together with no water, no privacy, and oppressive heat.

Their hostess closed the bedroom door and looked at the boys tenderly. "This time we've had a miraculous escape. God is good. Shall I serve you some milk? Do you have a place to stay?"

"Yes, thank you, ma'am, but don't go to any trouble. You've already done so much for us," Jacob answered.

"God help me if you leave here without a proper breakfast. I've lived alone since my husband died, and we never could have children, but my nieces and nephews used to come visit in the summer. Do stay for a bit." She brought out milk and a breakfast cake. As the fright subsided, the boys' stomachs awoke. They ate quietly until the woman spoke again.

"Are you all alone in the valley?"

"Yes, ma'am," Moses said.

"Well, you're handsome young men. I believe I saw you in church on Sunday. I never thought the gendarmes would be so brash, coming all the way from Le Puy to rob us of our peace . . . You could knock me over with a feather."

They finished eating and thanked the woman again before leaving. They felt calmer in the daylight. Though Moses's leg was still sore, he could walk on it. Jacob recognized one of the paths as leading toward the cabin up the mountain, and they followed it for a long time until they arrived. They were exhausted and cold in the chillier mountain air, but the sight of the sturdy wooden structure filled with the children from the boarding homes cheered them.

"Where have you been?" a caregiver asked, his voice edged with concern.

"I went to look for Moses, and it's a good thing I found him. The gendarmes were searching the Arnauds' farm."

"I'm still scared," Moses said, burying his face.

"Lucky for him, he was sleeping in the barn, not the house," Jacob explained.

"In the barn?" The caregiver's voice lilted up, perplexed.

Jacob had not had time to think much of it, but now he was puzzled at why Moses had not mentioned it.

"I had wet the bed a couple times, and Mr. Arnaud was angry with me. He told me that if I did it again, I'd have to sleep in the barn. He didn't want his kids to get dirty because of me. And he said that real men don't wet the bed."

Jacob gave a look of exasperation and put his arms around his brother.

The caregiver spoke up. "You're not a man, Moses; you're a kid. Mr. Arnaud shouldn't have done that. You can stay in our boarding-house from now on. We'll make room."

Moses flashed him a big smile at the best news he had received since arriving at the village. He would never have to leave his brother again.

They heard footsteps and looked up to see André Trocmé and Edouard Theis approaching the cabin. The caregiver went out to meet them. "How are things in town?" he asked.

"The gendarmes have gone. They took only Mr. Steckler and one other person. I was in Le Puy yesterday, talking with the chief of police. I told him most of our boardinghouses are under the protection of the Red Cross and are considered Swiss territory, but the Vichy regime cares little for international law or human rights," Trocmé said with a sigh.

"The prefect needs to turn in refugees to justify his position. He doesn't care about law or anything. Things are not going well for the Nazis in North Africa, and more people are joining General de Gaulle by the day," Theis added.

The caregiver nodded. "We need to get as many refugees as we can out of Le Chambon. They're not safe here anymore—at least not the foreign Jews."

"Last week when Charles Guillon returned from Switzerland with money, he told us that Jews could still escape through that route," Trocmé said.

"We should save all we can before the Germans occupy the entire country," the caregiver said.

"We've got to take them in small groups. It'll take us months to get even half of them over the Swiss border. We'll take precautions for new raids, and eventually the police will tire of coming all this way and going home empty-handed," Trocmé replied.

The pendulum of Jacob's emotions swung back into the hazardous zone of fear. Le Chambon no longer felt safe for them. He would miss seeing Anna, but he and Moses had to try to get to South America.

The three men continued talking in worried tones. "I think Officer Praly is behind all this. The prefect must have sent him to sniff around. They still haven't opened a permanent commissary, but I'm afraid it won't be long," Theis said.

"We'll keep a watch out for him," the caregiver answered.

"Léopold Praly was in church on Sunday," Trocmé added.

"He's surely reporting everything we say to the prefect. Several members of the congregation have told me the police have questioned and threatened them."

"Let's not allow our worries to get the best of us. It's better to trust than to fret. Let's keep the children hidden in homes tonight and then bring them back up the mountain in the morning. We'll keep a low profile and won't hold classes until things calm down. None of the children should be out and about in town," Trocmé told the men.

The group of children followed the men as they headed back down the mountain. Trocmé let Jacob and Moses catch up to him.

"Jean-Pierre has asked after you two. When things calm down, we'd like you to come over for a meal. Magda is a wonderful cook."

"Thank you, sir . . . pastor," Jacob said.

Trocmé chuckled. "You can call me André. A few days ago I spoke with Mr. Perrot. He said they will continue their efforts, but as yet they have been unable to secure either visas or passage for you. Perhaps in a few months things will have calmed down in the country, but until then, it will be impossible to leave France."

Jacob was happy to hear their friends in Valence remembered them and were still trying to help them.

"He also told me he'd received a letter from your parents. They have arrived in Buenos Aires. In a few days, the letter will come for you sent by Mr. Vipond, telling you some details about where they have settled for now."

Moses whooped for joy, jumped, and clasped Trocmé in a euphoric embrace. The pastor, typically serious, burst out laughing. He had been raised in a rather strict Protestant family that kept a tight rein on their emotions. But Magda, with Italian blood in her veins, had slowly managed to loosen him up enough to express his feelings.

Jacob studied the town from their vantage point on the mountain. Scattered houses among trees eventually led to the few streets that made up the entirety of the commune that was Le Chambon-sur-Lignon. He could see the Catholic church, the town hall, the Protestant church, and the train station. The gray of the stone buildings stood out against the dark green of the forests. It was a small spark of heaven in the midst of war's inferno, a place of refuge for thousands of every tongue and nation.

Trocmé halted, Moses still in his arms, and held his hand out to Jacob. He was no longer a child, but even so, Jacob squeezed the pastor's smooth, soft palm. He admired the man. In that loving, pacifist heart, Jacob sensed a kind of courage it was hard to find on earth and that he desperately wanted to have when he was older: the courage to be willing to die for those he loved and to be able to love even his enemies.

Chapter 23

Le Chambon-sur-Lignon
November 20, 1942

The loss of Algiers to the Allies and the sinking of the French fleet led to the German occupation of the formerly unoccupied zone of France. The French officials at Vichy continued overseeing some aspects of governance, but the Germans controlled the nation's land, borders, and resources. The Gestapo commenced the purging of southern France, especially Marseille, where hundreds of refugees had hidden with the hope of fleeing to Africa or the United States.

The arrival of hundreds of exiles to Le Chambon-sur-Lignon and the surrounding villages had far surpassed the expectations of Trocmé and the coalition of pastors and organizations that provided assistance to the persecuted. There, the refugees hid in houses and hoped to continue their flight after the harsh winter that was coming.

Jacob and Moses spent a relatively peaceful couple of months in the Maison des Roches alongside their classmates, now under the care of André Trocmé's cousin Daniel, but they did not dare walk alone to the church or the pastor's home. Jean-Pierre came every afternoon to their boardinghouse and played until dark. The nights were getting colder and colder, the sunshine less intense in the day, and the first snows were accumulating on the mountaintops. Within a matter of weeks, winter would have completely isolated the valley.

That afternoon, the three boys were playing happily when Anna came up. She was trembling. Her brown dress and pink jacket were splotched with mud, and her eyes were raw and red from crying. When Jacob glanced up and saw her, he asked, "Anna, are you okay?" She threw herself into his arms and sobbed. "What's going on?" he asked, bewildered.

"They've taken my mother. I was with some friends. They came to the house, and the gendarmes and the policeman took her."

Jacob knew the policeman she spoke of was Léopold Praly. He had been lurking about the village all summer and had taken up permanent residence the week before. The refugees avoided all contact with him. With his leather jacket and hat pulled down firmly over his eyes, he seemed more like a movie gangster than an agent of the law.

"Have you told Pastor Trocmé?" Jacob asked.

"No, I didn't know what to do," she said, unable to stop crying.

All four of the children ran to the church and burst into Trocmé's office without knocking. Jittery, Jacob blurted out, "They took Anna's mother!"

Wasting no time, Trocmé grabbed his coat from the hook and

hurried with the children to the town hall. Praly did not have an official office but was staying in a nearby hotel. Trocmé spotted him sitting at a restaurant. Battling his anger, Trocmé approached the inspector.

"Reverend Trocmé, to what do I owe this honor? I thought you and your congregation were no friends of public officials."

Trocmé took a deep breath, carefully relaxed his shoulders, and mustered a smile. "I've come to speak to you about an important matter. It seems the police have detained Mrs. Emdem, an upstanding member of our community—"

"And a Jew," the inspector spat out.

"And since when is it against the law in France to be Jewish?"

"Where have you been all this time, Trocmé? Back in October 1940, the president signed laws limiting the freedom of Jews—but the woman of which you speak was detained under the auspices of the Jewish Statute passed on June 2, 1941, thanks to the Commissariat for Jewish Affairs. All resident Jews lose their rights and will be deported to their country of origin. So it must be that you are in breach of these laws out of ignorance, not outright rebellion. Forgive me, I had assumed your congregation was a nest of communists. You were one of the first conscientious objectors among the clergy, refusing to serve your country, and you all have created a sort of Christian socialism, with your cooperatives and communist values. Are you still unaware of what communists do with Christians?"

Trocmé was not there to argue with the inspector. He frowned away Praly's monologue and asked directly, "Have you already taken Mrs. Emdem away?"

"I fear she's on her way to Le Puy. There's nothing to be done for her."

Trocmé turned and walked out without saying goodbye. The

roads were in too poor a condition to travel close to dark, so he would have to go the next day to the prefecture and intercede on behalf of the poor woman.

The children waited outside the restaurant. Anna, her head propped on Jacob's shoulder, had not stopped crying. Trocmé approached and hugged her. "We'll get to the bottom of it. You all come back home with me, and we'll have supper together. Anna can sleep with Nelly tonight," he said, stroking Anna's hair to calm her. Nelly could help distract Anna enough to get her through the night.

They made their way slowly back to the parsonage. It was a cold afternoon, and the clouds announced impending snow. There had already been a few snowfalls that season, but they were due for a storm. Trocmé thought about how the whiteness of the snow could make even the most worn-down, ugly things look beautiful and new. Love was something like that, he reasoned, capable of covering a multitude of sins.

Magda surmised easily enough what had occurred when she saw them troop into the house. She greeted Anna with a kiss, bent down, and with a sweet smile said, "You and Nelly can help me get supper ready. Then I think we'll bake a cake. Tomorrow it's one of the children's birthdays."

Anna nodded, tears still in her eyes. It was hard for Jacob to leave her, but he eventually wandered back to the boys' room and started playing with them. An hour later, they were all called for supper.

The table was packed with children. Despite the heaviness of Mrs. Emdem's detention, they were grateful to be together. Trocmé marveled once again at the treasure of childhood innocence, then thought of his own childhood with a distant, demanding father who never forgave himself for causing the accident that took the life of Trocmé's mother. Childhood had been sad for him. Adolescence had improved things, as he found the answers to his existential doubts and discovered his vocation as a pastor. Life had not been easy. The Great War had shown him what atrocities the human race was capable of. And his stay in the United States for seminary while he also tutored the children of the multimillionaire John D. Rockefeller was a crucial turning point in his life, because it was then that he met Magda.

After the prayer, the children dug into the food. Trocmé and Magda asked them about their day, their classes, and the games they played before focusing on conversation between themselves.

"Things are getting more difficult with each passing day. We haven't faced any shortages up to now, but there are few supplies to be had. Some of the wealthier refugees are hoarding food. We have to do something. People could start complaining and even denounce someone out of frustration," Magda said, exasperated.

"I know," Trocmé said, "but it isn't that simple. I'll tell you one thing: Since the Germans took over the whole of France, the number of refugees has skyrocketed. People are coming from Marseille and all over. Some have gone into hiding in the parts occupied by Italy, but most have hidden in rural areas. Now there are police in the village, and there are Gestapo raids in Lyon, Valence, and even Le Puy. It won't be long 'til they come here."

Magda shuddered. She was nothing but brave, but even so, the word *Gestapo* sent chills up her spine. She was exhausted, and it had begun to affect her health. "I'm afraid," she said in a wearied, unfiltered moment. She tried to be strong at all times, but even she was wearing down.

"Nothing's going to happen to us. We must have faith."

"Yes, but I'm not afraid for myself. What happens if they arrest you? What will people like that do to the children?"

Trocmé made a gesture for them to change the subject. He knew the children had ears for such comments even if they acted like they were paying no attention. "We've managed to overcome all the obstacles up 'til now. Do you remember when we were stationed in Maubeuge, how hard things were there? We were so young . . . Those workers endured subhuman living conditions. Then the pastoral commission denied us a pastorate in several different churches, until they sent us here to Le Chambon-sur-Lignon. God wanted us to come here. He has always guided our steps. What must happen will happen."

Jacob listened to the end of the Trocmés' conversation, worried about Anna but also for Moses. By the skin of their teeth they had escaped the raids in August and September. Now the Germans were all over the country, and the dreaded inspector Léopold Praly was always around town. He had the feeling that their little paradise was gradually turning into the hell that the rest of France and Europe had already become.

"I'd better take the rest of you back to your rooms. Anna, you can stay with us tonight," Trocmé said, getting to his feet.

The boys followed Trocmé's example, but Jacob crossed over to Anna before leaving the room. "It's going to be okay. You can always let me know if you need anything."

"Thanks, Jacob," she said, leaning over to give him a kiss on the cheek. The feel of her lips on his cheek overwhelmed him with a moment of inordinate happiness. He floated out of the room on a cloud. He did not even care that Moses mocked him.

The first snowflakes fell as Trocmé walked them down the street. He raised his hand and watched the snowflakes melt upon contact with his warm skin. "It's one of the most beautiful things in the world," he murmured, looking at the black sky.

The boys were excited, thinking about what they would find upon waking in the morning. The great white blanket would allow them to forget for a few days the black shroud creeping over more and more of their world. The war stretched from north to south and east to west, a great stain of death and destruction bound to devour everything in its path—even the secret valley of Le Chambon-sur-Lignon, where all hope had not yet been lost.

Chapter 24

From the beginning of December, the Germans were officially the rulers of the region. Commander Julius Schmähling had set up offices in Le Puy and, though he had not yet sent a detachment of soldiers to Le Chambon-sur-Lignon to take control of the city, the region had been declared a place of respite for some of his soldiers returning from the African and Russian fronts.

The Germans had taken over the Hotel du Lignon, right next door to the Tante Soly guesthouse, which was full of Jewish refugee children. The soldiers would at times duck under the doorway of the guesthouse to get out of the rain and wave to the children, unaware of who they actually were.

The residents of Le Chambon-sur-Lignon had not seen a German soldier at any point of the war until the Nazis requisitioned several hotels to lodge their soldiers in convalescence. Soldiers who were well on their way to recovery went out to restaurants or walked along the village streets in groups.

Over the past few weeks, the refugees had hidden more and more in their places of residence and were biding their time until they could escape to Switzerland after the difficult winter ahead.

Yet not everything was fear and worry that Christmas. Church members had hewn an enormous fir tree for the sanctuary, the women had decorated the walls and pews, and presents galore were piled at the base of the huge tree. The children were preparing a pageant for Christmas Day, and there was a joy in the air that, in such a difficult year, felt like a breath of hope in the midst of war.

Jacob walked into the church and marveled at the decorations. Moses's eyes darted back and forth every which way, taking it all in. The rather cold, austere building had become for a few weeks a veritable toy store. Moses was dressed as a shepherd, and Jacob, one of the members of the chorus, wore a suit and tie. Though they were Jewish, they did not want to miss out on a party that for them symbolized a time to share and show love to others.

Jacob spied Anna across the sanctuary and was starstruck. She wore a lovely white dress with pink ribbons, and her hair was pulled back beneath a wreath of flowers. Since her mother was taken, she and Jacob had become even closer. They would often spend the afternoons playing, and they sat together in church on Sundays. Anna was quieter and more melancholy than before, but when she was with Jacob, she was happy.

"Jacob!" the girl cried, waving at him from the other end of the room. Moses rolled his eyes and grabbed Jacob's hand. He was not as thrilled with this new arrangement. Since he had started seeing Anna more, Jacob played less with Moses.

"Hi!" Jacob hoped his greeting did not sound as nervous as he felt. Though they had known each other quite some time now and knew a great deal about each other, he still felt dazed every time the girl approached.

"Do you like my dress?" she asked, twirling so that the skirt billowed out like a bell around her.

"You look beautiful," Jacob answered honestly.

Anna leaned forward and kissed Jacob's cheek. Moses grumbled, so she bent down and kissed him too. "Don't be jealous, little one."

"I'm not little," Moses complained, looking altogether too adorable in his shepherd costume.

Magda called the chorus children while other teachers helped get the rest ready for the pageant rehearsal. The place was abuzz, everyone busy tending to this or that, and no one noticed a woman who came into the church and set two small suitcases on the floor. She was covered in snow and her shoes were soaked, but her face was kind and sweet.

Magda reviewed the songs for the evening with the chorus. When she noticed the woman, she recalled that André was supposed to pick up a new assistant sent by their denomination to give them a hand during the winter. Magda went up to her and asked, "Might you be Alice Reynier?"

"Yes, and you are Mrs. Trocmé?" the woman replied with a smile.

"I'm so sorry, I thought André would have remembered to fetch you. I told him your train would be arriving an hour ago. We're having a dress rehearsal, and . . ." Magda covered her face with her hands and shook her head.

"Don't worry about it in the least, Mrs. Trocmé. I've been helping in churches all my life. I know what a busy season it is," Alice said, still smiling.

"Well, it's a pleasure to meet you," Magda said, greeting her with two kisses.

"For me as well, Mrs. Trocmé."

"Do call me Magda," she said, able to smile again after the embarrassment of having forgotten the woman at the train station.

"Magda, I think I'm going to enjoy my time in Le Chambon-sur-Lignon very much."

"I'm sure you will. Let me show you the church. But first, let's take your luggage to the house."

Magda had been waiting for months for help. It had not been easy for her to get used to the village. She was only part Protestant. She had been raised Catholic in Italy, and part of her family had fled from Russia. It took her a long time to realize that her inability to totally fit in with Protestants was precisely what helped her get along so well with André and his way of understanding the world.

Magda led Alice to the room they had prepared for her next to the kitchen. Despite how small and narrow it was, Alice was delighted. Magda had never met anyone so positive and from whom flowed such natural goodness. When André had told her the denomination was sending them an aide, Magda had initially rejected the offer. She knew she was at the end of her strength, but she did not want some goody-goody making her feel that she was not good enough.

"They've told me you have four children," Alice said, unpacking her few things from the suitcases.

"Yes, three boys and a girl. They don't slow down one second the whole day. We always have two or three other children hanging about the house, in addition to meals with André's friends, visitors, visiting preachers, and everybody else who makes their way through town. Sometimes I think we run a hostel more than a church!" Magda said, immediately taking Alice into her confidence.

Alice nodded. "I work at a camp during the summers, and I'm used to cooking and cleaning the rooms. By the time I finish one and move to the next, the first one is dirty again. Homemaking is thankless work."

Magda had come across all kinds of women since her arrival in Le Chambon-sur-Lignon. Church women criticized her for not being a typical pastor's wife. Unlike them, Magda refused to cover her head in meetings or become the slave of her family and husband. Women had so much to give to the new society.

The two women returned to the chapel. The children were running to and fro while some of the church women put the finishing touches on the wall decorations. It seemed a more joyful ambience than a few minutes prior. No one seemed to be thinking about the war and its ensuing problems.

Alice helped Magda with the chorus, and after several runthroughs, the parishioners started heading home. The festivities would take place the next day.

"Anna, Jacob, Moses!" Magda called loudly. The children ran up to her. "I'd like you to stay for supper with us. The celebrations will start tomorrow, but it seems my children can't survive without you three." Feeding three extra children was more work, but she had to admit even to herself that she had grown fond of this bunch.

Jacob, Moses, and Anna jumped with excitement, then ran off to join the Trocmé children. When they were all together, Jacob, Moses, and Anna felt like they were part of a family again and could momentarily forget how far they were from their parents.

"See what I mean now?" Magda asked Alice with a wry smile.

Trocmé arrived home half an hour later, famished. He was surprised to find Alice there. He had forgotten it was the day of her scheduled arrival.

"André, you forgot to go pick Alice Reynier up from the station today," Magda reproached.

"Oh, I'm so sorry. It completely slipped my mind. I had several meetings, and Magda's reminder went in one ear and out the other. Please forgive me, Ms. Reynier. I want you to know we're very glad to have you."

"Please, call me Alice," she said with her customary smile.

"I think you're going to be an enormous help, Alice," Magda said. Trocmé arched his brows in surprise at the change of attitude. Magda had vehemently resisted having a helper, but he was familiar with his wife's temperamental disposition.

It was a happy supper, everyone excited about the next day's festivities. Nothing could keep them from celebrating Christmas.

All the next day, the parsonage and church were a beehive of activity. Women were fixing costumes, children were running wild, and by midafternoon the parishioners had arrived in small groups to save the best seats and sit next to their guests.

"Will you be ready soon?" Trocmé asked, somewhat nervous. It was almost time, and it looked like there was a lot left to get done.

Magda nodded, a pin in her mouth. She was fixing Moses's wool vest in their living room while the boy kept his eyes trained on her. Noting the child's intense stare, she asked out the side of her mouth, "You okay?"

Moses's face crumpled, and he began to cry. Magda hugged him tightly and, in the process, accidentally poked him with the pin. Moses squawked and backed away.

"Oh, dear me, I'm so sorry!" she said, amused despite the circumstances. Moses smiled for a moment, but the expression soon morphed back into crying. "Moses, honey, what is it?" Magda pressed.

"I miss my mother."

It broke Magda's heart. Sometimes she caught herself forgetting that many of the church's children did not have parents in the village. She knew most of them would never see their parents again. The Germans were emptying the detention camps in France, taking the Jews north. Magda had no earthly idea what became of them, but the war was increasingly bloody, and the Allies were bombing German cities nearly daily. Even André was worried about his German relatives. He had no way of knowing how they were. Magda was conscious of the fact that the conflict grew harsher and harsher, and she did not know how much longer Le Chambon would be spared direct attack.

"I'm sure you'll see her again one day soon. At least you know where she is. When winter's over, you can go to Argentina."

Moses closed his eyes and pretended that the woman hugging him was his mother. He needed her kisses, needed to feel like he was the most important person in the world for someone again.

"Thank you, ma'am," he said, wiping his tears as he walked away.

Moses headed for the chapel. The pews were packed, but the first few rows had been reserved for the children. He wiggled in beside Jacob and waited for the ceremony to begin.

The music started, and Trocmé walked out with a black robe, a white collar, and a stole. Theis and some of the deacons followed. The congregation stood as the leaders took their positions.

"My friends, brothers, and sisters, it's a pleasure to begin this beautiful Christmas feast. Many think that in times like ours we have little to celebrate. People all over the world have nothing to eat; others suffer illness or injury in hospitals or are living out the consequences of war. But today we want to celebrate peace and love toward all mankind," Trocmé began as the children's chorus approached the podium.

The congregation listened as the angelic voices of the children's choir sang several Christmas carols. Fathers smiled and mothers mouthed the words along with the children. Everyone had worked hard on the service, and as the voices floated up the church walls, the snow outside resumed falling to remind the world it was still winter. The lights on the tree and the walls trembled in the wind that found its way under the doors and through the cracks. The cold of the past few weeks had put the villagers' hearts in dormancy, but for a moment in the Christmas service, peace reigned once again in the soul of Le Chambon-sur-Lignon. The community that had suffered so much now sought to heal its wounds by candlelight, at the foot of the immense fir tree presiding over the stacks of presents while the music assuaged their grieving, terrified hearts.

When the children finished their repertoire, Trocmé took an accordion from a nearby chair and led the congregation in a song. When they were finished, Jacob's eyes were cloudy with tears. Moses and Anna were each holding one of his hands, and they stayed that way as Trocmé led the congregation in two more songs.

They all sat. Trocmé set the accordion down, cleared his throat, opened an ancient Bible on the pulpit, and began to speak.

"A couple of years ago, most of you who are with us in Le Chambon-sur-Lignon today would never have imagined you would be celebrating Christmas with us. Back then, we were complete strangers to you. We walked entirely different paths of life, and many of you lived in foreign countries or faraway lands. But today we are all gathered in the shadow of this great Christmas tree. We are looking out at life with uncertainty about what the next year will hold—our hearts cowering in fear, ignorant of the fates of our loved ones. Perhaps you have felt that you've been walking all alone in this world, that no one cared about you, but this is not true. You are a gift to us.

Many of you have been kicked out of your homes, you've been spit upon, you've been cursed; but we want to bless you and call you our brothers, our sisters."

Trocmé's voice resounded from every corner of the sanctuary, and the congregation paid rapt attention to his every word.

"Hurt, abandoned, countryless—many of you feel like the scum of the earth. You were the disinherited, wandering through the desert of life, but you have come to a promised land. A promised land that is not the beautiful green valleys of Le-Chambon-sur-Lignon, nor the dense forests of Auvergne, nor the lovely Loire River. You have come to our hearts. You have conquered with your laughter and tears. We will never be the same. Someday you will return home; you'll break bread beside your loved ones again; and I'm convinced you'll remember us in those moments. God has brought us together for a time, and together we will communicate the message of fraternity."

Sniffles and sighs punctuated the congregation. People nodded and slipped an arm around the shoulder beside them.

"Our beloved country rests on three unshakable principles, three longings that have made us what we are: equality, liberty, and fraternity. For centuries, we have attempted equality among all citizens; equality in matters of justice and opportunity, regardless of our faith, ideology, race, or sex. Liberty is another key player: the freedom to improve, to build a nation of people who are the masters of their destiny. But we have neglected fraternity. It's been taken for granted that we all belong to one great human family of humanity, but that is not the case. The human family must be built. Love is a decision more than it is a feeling. And tonight I have decided to love each of you. You are now my brothers and sisters, and I'll never be able to forget you."

As his words died away, a gust of cold air blew through the sanctuary. The main doors had been opened. Boots slapped against the stone floor. A murmur ran throughout the room. With no space left in the pews or along the walls, the group of Germans stood tall toward the back, in the center aisle. Those seated nearby crouched as far as they could away from the Nazis. The officer took off his hat, and the other soldiers followed suit. With their gray uniforms, black leather boots, and silver insignia, they looked like angels of death.

Trocmé looked them straight in the eyes and recommenced his sermon. "So now we are brothers and sisters. It may be that today in the faraway lands of Russia or Africa, in the Pacific Islands or the Syrian Desert, brothers are killing brothers—but that does not change anything. This is why we are here today, celebrating the birth of the one who became man for the love of mankind. A baby in a humble manger who, like many of those gathered here today, was far from home. There was no room in any inn for him either. Tonight, a star shines in the sky and its light brightens our world. Perhaps you fear that darkness will never again be dispelled, but soon we will once again see the star heralding peace and love for all men and women of goodwill."

The church stood as one and sang "Silent Night," their voices welling up from the depths of their being. Dozens of different accents, faces with unique features, and people of all ages sang as of one heart.

When the hymn concluded, Magda and the other teachers led the children out for the pageant. Moses pronounced his one line in such a precious way that the onlookers chuckled. Afterward, they handed out Christmas presents to all the children. One by one the children approached the raised platform, while Trocmé and Theis kissed them and gave them each a gift.

When the ceremony came to a close, several church members set up tables along one side of the church and laid out the food. The parishioners left the pews and started greeting one another with "Merry Christmas!" They hugged and kissed; some spontaneously sang carols in foreign languages; and they circled around the tables with the trays of food. The Germans remained quiet, serious, and inexpressive as they stood in the middle of the sanctuary. No one approached them. The officer motioned for them to leave, but just then Trocmé, who had had to greet half a dozen parishioners on his way toward them, approached.

"Merry Christmas, Captain," he said in perfect German.

The captain's brows knit together. His blond crew cut and leather jacket gave the thirtysomething man a formidable look. "Merry Christmas. You speak German, pastor?"

"My mother was German."

"I never would have guessed. That was a good sermon. You may think we're barbarians, but in Germany we also have churches and celebrate Christmas."

"I don't think anyone considers you barbaric. At least, that's not what I think. We've just been given difficult times to live in, Captain. You have your army, you order your men, and they obey. We are also an army, but our weapons are different, as are our battles."

The captain retained his serious look. Perhaps his mind wandered back to a time when he still believed in peace and love. He had seen and done too much for a few Christmas carols to change anything, but something still flickered inside him. Finally, he spoke. "It's hard to be far from family, to not know if tonight some airplane will fly over your house with the colored Christmas lights. But we know we're here for a reason, and we're proud of it. God is always with the strong," he declared.

"The God I know said he was with the weak, with those who are despised and helpless."

"Clearly, we are not talking about the same God. Someday we'll know which one ends up winning this war."

"Indeed we will, Captain."

"Merry Christmas."

"Merry Christmas," Trocmé said, a chill running up his spine at the exchange. He sensed that someone or something more than a simple German captain had come to visit that night, and he foresaw a battle to the death between good and evil.

The soldiers turned and their boots once again resounded over the stone floor. Everyone in the church let out a long breath as soon as the doors shut behind them.

Jacob, Moses, and Anna sat on a pew and opened their presents. Moses ripped off the silver paper and took out a small tin steam engine.

"Wow!" he said, showing it to Anna and his brother.

Jacob opened his box and took out half a dozen lead soldiers from the Napoleonic era. He held them close to his eyes to study every detail of their painted blue jackets, white pants, and long gloves. It reminded him of the toy soldiers they had played with back at the Magnés' house in Nouan-le-Fuzelier.

From her box, Anna drew out a rag doll and set to braiding her hair.

Despite the joy that permeated the village that night, Jacob could not help thinking about his parents. He tried not to, so as not to bring Moses or Anna down, but he could not get them out of his mind. Christmases in the past had been hard. They had not had much to eat or many presents, but at least they had been together. He thought of his parents in Buenos Aires, thinking about him and Moses. Even though they were Jewish, Christmas would still evoke memories of being together as a family and would still drive home how far they were from each other at that moment.

Moses ran his train back and forth on an imaginary railroad on the pew, and Anna tended to her doll. Joseph put his soldiers on the pew and arranged them for a while. Then he looked up and watched the people laughing, joking, eating. For just a moment he felt *home*. These people might not be his family, but like the pastor had said, they were now his brothers and sisters. He would never forget this place or this Christmas. He would always carry deep in his heart the village of Le Chambon-sur-Lignon, Anna, and the Trocmé family.

The great Christmas tree, alight with candles and crowned with a star, seemed big and strong enough to shelter everyone with its branches. But a long, dark shadow was stretching over the valley: the shadow of death and fear, darkness and hatred, which bided its time for the chance to overtake each home, field, and byway until it devoured the last ray of hope in the hearts of the women and men of Le Chambon-sur-Lignon.

Chapter 25

The most challenging days tend to start out calmly enough. Winter still had plenty of time left to go, but the sun had managed to warm the air throughout the day. News arriving from outside the valley was every day more dire. All escape routes for refugees from Marseille or any other point on the Mediterranean coast were closed. The January 3 attacks in Marseille against members of the German army resulted in only intensified persecution of dissidents and Jews. On January 22, more than twelve thousand police and five thousand German soldiers combed the city hunting down Jews and members of the Resistance. Over eight hundred people, primarily Jews, were arrested. Perrot had let Trocmé know that the evacuation of Jacob and Moses from Le Chambon-sur-Lignon was, for the moment, impossible. The children were so involved in their school activities that they hardly had time to think about traveling to South America. The days were too short, and by night they fell into bed exhausted.

A thick blanket of snow covered the fields and forests that bitterly cold winter. The children got up quickly, completed their morning routines, and then went to class. That morning, Jacob had particularly enjoyed their morning exercises, the schoolwork, and the company of friends. Daniel had congratulated him on his progress, and he was eager to tell Anna and Moses about his day.

Jacob ran from his school building to where Moses had class. He waited impatiently at the door until he saw Moses with Jean-Pierre, his constant companion. It was Saturday, but during the winter they spent Saturdays reviewing the week's material and putting their new knowledge into practice. Since they could not go to the river or explore the fields and forests, they spent their time in school.

Moses greeted his brother as soon as he saw him. "Hi, Jacob!"

"Hey! Do you want to go sledding down the mountain? I found this at school," he said, proudly holding out an old wooden sled.

Moses's and Jean-Pierre's eyes popped with excitement when they understood what Jacob was holding. The children of Le Chambon-sur-Lignon often went sledding on Sunday afternoons, but there were so many children and so few sleds that they rarely got more than a couple turns. But now they could spend the whole afternoon with their own sled.

"Let's get Anna, but don't tell anybody else," Jacob said.

"Sure. But tonight you should all come to dinner. My mother told me to invite you."

"I love everything your mother and Alice make," Jacob said, pleased at the thought. They walked down a parallel street so the rest of the children would not follow them and want to share the sled.

Jacob went up to the second floor of the house where Anna took classes. That afternoon she seemed more melancholy than usual. It had been almost three months since her mother had been taken, and no word of her had come. Yet the news that did arrive of what was occurring to Jews deported to the north was horrifying.

"I have a surprise," Jacob announced behind her, putting his hands over her eyes.

"A surprise? You're nuts," she retorted.

"Well, we already knew that," he joked, letting his hands fall.

"But where's the surprise?" she asked, let down.

"I didn't bring it up here, but if you hurry up, you'll see it in just a minute." They ran down the stairs, out of the building, and across the street to meet up with Moses and Jean-Pierre in the alley.

"A sled!" Anna cried when she saw the bundle behind the boys.

"Yes, and all for us. I have to return it tonight, but we can enjoy it until we go have dinner at Jean-Pierre's house."

The four of them headed toward one of the steepest slopes outside of town. It was hard to climb in the snow, and once on top, they were surprised to see the drop below them.

"Don't you think it's dangerous?" Anna asked, her stomach tightening at the steep descent.

"I'll go first to make sure," Jacob said. He climbed on the sled and without a second thought shoved off at full speed. As it descended, Jacob whooped and hollered with glee, fighting to keep his balance. He was down the hill within seconds, then turned and ran the sled back up.

"It's incredible!" he panted. "You've got to try it. Though, to be safe, we should go in pairs. Who wants to go first with me?"

Moses and Jean-Pierre both raised their hands and ran to get on the sled.

"Oh, come on, be gentlemen. You should let Anna go first."

The boys briefly pouted but finally let Anna go. She sat behind Jacob, and Moses and Jean-Pierre gave them a push. With the extra weight, the sled descended even faster than before. They spent the next hour going up and down the mountainside until it was nearly time for supper.

"Okay, this will be the last ride," Jacob said, moving the sled into position. Anna sat behind him, and they were off. At the end of the ride, the sled tipped and dumped them out onto the snow. Jacob rolled over but before he could get up, Anna leaned over and gently kissed his lips. It lasted only the briefest moment, but for Jacob it was a delightful eternity.

Moses and Jean-Pierre came tumbling down after them and, seeing the kiss, cried out and started pelting them with snowballs. "That's disgusting!" Moses yelled.

Jacob chased and caught him, commencing a snow battle that left them all completely soaked. "We've got to get going," Jean-Pierre finally said. "Father will be home soon, and they'll be waiting on us for supper."

They picked up their bags, straightened out their clothing, and brushed the snow as well as they could off their coats and hats. Then they took off running for the parsonage. It was already dark, and the light from the street lamps lit up the spotless snow behind the church. They wiped their feet before going inside and hung their coats in the hallway. As soon as they crossed the threshold, the comforting warmth of the fireplace reached them. All four of the children, shivering with cold, went to warm up by the fire. Nelly, Jean-Pierre's older sister, was peeved.

"I had to set the table and get everything ready by myself. Where have you all been?"

Jacob had hidden the sled outside the house and had warned the others not to mention it, so he would not get in trouble at his boardinghouse.

Magda came out of the kitchen carrying a huge white soup pot. She chatted with Alice and seemed to be in such a good mood she hardly noticed the children's clothes. "Have you washed your hands?" she asked distractedly.

They all four ran to the bathroom, scuffling to be first, then returned noisily to the dining room.

"André is at a meeting with the youth leaders, and he might be a while. So you children go on and eat. I don't want you up all night. And you boys will have to get back to your homes soon," Magda said. Her tone made them feel like they were just three more Trocmés.

"If you'd like, I can take them back to their homes," Alice offered. She was always willing to help. Since her arrival at Christmastime, Magda had regained her former energy and upbeat spirits. Though she never shook the concern for what might happen to her husband and the other leaders of the civil movement against the Nazis, it did not keep her from working tirelessly.

The children threw themselves into the chairs around the table and, the moment the prayer was over, grabbed their spoons and dug into the soup. Within minutes, they were on their second helpings.

Alice and Magda returned to the kitchen. Seeing the children eat heartily made them glad, but they had much to do to get ready for the next day. They had only been working a few minutes when they heard a knock at the door.

Magda went and opened it, unconcerned. A cold gust blew a few snowflakes into the entryway, and Magda was still smiling when she saw the dark, imposing figures of two gendarmes.

At first, she did not know how to react. It was unusual for them to drop by to visit André at this time of night, especially in winter.

"Can I help you?" she finally asked.

"Is this where the pastor André Trocmé lives?" one of the policemen said.

"Yes, but he's not here at the moment. Why do you want to see him?" she asked, curious.

"It's a personal matter."

Magda presumed it had to do with a transfer. When children were rescued from a refugee camp, the gendarmes often oversaw the transfer.

"My husband is a rather busy man, but you can come in and wait in his study. He should be home soon."

The men politely removed their hats and followed her down the hall to Trocmé's office. Magda left them and returned to the kitchen.

Alice had not seen who came in. "Who was it?" she asked.

Magda shrugged it off. "Some gendarmes looking for André."

The women went back to their work, unaware that Trocmé had come to the house through the door by the church and gone directly to his office, meeting the gendarmes.

"Good evening, gentlemen," he said, taken aback. He had not expected visitors at that hour.

"Are you the pastor André Trocmé?" the corporal asked.

"Yes, sir. May I ask why you need to know?"

"I'm sorry, but we've been sent to arrest you."

"Arrest me?" Trocmé asked, surprised. He had envisioned this moment for months yet had always imagined it playing out differently, not in the late evening, not with two gendarmes in his office.

"And why are you arresting me?" he asked.

"We're just following orders. Please, gather your things and we'll be on our way," the gendarme answered flatly.

"May I say goodbye to my family?" Trocmé was worried about how Magda and the children would react, but he could not leave without saying goodbye.

"Yes, but please don't drag it out. It'll be better for everyone if it's brief."

The three men walked to the dining room, but the gendarmes waited at the doorway. Trocmé went into the kitchen, and Magda turned to greet him. "Oh, hi! Two gendarmes are waiting for you in your office," she said, having nearly forgotten about them.

"Yes, I've seen them," he answered calmly, as if it were the most normal thing in the world.

"Well, what did they want?" Magda asked, seeing that he was not offering any information.

"To arrest me. They've come to take me to the gendarmerie in Tence."

Magda's eyes widened. She thought she had misunderstood her husband, but his pained grimace confirmed the worst.

"But why are they arresting you?" she cried frantically.

"I'm not sure. Likely for not collaborating with the Germans or the prefect. I'd better get ready for a little trip." Trocmé kept his voice steady.

Magda flew from the kitchen to their bedroom, brought a suitcase down from the armoire, and was shocked to find it empty. She left it on the bed and went back out to the hall, where her husband and the gendarmes were waiting.

"The suitcase isn't packed! You'll have to wait just a moment. We've had one packed since the summer, just in case, but since it's been so cold, I've had to take the clothing out for us to use. Could you spare us just a few more minutes?"

The gendarme nodded. "Of course, madam."

"We were just about to eat, and now everything will be cold. I wonder, have you two eaten? How about we all have something since it's all warm and ready?"

This did take the gendarmes by surprise. Was she really offering to feed the officers who had come to arrest her husband? They looked at each other. The younger gendarme's voice quivered, and involuntary tears came to his eyes.

"Ma'am, you don't know how hard it is to do this. Everyone knows your husband, and—"

Magda cut in. "Oh, don't apologize, gendarme. You're just doing your duty."

The policemen felt like miserable heels and awkwardly wiped their eyes and cleared their throats. Alice appeared with two plates of food and held them out to the gendarmes. At first they waved off the food, but then they nibbled on a bit of meat and bread. At that moment, Suzanne Gibert, Trocmé's goddaughter, walked into the house and saw the gendarmes. She turned and ran back to town.

The young woman started calling all the parishioners of the village and the residents of the schools and boardinghouses. By the time the Trocmés and their gendarme guests had finished a quick meal, a small crowd had gathered at the church.

Meanwhile, the children continued their meal in the dining room. Eventually Jacob got up from the table, curious as to why the Trocmés were eating in the kitchen. He was startled to see two gendarmes eating at the front door. He ran to tell Magda.

"Magda, there are two gendarmes at—"

"Yes, we know. Don't worry. André needs to go with them."

Jacob was immediately worried, but he tried to be calm so as not to alarm Moses and the others. "But the pastor hasn't done anything wrong. Why are they arresting him?" he asked in a low voice.

"Sometimes justice and authority don't line up. The police typically arrest dangerous people and criminals, but we live in very challenging times, as you know. But God will protect him, don't you worry," Magda said, ruffling his hair.

Trocmé picked up his small suitcase and went to his children. They surrounded him in a tangle of hugs. "Don't worry about me," Trocmé said. "I'll be back before you can even think about it. Behave yourselves and obey your mother. Help her every way you can, so when I get back she can tell me you've been wonderful children."

Moses and Anna hugged him as well, and Jacob also ran to him. Trocmé had been a father to them all.

"Thank you," Jacob said, his face smashed against Trocmé's shoulder. "Without you, I couldn't have gotten through this time without my parents."

"Don't worry, Jacob, I'll be back. Take care of the younger ones," Trocmé told him. He was smiling, but behind his glasses, tears were trickling down his cheeks and moistening the collar of his shirt.

Trocmé wiped his face with a handkerchief. He did not want people to think he was afraid of whatever awaited him.

"Gentlemen," he said to the two gendarmes.

"Let's go out by the door of the church—make all this as easy and quick as possible. We don't want to cause a scene. Think of your parishioners," one of the gendarmes said.

"There will be no scenes on my account. The brethren of the church won't pull any stunts. They know I wouldn't stand for it."

Trocmé kissed Magda's forehead, squeezed Alice's hand, walked down the hall, and reached the door by his office. When they stepped out of the house and into the church, they saw the waiting crowd. The gendarmes each took one of Trocmé's arms. The parishioners' faces were painted with anger, but Trocmé motioned for them to stay calm.

"Don't stop walking," the gendarme told him.

Then the policemen saw that the people were approaching with all sorts of objects and placing them on a large table. There was food, a warm garment, gloves, pens and paper, and even a roll of toilet paper.

Trocmé was heartened to see their demonstrations of affection. People touched his arms and spoke words of encouragement.

Jacob and the rest of the children went out of the house and around one side of the church. When they got to the front, they saw the crowd, five police cars with armed gendarmes, and a group of students from the Cévenol school. The students had formed a protective tunnel, and at the end of it stood Daniel Trocmé. Jacob ran and joined the group.

Inside the church, Trocmé gathered up all the gifts from the parishioners into his suitcase. But before closing it, one of the gendarmes touched his shoulder and held out a pack of matches.

"Please, accept this from me."

Trocmé was heartened again, sensing the strength of love operating in that moment despite the concurrent suffering. He thought of his parishioners and wondered if they would have the courage to continue the struggle. Immediately he knew the answer was yes. They were all there—men, women, children, and the elderly—as a sign of their bravery. With tears in their eyes, showing their respect and affection, these people would not give up easily. Trocmé knew they were the ones teaching him in that moment, showing him that, despite all the sacrifice and the many sleepless nights, he had always received much more than he had given.

"Thank you," he said to the gendarme and put the matches in his pocket.

The freezing air of the street brought back to him the full weight of reality. The crowd that had gathered outside the church was even larger than the one inside. He heard words of encouragement, recognized several voices, and could imagine all their faces, the same faces he had seen Sunday after Sunday. He was momentarily distracted with the thought of who would preach the next day in church. It was Saturday, and he had already prepared his sermon. Someone would surely stand in for him.

The students started singing a hymn written by Martin Luther over four hundred years before, "A Mighty Fortress Is Our God":

A mighty fortress is our God,
a bulwark never failing;
our helper he, amid the flood
of mortal ills prevailing . . .

As Trocmé walked to the car, he saw his good friend Edouard Theis had also been arrested and, beside him, Roger Darcissac. It pained him more to see those men taken than himself. He closed his eyes and kept walking. Jacob stretched out his hand and gave him a pencil. Not just any pencil, though. Jacob had brought it from Paris and kept it safe in his pocket for months. It was the pencil his father had used to mark up the books he read. It was the last physical thing Jacob had that linked him to his father—but he wanted to somehow express to Trocmé his love and respect.

Trocmé nodded at him and mouthed, "Thank you, Jacob." His tearstained face smiled. Jacob impulsively jumped out of the line of students and hugged Trocmé again. The gendarmes stopped short, but the pastor merely stroked the boy's hair and kept walking.

"I'll see you soon. Thank you for the pencil," he called. He walked the last few yards to where his fellow detainees awaited. He, Theis, and Darcissac embraced before climbing into the cars. It was quiet until the motors revved to life.

The crowd was silent as the police cars drove away. The sky was a frozen black expanse above. Little by little, everyone returned home. Daniel Trocmé called to Jacob, Anna, and Moses.

"Let's go," he said, his head hung low. He had no words to cheer them out of their mutual gloom.

They dropped Anna off first, and Jacob stepped ahead of the group to say goodbye at the door.

"I'm scared," she confessed, trembling.

Jacob hugged her, noticing how wet and cold her coat was, then stepped back to look at her. "André told me he'd be back, and he always keeps his promises."

Anna gave him a soft, sad kiss, turned, and went inside. Jacob stood, paralyzed. The day had held the highest highs and the lowest lows. He loved Anna, though he hardly knew what that meant. And though he had acted calm, he was also terrified. Jacob felt that, though Trocmé was just one man, the pastor had become a symbol for all of them and somehow represented the courage they could have if they united themselves instead of fighting the fear alone.

"You all right?" Daniel asked, seeing Jacob's lost look.

"No, but I think I've learned something tonight," the boy answered.

"I think we all have," Daniel said in a broken voice.

The three of them walked slowly, willing time to hurry so they could cheat it; but time would not have it. The evil that had spread like a black fog all over Europe had finally arrived in Le Chambon-sur-Lignon. As long as the light kept shining in each of their hearts, they could—together—keep battling the demon of war. But something had broken into the heart of the community that cold winter night.

PART 3

PART 3

Chapter 26

Le Chambon-sur-Lignon
June 29, 1943

The sound of motors woke them. Jacob went to the window and saw two Citröens, a dozen German police, and a truck with a canvas cover at the end of the road. He jumped out of bed, threw on his shorts, and called for Moses. "The Germans are coming!" he said, scrambling into his shirt and shoes.

It took Moses a minute to react, but then he got dressed as quickly as he could. Jacob helped him tie his shoes, and they ran downstairs. When they got to the living room, they heard a loud bang and saw the door burst open. The Nazis entered screaming, "*Raus, raus!*"

They ran up the stairs beating on doors and dragging the children out of bed. Jacob and Moses tried to slip out the back door, but the Germans had surrounded the building. One huge soldier grabbed them by their clothes and carried them back inside.

The terrified children and adolescents found themselves surrounded in the living room. Some were crying, some yelling, but most just hung their heads and hoped this was nothing more than another scare, a show of force.

"Where is Daniel Trocmé?" one of the soldiers demanded.

Jacob dared to raise his head and look around, but he did not see their tutor.

"What are you looking at, swine?" a soldier asked, and the back of his hand met Jacob's face. The blow stunned the boy, and his nose started to bleed. Moses went toward him, but the soldier pushed him hard to the ground.

Just then Daniel appeared at the back door. The night before, he had stayed at another of the boardinghouses and was on his way back when he heard the screams of the children. He could have escaped to the woods, but he hurried to the house. He could not leave the children at the mercy of the Germans.

"Are you Daniel Trocmé? We have suspicions that you are hiding members of the Resistance and Jewish refugees here. Tell us which of the children are French and which are Jews."

Daniel answered calmly, "For me, they are all simply students."

The Gestapo leader stepped forward until his face was an inch from Daniel's. He screamed, "Don't come at me with your stupid pacifist morality. Those terrorist cowards are murdering our men. You denounce the Jews and the members of the Resistance, or I'll take the whole lot of you in. Understood?"

"The children are under the protection of the Swiss government, which provides for their upkeep. If you detain any of them, you'll be contravening international treaties . . ." But before Daniel could finish, the officer hit him in the face.

"Take him to one of the rooms in the back to question him," he barked.

The noise of the trucks had gotten the attention of a young Resistance worker named Suzanne Heim. When she saw what was happening at the Maison des Roches, she turned and went straight to the church. She was out of breath by the time she entered the presbytery.

"What in the world is going on?" Magda asked, taking in the girl's nerves at a glance.

"The Gestapo are at the Maison des Roches!" she gasped out.

"Oh, dear God, no," Magda cried. She ran to the front of the church, grabbed her bike, and pedaled as fast as she could to the boardinghouse.

She arrived, threw down her bike, and marched into the kitchen. Assuming she was a cook, the Germans did not stop her. She busied herself getting some food ready while watching the Gestapo calling the children in one at a time to Daniel's office to document their identities. It twisted Magda's heart to see their scared, confused faces, still half-asleep.

Magda served the Germans some food, then made her way to Daniel.

"Daniel, do you remember what happened a few weeks ago? The little Spanish boy who saved the German who was drowning in the river? That might help us here," she whispered.

"It's worth a shot," he said under his breath.

Magda left her apron on a hook and went back out, hopped back on her bike, and headed into town, straight for the Hotel du Lignon, where convalescing German soldiers were housed. She hopped off her bike and marched up the stairs, but the guard at the door stopped her. In German, she explained that she needed to speak with a certain soldier. The guard knew who Magda was and allowed her in.

In the great hall of the hotel, she spotted three soldiers drinking and talking and marched right up to them.

"Have any of you been in Le Chambon-sur-Lignon for more than three weeks?"

Her question took them all by surprise. "Why do you ask?"

"Three weeks ago, a German soldier was on the verge of drowning in the river, and one of the students from the Maison des Roches saved him," Magda said, praying the officers would remember the incident.

"Yes, I remember. I was there that day," one of them said.

"This morning the Gestapo went to that boardinghouse and they're aiming to arrest the school. Could you come help us?"

The Germans looked at one another. They could not understand what she was after. The oldest answered, "We're not part of the Gestapo, ma'am. I don't see how we can be of help."

"I'm asking you as officers and gentlemen to testify on behalf of the children. We can't let them be taken away."

Two of the soldiers got up, put on their hats, and followed Magda. It was a surreal image: Magda walking down the main street of town, pushing her bicycle, escorted by two German soldiers. They had not gotten far when they ran into two girls from the church on their bikes.

"Girls, could you lend me your bikes? I need them for something important," Magda called.

The girls looked up, surprised, but they got off and handed their bikes to the officers. The party of three set off at full speed toward the Maison des Roches.

When they arrived, they were stopped at the door.

"We'd like to speak with the officer in charge," one of the soldiers said, unintimidated by the Gestapo. When the guard hesitated, the soldier repeated his intention, and the guard finally went inside and alerted his supervisor.

"What's going on?" the Gestapo officer said as soon as he walked outside. "This is none of your business."

The soldier answered coolly, "We wanted to make it known that a student from this house saved one of our men from drowning a few days ago. We do not believe they are members of the Resistance."

"Thank you, but we have information about this house, including the criminal activities of some of its members and the teacher Daniel Trocmé."

The soldiers shrugged, left the bicycles beside the house, and returned to the hotel. There was nothing more they could do for the children, but at least they had tried.

Magda stared at the Gestapo official and said, "I want to speak with Daniel Trocmé."

"You can't right now, but come back this afternoon." He turned to go.

Magda stood on the stoop for a moment, gathering her thoughts. Then she took her bike and walked it down the hill. The devastation sometimes threatened to swallow her whole. She had been separated from her husband back in February. Trocmé, Theis, and Darcissac had been held at the Saint-Paul Camp, but just before most of the camp's prisoners were transferred to Germany, the three men were released thanks to intervention from various public officials. But what would happen now with Daniel and the children? Would they face the same fate? Would they return safe and sound?

At home, Alice had been watching the Trocmé children and waiting for Magda to return. Seeing Magda's dejected face, Alice went to the kitchen and made tea.

"How are the children?" Alice asked.

"I don't know. They wouldn't let me in. I'm sure they haven't eaten since early this morning. They must be terrified. We've got to get them out of there."

Alice groped for comfort, though her face was as downcast as Magda's. "Rest for a bit and save your strength. In a couple hours things might look different."

Magda sank into the chair and began to cry. Then she knelt and prayed, "Oh God, God, God!"

Two hours later, she returned to the Maison des Roches with Jean-Pierre, whose friends Jacob and Moses were among those being questioned. As they approached, they saw all the children lined up with Daniel at the head. The Gestapo did not let them approach, but Magda called to him, "Daniel, don't be afraid!"

His clear voice ran out, "It's all right! I'll go with my students and protect them."

The tears returned to Magda's eyes, and she clung to Jean-Pierre's hand. "Why are they taking you?" she called back.

"They're accusing me of being a Jew and of helping the Resistance."

"But that's ridiculous," she protested, desperate.

"Tell my parents that I love them and that I'll be fine. As soon as I can, I'll get in touch with them," Daniel said, raising a hand. Jacob, Anna, and Moses were beside him. Jean-Pierre saw them and started hollering for them.

"Where are they taking them, Mother?" he asked, distraught.

Magda did not know how to answer. She bit her lip and shifted her weight from one foot to the other while the soldiers pushed the students toward the truck. One by one they climbed in, but when it was Moses's turn, Jean-Pierre ran up and hugged him.

"Don't go, don't go!" Jean-Pierre begged between sobs.

Magda ran up to her son as the Gestapo inspector cracked his whip at them.

"These two are very young," she protested, pointing to Jacob and Moses.

"They're Jewish swine. It's hard to believe you're the wife of a Protestant pastor," was his disdainful reply.

"They're children, not Jews. They're just orphans," she answered.

The inspector scared her with his dark eyes. "Don't you know a preacher's wife shouldn't lie?"

"I'm not lying, inspector. They're just orphans from Paris, innocent children," she said, weeping.

Jean-Pierre clung to Moses. Their sobs were audible, as were Jacob's, coming from inside the truck. The inspector hesitated briefly, then gave the order for the boys to be released.

Jacob grabbed Anna's hand, and she held on tight, but their fingers separated as a soldier pulled Jacob out of the truck. Magda saw Anna, the child with light eyes, blond hair, and panic all over her face.

"She's not Jewish either!" Magda cried, reaching for Anna's hand.

"Not the girl!" the Gestapo officer shouted, pushing Anna farther into the truck.

Two soldiers dragged Magda back. Jacob, Moses, and Jean-Pierre ran to help her, but other soldiers blocked them. The students of the Maison des Roches continued filing into the truck until it was nearly full. Besides Daniel Trocmé, the Gestapo detained eighteen students: Spaniards, Dutch, Belgians, Germans, Austrians, Romanians, Luxembourgers, and French.

A soldier shut the doors and smacked the back of the truck. The rest of the soldiers returned to their vehicles, and the party was off in a cloud of dust. Jacob tore off running behind the truck. He could see Anna's pale face looking out the back. He ran faster and faster, but the truck moved farther and farther away. As soon as the convoy turned onto the main street, Jacob fell too far behind and stopped to catch his breath. Anna's face turned into a white speck and then disappeared. Jacob collapsed and beat at the ground with his fists.

He later walked back to the house, head hung low. There was no one outside. Inside, he found half a dozen of the older boys in absolute silence. The Spaniard boy who had saved the German soldier was there. The Gestapo had pushed him out of the line headed toward the truck at the last minute. Magda stood, silent, pouring water into cups for everyone.

"They took her?" Moses asked.

Jacob squeezed his brother tightly to him. He had not been able to keep his promise to protect Anna. She had been his first love, the only girl he had kissed. And he had lost her forever.

"I couldn't help her," Jacob said before his voice cracked and all the grief poured out in sobs. He knew right then that they could not wait any longer. They had to get out of France as soon as possible, even if they got caught in the attempt. The only thing that mattered now was getting his brother to safety and seeing their parents again. In many ways, the Jacob who had left Paris almost a year ago no longer existed. Standing in his place was a young man who had wiped his mind and heart clear forever of the magic of childhood, the age when everything is possible and imagination is powerful enough to transform reality and start all over with a snap of the fingers. That magic had disappeared. The only thing Jacob felt was loneliness and shame, like Adam the day he discovered the terrible difference between good and evil.

Chapter 27

Things did not lighten up in the valley. At his wife's request and the insistence of some of their coworkers, André Trocmé had been in hiding for over a month. Violent resistance was more and more frequent, which provoked the Nazis and the French militia to respond with a heavier hand. The roads were watched more closely than ever, and the borders were nearly impenetrable. Switzerland had closed its borders to Jews and other exiles. The route to Spain through the Pyrenees was incredibly difficult in winter and, in the summer, Spanish authorities would hand fugitives back over to the Germans.

Magda had tried to dissuade the Stein brothers from their risky journey to South America. Everyone was waiting on the Allies to land in the country, and the Germans were losing battles on nearly every front—but the more trapped they felt, the more dangerous the Nazis became.

Jacob had not been able to eat much since the raid. He would disappear in the afternoons to go watch the sunset from the same hills where he and Anna had watched them. All the community's efforts to save the students the Gestapo had taken from the Maison des Roches had failed. Even the prefect Bach had intervened on their behalf with the Germans, but he had not gained their freedom. Daniel Trocmé had sent his parents a letter to send to the children of Le Chambon to comfort them, but with each day that passed, the possibility of their returning alive was more and more slim.

Convalescing German soldiers were not as numerous in Le Chambon-sur-Lignon as a few months prior, as the valley was no longer the peaceful respite it once had been. Resistance fighters were hiding in the forests trying to wear down Nazi morale with attacks against military men and materials. Trying to leave the valley in the current conditions would be dangerous; reaching the coast would be impossible.

Magda and Alice finished packing the boys' suitcases, small cardboard things with worn-out closures, but it was enough for a few changes of clothes, some food, and a couple of books.

Jacob still had the money their friends in Valence had given them. At first, he had thought about traveling alone with Moses, but as soon as Vipond and Perrot were informed of their plans, they offered to help.

Magda took the suitcases to the door, and some children gathered outside the church to bid farewell one last time. They were all vaguely aware that the village in the middle of France had offered them temporary shelter and that most of them would return home sooner or later. The memory of Le Chambon-sur-Lignon would fade into the realm of dreams, a brief interruption in the long life that lay ahead of them.

Alice kissed the boys, then Magda bent down before Moses and whispered, "Take care of your brother, behave yourself, and when you see your parents, tell them they have two wonderful sons they should be very proud of."

Moses stared at her with his big, expressive eyes, then hugged her. He swallowed back his tears, not wishing to cry in front of his classmates.

"Goodbye, friend," Jean-Pierre said, holding out his favorite slingshot.

"Oh, no, I can't take it. It's yours," Moses said.

"I want you to take it to South America. Every time you use it, you'll think of me." They hugged one last time, and Moses picked up his suitcase.

Magda bent down to kiss Jacob's cheeks repeatedly. "You're not a little boy anymore. You've grown and are quite the young man now. Don't forget us. Carry us in your heart. Don't worry about Anna. God brought you together for a time, and maybe he'll let you see her again. She would want you to be happy. The people who love us, even if they have to leave us for a while, will always be in our hearts."

"Thank you for taking care of us, saving us, the meals, everything. Tell your husband goodbye from us someday, and please thank him for everything he's done for us," Jacob answered.

"Be smart now. Wait for the right moment, and never stop trusting. Someday you'll be a great man and can help others find their way in life. Though these months have been very hard, they've taught you valuable lessons—the importance of friendship and the power of the common man. Don't forget what you've learned."

A car drove up the street, crossed the bridge, and parked in front of the church. Jacob and Moses recognized the driver immediately. It was Perrot. Except for more white hairs in his sideburns and beard, he looked practically the same as he had a year before.

After greeting the boys, Perrot loaded their suitcases, and they all climbed in. As the Renault drove away, the boys stuck their heads out the window and waved goodbye to their friends.

The granite houses gave way to beautiful fields starting to yellow in the heat. The forests were as thick and foreboding as in winter, but flowers grew up and down the highway. The sun was hot overhead.

"You'll miss them," Perrot said.

The boys looked out the windows in silence. Le Chambon-sur-Lignon had been more than a place of refuge for them, more than a secret valley, more than a village full of brave, generous people. The town embodied the reality that people could always find a way out, and the impact of one good deed was infinitely more powerful than that of evil.

They drove in silence the whole way to Valence, watching the landscape slowly morph into wide plains and cropland. The car came to a stop near Vipond's house, and they all got out, without taking the suitcases.

"I didn't know we'd come back here," Jacob said, puzzled.

"Mr. Vipond wants to speak with you," was Perrot's only reply.

They went up to the top floor. The stairway was dark and quiet, but when they got to the landing before the attic apartment, a light shone directly on the door. They knocked, and Vipond answered right away, as if he had been waiting at the door.

"My dear boys, how big you've gotten! Moses is practically a young man now!" Vipond managed a smile, but the boys could see he was much older and weaker than when they had left him.

"We're so happy to see you, Mr. Vipond," Jacob said, giving the man a hug.

"Come in, come in. I'm sure you're hungry. At your age I could never stay full, though, truth be told, I still eat too much, but that hardly matters anymore."

The house smelled closed up, as if the outside air dared not flow through territory so closely guarded by death. Jacob and Moses sat on the sofa, and the old man brought out two passports.

"So, we've got you forged passports, authorization from your parents to travel, and a letter of safe passage. Of course, your father's family lives in Spain, which is why you've got a Spanish last name, Alejo. You can get into Spain and go to Barcelona. These are the tickets for a passenger ship headed for Buenos Aires with the Spanish Line. The ship sails in five days. We think that's enough time, but it's also not a good idea to stay in Spain too long. Franco's police would get suspicious."

Jacob was overwhelmed. "Thank you so much," he said, taking the papers.

"Mr. Perrot and I think it best that I take you. I hope I don't slow you down, but we can't rest knowing you're traveling alone. It will be very challenging to make it to the Spanish border, but crossing the country and then an ocean is another matter altogether, so we think one of us should go with you. Mr. Perrot has his obligations with the theater. But I, I've nothing keeping me here on earth anymore. I'd rather die somewhere else, not here where the walls only remind me how old and weak I am. Besides, it would do me good to see your parents again."

The boys were flabbergasted. They had never dreamed of something so kind. They were overjoyed not to have to travel alone. The world was too dangerous for two children on their own, especially amid the times they were living. And they knew nothing of Spain, not to speak of the awful possibility of never actually finding their parents in Buenos Aires.

"When do we leave?" Jacob asked.

"Tonight. The raids are almost constant now. At first, we had thought to get you out through Marseille, but the Nazis have destroyed the place, rounded up all the refugees and dissidents, kicked out the consulates, and closed the port. The only chance is to go through Spain. Some boats sail straight to Buenos Aires, though they make stops in Brazil and Uruguay."

"How long will it take?" Moses asked. "I'm scared of being on a boat for a long time."

"Four or five weeks. If everything goes well, you might see your parents by the end of September," Vipond answered.

It was a lot to take in. The boys had waited so long that it was hard to believe they might actually see their parents in just over a month.

Jacob and Moses helped Perrot bring some food from the kitchen, and together they had lunch. As they ate, the men asked them about their time in Le Chambon-sur-Lignon. Jacob and Moses explained how it was when they first got there, the visit of the minister Lamirand, the gendarme raids the summer before, Christmas in the village, the arrest of Pastor Trocmé in February, and the arrest of the students and Daniel Trocmé a few weeks prior.

"We heard about what happened to Pastor Trocmé and his cousin," Perrot said. "People are more and more outraged as time goes by. If they didn't have to pay dearly for it, I think the whole world would be out in the streets hunting down Nazis, but it's just a matter of time. The Germans have lost in Stalingrad and Tunisia. The fascists in Italy overthrew their own Mussolini and have asked for an armistice.

The Allies recently landed in Sicily, though we were all hoping they would come to Marseille."

Vipond nodded. "And now there's talk of another Allied landing on the Atlantic. With any luck, France will be free again before the end of the year." He hoped he would live to see it. The journey to Argentina was, in a way, his own personal bon voyage.

Great actors know when to get off stage. Accordingly, Vipond had spent the past few weeks closing his hostel, selling off his property, and securing his money in a trust as an inheritance for Jacob and Moses when they grew up. He had never had children of his own. With his strength leaving him for good, he was more aware than ever of how selfish he had been: always living for the applause of an adoring public, allowing himself to be loved and adored, and incapable of returning that love to others. Yet now he felt deep tenderness toward Jana's children.

"I'd better lie down for a while. I've got to drive all night, and at my age, that's an epic feat," the old man said.

When he had gone to the bedroom, Perrot stood and took his hat. "I hope you have a good journey and that you find your parents very soon. They were so kind while they were here in Valence. It's not easy finding people like that. We live in a world in which men have become wolves for other men."

"We'll greet them for you. Thank you so much for your help. You've risked your life for us," Jacob said, also getting to his feet.

"Life's not worth living if you don't give it to others. We can't take anything with us. I hope we've at least been able to teach you something worthwhile in the time you've spent with us."

Perrot held out his hand and shook with Jacob. The boy felt like a grown-up for the first time, as if he were bidding farewell to an equal. Moses stretched up and held out his smaller hand too.

"You boys have helped me remember so many things, in particular why I love life," the man said somewhat dramatically. Jacob wondered if he were quoting a line from one of the many plays at his theater.

"Goodbye, Mr. Perrot," Jacob said.

"Yes, well, it's time to lower the curtain." And with a nod, he made for the door and closed it quietly behind him. The house was cloaked in silence.

Jacob and Moses made themselves comfortable on the couch. They tried to sleep, but they were jittery and excited and could hardly be still.

"In a month," Moses said, repeating the words of their bene-factors. "We'll see them in just over a month."

"We've already got tickets for South America and papers to get out of France," Jacob said as if to confirm reality. He was flipping through the passports and other documents. "Plus, Mr. Vipond is coming with us. I'd so much rather he come than have to make this trip on our own."

Moses nodded thoughtfully, as if holding his tongue.

"What is it?" Jacob asked him.

"Nothing. I just wonder if he'll be able to survive a trip like this."

Jacob stood up and looked through Vipond's bookshelves until he found a map of France, then he stretched it out over the coffee table. Next, he stood on a chair and brought down the globe. He put it by the map and studied them.

"Look. This is about where we are. The border with Spain is really far, at least two days away. I don't know where we'll stop at night. Maybe here near Montpellier." He pointed. "Then we'll cross the border probably here at La Junquera, and then go straight to Barcelona. We'll have to stop for the night again somewhere near the border and in the city."

Moses stared at the map, his jaw slack, and then got excited when Jacob reached for the globe.

"This is Spain. The boat will go along the coast to the Strait of Gibraltar, then out to the open sea. From there we'll head for Brazil, then Montevideo, in Uruguay, to our final destination, Buenos Aires," he explained.

Moses's face was inches from the globe as he studied every detail and imagined himself crossing the wide ocean. "We'll be like pirates," he concluded with a smile.

"Exactly, like pirates!" Jacob giggled.

Jacob, still a bit hungry, went back to the kitchen while Moses kept imagining the impending adventure. Before they realized it, it was the dead of night. They waited in the dark for Vipond to wake up, but there was no sign of him. At first they were just impatient, but then they grew worried, wondering if something had happened to him.

"Should we wake him?" Moses asked Jacob.

"Let's let him rest a little longer."

Not two minutes had passed before they heard a noise and approaching footsteps. Vipond emerged dressed and ready.

"Let's go, boys. We'll be on the road until dawn. I don't want my neighbors to see me go. One of them might inform the Germans."

They went out to the landing and walked down the stairs as carefully as possible. The heat was palpable even at that late hour. Vipond went out first, made sure no one was around, and motioned for them to follow. Then they got in the same vehicle that had brought them from Le Chambon-sur-Lignon.

Vipond turned the key, and the typical motor noise sounded particularly deafening in the late-night silence.

"There's a curfew, so we've got to get out of the city as quickly as we can. We'll go by back roads. It'll take longer, but they're safer.

We won't see many Germans, and hopefully the gendarmes will let us through without much hassle."

The car wound its way through mountain roads, avoiding the highways and busier streets of the plains. Vipond was an excellent driver, just very slow. The headlights were uncomfortably dim, and the roads were in deplorable shape. Some curves were so sharp Vipond brought the car to a near stop in order to make them. They hugged the edges of cliffs and traversed dozens of miles without passing a single car or even going through a town.

Jacob tried to keep up conversation. He was afraid their chauffeur might fall asleep at the wheel otherwise. He could hear Moses's snores behind him.

"I went to Spain once, a long time ago," Vipond was saying.

"You did? For a play?"

"You're not going to believe it, but it was for the only woman I ever loved. What happened ended up being so terrible, you couldn't even imagine. It's perhaps why I gave up on love and never remarried."

This took Jacob by surprise. "You were married?" he asked. He had always presumed the man was a hardened old bachelor.

"It was a long time ago, after great success on the stage in Paris. One of the dancers in our company was a young Cuban woman named Mercedes. She was mixed race. Beautiful. The most beautiful woman I've ever seen, truly. She had enormous dark eyes, copper-colored skin, curly black hair, and a figure to give a man a heart attack . . ." Vipond remembered suddenly that he was talking with a boy, though Jacob was thirteen now.

"Mixed race?" Jacob asked.

"Yes, her mother was black and her father was white. He was from Catalonia and had gone to Cuba to make his fortune. He married a Cuban woman and they had five children. Mercedes had been born an artist. She was a stunning dancer and actress, though there weren't many roles in Paris for an actress who was half black. She did a bit with movies and then landed in the theater where I had been acting for two years. It was love at first sight for me—a direct shot from Cupid. I couldn't resist her!"

Jacob did not necessarily understand all the vocabulary the old man used, but he liked hearing stories. It made him feel like he was living them too.

"She put me off at first. I imagine she thought I was rather green. She was two or three years older, had lived in different countries, knew people all over the world. For her, Paris was just one stop in her life, while I planned on staying there forever, especially if I kept making it big in the theater. One night, after the last show, I worked up my courage and asked her to dinner. I'll swear to you: Nights in Paris are magical. We went to a lovely restaurant in the Latin Quarter, then walked along the Seine and ended up at the Avenue des Champs-Élysées. The night was beautiful—clear, with a huge moon that must have driven us a bit mad. At the end, I kissed her. She was not the first woman I had ever kissed, but she was the first I had ever truly loved. I'd always been rather narcissistic; it's hard not to be when you want to be an artist and leave everything else behind. But in that moment, she was the only thing that mattered to me."

This was something Jacob could understand all too well. He had also known what it felt like to love. Every day that went by, he missed Anna even more, though he had decided to follow Magda's advice and be happy. He knew that is what Anna would have wanted.

The car emerged from the more mountainous roads as they reached the area of Nîmes, with wide meadows and small forests dotting the way. It was still night, but the horizon was starting to lighten.

Vipond yawned before continuing his tale. He thought that this was precisely what it meant to be old: to have a long past and no future. As he relayed his life to Jacob, he felt that, in some way, it had all been worth it, though it had gone so fast, and death had become a constant companion for the journey. Nearly all of his friends were dead, as were his parents and most of his relatives. He was the last witness of a world that was going extinct, never to be seen again.

"What happened next?" the boy asked, impatient. Jacob, on the other hand, barely had any past. Uprooted from his home country and from his Jewish roots, he needed to feel that the ground beneath his feet meant something. Should he disappear tomorrow, he wanted to know that somebody would remember him.

"Patience, my boy. We've got a long road ahead of us and I don't know that your mother would want me to tell you this story. She knows it, of course. Old men repeat themselves constantly."

"Please, Mr. Vipond, go on," Jacob begged.

"I don't suppose Jana would get too mad at me. It's just life, the wonderful and terrible existence we all share."

Jacob was quiet. He wanted the old man to keep telling his love story about Mercedes, the exotic and beautiful Cuban dancer. In a way, that was how Jacob envisioned South America: a world so different from his own, full of new colors, smells, and tastes.

"A while after that first kiss, we got engaged. She was very reluctant to get married. She had always been free. She'd had any number of lovers and somehow felt I had tamed her, but she did love me in her own way. Two months after we got engaged, she disappeared one day. She didn't come to the theater, and when I went to her apartment, they told me she'd gone to Madrid. I thought I would lose my mind. How could she have abandoned me like that? I took the train to Hendaye that very day, traveling all night. Then I took another train to Madrid. I had no idea where to look for her, and I didn't speak the language, but I finally found her. She was working at the Teatro Español, a beautiful spot in the heart of the city. One night, I showed up at her show and watched her act. She was playing Desdemona, Othello's lover—a role that suited her perfectly."

"What happened?" Jacob asked again. The sky was almost fully light. The night had frittered away as they talked.

"I waited for her at the door. She didn't seem surprised to see me. The actors were going out to eat, and she told me to come with them. The whole night she flirted with the main actor, and I was eaten up with jealousy. You haven't experienced it yet, but it's like fire burning you up inside. I decided to go back to Paris, but she was toying with me. She showed just enough interest, gave me just enough affection, for me not to leave her. Finally, one night during a terrible rainstorm, after her show, I made up my mind for sure to leave. She ran through the streets of Madrid, coming after me. We got married the next day at the French embassy, but she made me promise not to consummate the marriage until we were back in her country. It was insane. We sailed to Cuba for me to meet her family. We arrived in Havana about a month later. I was as happy as a clam. The journey on the boat had truly been a pleasure cruise.

"So we got to Cuba, and she introduced me to her family. They all received me warmly and called me *el francés*. I thought about staying there to live. It was beautiful and peaceful, far from the ruckus of Paris. That night we had a reservation at the nicest hotel on the island, for just the two of us. We enjoyed a candlelight dinner, and when it came time to go to bed, I was nearly beside myself. We got to our room, and just as we were finally naked together, she began to laugh. I didn't understand what was going on. Then she told me she didn't like men, that she hated men, that she didn't love me, that she would never sleep with me."

Jacob was shocked and confused. Why would any woman do that to Vipond?

"I returned to Paris completely destroyed. At least my profession helped me keep going. I never fell in love again and only had passing relationships. Mercedes made me distrustful of women, until I met your mother, actually. She is such a beautiful soul . . . She was like a daughter to me."

They were approaching the region of Montpellier. Vipond stopped the car behind a tree-covered area. "I think we can rest safely here. We'll start up again in three or four hours. Some friends will help us in Carcassonne. We'll spend the night with them and cross the border the next day, leaving France forever," he said. His words sounded sad. He mused on how aging implied doing many things for the last time. Under the unstoppable clock, life slipped away so quickly that one day you woke up and found there would be no tomorrow.

Jacob looked toward the back seat. Moses was sleeping peacefully. Then he stretched out and fell into a dream of Anna. She was at the port in Barcelona, on the ship's deck, her blond hair flying free. She was smiling at him, but each time he tried to get close to her, she evaporated like a passing mist, like ashes blown in the wind.

Chapter 28

They ate before leaving the outskirts of Montpellier. Besides some cheeses and a bit of fruit, Vipond had brought them one piece of chocolate cake each. Moses savored it to the last bite, then picked the crumbs off his shirt and the back seat and ate them all.

"We should keep going. I don't want to get to Carcassonne too late," the old man said.

Jacob considered staying up front but finally opted to stretch out in the back seat and try to sleep more, leaving the passenger seat to Moses.

Moses spent most of the ride studying the car's gearshift and other features, touching everything and imitating Vipond's driving. Vipond glanced at him frequently in amusement. He had always marveled at the power of a child's imagination.

"Are you driving your own car, Moses?" he asked.

"Oh yes, I love driving."

The old man smiled, then studied the surrounding country again. It had been years since he had ventured out of Valence and had hardly even left his apartment building in recent years. He had forgotten that he loved nature, the interminable forests, the beautiful prairies. He was anxious to see the Pyrenees again. He remembered how beautiful they were. He thought about his trip to Cuba and wondered how Buenos Aires would compare. He chuckled to think that here he was, as old as could be, making the longest trip of his life. Yet the even longer journey was yet to begin.

Vipond's thoughts wandered back to his childhood, when he was a boy like Moses. He had been so afraid of hell, a childish notion he had since disabused himself of. He had not been overly concerned about his soul in recent years, nor about the fact that his body was old and sick. He had simply been carried along by the impetuous rush of life. One day followed the next, without giving the impression of leading anywhere in particular. He still had that impression, which worried him a bit. How was it possible that, being as close as he was to death, he gave it such little thought? Since childhood, Vipond had intuited that at a certain age people stop asking hard questions— not because they are no longer interested in the answers but rather because they are afraid of them.

"What're you thinking about?" Moses asked.

Vipond was not sure how to answer. "I don't think you'd be able to understand if I explained it. You're still in the world of fantasy. You make reality fit with what you want to see . . ."

"Do adults not do that?" Moses said. At first Vipond chuckled at the boy's innocence, but then he thought, perhaps, that is exactly what adults did. They lived in their imaginary worlds, worried about the problems that were never going to materialize, wishing for things they were unwilling to fight for, and ignoring the eternal question of the real meaning of life.

"Maybe we do," the old man finally mused. "I'd just never thought of it like that."

"You know what? Sometimes I imagine what South America and Buenos Aires are like," Moses said, suddenly serious.

"And what are they like in your imagination?" Vipond asked, expecting a fantastical description.

"I imagine everything is new, which is why they call it the New World. The streets are clean and straight, the buildings look all shiny and pretty on the outside, like parts of Paris. The people are rich. The country's so young the rich people won't have had time to rob all the poor people. I heard that over there nobody asks you where you're from because everybody's from somewhere far away. The days will be really long, and I don't think it's as cold as here. And, best of all, my mother and father are there." Moses finished his pronouncement with great satisfaction.

"Well, I think you've painted a pretty picture," Vipond answered. He did not know much about Argentina either, other than the fact that it had been a Spanish colony, that the English had wanted it, and that it had vast tracts of virgin land.

"I think they speak Spanish, but in a different way than in Spain. They're all really pale and they don't hate Jews."

Moses's last prediction took Vipond by surprise. "And why do you say that?"

"The French hate Jews, like the Germans and Swiss, but the Argentines don't. They let us come live with them," was his naïve conclusion.

They were so wrapped up in the conversation that they did not notice a checkpoint of the paramilitary French militia, the Milice Français, some two hundred yards ahead.

One of the militiamen raised his hand for the vehicle to stop. For a brief moment, Vipond was tempted to speed up and run the fascists over, but he braked. They had nothing to fear; all their papers were in order.

"Documents for yourself and the children, please, sir," the militiaman barked. He wore blue pants, a brown shirt, and a blue beret. His fellow militiamen kept their machine guns trained on the vehicle's occupants.

Vipond reached for the identification papers and removed their three passports from the glove compartment, then handed them over.

Jacob woke and sat up in the back seat. Moses looked nervous, but he did not speak. He kept his eyes on the men's guns.

"Where are you headed?" the militiaman asked.

"To Carcassonne," Vipond said, volunteering no more information than what was required.

"For what purpose?"

Vipond ran his hand across his bald head, noting the sweat. It was very hot. It was late afternoon already, and the farther south they got, the hotter it became.

"I'm taking the children to see some family, then I'm heading back to Valence," he said.

"Why have you come this way? These roads are dangerous, overrun by partisans."

Vipond was tempted to say he was happy to hear that and hoped that very soon all the collaborationists would pay for their crimes, but he simply looked at the militiaman with the tired eyes of an old man who has seen too much. The militiaman frowned, opened the passports, and studied the faces of the three passengers. Then he walked to the makeshift guardhouse fashioned from decaying wood, said something to a superior, and returned with the passports.

"Your papers are in order, but these boys are the children of Spaniards."

"Yes," Vipond answered, puzzled. That was the identity he and Perrot had chosen in order to cross the border more easily.

"All Spaniards must be registered at the Gurs camp. You'll have to come with me," the militiaman said, handing the passports back.

"I think there's been a mistake. The boys are French. Their parents have been in France for over twenty years. They aren't Republican immigrants," Vipond said.

"We'll need to confirm that with the records. If it's true, you can continue on your journey."

Vipond's mind raced. He had to react, had to do something. He looked around wildly and noticed no cars or motorcycles in sight. Could the militia possibly be there with no means of transportation?

Without thinking more, he pressed the accelerator and the old motor roared to life. He swerved around the large drums blocking the way and drove straight toward one of the militiamen, who dove into the neighboring field.

"Get down!" Vipond barked, and he himself ducked, keeping his eyes just level with the steering wheel.

They heard rounds of machine-gun fire, and Vipond swerved violently to protect the tires. Then he sped up and tried to clear his head. Traveling to Carcassonne was now out of the question, as he had given that information to the militiaman. Plus, German military force would be waiting there. The militiamen would send a description of the car and its passengers. They had to switch routes, go by some other road. It would not be very hard to find two boys and an old man in an old Renault. But could he drive without stopping to the border before their description reached it? He had no choice but to try.

The shots followed them until they rounded the first curve. Vipond drove as fast as he could along the back roads while Moses wept in the front seat. Jacob eventually reached and pulled him into the back and climbed clumsily into the front.

"What are we going to do?" His voice shook.

"Head straight for the border," Vipond said, his eyes glued to the road.

"But how far is that?"

Vipond tried to calculate the distance in his head. Unsure of a definite route, he did not know exactly how many miles it would be.

"I think it's around two hundred miles. There's a pass at Molló. If they don't have a telephone, our description won't have reached them," Vipond said. He was shaken by the turn of events.

"Can the car make it that far? It's a long way," Jacob said.

The old man thought it over and finally nodded. His legs and back ached, but he could rest once they got to Spain.

For hours the old Renault raced along the winding roads of southern France, as Vipond eschewed towns and main roads. He and Perrot had foreseen the need to travel without stopping even at gas stations and had filled the trunk with extra cans of gasoline. It was almost night by the time they approached the Pyrenees. They would not reach the border during daylight. His body felt weaker as the time dragged on. His left leg was cramped and sore. He touched it and felt wetness. One of the bullets had found him, draining him of strength and blood. Cold sweat prickled at his spine, and he could barely resist the urge to close his eyes.

"Are you all right?" Jacob asked. In the dying light, Jacob could see beads of sweat running down their chauffeur's face.

"Yes, don't worry. We'll be at the border before long."

"Will they let us through at night?"

"I suppose. I've never driven a car across a border," Vipond mused.

Moses was asleep again. He had exhausted himself crying after the fright at the checkpoint and had fallen into a fitful rest.

Jacob's eyes went back and forth between Vipond and the road. Jacob held his breath every time it seemed they would veer off the narrow streets, but Vipond always straightened at the last moment.

"The papers are in the glove compartment," Vipond began. "The suitcases are in the back. The boat passage is in my wallet. You'd better get the tickets out."

Jacob reached his hand into the inside pocket of Vipond's jacket and gingerly pulled out the tickets.

Vipond grimaced in pain but remained calm and resolute, as if seeing the end of a long journey.

"Why are you telling me all this? You're coming with us. You're going to South America. My parents will be so happy to see you." The quivering words rushed out of Jacob.

The old man turned his head slightly and touched his hand to Jacob's hair. "You're a good boy, Jacob. Don't ever change. Sometimes this world can turn us into something we shouldn't be. Take care of your brother and your parents."

They could not see more than a few yards in front of the car. Vipond thought of how he would not, after all, see the Pyrenees again. He thought of all the things he had left undone and how many places he would never get to see. He regretted his many years of apathy, closed up in his Valence boardinghouse, licking the wounds of old age. He told himself he really should have lived more, and he understood clearly that the only true reason to go out into the world was to love. His heart, withered by bitterness and selfishness, had undermined his ability to give of himself to others. Jana and Eleazar had managed to penetrate his apathy. Now, their children had provided him a grand adventure, and he was profoundly grateful. True love welled up in his heart for the two boys. He would live on somehow in their memory. The boys had to get out of there and start all over with their parents.

Vipond started crying when the dim Renault lights showed a sign indicating five miles to the border. He had to hold on. Just a little longer now and they would make it.

"I won't be crossing the border," he told Jacob at last.

"What?"

"I wouldn't make it far. You'd have to take care of me, and you'd miss the boat. The police would question you about my wound. I'm going to leave you at the border."

Jacob was speechless. He squeezed Vipond's arm, soaked in sweat, then studied his pale, sick, fragile face as best he could in the dark.

"I thank heaven I had the chance to know you two. You've made me remember the sweet taste of happiness, and I'm satisfied. Now you mean more to me than my own life. This old bag of bones doesn't have any more fight in it. Maybe we'll see each other in eternity."

The car swerved dangerously. Vipond lost consciousness momentarily but awoke with a jerk. Jacob grabbed and steadied the wheel to keep them from plummeting over the edge of the cliffs.

Then they saw the border checkpoint. Vipond rolled the car off the road and hid it as best he could among some trees, about three hundred yards from the guardhouse.

"We can't leave you like this," Jacob said.

Vipond turned on the car's interior light and looked at Moses's sleeping body. Then he turned his tear-filled eyes to Jacob.

"It's been a true pleasure to know you. Don't ever grow up. And if you do, don't ever forget the boy you were. Kiss your mother for me and give your father a big hug."

"We won't leave you."

Vipond put his hand on Jacob's shoulder. He was so pale the light bounced off his face. Moses sat up suddenly, confused about where they were and what was happening. Vipond smiled at him, then closed his eyes. He was so tired. Whatever strength remained was quickly vanishing. He thought about saying something else, but it was too hard. He leaned back and let himself go.

"What's happening?" Moses asked.

Jacob wiped the tears from his face and said in a dry voice, "Mr. Vipond is just really tired. He's going to stay here and rest for a bit."

Jacob got out of the car and took their suitcases, passports, letter of safe conduct and authorization for travel, and the money. Then he turned off the car lights and the motor.

"Come on, Moses."

The boys walked slowly toward the guard station, Jacob carrying their suitcases. A half-asleep gendarme sat in the guardhouse, and he jumped when he saw the boys. This particular border point got little traffic, and there were no Germans there at night. Most fugitives avoided the roads in their attempts to cross over, and the Nazis concentrated their efforts on the surrounding countryside. If the Spanish caught the fugitives who managed to slip through and they did not have their papers in order, they would be shipped back to France.

"Where are you going at this hour of the night?" The guard had not recovered from the shock. He turned the flashlight on them.

"We need to cross the border. We have family waiting for us in Spain," Jacob said with as much confidence as he could muster.

"Are you Spaniards?" he asked, checking their passports.

"We aren't, but our parents are. They're sending us to stay with family for a while."

"Makes sense. Things have gotten pretty ugly here. Who wouldn't send their kids away?" the gendarme muttered.

Jacob and Moses stayed quiet. The gendarme studied the rest of their papers, then looked down the road and was surprised to see no car anywhere.

"Who brought you?" he asked.

"A friend dropped us off a couple miles back and we walked the rest of the way."

The gendarme stamped their passports, stood up, and raised the barrier. When the guards on the other side saw the French barrier raised, they raised the Spanish barrier and turned on the lights.

The boys walked calmly through the short stretch of land that belonged to no country. Though they walked away from danger, sadness gripped them. They were also leaving so many other things behind: people who had helped them and who, while the war lasted, would still be in danger. But mostly they thought of Vipond. They had once more been abandoned—they were on their own again—yet they knew it was not really like that. The old man had left this world with a smile on his lips. Love was the only thing that kept people from suffering the eternal disappointment of life.

The boys reached the Spanish side. Officers wearing capes stood with their hands on their hips and watched them approach. They were annoyed at having been wakened from their post.

"Stop there," the customs officer said in Spanish.

Jacob held out their papers. The man scrutinized their documents, then looked up at the sad, exhausted faces of the boys. "Spanish family. Fine. Go on."

Jacob stepped forward and his right foot came down on Spanish soil. He breathed out a long sigh of relief. Moses followed and, before they knew it, they were walking in the outskirts of Molló, a picturesque stone village that reminded them of Le Chambon-sur-Lignon. This was the beginning of safety.

Chapter 29

Molló
August 12, 1943

Though it was summer, the night was cool. Jacob and Moses huddled together in the doorway of a church. There was nothing they could do until the next day. Moses soon nodded off on Jacob's shoulder, but Jacob was alert all night. Guilt for what had happened weighed on him. Vipond's corpse now lay in an abandoned car on the other side of the border. It would not take the authorities long to find him, but Jacob would have preferred to bury him in a beautiful cemetery in the Pyrenees, where Vipond could rest under the care of the mountains. Had Vipond not driven them across France, he would still be alive.

Jacob could not stop asking himself how they had managed to escape. Countless Jewish children and adults had ended up in

Germany or Poland, enduring humiliating work, the deathly winter climate, and the cruelty of the Nazis. Who or what sent some to an unjust death but saved others against all odds? The fact that this question had no answer brought no comfort. He wept silently for a while. As dawn approached, Jacob gently lowered Moses's head onto one of the suitcases and stood up to greet the colorful changing of the guard.

It was Spain—and yet the mountains, the trees, and the horses grazing in a nearby field were the exact same as in France. The border, the only thing distinguishing one place from the other, had been imposed by humans alone. Adults were always judging one another based on appearance, religion, skin color, or wealth. Children were not like that. For them, everyone was equal, and they hardly noticed differences between peers.

Jacob heard footsteps on the gravel behind him and turned quickly, assuming Moses had woken up and was hungry for breakfast. Instead, he found himself looking into the round face and small, square-framed glasses of a priest who was studying him with evident curiosity.

"I've never found a sunrise as beautiful as in Molló," the man said with a light, elegant voice.

Jacob did not understand Spanish, though in Le Chambon-sur-Lignon he had picked up some basic phrases with the help of some Spanish-speaking friends.

"I'm sorry, Father. I don't understand what you're saying," Jacob answered in French.

The priest switched to a very rudimentary French, but it was enough for Jacob to understand.

"I saw the other boy sleeping. You are alone? You spent the night outside?"

Jacob was not sure how he should answer. Could he trust this man, or would he go to the authorities?

"I won't do anything to you. I just want to help," the priest said.

Jacob crossed his arms. He knew they would need help getting to Barcelona but did not know how far away it was. Perhaps an entire day's drive. Yet he intended for them to keep their distance from the Spaniards, who were likely to turn them in. Jacob had heard that Franco's government was allied with the Germans and that the Spanish police had turned any number of Jews over to the French authorities.

"We're traveling to Barcelona. We need to catch a ship to Argentina," he finally said, continuing in French.

"And when does the ship sail?" the priest asked. He pulled a cap out of the pocket of his cassock and put it on, then checked his pocket watch.

"In two days, from the port in Barcelona."

The priest was intrigued. "You don't have much time. Why are you going to Argentina?"

"Our parents are there," Jacob said. He started to relax, sensing the man was sincere.

"I can get you to Vic, and from there you can take a bus. I think they only leave in the mornings, so you'll have to spend the night in the city. I know some nuns who would let you stay the night. I'd like to do more, but I need to get back by the afternoon, to celebrate the mass. There's no one who can take my place."

Moses woke and stretched and rubbed his eyes, still dazed by sleep.

"This is my brother, Marcel," Jacob said, using the names on their passport.

"I'm pleased to meet you, Marcel. I'm Father Fermín."

Moses shook hands and then, with a moment's pause, declared, "I'm hungry."

"Well, we can take care of that," the priest said. He returned to the entryway of the church. The priest set their suitcases inside and then walked the boys to a nearby café.

"Jordi, please bring breakfast for three," he said in Spanish.

A few minutes later the waiter brought two glasses of milk, one cup of coffee, and a tray of something that looked like long, fried sticks.

"What's that?" Moses asked.

The priest smiled and said, "Churros." Jacob and Moses soon discovered the universal appeal of churros and gobbled up every last one of them.

The priest sipped his coffee, softened with cream. When the boys were satisfied, he led them to his car. "I'll be right back," he said, leaving them to wait in the car. He retrieved their suitcases, then locked the church, rolled up the sleeves of his cassock, and sat behind the wheel. The car was an old, beat-up 1927 Fiat that threatened to fall apart if its occupants breathed too deeply. It started with strange popping noises, black smoke billowing from the exhaust pipe.

"She's old and it's hard to find gas for her, but don't worry—she'll get us to Vic. I don't think she'd make it to Barcelona," the priest said.

The boys remained silent for the whole ride. The priest kept his word and took them to the convent in the middle of the city. He parked at the entrance and helped them with their suitcases, then knocked at the wooden door. It looked like it had been closed for centuries, but they heard footsteps, then the rattling of keys, and finally the heavy door creaked open.

"Sister Clara, I've brought two boys who need somewhere to stay tonight. Early tomorrow they need to take the bus to Barcelona."

"Father Fermín, how wonderful to see you again. God bless you. The Mother Superior will be delighted you've come to visit."

They followed the nun into the building, walked along the cloister, and through the archways saw the inner courtyard with a well in the center. They reached another building and went up a stone staircase, at the top of which the nun stopped before a door. She knocked and entered without waiting for an answer.

Jacob and Moses were surprised to see the Mother Superior was rather young and pleasant-looking. She received them with a smile, clucked over the boys affectionately, and asked them to have a seat. The priest briefly explained what the boys needed, and she agreed to house them.

"Tomorrow morning we'll take them to the bus station," she said.

"They don't speak Spanish," the priest warned.

"What do they speak?" she asked with her pretty smile.

"French, though the older one understands a bit of Spanish."

"How fortunate. I speak a bit of French, and we have a French sister among us."

"Thank you so much, Reverend Mother," Fermín said. He turned to the boys. "Be good now, my boys. The sisters are not in the habit of receiving strangers."

Jacob nodded seriously. Father Fermín bid them farewell and left the room, leaving Jacob and Moses alone with the Mother Superior.

"You can share one of our cells," she said in French.

"Thank you . . . Mother," Jacob said, unsure how to address her.

"Reverend Mother," she corrected him gently. Jacob smiled, and her heart melted to see the helpless boys. She wondered how much they had been through to get where they were and what all lay ahead of them.

"Why don't you go out to the courtyard and play, and we'll call you when it's time for supper."

They left their suitcases in her office, but Jacob kept their documents, tickets, and money on him. He would never part with the precious pieces of paper that would allow them to escape the continent.

They spent the rest of the afternoon exploring the courtyard and the buildings around it. They found a fountain and had a drink. While they were sitting down to rest, a nun came up to them. She was hardly more than a girl.

"Good afternoon, I'm Sister Ruth," she said in French.

"Good afternoon, Sister," Jacob answered.

"It's time for supper. Please follow me."

The boys received the news happily, as it had been a long time since the churros that morning. They followed Sister Ruth down several hallways to the cafeteria. It was a large room with an intricately painted dome and columns built into the wall.

"We take our meals in silence," Sister Ruth explained, "and one of the sisters reads from that book." She pointed to a lectern.

They were the first to arrive. Sister Ruth sat them at one end of a long table. "What part of France are you from?" she asked.

"Paris," Moses answered.

Jacob gave his brother's leg a squeeze under the table. They had to be careful, being a long way from the boat still.

"I've never been to Paris. I grew up in a small town called Roussillon. I've been in Spain for two years. My order sent me here. After the civil war in Spain, many convents were practically empty, and they're trying to fill them again."

"We really appreciate your hospitality," Jacob said.

"It's our Christian duty," Sister Ruth answered. Her hair was hidden beneath the habit, but from her freckles and red eyebrows, Jacob figured she was a redhead.

"I'm really hungry," Moses said in his frank way.

"It won't be long now. Then you can go right to bed, and I'll take you to the bus station early in the morning. I think it'll take about three hours to get to Barcelona. It's a big city. You'd better go right to the ship and speak to the captain to see if you can stay on the ship tomorrow night. I doubt that would be a problem."

Over a hundred nuns filed into the cafeteria and, without saying a word, all sat down at the same time around the table. One of the sisters went to a large lectern, prayed over the meal, and then started reading with a tired, chantlike voice. As the novices served the water, the bread, and the rest of the meal, the reader's monotonous voice was the only sound to be heard in the enormous hall.

Jacob and Moses gobbled up everything they were served, then waited patiently for the sisters to finish. Every now and then a nun would look over at them and smile, but no one came up to them after the meal.

Sister Ruth led them to their cell. There were two beds with white sheets and a rough brown blanket. The only decoration on the bare walls was a crucifix. Their suitcases were waiting at the foot of the beds.

"I hope you rest well. We'll get an early start tomorrow. We won't have time to eat breakfast, but I'll pack you something for the road," the nun said before turning off the light and locking the door with a key.

As soon as they heard her footsteps die away, Moses sat up and started talking. "This place gives me the creeps. Can I sleep in your bed?"

"Of course." Jacob pulled his blanket back.

"One more day and we start our journey for South America," Moses said, sighing. He could not stand the waiting.

"I'm impatient for it too," Jacob said, hugging Moses to him. Despite the heat of the day, it was quite cold in the cell—yet the boys were glad to get cooled off. The silence of the convent was as complete as the darkness. Jacob had the sensation of being in a tomb. This made him think of Vipond. He presumed the authorities had found Vipond's body by now and had, he hoped, buried him. No one would ever know where the man's tomb was, but Jacob vowed to come back when he was older to visit the spot where the actor had died. He felt weariness slowly and pleasantly stealing through his body and mind until he was fully asleep.

They woke at the sound of keys jingling. It was still dark, and when the sister turned on the light, they were momentarily blinded. They had slept in their clothes and only had to put on their shoes and follow the nun in silence. They walked back down the cloister to the big wooden door and out to the street. Moses let out a deep breath. He had not liked the feeling of being locked up in the convent. After a few minutes of walking, they came to a small vacant lot where some people were gathered around two old buses.

Sister Ruth made sure all the details were correct, bought their tickets, helped them load their luggage, and took them to their seats.

"The bus goes straight to Barcelona. Then you'll walk to the port. It isn't too far."

"Thank you, Sister Ruth."

The nun smiled at them, stroked their hair, and made her way out of the bus. Jacob and Moses remained sitting while the rest of the passengers filed in. Fifteen minutes later, the vehicle eased out of the vacant lot and headed down the main road. By the time the sun could be seen on the horizon, they had left Vic behind.

The bus rumbled leisurely through the mountains, taking the tight curves slowly. The landscape gradually changed from mountains to an endless succession of pine forests, croplands, grapevines, and small red-roofed villages.

Within two hours, the bus stopped in a town called La Garriga. The rest of the passengers got out to stretch their legs, but Moses and Jacob stayed glued to their seats. They pulled out the sandwiches the nuns had prepared for them and started to eat. The sandwiches tasted good, and the boys were enjoying them when they heard voices behind them. Two older teenage boys were talking to them, and Jacob turned around to look.

"Can I have a bite?" one of the boys asked.

Jacob made a sign to show he did not understand what he had said.

"Eat. Hungry," the boy said slowly, touching his mouth and rubbing his stomach.

Jacob nodded and gave him a bite of the sandwich, and the two older boys came closer to them. "Where are you going?" they asked.

Jacob could understand that much and replied, "Barcelona."

"Yeah, we're all going to Barcelona. I mean where exactly?"

"To Barcelona. Boat . . ." That was as far as Jacob could explain in Spanish.

"Ah ha, you're going to take a ship. Did you hear that, Ramón? The French boys are going to hop on a boat," one of the teenagers said.

"We can take you there when we get to Barcelona," Ramón offered. "We're not in any hurry, and you might get lost."

Jacob could guess more or less what they were saying. At first he shook his head, but then he shrugged. Perhaps, he thought while finishing his sandwich, the teenagers might be able to help them after all.

The rest of the passengers returned to the bus, but when the driver turned the key, the motor gave no sign of life. He tried starting several times, but to no good end. He shouted something and motioned toward town. The teenager who had tried Jacob's sandwich said, "He's going to get another battery. We have to wait."

Jacob understood "wait" and started to worry. He stayed pressed into the seat beside Moses while the rest of the passengers got back off the bus.

Jacob didn't know whether to stay or go. What would they do if the bus never started? They would miss the boat if they had to spend the night in La Garriga.

They had to wait four hours total before leaving. Jacob and Moses let out their collectively held breath when the driver turned the key and the bus finally came to life.

They entered the outskirts of Barcelona in the late afternoon. Jacob and Moses had not seen such a large city since they had left Lyon. Their faces were pressed up against the glass and their eyes drank in every building and street until they arrived at a large plaza in what must have been the heart of the city.

The other passengers started gathering their things. Jacob and Moses got their suitcases and left the bus amid general confusion. They did not know which direction to go. The teenagers who had spoken with them earlier caught up with them.

"We can carry your bags," one of them said.

Though the boy's words were incomprehensible to Jacob, the meaning was clear enough. He shook his head and held the suitcase tightly to him.

They headed down a narrow street. It was starting to get dark. There were still people on the streets, but things were slowing down, shops were beginning to close, and soon it would be night.

"Where are you going to sleep?" one of the teenagers asked.

Jacob was starting to get nervous. He could understand the Spanish word for "sleep" and shrugged the question off. He did not have a good feeling about these strangers.

"You can stay with us. Uncle John would happy to have you. We don't live far from here. The port's about twenty minutes away, but it's not the best place to spend the night."

They came to a wider street, full of women talking with sailors and bars with their doors open. At the end of that street they could see a bigger road ahead. Jacob decided that was where they should go. He motioned to Moses and started running. Moses followed, his suitcase in hand. The teenagers started shouting after them, but Jacob and Moses ignored them. Jacob sped up and reached a covered shopping arcade. He looked back and saw that Moses had fallen behind. The older boys had almost caught up to them. He ran to Moses and grabbed his hand.

"Throw your suitcase down," he said.

"What?" Moses asked, still running.

"Throw it!" he repeated, throwing his own suitcase in the middle of the street.

The teenagers stopped to pick them up and started rummaging inside.

Jacob's heart was in his throat as they ran. It was not far 'til the bigger road. But Moses tripped and scraped his knee, whimpering at the pain.

"Run, Moses!" Jacob said, seeing the teenagers resume the chase. Finally, they reached the wider avenue and ran down it. A few people milled about, but Jacob spotted a policeman and ran near to him. When the thieves saw where the boys had gone, they turned and ran back down the alley.

"What's going on, boys? Everything all right?" the policeman asked.

"Mr. Policeman," Jacob stuttered in very bad Spanish. "Bad boys. We run. They take things."

The policeman looked all around but saw no one suspicious. "Where are you from?" he asked.

"France. Tomorrow boat Argentina. Mr. Policeman, please. Where boat?" Jacob answered.

"The port's not far. You can almost see the ocean from here," he said. The boys just stared at him with their wide eyes. He sighed and shrugged. "Fine, I'll take you, but we have to be quick. I'm on duty and can't get far off my round."

Jacob understood enough to know they should follow him. They had no luggage, but Jacob still had their tickets, their identification, and their money. He hoped the captain would let them board.

The sight of enormous ships announced their arrival. They shimmered in the lights of the port and cast their reflection over the dark water.

"What's the boat called?" the policeman asked.

Jacob pulled out their tickets and read the name, *La Habana*.

"The Spanish Line? It's that big white one there," the policeman said, pointing. He walked them up to the deserted gangway. "Go on up. I'll wait here. If everything's okay, look over the deck and give me a wave." His hands pantomimed everything he said.

Jacob and Moses made their way up the gangway to the main deck. Sailors were busy all around them and paid no attention to the boys.

"Sir," Jacob called to one, a very dark man with severe features. He wore a black-and-white striped uniform and a cap.

"What is it, little man?" He spoke fast, as if he had no time to lose.

"We, this boat, tomorrow." Jacob held out their tickets. "In Barcelona, nobody. Talk captain."

"The control room is that way." The man pointed toward some windows on an upper deck.

Jacob and Moses went up a set of stairs to the upper deck and opened a door. The helmsman and some other officials stared at the boys as they entered the control room.

"Good evening. We talk captain?" Jacob attempted.

"What's going on?" asked a bald uniformed man with a large mustache.

"Captain, we brothers, the Alejos. Tomorrow, boat to Argentina. Tonight, Barcelona, no sleep."

The captain frowned. "You're traveling alone? Do you have authorization to travel?"

Jacob presumed the man was asking for their papers and handed them over. The captain studied them, including their tickets.

"Your room won't be ready until tomorrow, but if you can pay for the extra night, we can move you to one that's already prepared. Where's your luggage?" The captain made a gesture like carrying something.

Jacob shook his head. "Bad boys. They take things. We run."

The captain nodded in disgust. There were always parasites lurking about the port seeking out people to exploit. It was the same all over the world.

The captain looked to one of the other men standing near. "Take some clothing to the room where the boys will stay." Looking back at Jacob, he said, "Sometimes passengers leave luggage and other things on board. You can't wear the same clothes for four weeks."

Jacob did not catch it all, but he could tell it was good news for them. "Thank you, Captain, thank you," he said.

"Captain García Urrutia, at your service." He bowed.

Jacob and Moses were escorted out of the control room by a sailor. They peered over the deck and waved to the policeman, who waved back before turning and walking away.

The sailor led them down two decks and through a hallway to a room. He opened the door and stepped aside for them to enter. Jacob and Moses were dumbstruck. It was a big suite with a private bathroom, a small living room, and two bedrooms.

Jacob waved to take it all in, then pointed to himself and Moses with a puzzled look. "This? Us?"

"Yes, little man. You've got first-class tickets. The dining room is one floor down, and across from it is the game room, a bar, and a restaurant. It's already past dinner, but if you order something, they'll deliver it to your room. Use the bell," he said. When the man pointed to a red button, Jacob understood enough to piece together that pushing the button would bring dinner.

After the sailor left them, Jacob and Moses just stared at each other in silence. Then they burst out laughing, shouting and jumping up and down. They kicked off their shoes and jumped on the beds until they were exhausted.

They did not end up eating that night. After the initial surprise wore off, they melted into the soft feather pillows and fell into sweet sleep. They dreamed of Buenos Aires, of their parents, of the future awaiting them in Argentina. The long, dangerous journey across Europe was almost over. Nothing could keep them from being together with their parents again for forever.

Chapter 30

Montevideo
September 9, 1943

The weeks at sea went by more slowly than Jacob and Moses had envisioned. The boat made its first stop in Valencia, then Cádiz. After three days in the Mediterranean Sea, they finally entered the immeasurable Atlantic Ocean. In two more days, they passed the Canary Islands and then bid a long farewell to land. For nearly two weeks, they saw nothing but an interminable blue that changed according to the intensity of the light and the time of day. A week after setting sail, they hit their first bad storm. The boat rocked so violently that Jacob and Moses vomited for two days straight.

In the evenings, they ate dinner at Captain García Urrutia's table. He was an experienced sailor who had sailed every ocean and sea on the globe and who would soon be retiring. He was from Spain but had spent most of his life in Uruguay. He had a wife and three children in Montevideo. A friendly but reserved man, he was well respected by both his crew and the passengers. He had taken a liking to the Alejo brothers and took them under his wing for the whole long journey. Whenever he had a free moment, he would visit their suite or invite them to his to work on their Spanish. Moses picked it up very quickly. After a few weeks, Jacob could understand everything but spoke with a strong French accent.

Jacob and Moses also became friends with the children of several other families on board, especially the children of the Spanish vice-consul to Buenos Aires. They kept a tight lip about their true background and recent journey through two countries, though they were often tempted to tell the new friends they made, especially the captain.

There on the boat, the war seemed far away. Jacob had the sense that they were going to another world, with different problems and concerns. Though many refugees from France, Germany, and Belgium traveled on the boat, most of the passengers were Spanish or Argentine.

During the journey, Jacob and Moses thought often about their friends in Le Chambon-sur-Lignon, wondering how they were. Not a single day passed for Jacob without thoughts of Anna. He wanted to write the Trocmés as soon as they arrived in Buenos Aires to see if they had news of her.

On the morning of September 9, after a turn at Punta del Este, Jacob and Moses were with the captain on the ship's bridge when the boat came into view of the city.

"Look! My beloved Montevideo," the captain said, a smile of excitement playing on his lips. He had seen the brilliant scene of the city rising up from the mouth of the Río de la Plata dozens of times, and it never ceased to stir him. He loved this place, his home. There he would eventually drop anchor for the last time.

"Is the city very pretty?" Moses asked in clean Spanish with a Uruguayan accent, thanks to his tutor.

"Montevideo itself is beautiful, but the people are what make it wonderful. It's a pity you won't be able to really get to know the city. We'll only be docked today. We'll leave for Buenos Aires early tomorrow morning."

"How far away is Buenos Aires?"

"Not far, hardly four hours from here."

It was a gray morning, with a light drizzle falling over the river. The ship went through the necessary maneuvers to dock. The passengers who would be staying in Montevideo were already on deck with their luggage by the time the boat was in position and the gangway was lowered.

The captain had promised to show Jacob and Moses the city. The boys wanted to buy clothes as well. The clothes they had worn on the ship were not their own, and they wanted to look their best when they met their parents.

An hour later, the captain was escorting the two boys through the streets around the port toward his home near the Plaza Zabala. They knocked at the bars on the door, and a black woman with curly white hair opened. She jumped with gladness when she saw them.

"Good heavens, it's the captain!" she said, welcoming him with a hug. Next came the captain's wife, Charlot, and two of his children, Claudia and Martín. The oldest son was already married and lived in Santa Lucía.

Jacob and Moses felt a sort of happy, nervous jealousy watching the scene of affectionate greeting. Now that they were so close, they could hardly breathe for the anticipation of finding their parents. The moment was only hours away, yet they worried it would never come.

"These are the Alejo brothers, Jean and Marcel. They're on their way to Argentina to find their parents."

"It's a pleasure to meet you," Charlot said. She was elegant and beautiful with her blond hair and fine blue dress.

"Thank you, ma'am."

"They'll see their parents tomorrow, and the boys want to make a good impression. Perhaps you could help them shop for some clothes," the captain suggested.

"Of course. But first let's celebrate their arrival with mate," his wife responded.

Jacob and Moses followed the family inside and sat down while the maid prepared the mate. The day was starting to clear up, and shy rays of sunlight filtered through the windows. The captain's family asked all about the trip and the war in Europe, as news was slow in reaching them. The newspapers reported German losses, but no one knew for sure what was going on.

"At least in Spain there's no war," the captain joked.

"Mm-hmm," Charlot snorted. Second-generation Polish, she was concerned for family members who were still in Spain.

"The Allies are slowly making their way through Italy, driving the Germans north. The Russians are recovering their positions, and German cities are bombed day and night," the captain summarized.

Charlot nodded stonily. "Those Nazis deserve it. They've destroyed my grandparents' country and killed tens of thousands of people."

The captain's daughter, Claudia, handed Jacob the mate. He looked at it suspiciously, sniffed, then took a cautious sip. As the hot water hit his tongue, he winced at the bitterness, and everyone laughed.

"You'll get used to it," the girl said.

On the side, Charlot asked her husband, "Have you heard what's going on in Argentina?"

"What do you know?" he said, intrigued.

"There's been a military coup, and they deposed President Ramón Castillo," she said.

"Well, they finally dropped the pretense of presidents handpicked by General Uriburu, though I doubt another coup d'état will fix the country."

"May God protect Argentina from her leaders!" Charlot said with a wry smile.

"Well, and let's not even start on Uruguay. Our leaders could not exactly be accused of decency, you could say," the captain retorted. While Uruguay was known as the Switzerland of the Americas, the crisis of 1929 and poor governance had squandered nearly all the country's wealth.

After several rounds of mate, the captain's wife and daughter took Jacob and Moses out to buy shirts, pants, and jackets. Jacob was euphoric when they returned. He was wearing his first long pants, and the boys felt like princes.

The captain's eyebrows rose as he took in the new elegance of his young friends. They packed their clothes in a suitcase Charlot gave them, said their goodbyes, and headed back to the boat.

"Won't you sleep at home tonight?" Jacob asked the captain.

"The day after next, I'll be back in Montevideo. A captain never abandons the ship 'til he's brought her safely home," he answered, smiling.

They walked back up the gangway of *La Habana* and dined together one last time in the main dining room. The next morning, the ship would sail for Buenos Aires, and that very day Jacob and Moses would try to find their parents.

"Dinner has been delicious," the captain said, dressed in his formal uniform.

Jacob finished off what was left on his plate and looked all around at the luxurious tables. He thought of the miserable people crammed into the velodrome, the detention camps, the needs overwhelming the provisions in Le Chambon-sur-Lignon. His stomach grew hard.

"Lots of people in France won't have supper at all tonight," he said quietly, needing to give voice to the guilt.

"That is true," the captain said. Then he stood and asked the boys to follow him to the deck. They looked toward the port, where the lights of Montevideo were shining. It was a beautiful scene the captain did not want them to miss.

"They call this the New World, but don't be deceived, boys. People are the same here as in the Old World. Greed, envy, hatred, violence, and injustice also control the streets of South America. We're a mixture of Spanish, Portuguese, Italian, Russian, German, Polish, British, African, and natives. But we've all got the same ambitions and passions in our hearts."

Jacob felt more confused. "But people say Argentina is a land of opportunity, where you can be truly free." For months he had dreamed of South America as something new and different.

"It certainly is a land of opportunity, without a doubt. There is much to do; people adapt easily to their new home with the support of their communities. But the politicians and the powerful always get the best slices of the cake."

"That's not fair," Moses complained.

"No, but it's reality. When you're young, you dream about making the world a better place, overturning injustice and inequality. But within time you just settle for getting by. I don't mean to discourage you. What would the world become if each generation didn't dream of changing it?"

Jacob leaned his chin on the cool metal of the rail. He understood what the captain was saying, but he knew it would be different with his generation. All they had suffered with the war, the death, the desolation . . . It would not be for nothing. As soon as the Allies beat the Germans, they would build a just land. Jacob was confident but did not share his thoughts with the captain.

"The important thing is that you'll find your parents tomorrow. You already know where I live, so if you run into any trouble, you can come to my house or send me a letter. If I'm away, my family will help you."

"Thank you," Jacob said.

"Yes, thank you so much, Captain," Moses echoed.

The captain chuckled and stroked Moses's cheek. "Your Spanish is flawless now!"

"We'll miss you very much," Jacob said, straightening up again. He had grown much taller even since leaving Le Chambon-sur-Lignon.

The captain held out his hand to shake, then made a military salute, which the boys clumsily imitated.

"Tomorrow you reach your destiny. I do hope you'll be happy. Though the world is full of injustice, don't ever give up hope. There's a lush valley behind every new mountain."

The captain walked away, but the two brothers stayed watching the city lights a bit longer.

"Will we be able to find them?" Moses asked hesitantly.

"We didn't come halfway across the world for nothing. Of course we'll find them," Jacob said, slinging his arm around Moses's shoulders. Their eyes shone with the lights of the port, and the cool breeze and smell of the sea made them feel fully alive. They had so often feared this day would never come, that they would not make it—but here they were in the Rio de la Plata, in South America, and they would never have to be afraid again.

Chapter 31

L*a Habana* docked at the port of Buenos Aires at ten o'clock in the morning. The captain had said a final goodbye to Jacob and Moses after breakfast. The boys packed their belongings in the suitcases provided by the captain's wife, cast a final glance around their comfortable suite, and closed the door. Nerves and excitement propelled them toward the gangway, where a long line of passengers waited to disembark. A few policemen and a man in a white coat walked up the gangway. The police sergeant gave instructions, and the passengers presented their documentation. Argentine citizens got off first and were met with the hugs and kisses of friends and family members.

Jacob and Moses waited on deck and watched the process over

and over: a traveler carrying more luggage than would seem possible would walk down the gangway looking all around the crowd waiting on land. Someone would shout the traveler's name and start waving his or her arms, and the traveler would speed up and run into the outstretched arms of the loved one, dropping the suitcases, and smothering the person in kisses.

Meanwhile, on the boat, once the Argentine citizens had all disembarked, the police ordered the immigrants to have their papers ready. Jacob and Moses waited patiently in the long line until it was their turn. The agent took their papers and scrutinized them, studying the photos carefully before returning them.

"Origin?" the officer asked, filling out the forms.

"Paris, France," Jacob answered.

"Relationship?"

"I'm sorry, what was that?" Jacob did not understand the question.

"Are you two related?" the man asked blandly.

"Yes, brothers. Our parents—"

"Wait for the questions," the agent said.

"I'm so sorry," Jacob answered.

"Ages?"

"I'm thirteen, and my brother is nine," Jacob said, pointing to Moses.

"Religion?"

Jacob was quiet for a moment. He had thought it would no longer matter in South America.

"Religion?" the agent repeated, looking up this time.

"Well, our parents are Jewish, but—"

"Fine, Jews," the man said, ticking a box and licking his thumb to turn the paper over. He continued the questions in his monotonous voice. "Reason for traveling to Argentina?"

"To be reunited with our parents, who came to Buenos Aires a few months ago."

"You have their current address?"

"Yes, sir."

"And they will take charge of you?"

Jacob squinted, not sure what the question meant. The agent paused from his routine to explain. "Many parents don't come for their children or take charge of them when the children arrive. But don't worry, there are plenty of shelters for immigrant children, including Jewish shelters. We'll attempt to alert your parents of your arrival, and if we can't find them, we'll take you to one of the shelters, though you might not both be able to go to the same one."

"My parents will take charge of us," Jacob answered with absolute conviction.

After assigning them a number, the policeman went to the next passenger, and the boys were passed to the doctor, who asked them several questions, examined them quickly, and told them to go down to the port.

Immigrants were directed to one side. Once there was a sizable enough group, a handful of policemen took them to a large building not too far away.

"What is that place?" Jacob asked a boy in front of him.

"The Immigrant Hotel. We'll stay there until someone comes for us or until we find work."

"It's not a jail, is it?" Moses asked.

"Nope. They feed you decent food, and it's clean enough, though there isn't much privacy. Men and women are separated, and dozens of people sleep in the same room. But you can come and go, as long as you're back by supper."

Jacob and Moses breathed a sigh of relief. Their arrival in

Argentina was not turning out to be like they had pictured. It was much less exciting. They knew their parents were unaware of their arrival, but even so, they had envisioned the impossible sweetness of an immediate reunion.

The Immigrant Hotel was a gigantic building with a huge entryway, an enormous dining hall with long marble tables, and a complex system of kitchens, laundry rooms, bathrooms, showers, and yards.

Caretakers divided the group of recent arrivals and led them to their rooms. Jacob was amazed at the size of the dormitory with countless bunk beds. He jockeyed to get beside the boy they had talked with in line.

"What's your name?" Jacob asked.

"Andrea," the boy said.

"Are you Italian?"

"Yes. My father is sending me to stay with one of his brothers in Rosario. Things aren't going well in my country. I figure my uncle will come get me soon. You can only stay here in the hotel five days for free. After that, you have to pay. You'd better find your parents as soon as you can. I heard that government employees work as slowly here as they do in Italy."

Jacob and Moses placed their suitcases on their beds, then sat down. The Italian boy pulled out a cigarette and offered them one.

"No thanks, we don't smoke," Jacob said.

"Your loss!" the boy joked.

"Do you think it's safe to leave our stuff here?"

Andrea shrugged. "I wouldn't leave it if I were in Italy, and they say that half this country is made up of Italians."

Jacob instinctively touched the belt inside his shirt where he kept their papers, money, and their parents' address strapped to his body.

"I'm going out to see Buenos Aires. After so many days at sea, I need to walk on solid ground," Andrea said.

Jacob and Moses nodded. "We'll come too." They stood and put on their jackets and a hat.

When they got down to the port, a policeman wrote their numbers down, and they walked out onto the bustling street, where they hopped on a trolley headed downtown. They were balanced on the outside, holding on to an exterior rail, so they could hop off as soon as the inspector came for their ticket. The streetcar traveled slowly, and the traffic seemed worse than in Paris, Jacob thought. Double-decker buses made their way through the city, and the sidewalks were packed with well-dressed people.

"Where do you want to go?" Andrea asked.

"I think our parents are in Once or Balvanera. One of those neighborhoods," Jacob said.

"I'll go ask how to get there." Andrea asked one of the other passengers, and fifteen minutes later, the boys jumped off the trolley.

"It's southwest of here. We'll take a bus to the Plaza Miserere."

Andrea moved about the city as if he had lived there his whole life. Jacob and Moses followed him like two blind men led by a seeing-eye dog. The bus took them to the plaza, and they started looking for Moreno Street. The buildings were not very tall, just two or three stories, and had balconies or terraces decorated with wrought-iron rails. Some had businesses on the street level. They were painted with lively colors, but the streets were calmer than the area around the port.

The three boys stood in front of the number written on Jacob's paper, and they studied the façade. The building was a bit old and could stand a fresh coat of paint, but the door looked new, with a pretty, colored window above the door frame. They stood there a while as Jacob and Moses hesitated, unsure whether to ring the bell. They were afraid of once again not finding their parents.

Finally, Andrea sighed and knocked loudly at the door. They waited again and then heard the sound of bolts sliding back. A young woman looked out at them, curious.

"What do you want, boys?" she asked.

"We're looking for Mr. and Mrs. Stein," Andrea said.

"Stein?" the woman asked, scrunching up her eyes.

"Eleazar and Jana, they're a German couple . . ." Jacob began. He had managed to get control of himself again. He dearly hoped his parents had not taken fake names in Argentina.

"You mean the Ashkenazim? They moved a couple of months ago. They were living on the top floor, but I hardly ever saw them. They didn't speak much Spanish. I'm Sephardic," she explained.

As she spoke, Jacob and Moses sank deep into themselves, hardly seeing the ground they were staring at. Finally, Andrea asked, "Do you know anyone who might know where they are?"

"They didn't have many friends, or at least if they did, they didn't bring them around here. I think sometimes they would go to Café Izmir. It's on Gurruchaga, in Villa Crespo," the woman said, ready for the conversation to be over.

"Thank you, ma'am," Andrea said.

As soon as they heard the bolts sliding back into place, Moses began to sob. Jacob hugged him and tried to calm him down.

"Don't worry, we're going to find them. They just had to move for some reason."

"It's late, but we could try looking for them at the café," Andrea offered, trying to cheer Moses. "Then we should get back to the hotel." Though Andrea could look and act tough, he knew what it felt like to be a long way from the people who loved you.

The three boys walked back to a main avenue and took another bus. They were on Gurruchaga a short time later, in a neighborhood that was rather different from the one they had just left. Many of the storefronts had a Middle-Eastern look to them, and the aroma of tea and spices filled the air. As Jacob, Moses, and Andrea approached the café, they saw it was very different from what they had imagined a city café might be. A thick cloud of smoke enveloped them as they went inside. Turkish music wafted up from the back of the room, and people dined on little bites of meat and vegetables served with round, flat bread.

The boys headed for the bar, where a girthy, dark-skinned man glanced at them out of the corner of his eye. He was used to boys sneaking in to rob clients or pocket food.

He turned to them and asked, "What do you want?"

"We need to ask some of the people in here about a man and a woman," Andrea said.

"Sorry, spaghetti. You're not going to bother my clients."

Andrea frowned. "These boys are looking for their parents. We were told they used to come here a lot."

The man stared the boys down while taking a sip of very black coffee. Finally, he decided they were not ruffians after all.

"What are your parents' names?" he asked in a bored voice.

"Eleazar and Jana Stein." Jacob's voice trembled as he pronounced their names.

"The Germans? They didn't talk much. Most people around here are Turks or from the Middle East. But they used to sit with Juan Prados sometimes—the playwright. He likes this place and comes by in the afternoons, but he's already gone home," the man said.

"Could you tell us where he lives?" Jacob asked eagerly.

"Somewhere by the Regio Theater, but I don't know where exactly. If you come by any day around six o'clock, you'll find him. He's like clockwork."

The boys thanked him for the information and headed back to the Immigrant Hotel. They spoke little on the bus or the trolley. They crossed the wide street that separated them from the railroad, gave the policeman their numbers, and reentered the building.

They went straight to the big dining room, having made it in time for the very last round of supper. Even so, the place was packed. Nearly a thousand people jockeyed for a place to sit. When all were seated, women carrying enormous pots started serving meat and potatoes. Andrea finished his plate and a second helping, then mopped up the dregs with a piece of bread.

"Tomorrow we'll go back to that café. We'll find that man, and surely he'll tell us where your parents are," he said to cheer up Jacob and Moses.

"We've been waiting so long . . . We've traveled hundreds of miles and gone through countless cities to see them. I just don't understand. It really feels like we're never going to find them," Jacob lamented. His shoulders dropped, and he buried his chin in his chest. Moses began to cry again, and Jacob no longer had the heart to try to comfort him.

"Tomorrow you'll figure out where they are. I don't think my uncle will show up until the day after tomorrow, so I can help you look for them. Buenos Aires is big, but I'm sure we'll find them," Andrea said.

"Thank you, Andrea. But maybe we should give up. The officer on the boat said there were shelters for Jewish children. We can stay at one of those and wait until they find us. If they get in touch with our friend in France, Mr. Perrot, he'll tell them we're here." It seemed a reasonable conclusion to Jacob, who was out of ideas.

"Well, still, we'll go back to the café tomorrow afternoon," Andrea insisted. Then he grabbed another piece of bread and started nibbling it.

They went to the bathroom on their way out of the dining hall, and by the time they got to their dormitory most of the bunk beds were already occupied. The sounds of breathing, coughing, gas being passed, and snoring reached them. They went to their bunks and lay down.

"Jacob," Moses said, "can I sleep with you?" Jacob climbed down from the top bunk and lay down next to his brother. Moses was breathing hard, and his cheeks were wet with tears.

"I can't take it anymore. I can't take it. I just can't take it," he said over and over.

Joseph sighed. "Andrea's right. We should try one last time. Steins never give up. You're a Stein, aren't you?"

"Yes."

They put their arms around each other. Though they were no longer at sea, they still felt the waves rocking the boat, the ocean one great lullaby. They had been on their own for so long that sometimes Jacob believed they would never see their parents again. He prayed a short prayer that night. He did not know whether he should address the God of the Jews or the God of the Christians—he had hardly ever learned to pray—but he asked that God would help them find their parents. When he finished, he had the sensation that somehow, all throughout their long, lonely journey, they had never been fully alone.

Chapter 32

The Stein brothers let the clock run down as they wandered aimlessly in the hotel yards and stared unseeingly at the river. Andrea had a hard time shaking them out of their lethargy. How were these boys willing to throw it all away when they were so close?

"The hardest fall an athlete will take is right before the finish line, but they get up again and finish the race," he said to bolster them.

Jacob thought back to all the people who had sacrificed themselves for him and his brother. He thought about Vipond's dying in order to get them across the French border. He felt wickedly selfish. Why had he dared challenge fate? Why had he not settled for mere survival like the rest of the human race?

Those months had held betrayal, unconditional love, disdain, falling in love, and the abyss of loss. He was no longer the boy who had left Paris hoping for a brighter future, longing to be reunited with his family. Now he was almost an adult struggling desperately to hold on to the final sparks of hope.

After the noon meal, Jacob and Moses changed their clothes and looked for Andrea, whom they soon found playing cards with some of his countrymen. At first Andrea paid them little attention, but he eventually left the cards and walked with them to the trolley.

"I didn't want to come today. I know you're down in the dumps, which is why you can't see how lucky you've been. You managed to escape from the Nazis, you went across an entire country in the middle of a war, and you managed to cross an international border and a whole ocean. You've got each other and, besides, sooner or later, you're going to find your parents. I'm all alone. I don't know if I'll ever see my family again or if I'll ever go back to Italy." For the first time they heard sadness in their new friend's voice, his confident vigor dissipating with the smoke of his cigarette.

"I'm sorry," Jacob said, sighing. "You're right. Though you have to understand what a blow it was to not find them yesterday. We were so hopeful. I've imagined it a thousand times . . ."

"Of course I understand, but life isn't the sum of our expectations. It's the outcome of our decisions. If you've decided to find them, nothing's going to stop you. I'm sure you'll do it. But if you give up now, you might spend the rest of your life regretting that you didn't keep trying."

The trolley came, and the three boys hopped on. They traversed a muted city covered in black umbrellas and gray raincoats. It looked like the saddest day in the world, but a few rays of sunlight filtered through the dark clouds when they arrived at Café Izmir.

There were not as many people as the day before. That must be why the playwright preferred six o'clock, a quieter time before most

CHILDREN OF THE STARS

customers came for supper. After a quick glance at the tables, they knew exactly which one Juan Prados was. He was a thin man with yellowish skin and a short beard. He held a book too close to his face, as if his glasses no longer worked.

The boys went up to him slowly and stood near him for a while, not saying anything, until he finally looked up from his book.

"Are you Mr. Juan Prados?" Jacob's voice trembled again.

Juan Prados raised his eyebrows, unaccustomed to being approached by strangers in public. "Yes, little squirt, and why do you ask?"

"We don't mean to bother you, but we're looking for two people we think you know," Jacob answered.

Andrea was fed up with Jacob's caution. He stepped forward and said, "Do you know where the Steins are living? These are their children, Jacob and Moses, who've come from France to find them, but they aren't at the place they used to live."

Prados closed his book, set it on the table, and gave a slight smile. "Jana and Eleazar's boys. I've heard of you. And you've come from France to find them? Dear boys . . . Rafael, bring some coffee for these squirts!" he hollered. Then he motioned for them to sit down.

"So do you know where they are?" Moses asked impatiently.

The playwright put his bony, ink-stained hands on Moses's shoulders. "Yes, lad. Don't worry."

The waiter arrived with coffee and set it on the table. Andrea, long accustomed to coffee, downed his in one gulp, but Jacob and Moses eyed theirs warily.

"Come now, coffee is like life! A little bitter at first, but the last sip leaves you wanting more."

Jacob took a sip, involuntarily grimacing, but finished the cup.

"Your parents are in Rosario, a city along the Paraná River. I got

Eleazar a job at El Círculo, a theater. They were in rather dire straits here in the city. Sometimes Buenos Aires can be a good stepmother but a very cruel mother."

"Rosario?" Moses asked.

"It's where my uncle lives," Andrea said.

"It's not too far, considering how big this country is. You can take a train there tomorrow. You could go on your own, but I'd feel better if I went with you. The good thing about being a writer is the only thing you've got in abundance is time, and plenty of it, kiddos."

"You'd take us to Rosario?" Jacob asked, his weary spirits starting to rise.

"Sure. The Rosario train leaves at nine o'clock, and we'd get there around five in the afternoon," Prados said.

Jacob and Moses whooped for joy. They were back to believing everything was going to be okay. After talking with Juan Prados a bit longer, they left the café and walked back to the trolley instead of taking the bus.

They were filled with joy, talking and laughing the whole way. The gray clouds had cleared away, and the stars were already shining, shimmering with the news of their imminent reunion with their parents. They were so close!

At the trolley, they sat down for the first time on one of the wooden seats and let the city caress their cheeks with the breeze coming in from the river. They hopped off as soon as they saw the huge building and ran to the entrance. They could hardly swallow their supper for all the talking and laughing. They went to bed late, trying to wear the clock down as much as they could. Andrea was very happy for them, but when it was time to say goodnight, just before entering their dormitory, he hugged them and, his eyes watering, asked them not to forget him.

"We'll never forget you, Andrea. You gave us the final push to find our parents. You gave us your kindness and your strength. And we'll see you again," Jacob said, sharing his friend's sadness.

That night they did not sleep a wink. Jacob and Moses huddled together, wide awake, until the morning. They wanted to get to the train station as early as possible, before dawn reminded them they were still far from their parents.

Chapter 33

On the way to Rosario
September 12, 1943

The morning light poured onto the giant Retiro station. The gray exterior in no way diminished the building's magnificence. Jacob and Moses entered it as they would a sacred temple. Despite the hour, hordes of people ran this way and that. The Stein brothers felt miniscule and unimportant amid the crowd's hustle and bustle. When they reached the platform of the train to Rosario and saw Juan Prados, they sighed with relief. They had feared any number of accidents might have forbidden him to travel.

"I'm glad to see you're timely, little squirts," he said. "We've already got our seats." Wearing an old suit, a light coat, and an English hunting cap, he led them to the car.

They climbed aboard the second-class car. Though not luxurious, it was much more comfortable than the cattle car of their most recent train ride. Moses did not want to miss a single detail of their trip, so he settled in next to the window. He had seen so many things in the past few months that he wondered if the time would come when his eyes would wear out and he would be left blind. But so far, his eyes had not yet had their fill of seeing, nor his ears their fill of hearing.

As soon as the train started and they felt the comforting rhythm of its chugging along, Prados leaned his arm against the window frame and observed the city. "I can't live there, but I don't know what I'd do if Buenos Aires didn't exist. Chaotic, dehumanizing, dirty, anarchic—but she's my mistress, my lover. I love roaming the streets on the outskirts, so calm, unpretentious, not clamoring to be known. I think about the people who live in those houses; I imagine what part of the world they're from and what they left behind to reach some little dream. Buenos Aires is one street I'll never come to the end of. There's always something more to discover in the heart of a human and in the heart of a city," he mused, somewhat melancholy.

After a while, the landscape became monotonous, interminable flat fields that simultaneously announced the country's wealth and the poverty of the human landscape, always transformed by economic interest and the love of money. The river, separating the wetlands from the croplands, was now distant, like the last vestige of a countryside growing extinct as humanity advanced.

"Argentina is great!" Moses exclaimed.

"You can't measure the greatness of a country by acreage, my boy. The souls of men and women make a country great. There are many, *many* good souls in Argentina. But there are also many speculators who are only out to exploit her. Don't confuse flags for patriots. You can't love a symbol and hate what it represents. The people *are* the nation: every last dark or light face, every blond- or black-haired person, the Russians, the Poles, the Italians, the Galicians. To be Argentine, you just have to love things from all over the world and make them yours. Being Argentine isn't a nationality. It's a state of mind."

Prados eventually succumbed to the rocking of the train and closed his eyes, snoring lightly. Jacob and Moses enjoyed the silence of the endless plains until Rosario subtly arose, unpretentious, before their eyes. For many, it was just a stop between Córdoba and Buenos Aires, but human contact after the endless plains and the simplicity of the streets invited newcomers to get lost among Rosario's inhabitants.

The train station in Rosario was a simple white building with a small clock in the center. Jacob and Moses, carrying their suitcases, and Juan Prados, using his umbrella as a cane, disembarked, left the station, and walked toward a trolley.

They went down Mendoza Street and walked slowly toward the beautiful Teatro El Círculo. Through a side door, they approached the orchestra level and saw the curving walls lined with gold and bloodred box seats. Jacob and Moses stared up at the domed ceiling, still clinging to their suitcases. Then they lowered their gaze to the stage. A small group of actors was reading a play called *Life Is a Dream*. One man, standing, had his back to them. Beside him, a blond-haired woman leaned over, taking notes.

Moses dropped the suitcase and started running. Jacob followed. Their feet slapped down the red carpet. They bounded up the stairs to the stage and stood waiting, breath bated, incapable of speech.

The man who was standing up turned to see what all the actors were seeing. The woman lifted her head and her sweet gaze fixed on the faces of the boys. For a moment, time stood still; nothing happened; eternity poised all its intricate movement on that one moment. Then the man threw the papers he had been holding into the air and ran toward the children. The woman stood, clapped her hands to her mouth, and followed. They all four ended in a tangle of hugs on the floor, arms groping to confirm reality. Tears spilled out of closed eyes and mixed with the tears of the faces pressed against them. Four hearts beat as one in that inseparable embrace.

Everyone watching was surprised and delighted. Observing the happiness of others always makes the world make a little more sense all of a sudden, makes suffering a little more bearable, makes grief a little less suffocating.

"My God!" Jana kept shouting as her children kissed her like desperate puppies, trying to make up for the thousand longed-for yet delayed kisses during their separation.

Eleazar seemed to have gone mad. His animal instincts kicked in. He beat his chest and was sweating, both overjoyed and overwrought with guilt for having abandoned them when they most needed him. But the children brought no reproach. They loved their parents so deeply and needed them so wholly that the reunion was the best moment of their lives. On that stage, surrounded by the invisible audience of all the people who had helped them since May 1941, the children finally felt secure. They could hear distant applause, but it did not come from the small group of actors who wept to witness the emotional encounter. The echo came from much farther, from the streets of war-besieged Paris; from the infamous Vél d'Hiv that reaped so many lives with its cruel confinement; from the Vichy's concentration camps; from the dusty streets of France; from the trains full of the fear of the refugees; and, more than anywhere, from the green valleys of Le Chambon-sur-Lignon, where a village of men and women set their faces against the horror and showed that, armed with the Spirit, the noblest hearts are always capable of overcoming and that the shadows of evil will finally be dispelled until light invades everything once more—for a new generation to believe it can change the world, or at least try.

Epilogue

Rosario, Argentina, October 15, 1943

Dear André and Magda,

We've reached the end of our journey. Many times we doubted we would make it, but hope never fully abandoned us. It's bad for people to lose hope, because it's the only thing that keeps us tied to our dreams.

My parents are so grateful to you. We told them about your courage and how much you love people. We know a lot of people have sacrificed themselves for complete strangers, but you all understood a long time ago that human beings are part of the same family and that we're all brothers and sisters.

Over here, the war seems like a faraway ghost, but we know it's still a very real monster in France. You two taught me to trust. I hope this trust doesn't let you down during the hard times you're going through.

The sky looks just as blue in Argentina. The prairies are just as green, and the same stars shine every night here—but we never forget Le Chambon-sur-Lignon and all the children who dream of reaching what we have. Keep encouraging them; help them know they can change the world.

I hope you have news of Anna? I haven't forgotten her.

Moses is doing well. He never leaves Mother's side, doesn't even let her go to the bathroom by herself! I wear long pants now, but I'm still avoiding the world of adults. I think I'll be happier if I always stay like a child, plus it'll help me be braver about the future. The world is full of cowards who give up on their dreams, but I'll never stop. I owe it to those who didn't reach their dreams, those who died in some forgotten ditch; the people from whom the Nazis stole their will to live; and the people who have become a ghost of themselves.

Sometimes my heart is full of things that words can't fully express, but I'll always walk on the edge of the impossible without being afraid of falling. And if I trip, I'll get back up again. I understand now that all of us have a deep desire for eternity in our hearts and that someday I'll see again all those who helped me on this long journey.

I hope all the best for you and send my unconditional love, the same kind of love that you gave to this stranger and his little brother.

Your son forever,

Jacob Stein

Clarifications
from History

Jacob and Moses Stein themselves are fictitious characters, but the story about them is based on the experiences of real children who traveled all over Europe during the dark years of World War II. In a way, the brothers are a tribute both to all those who managed to escape the bombs and the cruel grasp of the Nazis, and to all those who did not—to those whose innocent lives were devoured by the insatiable hatred of fanatical, inhumane humans.

The events described in the Paris roundup and the Vélodrome d'Hiver are true. Thousands of people were crammed into the velodrome for days, waiting to be shipped to an uncertain destiny up north. Thousands of Jews living in France died in gas chambers or as a result of the mistreatment and abuse of their captors. France deported some seventy-six thousand Jews between 1942 and 1944; only an estimated three percent survived, though some sources report that up to ten percent of those deported were eventually able to return.

The French Resistance and several anonymous French coalitions helped thousands of Jews hide during the war, thus lending dignity to the history of a country subserviently given over to Nazi whims.

The story of Le Chambon-sur-Lignon and its residents is true. A simple village in the middle of nowhere served as the refuge for thousands of persecuted people. The Protestant pastor André Trocmé, his wife, Magda, and most of the Le Chambon characters mentioned in this novel are real. After the war, André and Magda held positions in several organizations that worked for peace.

Daniel Trocmé, along with most of the students detained with him in the summer of 1943, died in a Nazi extermination camp.

Hope for many immigrants, especially Jews, lay across the Atlantic Ocean. They were not wanted in their own countries and had to fight to escape the Nazi nightmare. Argentina was one of the countries that accepted the most Jews, becoming a sort of promised land for them.

Buenos Aires is magic, a little piece of heaven on earth. It welcomed millions of people from all parts of the world, restoring their dignity as human beings. Yet it is as complex as it is magic: it also welcomed countless Nazis and fascists fleeing the justice demanded after the war. The way I see it, being Argentine is—as one of the characters says—more than a nationality. It's a state of mind, which allows me to feel like I, too, am a bit Argentine.

Finally, I want to pay the highest tribute to those who, not for lack of trying, never finished the journey and never saw their dreams come true.

Timeline

September 1, 1939

Germany invades Poland, initiating World War II in Europe.

September 3, 1939

Fulfilling their commitment to safeguard Poland's borders, Great Britain and France declare war on Germany.

April 9, 1940–June 9, 1940

Upon German invasion of Denmark and Norway, Denmark surrenders immediately; Norway resists until June 9.

May 10, 1940–June 22, 1940

German invasion of western Europe: France, the Netherlands, Luxembourg, and Belgium, all of which eventually surrender. On June 22, France signs an armistice agreement under which the Germans occupy the northern half of the country and the entire Atlantic coast. A collaborationist government for southern France is established in the city of Vichy.

June 10, 1940

Italy joins the war and invades southern France on June 21.

June 16, 1940

French Premier Paul Reynaud offers his resignation, and his successor, Marshal Philippe Pétain, immediately establishes communication with Germany.

July 10, 1940

Complete governmental powers are given to Marshal Philippe Pétain in the new constitution for Vichy France.

December 1940

The first Jewish woman seeking refuge arrives in Le Chambon-sur-Lignon.

June 22, 1941–December 6, 1941

Germany and the Axis partners (except Bulgaria) invade the Soviet Union, taking control of many cities. A Soviet counteroffensive pushes the Germans out of Moscow.

December 7, 1941

Japan drops bombs on Pearl Harbor.

December 8, 1941

The United States of America declares war on Japan and enters World War II.

May 30, 1942–May 1945

The British bomb the German city of Cologne, taking the war into Germany for the first time. For the next three years, British–US bombings reduce German cities to rubble.

July 16–17, 1942

The Vélodrome d'Hiver roundup in Paris.

August 10, 1942

The Vichy minister of youth, Georges Lamirand, and the prefect Robert Bach visit Le Chambon-sur-Lignon.

August 25, 1942

Raids begin in Le Chambon-sur-Lignon.

November 8, 1942

Vichy forces fail to repel US and British troops that land at various points along the coast of Algeria and Morocco in French North Africa. This Vichy failure allows the Allies to reach the western border of Tunisia, which precipitates the German occupation of southern France on November 11.

November 23, 1942–February 2, 1943

Soviet troops launch a counterattack and trap the German Sixth Army in Stalingrad. With Hitler's prohibition of retreat or escape from Soviet territory, survivors of the German Sixth Army surrender.

February 1943

The compulsory labor service program is created, through which some six hundred thousand French were sent to work in Germany.

February 13, 1943

André Trocmé, Edouard Theis, and Roger Darcissac are arrested and held at the detention camp at Saint-Paul d'Eyjeaux.

June 29, 1943

Raid at the Maison des Roches: the Gestapo arrest eighteen students and Daniel Trocmé.

September 8, 1943

With Mussolini internally deposed and imprisoned, the Italian marshal Pietro Badoglio leads Italy and surrenders to the Allies. The Germans take control of Rome and northern Italy, free Mussolini, and install him as a puppet leader.

June 6, 1944

Allied invasion of Normandy, France, in which combined British, US, and Canadian forces land on beachheads along the Atlantic coast of France.

August 26, 1944

General Leclerc's troops march through Paris, proclaiming the liberation of France from Nazi occupation.

Acknowledgments

A trip in 2011 drew me in for the first time to the incredible story of Le Chambon-sur-Lignon. It was not the only town in France that helped refugees and hid Jews, but it did the most to rescue the dignity of a country fawning at the perverse force of the Nazis.

In 2016 I visited Le Chambon-sur-Lignon with my family. First and foremost, it was an internal journey that taught us the value of human life and the importance of never giving up.

I would like to thank the Lieu de Mémoire au Chambon-sur-Lignon for their kind welcome and the opportunity to visit the museum dedicated to those who helped fight for persecuted people during World War II.

I am indebted to Richard P. Unsworth and Pierre Boismorand for their biographies of André Trocmé and his wife, Magda. Also helpful in understanding the facts about Le Chambon-sur-Lignon and its protagonists were the books of Peter Grose, Albin Michel, Patrick Gérard Henry, Bertrand Solet, and Patrick Cabanel.

I also want to thank Pierre Sauvage for his magnificent documentary *Weapons of the Spirit*, which rescued the memories of what happened in Le Chambon-sur-Lignon at a time when French society still preferred to look the other way.

Jean-Louis Lorenzi's 1994 film *La Colline aux Mille Enfants* also included a helpful portrayal of some of what occurred in Le Chambon.

I want to thank Elisabeth, Andrea, and Alejandro, who went with me to the beautiful meadows of Le Chambon-sur-Lignon and were as excited as I was to see the story of those valleys come to life.

I cannot leave out all those who sent me throughout the Americas to promote my last novel, *Auschwitz Lullaby*: my good friend Ana Matonte, the creative and endearing Berenice Rojas, the kind and happy Karla Nájera, the dynamic and tireless Jorge Cota, and the always smiling and prepared Selene Covarrubias.

My gratitude goes to the publishers of Del Nuevo Extremo, Miguel Lambré and his wonderful sons Martín and Tomás, who hosted us in Buenos Aires, offering their friendship and affection along with a tour of the Immigrant Hotel. What exquisite Argentine beef! And what exquisite company!

To my dear friend, the author Eduardo Goldman, who received me so warmly in his lovely city.

To the entire team of HarperCollins Español, who work their fingers to the bone day in and day out to keep this great editorial ship moving forward: Graciela, Lluvia, Carlos, and so many others.

To my good friend Roberto Rivas, for that night of tangos and confessions.

To my dear friend Larry Downs, who still believes that books can change the world.

To the tens of thousands of bookworms inspired by my writing who will devour these pages with their insatiable eyes.

Discussion Questions

1. The Steins make the difficult decision to leave their sons behind in search of a safe place for their family to live together. Would you have made the same choice if forced into their position? If not, what would you have done?

2. Many people help Moses and Jacob along their journey, often to their own detriment. What motivated such people? What prevented others from protecting those in harm's way?

3. Describe how this novel depicts the atmosphere of Nazi-occupied Paris. Did the people of France understand what was happening to their country? Did denial, hatred, or fear play a role in how citizens behaved toward the vulnerable among them?

4. How does apathy play a role in this story?

5. Describe the moments of resilience in the novel. Are children more resilient than adults? Why or why not?

6. In a desperate time and place like Nazi-occupied France, what is the value of hope?

7. Who are the heroes of this story? Who are the villains?

8. Wise little Jacob proclaims, "We always have to choose between love and fear." What does he mean by this, and what happens when we choose fear?

9. What does this story tell you about the power of family? The power of love and sacrifice?

10. The author based this novel upon real people who lived in Le Chambon-sur-Lignon and protected the refugees of war. How does the truth of this story change the way you read and experience it?

Please enjoy this excerpt from *Remember Me.*

Amid the shadows of war, one family faces an impossible choice that will change their lives forever.

❧ Coming September 2020 ☙

Available in print, e-book, and audio

THOMAS NELSON
Since 1798

Prologue

Madrid
June 20, 1975

My hands shook with the letter I had just received, postmarked from Mexico. The memories of the sad, exciting journey of my childhood returned to remind me that, at the end of the day, I belonged nowhere. I wiped my tears with my shirttail and studied the sender's name: María Soledad de la Cruz. That girl had stolen my heart nearly forty years earlier. For a long time I had tried to convince myself I was a Spaniard, that my time in Mexico had been a kind of daydream. I had awoken from that dream as abruptly as the bombs had started falling over Madrid in the summer of 1937. I had gotten used to the black-and-white city Franco's followers ran like military barracks for nearly forty years—so used to it all that the memories of life in Veracruz, Mexico City, and Morelia were no more than distant, imagined ghosts. They were Don Quixote's loquacious deathbed visions after the entrance to his library had been sealed shut. I had spent the intervening years remaking my life, and I had a job I loved. I had inherited my father's printing press. For so many of us, the civil war had taken health, property, and existence itself. For me, it had also ripped away the future.

I thought about María Soledad de la Cruz's eyes, which still shone out bright from those eclipsed years. They were so black the light disappeared in her pupils but came back out through her thick lips in the first stolen kiss there in Cointzio.

I opened the envelope and read the short letter with a lump in my throat. Then I looked at the small black-and-white photo hidden in the mustard yellow envelope. It was the same girl with black braids and pearls for teeth, the one who had taken up shop in my heart and who reminded me yet again that, being fully Spaniard and fully Mexican, I could lay claim to no homeland. I still could not forget it. It was my bounden duty to remember, like my mother told me that day in Bordeaux, the last day of my old life and the first of a journey I never could have imagined.

Chapter 1

The Search

Madrid
November 14, 1934

For children, war feels like a game at first. They have no idea that behind the gunshots and uniforms, the marches and rallying songs, death clings like mud to shoes and leaves footprints of blood and flesh, forever marking the lives of whoever falls into its infernal clutch.

The Spanish Civil War began long before soldiers took up arms on July 17, 1936. At least it had begun for us, the children of poverty and misery.

First thing that morning, I heard someone beating on the door of our house in the La Latina neighborhood. We were still in bed, my two sisters and I, my parents, and the girl who watched us while my mother worked in the theater. Instinctively, my sisters and I ran to our parents' room. Isabel, with her white cotton nightgown, trembled and shrieked as she clung to our mother. Ana sobbed in my arms while our father masked his fear behind a smile and told us nothing was wrong.

María Zapata, the girl who helped around the house, also started to cry as she followed my father like a scared puppy to the door. The rest of us hunkered down in the main bedroom, but when I heard the shouting and skirmish in the hallway, I left my little sister in our mother's lap and headed for the door without a second thought. While not particularly brave, I wanted to help my father. I was still young enough that my dad was the invincible, mythic hero I longed to become. I stood trembling at the doorway of the small room we called the study, which was just a six-by-nine-foot room stuffed with books and papers. The walls were caving in and the shelves bowed, but to me that room was the hallowed halls of wisdom. However, right then it felt like the entrance to hell itself. Papers flew about as the gloved hands of the Social Brigade tore brightly colored spines from books yanked off the shelves. Nearly all the books were from Editorial Cervantes, a publishing house in Barcelona for which my father's printing press sometimes did work. My father raised his hands in despair, each ripped spine and crumpled page falling like the lash of a whip on his back.

"We don't have any banned books here!" My father's strangled shout interrupted the chaos of military boots and police barking. The sergeant turned and punched him square in the mouth. Blood gushed from my father's busted lip, and I, horrified, saw a terrified look on the face of the man I had always believed to be the bravest soul on earth.

"You piece of red trash! We know you're one of the leaders of the printers' union! On October fifth your people attacked the

State Department, and you're part of the Revolutionary Socialist Committee. Where are the books? We want the union's papers and the names of everyone on the committee!"

The sergeant was shaking my father, who, in his silly striped pajamas, looked like a marionette in the man's hands. I knew the books they were talking about were not in the study. A few days before I had helped my father hide them in the dovecote on the roof of our building.

"I'm an honest worker and loyal to the Republic," my father answered, more calmly than I expected. His collar and the front part of his shirt were red with his blood, but his eyes had recovered the courage that always guided his steps.

Yet he doubled over when the sergeant punched him hard in the stomach. The officer shoved him, and the guards fell upon him with their nightsticks. My dad sank to the floor, screaming and flailing his arms like a drowning man grasping for oxygen at the bottom of the ocean.

"Boy, come here!" the sergeant barked at me, and for the first time, I looked him full in the face. He was like a rabid dog with spittle flying from his mouth. His thick, black mustache made him look even wilder. He grabbed my shirt and yanked me out of the study to the living room and threw me into a chair. I landed abruptly, and the man crouched down to get his face right in front of mine.

"Look, kid, your daddy is a red, a communist, an enemy of peace and order. If you tell us where the papers are, nothing bad will happen. But if you lie to us, you and your sisters will end up in the Sacred Heart Orphanage. Do you want them to shave your mother's hair and lock her up in the prison of Ventas?"

"No, sir," I answered. My voice shook, and I nearly wet myself from fright.

"Then come out with it before my patience runs out," he sputtered, more foam gathering at the corners of his mouth.

"These are all the books my dad has. He's a printer, you know . . . That's why we have so many."

The sergeant lifted me up by the folds of my shirt and shook me with violence. My feet flailed aimlessly in the air until he dropped me onto the floor. Then he turned and raged back to the study with great strides.

"Let's go! We're taking the adults with us!" he snarled.

"What do we do with the kids?" one of the guards asked.

"The orphanage. Let them rot with the lice and bedbugs."

I ran to the door of the living room. One of the police officers was dragging my mother out of the bedroom, and I threw myself upon him, grabbed his neck, and bit one of his ears. Bellowing, the officer let go of my mother and tried to shake me off.

"Marco, please!" my mother yelled, terrified at seeing me on the police officer. The officer wrestled me off and threw me against the wall. He pulled out his nightstick and raised it to strike, but my mother grabbed his arm. "Please, he's just a child. Don't hurt him," she begged through her tears.

The sergeant appeared in the hallway. Two of his men were hauling my father off. His face, nearly purple, was covered with blood, his eyes swollen. He groaned in pain. My little sisters ran to him, but the sergeant shoved them back. Moving forward with the rest of the group, he called out, "Grab the brat!" But before the other guards could reach for me, I opened the door to the hallway and tore down the stairs.

The last thing I heard as I raced away was the voice of one of the policemen and my mother's screams as they flooded the entry stairway. Her voice swelled like thunder and lightning until it broke into muffled sobbing. Pain seared my chest as I raced down the street. I did not stop until I reached the Plaza Mayor, where the street cleaners were hosing off the cobblestones. I leaned against one of the columns in the plaza and wept bitterly.

The war started a long time before 1936. By then it was already coursing deep in the blood of the entire nation. That day I understood that people can be right and still lose; that courage is not enough to defeat evil; and that the strength of weapons destroys the soul of humanity.

About the Author

Photo by Elisabeth Monje

Mario Escobar has a master's degree in modern history and has written numerous books and articles that delve into the depths of church history, the struggle of sectarian groups, and the discovery and colonization of the Americas. Escobar, who makes his home in Madrid, Spain, is passionate about history and its mysteries.

Find him online at marioescobar.es

Instagram: @escobar7788

Facebook: MarioEscobarGolderos

Twitter: @EscobarGolderos

About the Translator

Photo by Sally Chambers

Gretchen Abernathy worked full-time in the Spanish Christian publishing world for several years until her oldest son was born. Since then, she has worked as a freelance editor and translator. Her main focus includes translating/editing for the *Journal of Latin American Theology* and supporting the production of Bible products with the Nueva Versión Internacional. Chilean ecological poetry, the occasional thriller novel, and audio proofs spice up her work routines. She and her husband make their home in Nashville, Tennessee, with their two sons.

9 780785 233039